Train Up a CHILD

Jean Ahern Lubin

HARVEST HOUSE PUBLISHERS
Eugene, Oregon 97402

TRAIN UP A CHILD

Published by Harvest House Publishers
Eugene, Oregon 97402

ISBN 1-56507-217-0

Printed in the United States of America.

94 95 96 97 98 99 00 01 / 10 9 8 7 6 5 4 3 2 1

To my dear husband, Ed

To my precious children,
Casey, Sean, and Alison

To my wonderful parents,
Joe and Celeste Ahern...

Thanks to all of you for
your encouragement,
patience, and love!

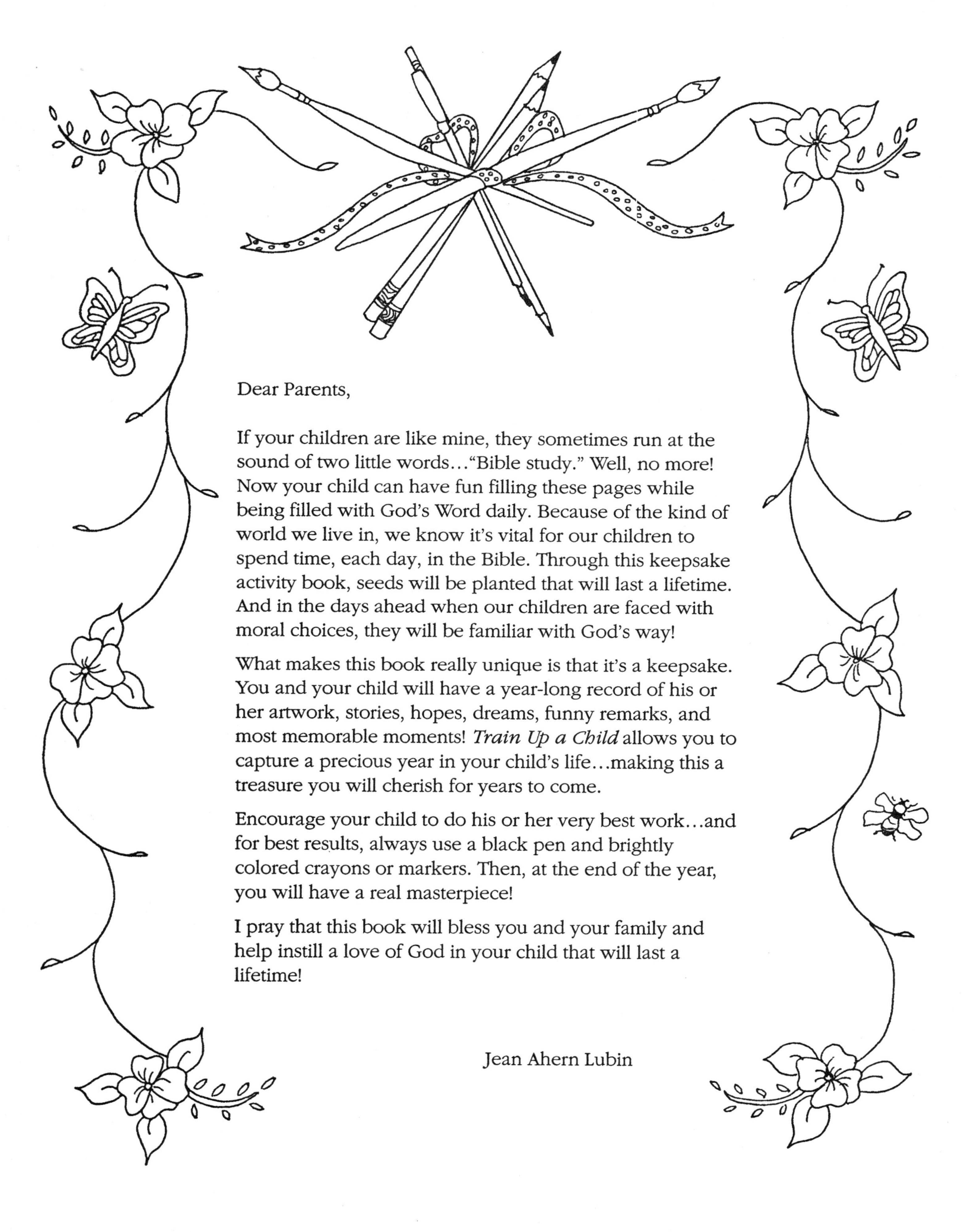

Dear Parents,

If your children are like mine, they sometimes run at the sound of two little words…"Bible study." Well, no more! Now your child can have fun filling these pages while being filled with God's Word daily. Because of the kind of world we live in, we know it's vital for our children to spend time, each day, in the Bible. Through this keepsake activity book, seeds will be planted that will last a lifetime. And in the days ahead when our children are faced with moral choices, they will be familiar with God's way!

What makes this book really unique is that it's a keepsake. You and your child will have a year-long record of his or her artwork, stories, hopes, dreams, funny remarks, and most memorable moments! *Train Up a Child* allows you to capture a precious year in your child's life…making this a treasure you will cherish for years to come.

Encourage your child to do his or her very best work…and for best results, always use a black pen and brightly colored crayons or markers. Then, at the end of the year, you will have a real masterpiece!

I pray that this book will bless you and your family and help instill a love of God in your child that will last a lifetime!

Jean Ahern Lubin

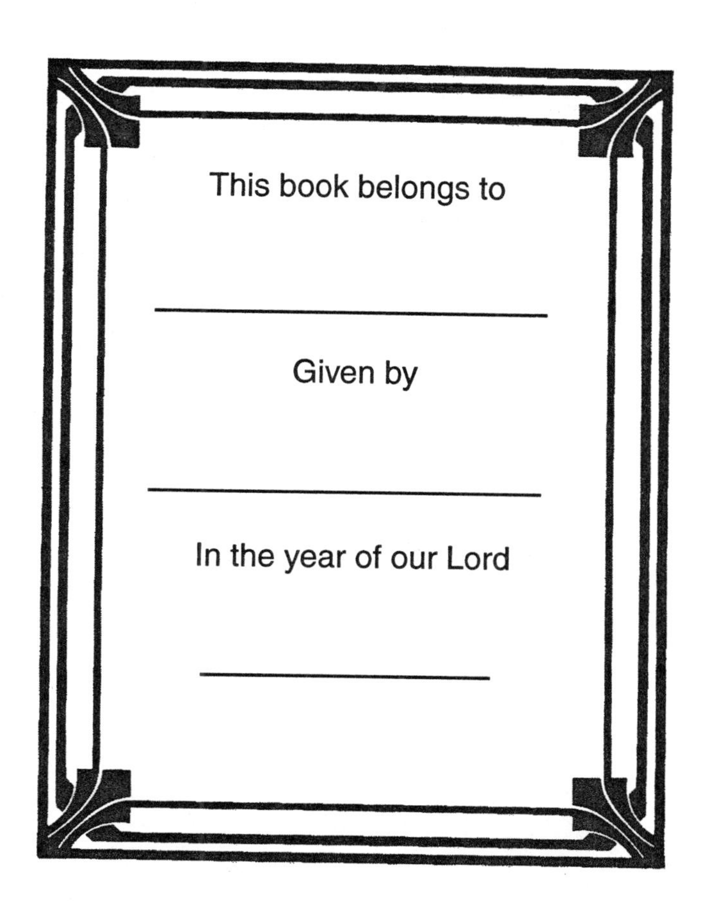
This book belongs to
Given by
In the year of our Lord

JANUARY

January 1

God is amazing! He made the whole universe...every planet, every star, and every moon! But God's most amazing creation...is you!

How do you think the earth looks from God's point of view? Color it!

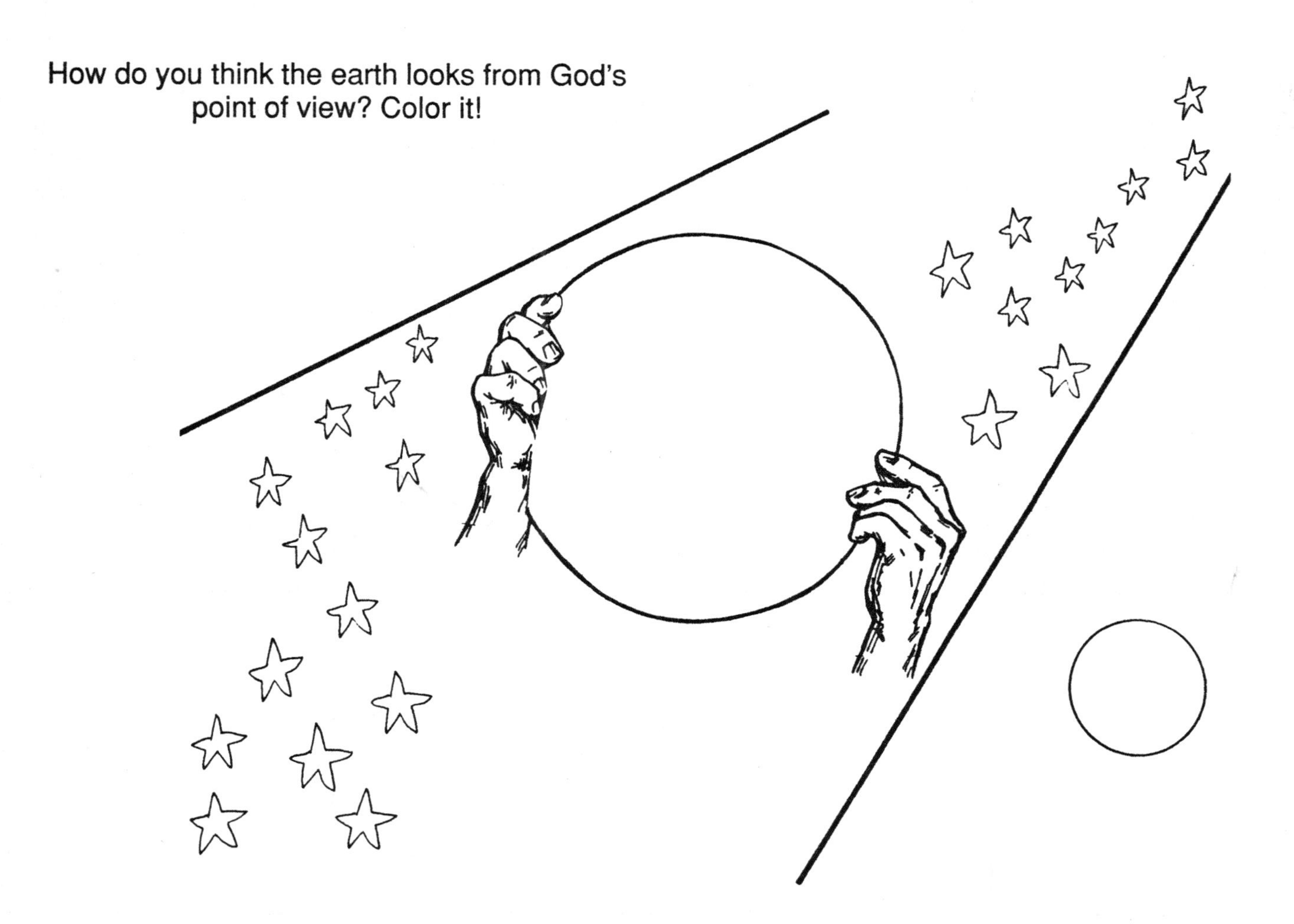

In the beginning, God created the heavens and the earth.

Genesis 1:1 (NKJV)

Dear God,

You are wonderful! Even though I am a small child in a gigantic universe, I know that You love and care for me!

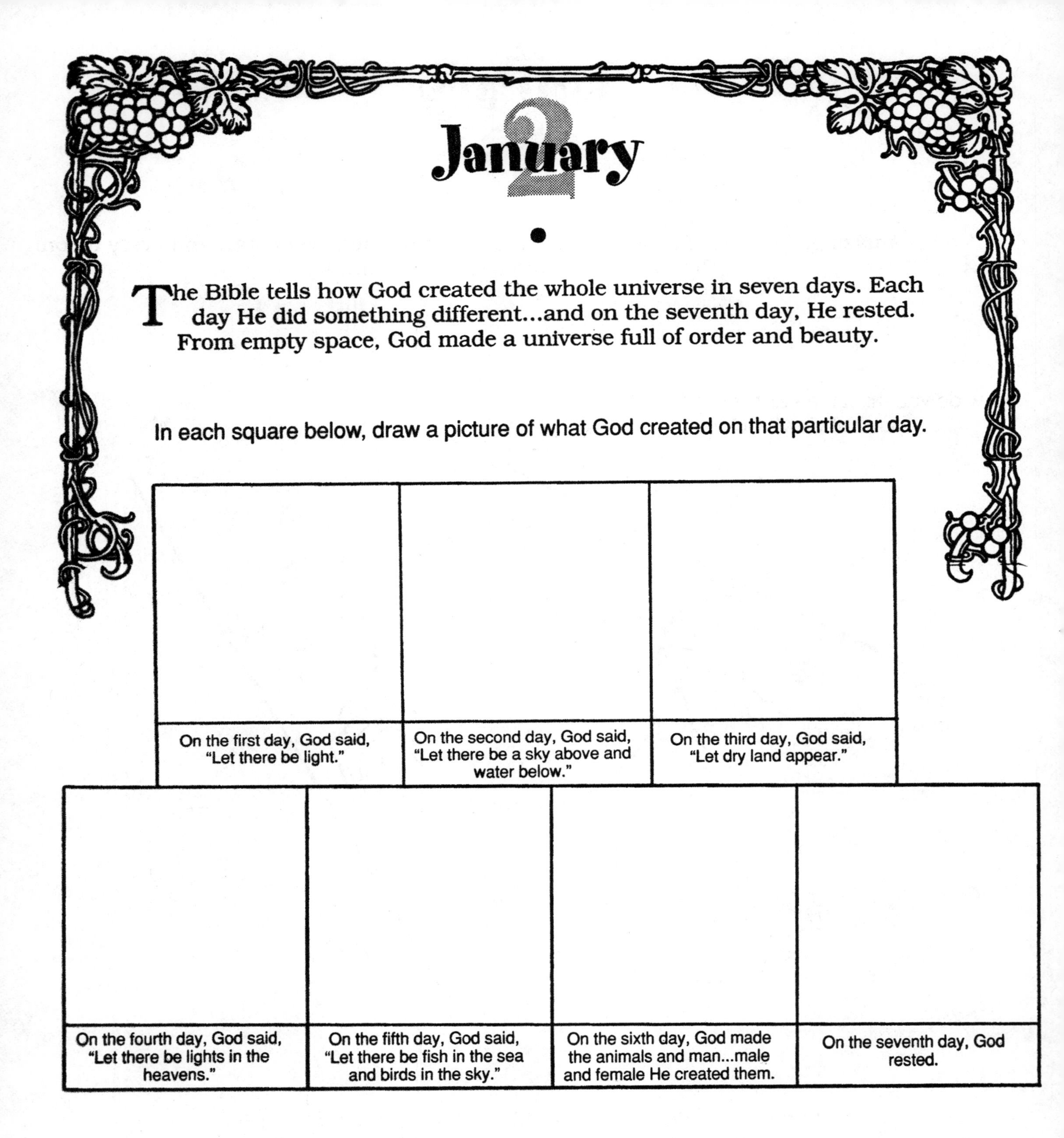

January 2

The Bible tells how God created the whole universe in seven days. Each day He did something different...and on the seventh day, He rested. From empty space, God made a universe full of order and beauty.

In each square below, draw a picture of what God created on that particular day.

On the first day, God said, "Let there be light."	On the second day, God said, "Let there be a sky above and water below."	On the third day, God said, "Let dry land appear."

On the fourth day, God said, "Let there be lights in the heavens."	On the fifth day, God said, "Let there be fish in the sea and birds in the sky."	On the sixth day, God made the animals and man...male and female He created them.	On the seventh day, God rested.

And so the whole universe was completed.

Genesis 2:2

Dear God,

Thank You for making such a beautiful world. And most of all, thank You for making me!

God made you. You are special because you are a child of God.

SELF-PORTRAIT

Draw a picture of yourself.

You created me.

Psalm 119:73

Dear God,

Thank You for making me and loving me so much. Thank You for being interested in every part of my life!

God will never forget His children—it could never happen! Our heavenly Father says He has written the names of His children on the palms of His hands.

Write your name on the palm of God's hand. Write the names of the people you love, too.

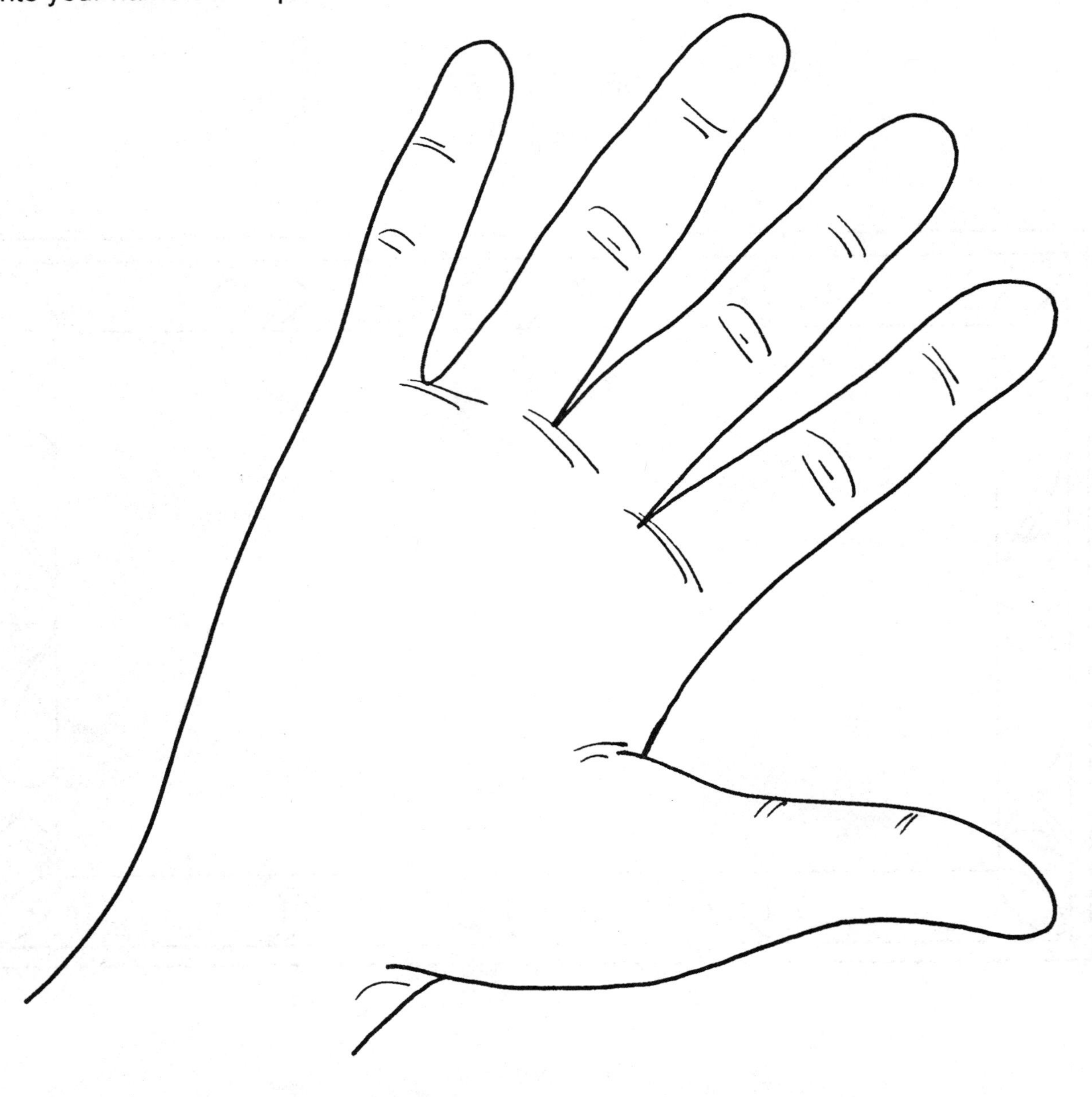

I have written your name on the palms of my hands.

Isaiah 49:16

Dear God,

I am glad that You will never forget me. I love You so much!

You love to eat all kinds of apples, don't you? They are delicious! Do you know that you are the apple of God's eye? That means you are very, very special to Him.

Write your name on the blank line.

For he who touches you touches the apple of His eye.

Zechariah 2:8 (NKJV)

Dear God,

Thank You for letting me know that I am so special to You. I am glad that You never forget me and that You will always love me. Thank You so much.

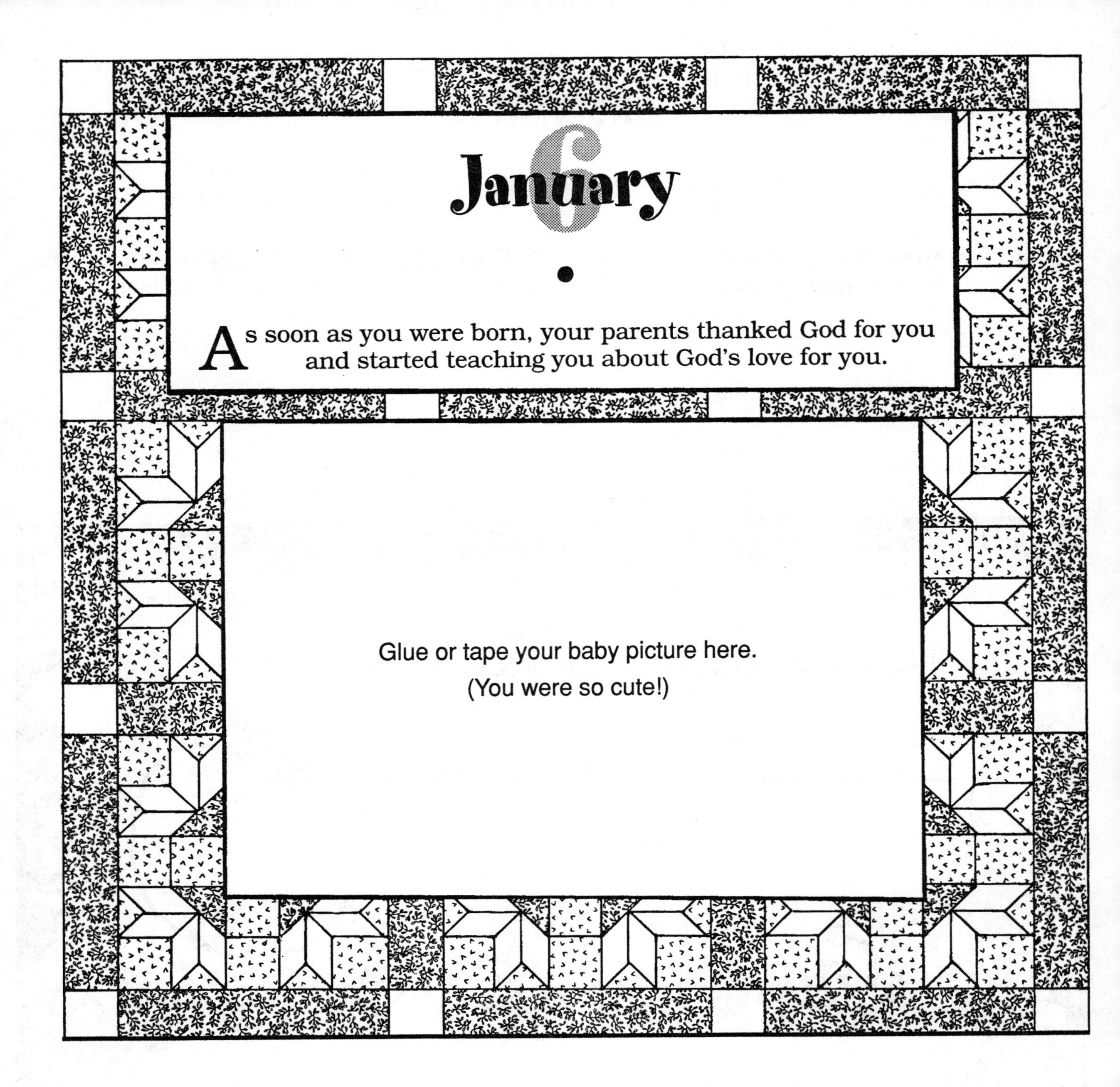

Ever since you were a child, you have known the Holy Scriptures.

2 Timothy 3:15

Dear God,

Thank You for my parents and all the people who have loved me since I was born. Thank You that I am learning the truth about You at a young age.

Do your parents ever tell you that you are growing like a weed? Weeds grow quickly, so when your parents say that, you must be growing fast! God is watching over you and making sure you grow just the right amount each year.

I will praise You, for I am wonderfully made.

Psalm 139:14 (NKJV)

Dear God,

Thank You for making sure my body works so well. I am glad that You know everything about me.

God has made us a wonderful promise! If we obey and honor our parents, God will help us live a long life. Isn't that wonderful?

MY LIFE STORY

Me Today	Me at Age 25	Me at Age 80

Do you think you will get married?_______ How many children will you have?________

Respect your father and your mother...so that you may live a long time.

Deuteronomy 5:16

Dear God,

Help me to always respect and obey my parents, and thank You for my wonderful life.

Your parents were blessed the day you came into their lives, and God knew about your whole life even before you were born!

ALL ABOUT ME!

Color this child to look like you and fill in all the blanks with answers about you. If you have a favorite outfit, color yourself wearing those clothes.

Eye color:_______________

Height:_______________

Hair color:_______________

Favorite toy:_______________
(Draw it in your hand.)

Weight:_______________

Draw yourself wearing your favorite shoes.

Shoe size:_______________

Children are a gift from the LORD.

Psalm 127:3

Dear God,

Thank You for doing such a good job of making me. Thank You also for my parents.

•

God loves you so much that He has sent angels to watch over you and make sure you are safe wherever you go.

God will put his angels in charge of you.

Psalm 91:11

•

Dear God,

Thank You for always being there when I need You. Thank You for sending angels to watch over me.

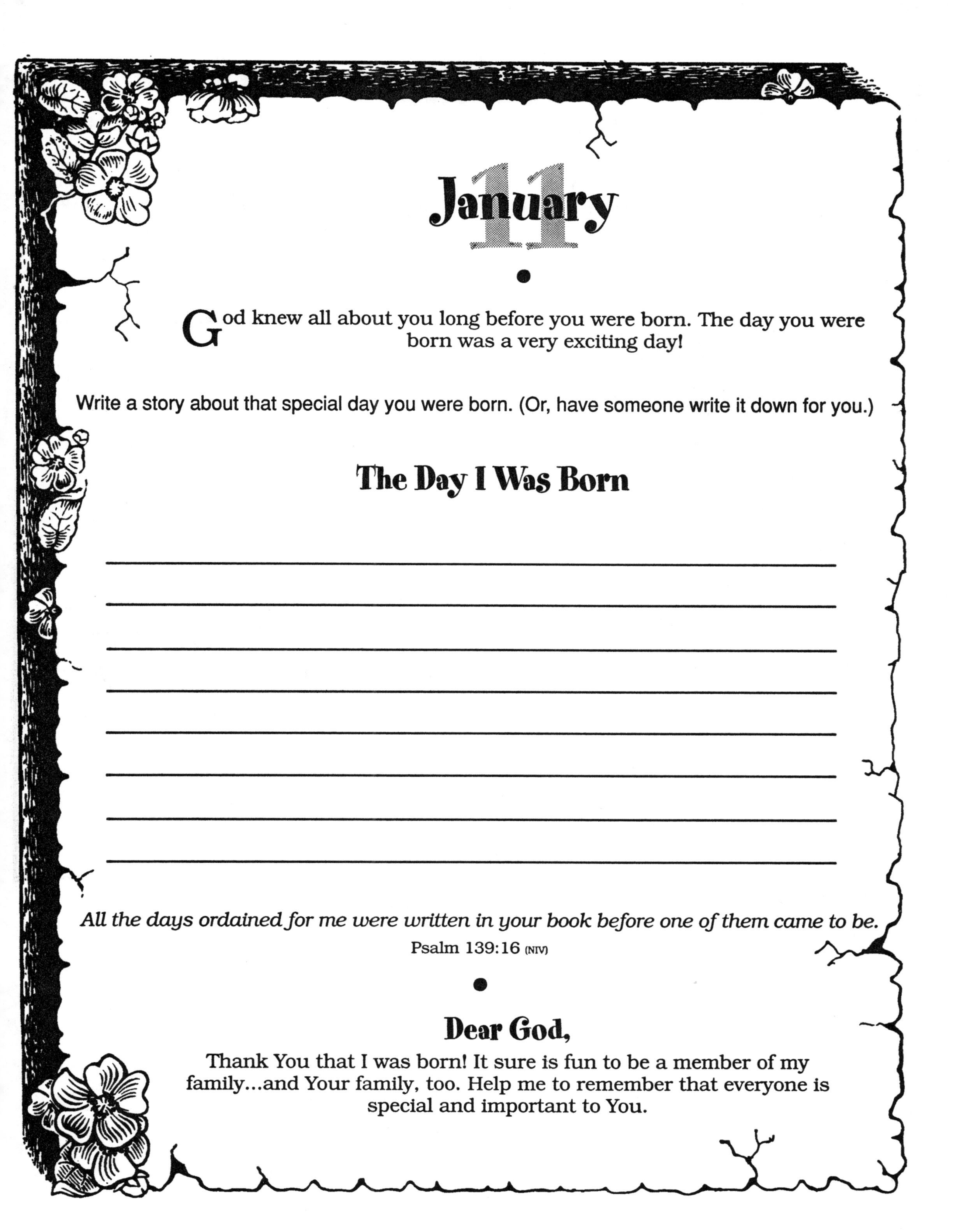

January 11

God knew all about you long before you were born. The day you were born was a very exciting day!

Write a story about that special day you were born. (Or, have someone write it down for you.)

The Day I Was Born

All the days ordained for me were written in your book before one of them came to be.

Psalm 139:16 (NIV)

Dear God,

Thank You that I was born! It sure is fun to be a member of my family...and Your family, too. Help me to remember that everyone is special and important to You.

Jesus loves children. He always had time to give them a hug. In fact, Jesus said that grown-ups should be more like little children—trusting God with open hearts.

Draw a picture of you sitting on Jesus' lap.

Let the little children come to Me, and do not forbid them; for of such is the kingdom of heaven.

Matthew 19:14 (NKJV)

Dear God,

Help me to always trust You in every part of my life.

You are very special to your parents. You are their gift from God!

Do you like to hear stories about when you were a baby? Write something that you did or said that was special: ______________________________

I was born on ____________________ I was born in the city of ____________________

I weighed ____________________ I started walking when I was ____________________

My first word was ____________________

Children are a gift from the LORD; they are a real blessing.

Psalm 127:3

Dear God,

Thank You for all the care You put into making me. Thank You that I was born and that my family loves me so much.

God knows everything about you. He knows where you live, and He knows what you think about. He knows what you hope and dream about. He loves you!

GETTING TO KNOW ME

In case you ever want to write to me, here is my name and address:

If you want to call me, here is my telephone number: ___________

You probably know that I am ____ years old. And so you can start shopping early, my birthday is _____________.

My absolute favorite color is, well, see for yourself!

(Put your favorite color inside this box.)

I am ☐ right-handed
☐ left-handed

I am ticklish: ☐ yes
☐ no

I live in a ☐ house
☐ apartment

I live in the ☐ city
☐ country
☐ suburbs
☐ town

I have a collection of ____________________.

I once walked _____ miles.

I once went on a long car trip. It was ____ miles long.

I once flew in a plane and traveled ____ miles!

LORD...you know me.

Psalm 139:1

Dear God,

I am glad You know all about me and love me so much.

January 15

As long as you love God and follow His directions for your life, you will be blessed. You can be sure He will love you, protect you, forgive you, and bless you all the days of your life!

How old are you? Draw that number...really BIG. Now turn that number into something. For example, a zero could be a pumpkin. Now color your picture.

Surely goodness and mercy shall follow me all the days of my life.

Psalm 23:6 (NKJV)

Dear God,

I know that You hold my life in Your hand. Thank You for every day of my life.

God made the whole world. He is in charge of everything. He knows how to make the sun rise and set at the right time, and He knows what is best for you.

Draw a beautiful scene.

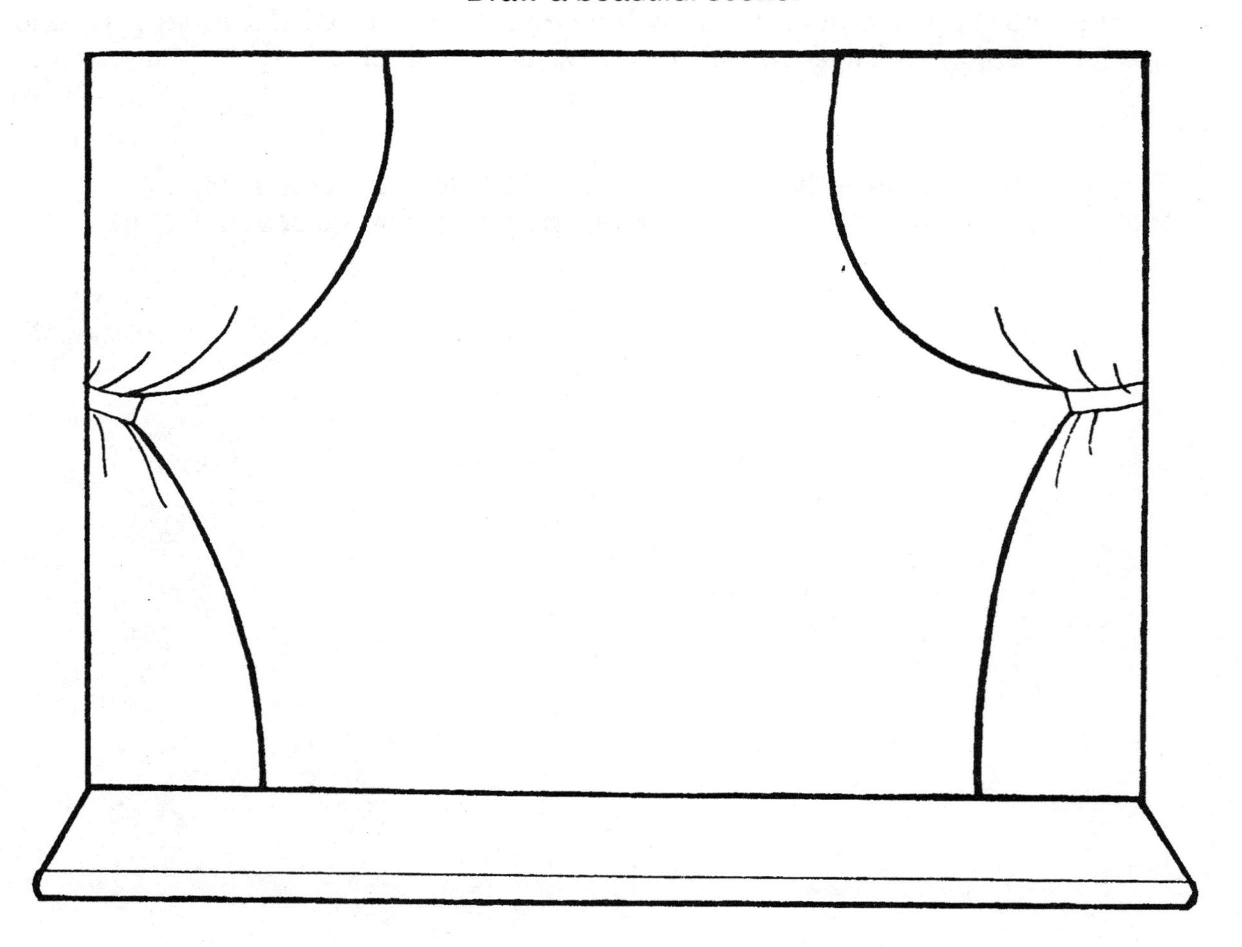

THE VIEW OUT MY WINDOW

God created the universe.

Genesis 1:1

Dear God,

You are so wonderful! You made everything in this world. Thank You for caring about us.

When you love God, your life will be blessed. You will be happy and God will give you everything you need.

Have you ever heard of a family tree? It is a record of your ancestors—that means your parents, and their parents, and on and on back. It shows all the people in your family, and ends with you! Family trees, or genealogies, are very important in the Bible. Fill in this family tree. Put your whole name on the bottom, then your parents' names above your name, and then their parents' names at the top.

They are like trees that grow beside a stream. They succeed in everything they do.

Psalm 1:3

Dear God,

Thank You for my parents and for all the people in my family who lived before me.

The Bible tells us not to worry or be anxious about anything. Just ask God to help you whenever you feel worried or scared. He will help you feel happy, strong, and brave.

Color these three friends who are helping each other

Don't worry about anything, but in all your prayers ask God for what you need, always asking him with a thankful heart.

Philippians 4:6

Dear God,

Thank You for always hearing my cries for help. Thank You for always being there when I need a friend.

A real friend will always love you and help you. You can notice when your friend needs something. It may be a kind word or a hug, or inviting your friend to join in a game with other children. And remember, a good friend is always quick to forgive.

This little turtle has everything he needs. But all of his friends are missing something they need. Give the other turtles what they need.

Do not forget your friends.
Proverbs 27:10

Dear God,

Help me to be a kind person who is always thoughtful and considerate to all my friends.

Some people look really different from you, don't they? When you are making friends, you shouldn't just look at them on the outside; look at them on the inside, too. A good friend is someone who has a loving heart.

Make these cats look fantastic, but all different! Give them hats, necklaces, bow ties, glasses, and anything else you would like.

The Lord does not look at the things man looks at. Man looks at the outward appearance, but the Lord looks at the heart.

1 Samuel 16:7 (NIV)

Dear God,

Thank You for looking at what really matters—our hearts. Help me to have a loving heart.

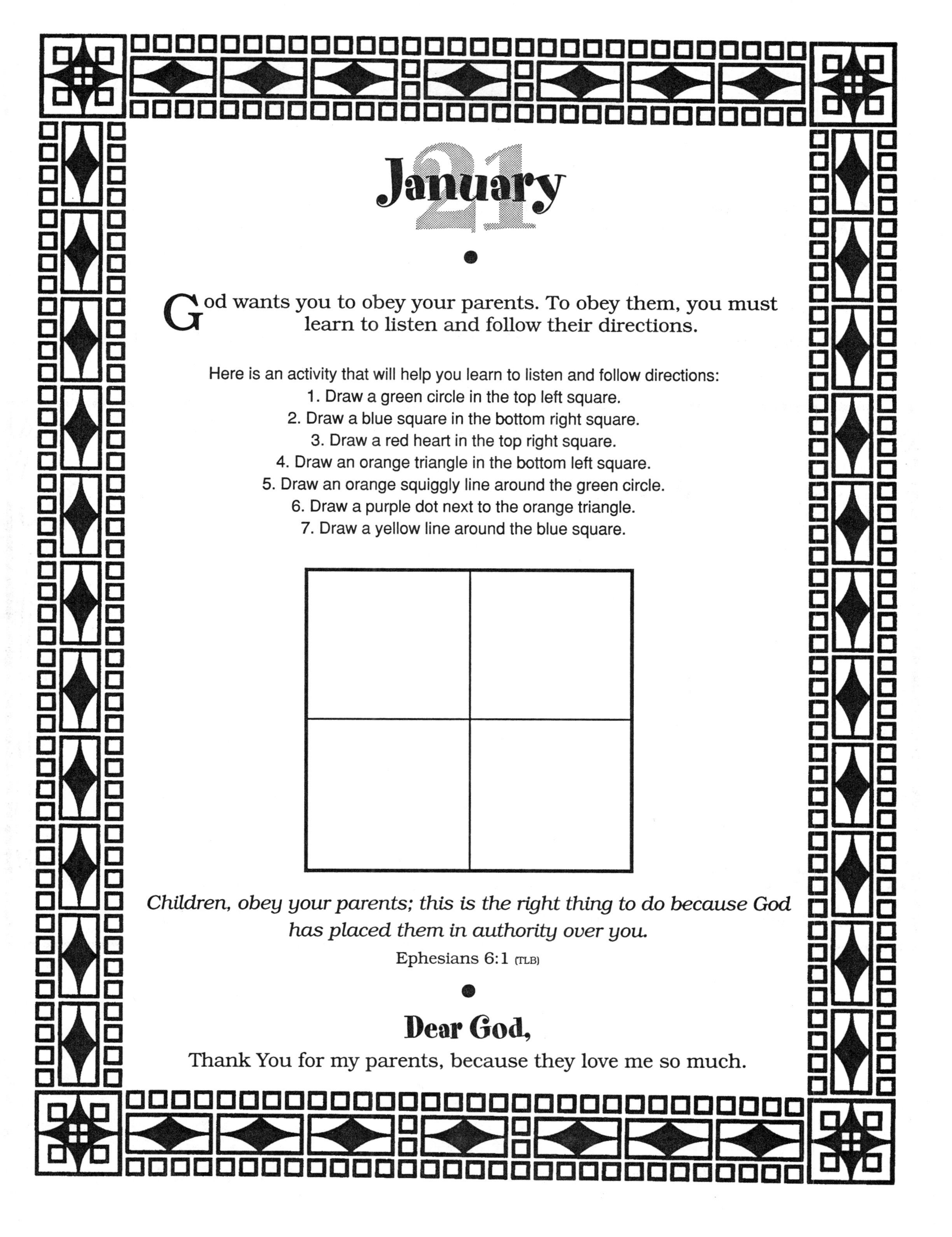

January 21

God wants you to obey your parents. To obey them, you must learn to listen and follow their directions.

Here is an activity that will help you learn to listen and follow directions:

1. Draw a green circle in the top left square.
2. Draw a blue square in the bottom right square.
3. Draw a red heart in the top right square.
4. Draw an orange triangle in the bottom left square.
5. Draw an orange squiggly line around the green circle.
6. Draw a purple dot next to the orange triangle.
7. Draw a yellow line around the blue square.

Children, obey your parents; this is the right thing to do because God has placed them in authority over you.

Ephesians 6:1 (TLB)

Dear God,

Thank You for my parents, because they love me so much.

God makes the rain so there will be beautiful spring flowers. God makes the summer hot so you can jump into the pool. God makes the autumn leaves change color right on time, and in the winter, the snow falls and makes a soft, white blanket.

Different seasons mean different kinds of weather...and that means different kinds of clothes! Draw yourself in the kinds of clothes you would need in each type of weather.

Who makes rain fall....So that grass springs up?

Job 38:26,27

Dear God,

Thank You for all the different kinds of weather. I love them all!

Sometimes it's easier to do the wrong thing especially if other kids are doing it, too. But real happiness comes from doing what God wants us to do.
Good deeds make us happy.

Your deeds bring shouts of joy.
Psalm 65:8

Dear God,

Please help me stay away from the bad things going on around me. Help me to always choose what is good. Thank You for watching out for me.

We should try to get along with everyone. That is how God wants us to live. Instead of getting angry at someone today, stop for a minute, then try to be nice instead. Then you both will have a great day!

Draw yourself holding hands with your friends.

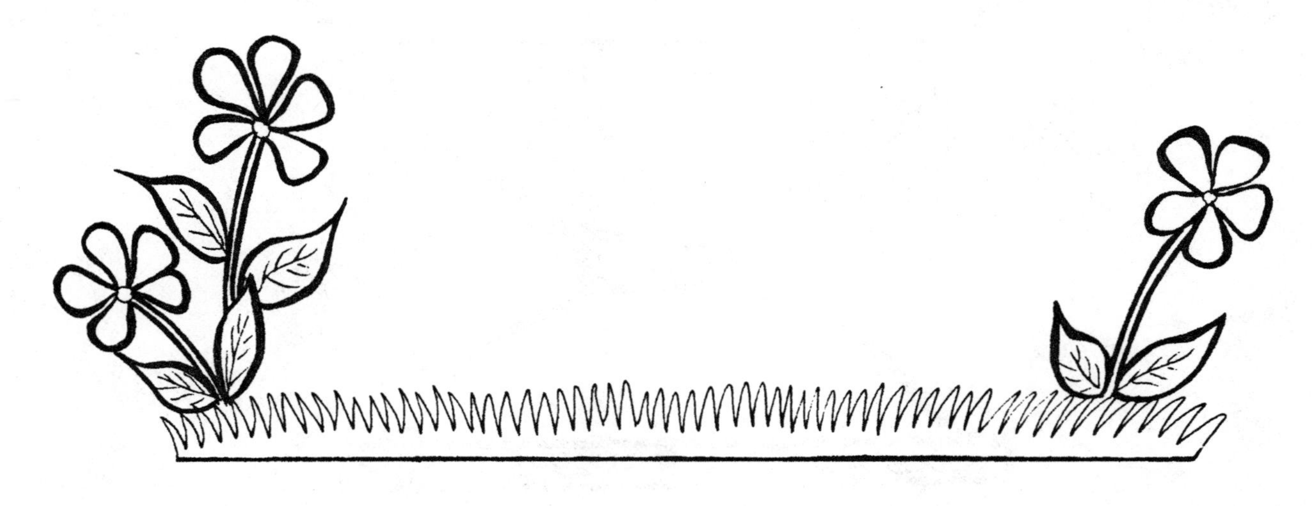

God's people...live together in harmony!

Psalm 133:1

Dear God,

Help me to show love and kindness to everyone, no matter how they treat me.
Help me to be more like YOU!

Doesn't it feel great to know that God is in charge of this world? Every day is a special day from God...there will never be another day quite like today again!

Fill in the times you do these things every day.

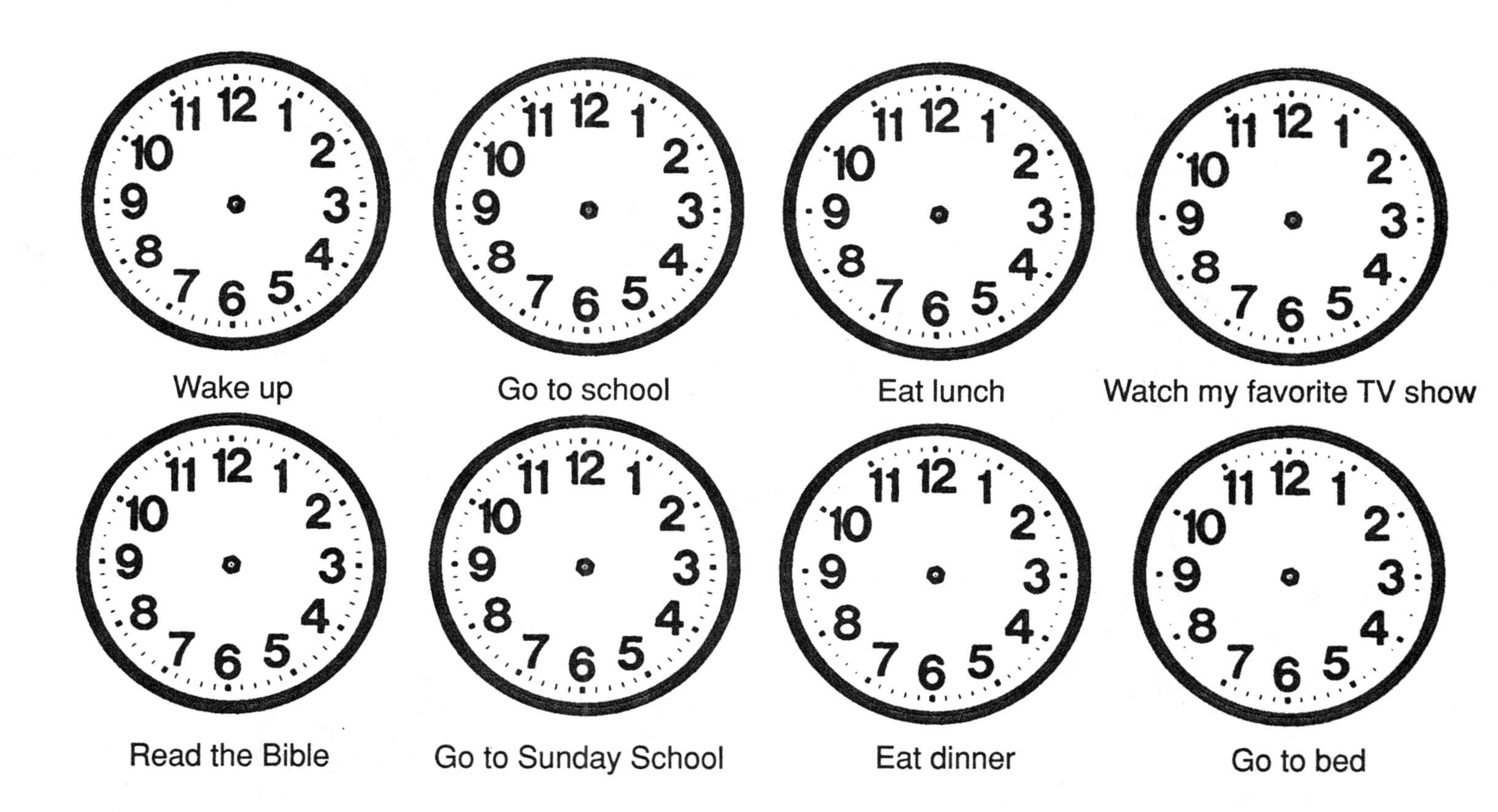

Everything that happens in this world happens at the time God chooses.

Ecclesiastes 3:1

Dear God,

Thank You for every brand-new day. Thank You also for always making the sun come up at exactly the right time.

It is important that we show kindness to everyone, wherever we are, every day. That is the best way to show them the love of Jesus.

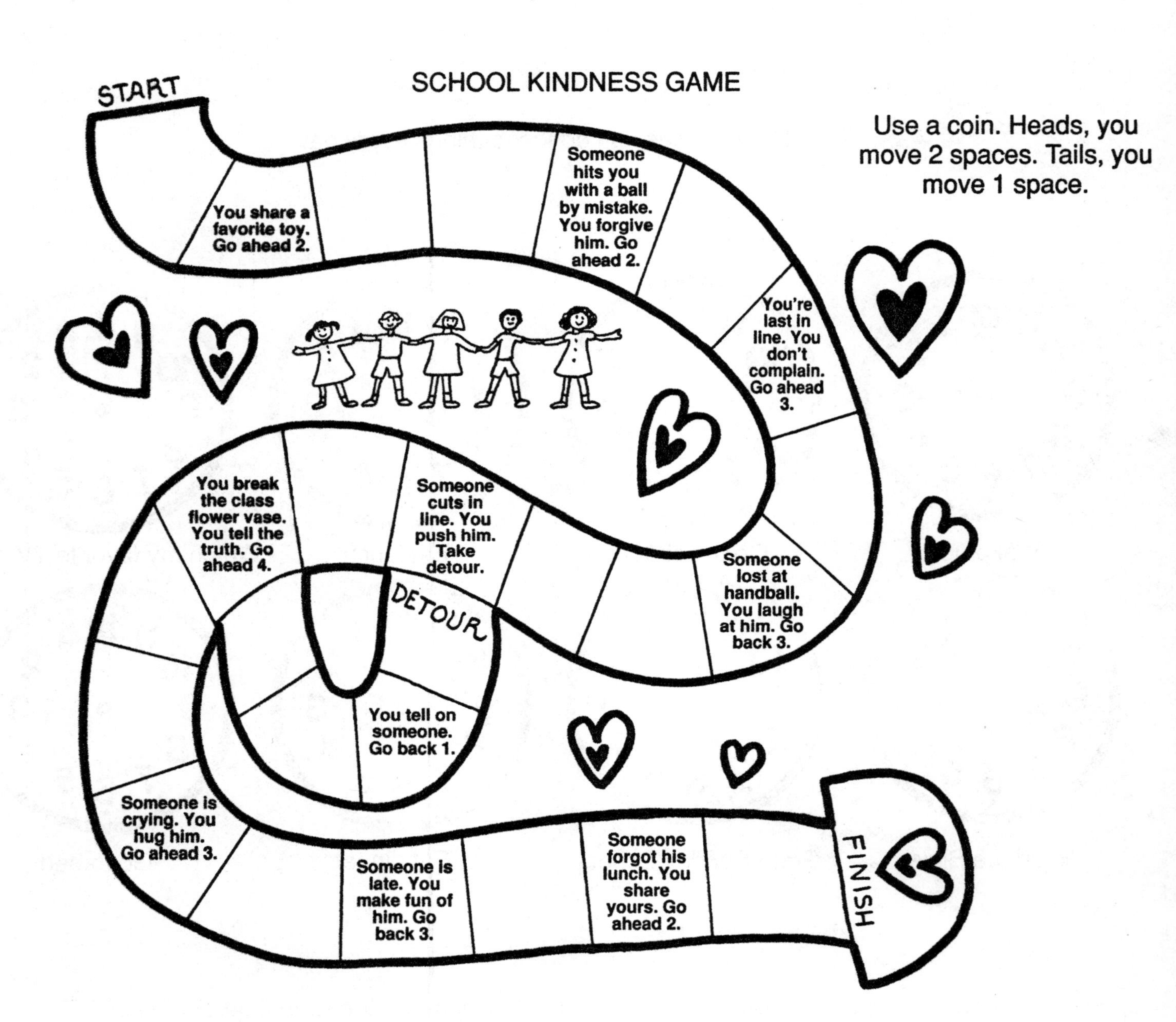

For I was hungry and you gave me something to eat.

Matthew 25:35 (NIV)

Dear God,

Help me to show kindness at school...and everywhere I go!

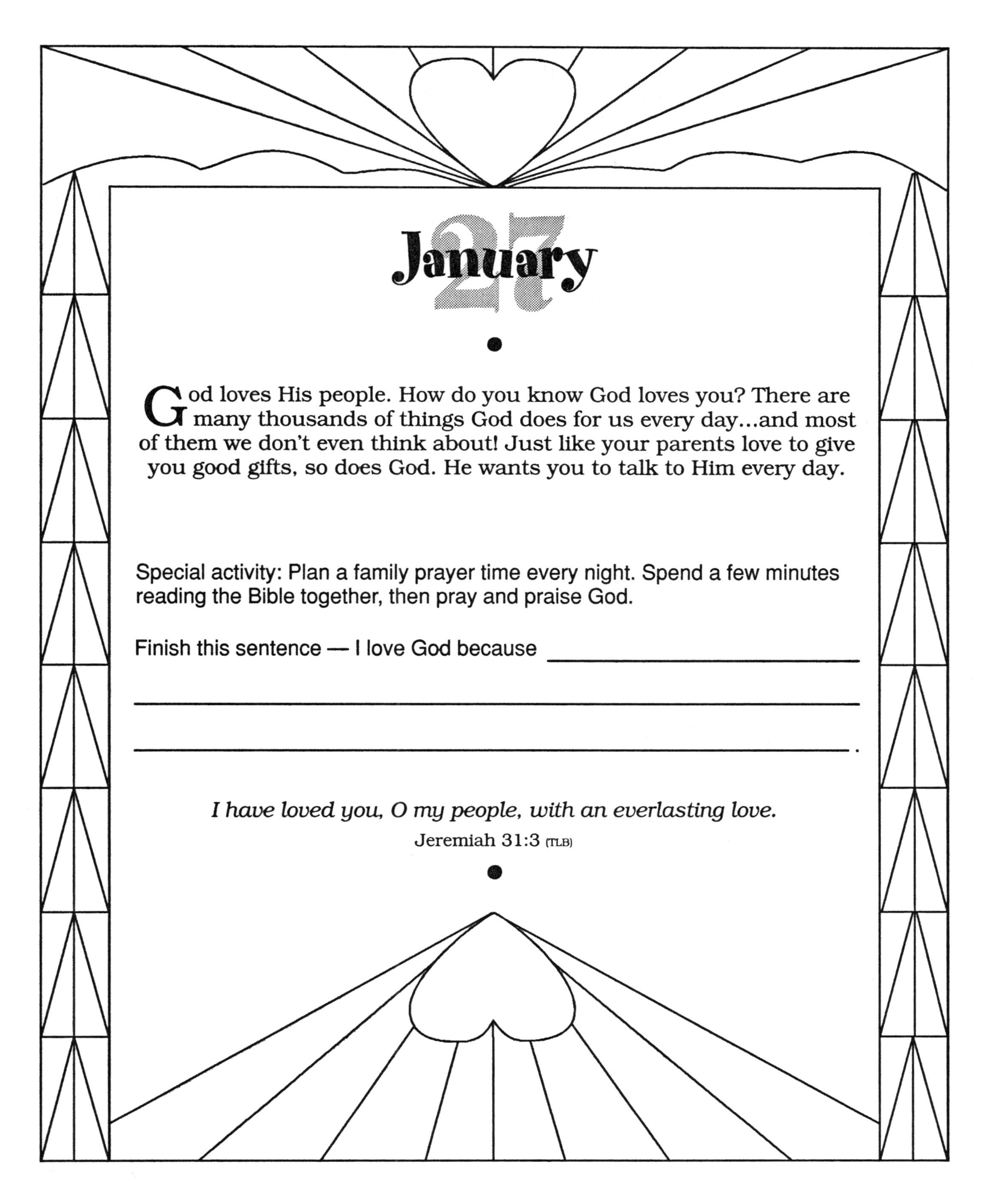

January 27

God loves His people. How do you know God loves you? There are many thousands of things God does for us every day...and most of them we don't even think about! Just like your parents love to give you good gifts, so does God. He wants you to talk to Him every day.

Special activity: Plan a family prayer time every night. Spend a few minutes reading the Bible together, then pray and praise God.

Finish this sentence — I love God because ______________________________

____

____.

I have loved you, O my people, with an everlasting love.

Jeremiah 31:3 (TLB)

Dear God,

Thank You for Your love for me.

Life is full of so many exciting possibilities. God made you special. You are one-of-a-kind. Always pray for God to guide you and show you His plan for your life!

Draw a picture of what you want to be when you grow up.

Ask the LORD to bless your plans, and you will be successful in carrying them out.

Proverbs 16:3

Dear God,

Thank You for all the talents and abilities that You have given me. Help me to always use them for Your glory.

There are many different ways to pray. Prayer is just talking to God, and you can talk to Him any time and any place. Wake up in the morning and thank God for a beautiful day. Tell God how wonderful He is when you look at the fluffy clouds He created. And when you are in trouble or you need something, you can always ask God for help.

Write a prayer thanking God for something today.

Write a prayer praising God or telling Him how wonderful He is.

What kind of praying do you do most? Remember to praise and thank God when He answers your prayers.

Write a prayer asking God for something you need.

Pray at all times.

1 Thessalonians 5:17

Dear God,

I'm so happy I can talk to You every day. We can talk as long as we want, and there is never a phone bill. The best part is that Your line is never busy!

God wants us to love Him and each other. There are many ways you can show kindness to each other: a kind word, a big hug, or doing something special can really make someone happy.

In each puff of smoke, write a person's name and something kind you can do for that person.

Be kind.

Ephesians 4:32

Dear God,

Thank You for Your love and kindness. Help me to be loving and kind to others.

January 31

•

Every month is full of many wonderful experiences and memories. Can you think of an especially wonderful memory you enjoyed this month? It could be something you did or said, or it could be an exciting place you went to or special people you visited.

Glue or tape a photograph or draw a picture of January's memorable moment in the space below. Then write (or have someone else help you write) about what happened.

Always remember...

Proverbs 3:1

•

Dear God,

Thank You for all my happy memories.

FEBRUARY

Adam was special to God. God hoped that He and Adam could be good friends. God put Adam in a beautiful place, the garden of Eden. The garden had everything Adam needed. Later, because Adam was lonely, God gave him a wife named Eve.

And the LORD God formed man of the dust of the ground, and breathed into his nostrils the breath of life; and man became a living being.

Genesis 2:7 (NKJV)

Dear God,

I know that You love me and I will have everything I need.

God gave Adam a job in the garden of Eden. He asked Adam to name all the animals. Do you think he had fun?

Let's pretend that you have to name some of the animals. What would you call each of these?

Lion ____________	Cow ____________	Cat ____________
Horse ____________	Swan ____________	Elephant ____________
Alligator ____________	Goldfish ____________	Zebra ____________
Camel ____________	Robin ____________	Bear ____________
Dove ____________	Dog ____________	Whale ____________

Now make up a funny story about some of these animals, using *your* names for them.

So [Adam] named all the birds and all the animals.

Genesis 2:20

Dear God,

Thank You for all the wonderful animals in the world.

February 3

Adam had to follow only one rule: He could eat no fruit from the forbidden tree. But Adam and Eve disobeyed God. God punished them and made them leave the garden of Eden. Now they would have to work hard to grow their own food. They would feel pain, get sick, and die. That's how it has been for people ever since.

Color this picture, and talk with your parents about the importance of obeying God.

The LORD God sent him out of the garden of Eden to till the ground from which he was taken. So He drove out the man; and He placed cherubim at the east of the garden of Eden.

Genesis 3:23,24 (NKJV)

Dear God,

Help me to always trust and obey You, because You know what is best for me.

February 4

What does it mean to follow in the steps of Jesus? It means to love Him with all your heart and follow His example. Jesus always showed love to others, He always told the truth, and always obeyed God. He always trusted God in every situation.

Outline the bottom of your foot on this page. Did you know that you walk about 10,000 steps in one day? That means that in your lifetime, your feet will travel a distance equal to four times around the earth. One time around the earth is 24,902 miles!

Everyone's feet are different. No one has a footprint exactly like yours!

Each foot has 26 bones, 20 muscles, 33 joints, and over 100 ligaments. There are also thousands of sweat glands. How's that for an amazing feet!

Put your heel here,
then draw the outline of your foot.

It was to this that God called you, for Christ himself suffered for you and left you an example, so that you would follow in his steps.

1 Peter 2:21

Dear God,

Help me to be more like Jesus.

February 5

How are we like God? We aren't as big or smart as God, and we can't do everything God can do. So how are we like God? We are able to love!

Draw yourself giving these flowers to someone. If you want, you can also write a nice note and give it to a friend tomorrow.

So God created human beings, making them to be like himself.

Genesis 1:27

Dear God,

Thank You for Your love, which never ends. Help me to love and get along with others every day. Help me to forgive when they hurt me.

February 6

God has always blessed people who love Him and obey His commandments. One of His blessings is giving people children.

Write about some special family memories. Talk to your parents and grandparents, then answer these questions:

How did your grandparents meet?

____

____

How did your parents meet?

____

____

____

God brought your grandparents and parents together so you could be here today!

He will love you and bless you, so that you will increase in number and have many children.

Deuteronomy 7:13

Dear God,

Thank You for taking care of my family for so long.

Every day we see people who are in need. Maybe they are hurt and need some help. Sometimes they feel left out and need to feel included. The Bible tells us that we should notice when a person needs help and do what we can for him or her. If you don't help, maybe no one will.

These boys are having a great time playing basketball. But the boy in the black shirt doesn't seem happy. What do you think he needs? How could the others make him feel better?

When God's children are in need, you be the one to help them out.

Romans 12:13 (TLB)

Dear God,

Thank You for giving me so much. Help me to notice when a person needs something... even if it is just a kind word.

•

Isn't it great to know that you can always count on God? He has promised that day and night will always show up right on time, and so will spring, fall, winter, and summer.

In the space above, draw a picture of yourself doing something you love to do in the winter.

As long as the earth remains, there will be springtime and harvest... winter and summer, day and night.

Genesis 8:22 (TLB)

•

Dear God,

Thank You for Your love in every season.

February 9

It's easy to love God with all your heart when you think about how wonderful He is! He loves you very much, and takes care of you every day.

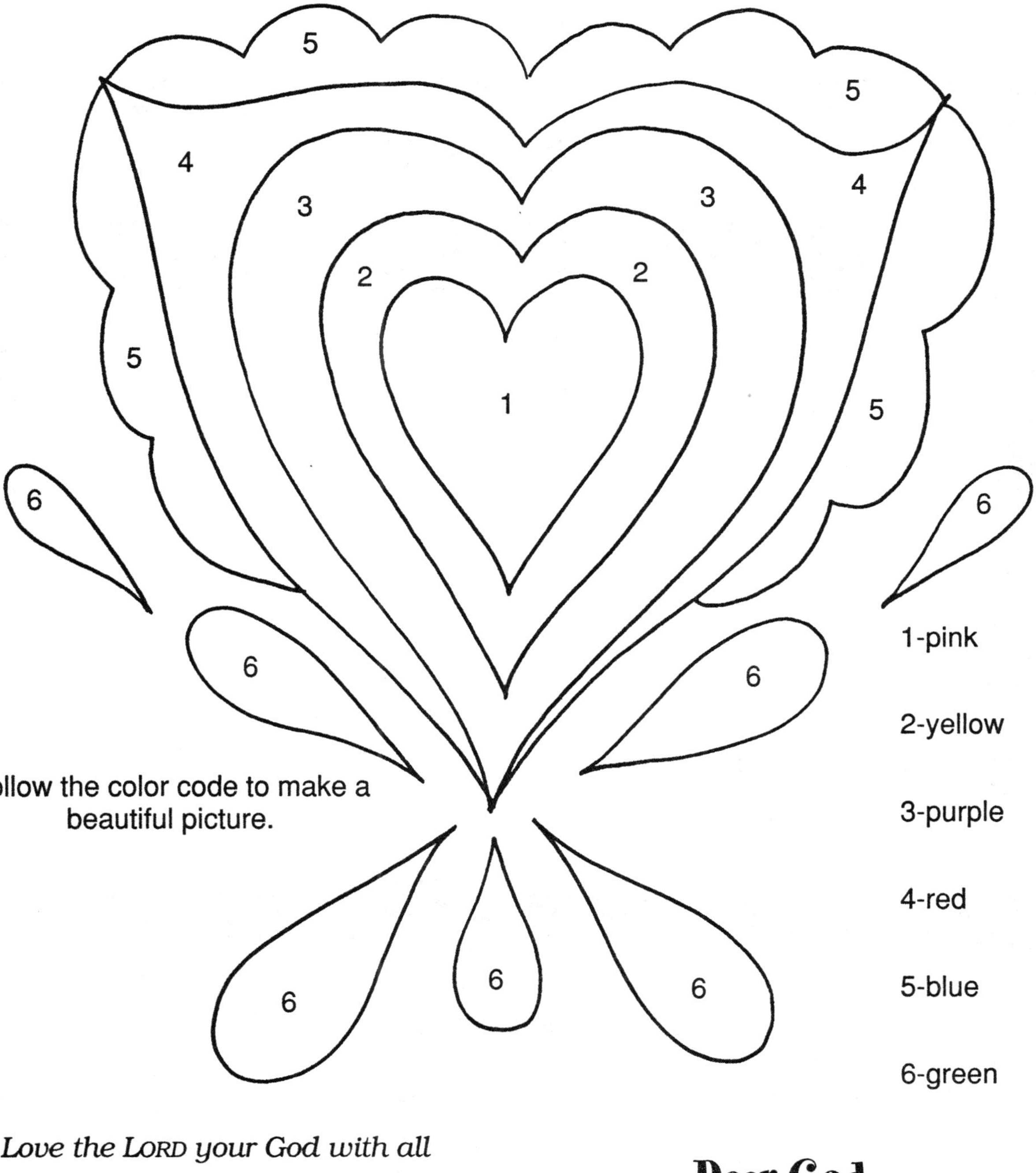

Follow the color code to make a beautiful picture.

1-pink

2-yellow

3-purple

4-red

5-blue

6-green

Love the L*ORD* *your God with all your heart.*
Deuteronomy 6:5

Dear God,
Thank You for Your love for me. I love You!

February 10

•

Has a friend ever hurt you or your feelings? Being a good friend means that you are willing to forgive the other person. Sometimes it also means saying you are sorry. Always treat your friends with love.

Special activity: Write a letter to a good friend. Tell your friend what you have been doing and decorate the letter and envelope with artwork. Tell your friend how much you miss him or her and have your parents help you mail the letter.

Draw a picture or tape a photo of you and one of your favorite friends doing something you love to do together.

See that no one pays back wrong for wrong, but at all times make it your aim to do good to one another and to all people.

1 Thessalonians 5:15

•

Dear God,

Thank You for my friends. Help me to always treat them with love and care.

•

The world is full of people who do not love God. We must be different from those kinds of people. We must stand out, just like stars shine brightly in a dark sky! We can give other people hope by letting them know about Jesus and how much God loves them.

Mirror writing is the opposite of regular writing. You have to write your words backwards, then hold them up to a mirror to read your message. On the blank line above, write your name...in mirror writing! Use the chart below for help. The top line is mirror writing. Remember to write from the right side of the paper to the left! Hold this page up to a mirror to read a speical message.

A	B	C	D	E	F	G	H	I	J	K	L	M	N	O	P	Q	R	S	T	U	V	W	X	Y	Z
A	B	C	D	E	F	G	H	I	J	K	L	M	N	O	P	Q	R	S	T	U	V	W	X	Y	Z

Do everything without complaining or arguing, so that you may be innocent and pure as God's perfect children, who live in a world of corrupt and sinful people. You must shine among them like stars lighting up the sky.

Philippians 2:14,15

•

Dear God,

Sometimes I think I have to copy everyone else to have friends. Help me to remember that the very best friends will want me to do what is right.

God wants us to be kind and loving to everyone we meet—even when they are not so easy to love! Remember that God loves everyone, and if we ask God to help us, we can love everyone, too. If you are having a hard time with someone, try praying for that person.

Whoever loves God must love his brother also.

1 John 4:21

Dear God,

Thank You for all the wonderful people in my life. I love them all, and I love You, too!

February 13

Did you know that angels are always busy helping people every day? The Bible has many stories of angels delivering special messages from God. And angels are just as busy today, watching over you and your family!

Color and name this angel.

This angel's name is

____

What are the angels, then? They are spirits who serve God and are sent by him to help those who are to receive salvation.

Hebrews 1:14

Dear God,

Thank You for loving and caring so much for me. Thank You that angels are watching out for me every day.

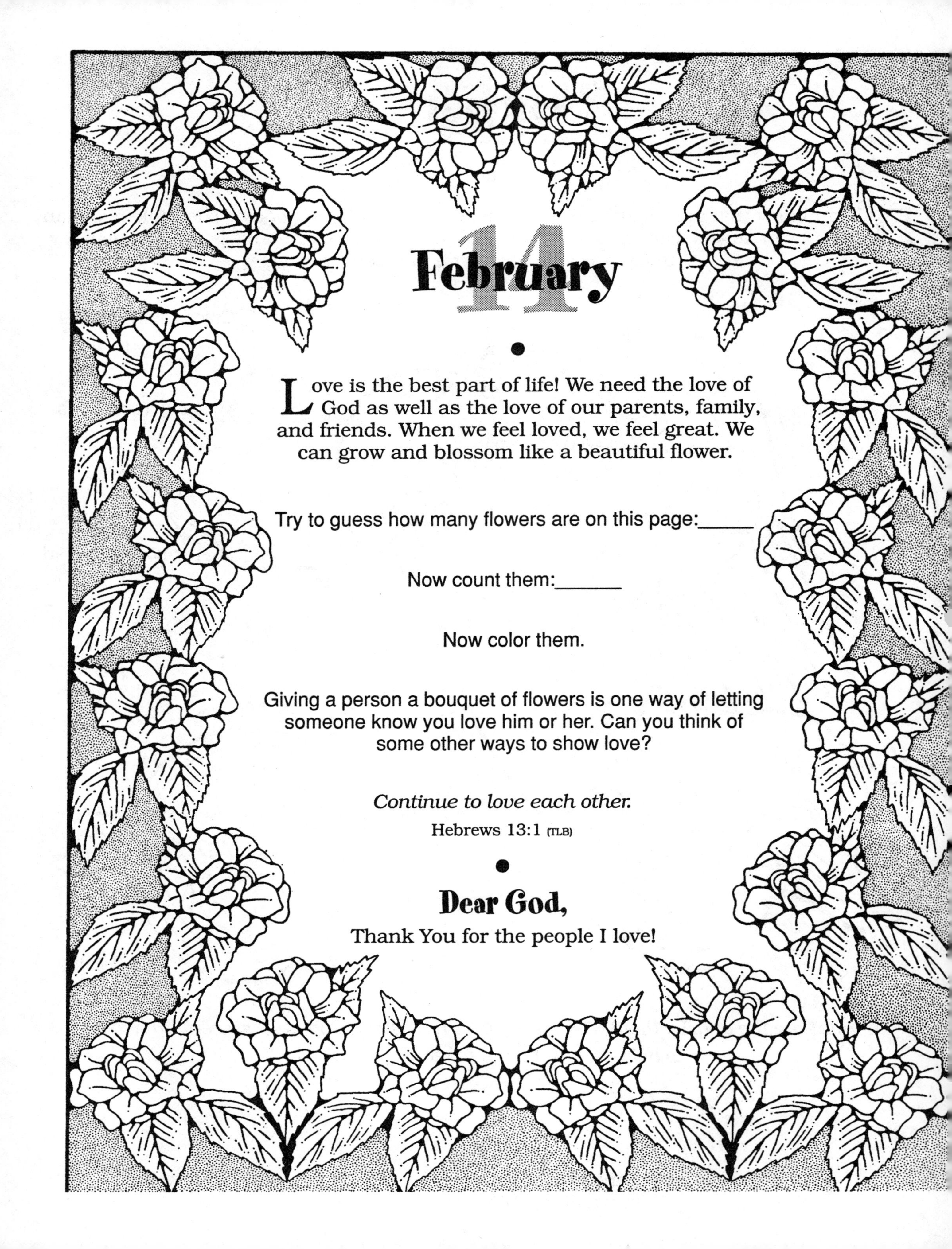

February 14

Love is the best part of life! We need the love of God as well as the love of our parents, family, and friends. When we feel loved, we feel great. We can grow and blossom like a beautiful flower.

Try to guess how many flowers are on this page:_____

Now count them:______

Now color them.

Giving a person a bouquet of flowers is one way of letting someone know you love him or her. Can you think of some other ways to show love?

Continue to love each other.

Hebrews 13:1 (TLB)

Dear God,

Thank You for the people I love!

February 15

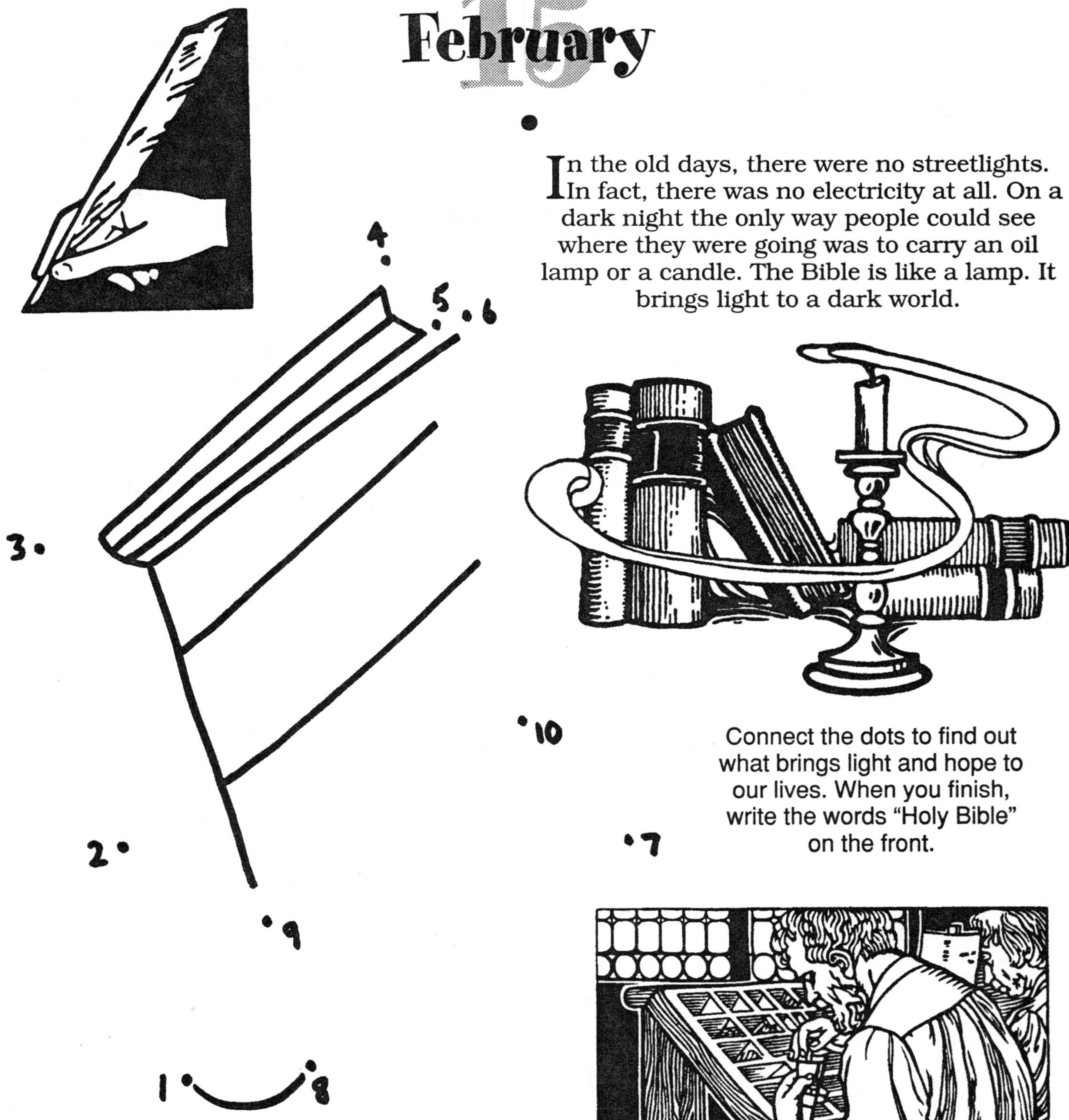

In the old days, there were no streetlights. In fact, there was no electricity at all. On a dark night the only way people could see where they were going was to carry an oil lamp or a candle. The Bible is like a lamp. It brings light to a dark world.

Connect the dots to find out what brings light and hope to our lives. When you finish, write the words "Holy Bible" on the front.

The Bible has come down to us by the careful work of people who copied the original text generation after generation.

Your word is a lamp to my feet and a light to my path.

Psalm 119:105 (NKJV)

Dear God,

Thank You for Your word in the Bible. It brings light to every situation in my life!

February 16

•

Every person is different. So how can we be at peace with everyone or get along with them? Well, when you know that God loves you, it helps you to love others. And when you love others, it pleases God.

CREATE THREE DIFFERENT PEOPLE. Choose whatever hair and facial features you want from the box below, and draw them onto the blank faces. You can pick features that belong together, or make someone look really silly!

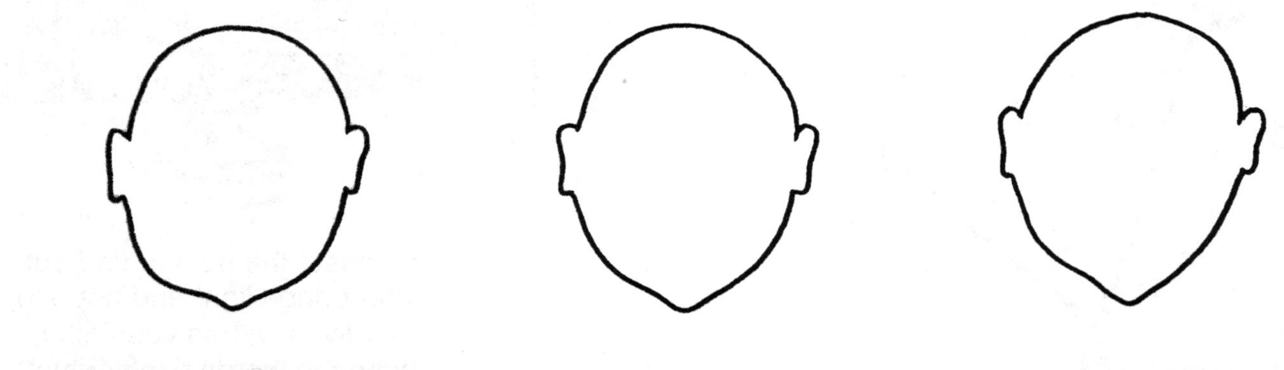

Try to be at peace with everyone.

Hebrews 12:14

•

Dear God,

Help me to get along with everyone. Some people I meet might not know how much You love them. Help me to show Your love to them by showing kindness.

February 17

Jesus told us to be at peace with one another. That means to avoid fighting at all costs. Try talking about your problems calmly. You can tell people how you feel without screaming, kicking, or punching...give it a try!

Learn how to say "peace" in several different languages:

Language	*Write it*	*Pronounce it*
French	paix	pay
German	Friede	free-deh
Hawaiian	maluhia	ma-loo-hee-ah
Hebrew	shalom	sha-lome
Irish	síocháin	shee-ah-kon
Polish	spokoj	spoh-koy
Spanish	paz	poz
Swahili	amani	ah-mon-ee

Now that you can say it, do it!

Be at peace with one another.
Mark 9:50 (NAS)

Dear God,

Help me to love You with all my heart and to treat other people the way I like to be treated.

Just as the little children talked to Jesus when He was on earth, you can talk to Jesus today! He loves you very much and is interested in every part of your life. Wouldn't you love to tell Jesus all the things you are thinking about? What would you like to tell Jesus?

Jesus Christ is the same yesterday, today, and forever.

Hebrews 13:8

Dear God,

I am so glad You love me. Thank You for Your Son, Jesus.

Do you know what self-control means? It means not to overdo anything—for example, you shouldn't eat too much candy, and you shouldn't watch too much television. Self-control also means controlling your actions and emotions when you become upset. When you feel upset or angry, take a minute to think and control yourself before you do or say something...you will be glad you did!

How can these children practice self-control?

Helen finds the cookie jar full of cookies.

Dwight watches TV all day long.

Ashley finds Amy wearing her brand-new outfit.

For the Spirit that God has given us does not make us timid; instead, his Spirit fills us with power, love, and self-control.

2 Timothy 1:7

Dear God,

I know that with Your help I can control myself in all kinds of situations. Then I will feel much better and have more friends, too.

What does it mean to be gentle? It means you speak softly, you don't hit or push or shove, and you use sweet, kind words and actions. God wants us to be gentle with each other. When you are gentle, you are showing love.

You can be kind to animals, too. Have fun coloring this cat. Follow the color key.

Show a gentle attitude toward everyone.

Philippians 4:5

Dear God,

Help me to treat other people gently so they will know how special they are to me.

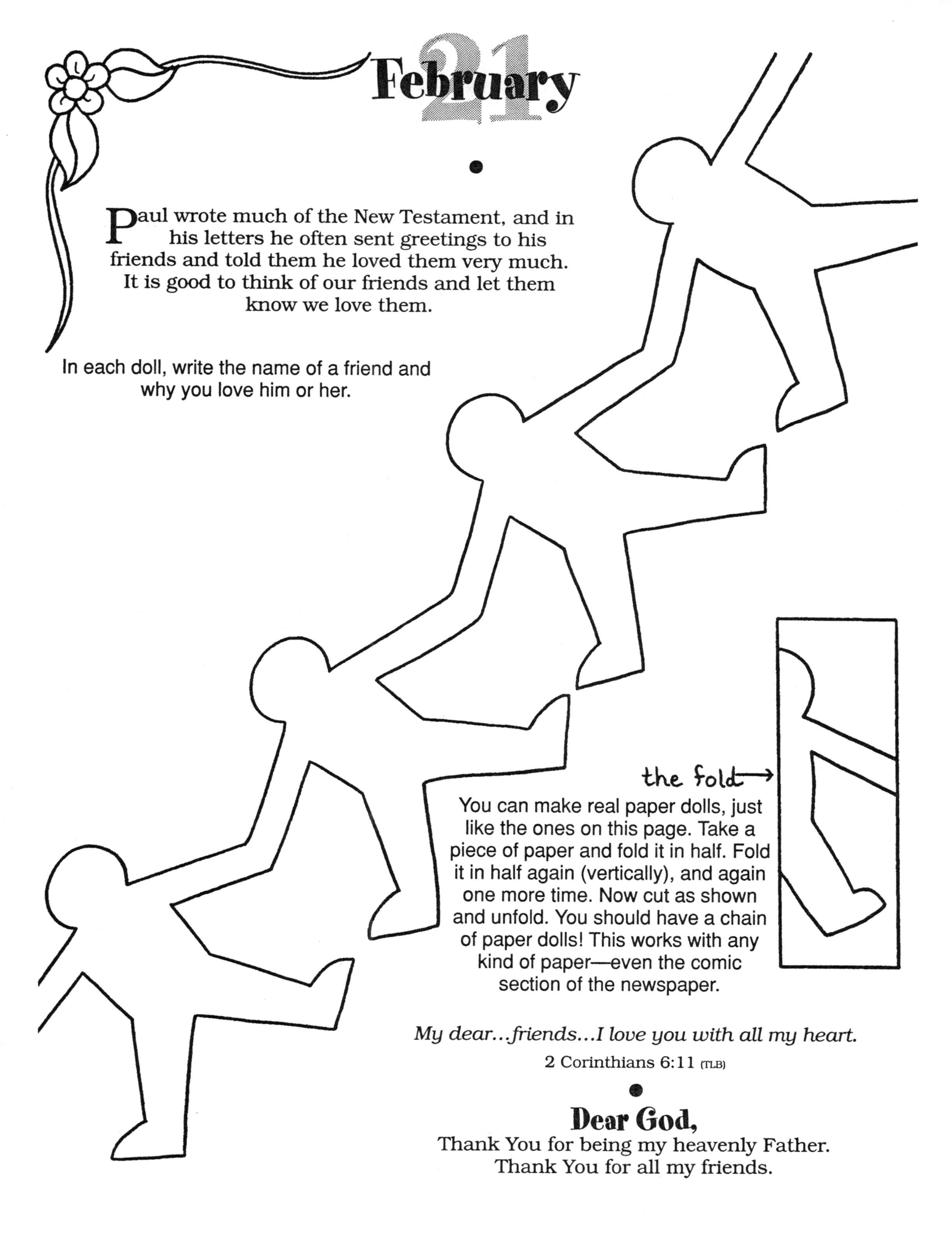

February 21

Paul wrote much of the New Testament, and in his letters he often sent greetings to his friends and told them he loved them very much. It is good to think of our friends and let them know we love them.

In each doll, write the name of a friend and why you love him or her.

You can make real paper dolls, just like the ones on this page. Take a piece of paper and fold it in half. Fold it in half again (vertically), and again one more time. Now cut as shown and unfold. You should have a chain of paper dolls! This works with any kind of paper—even the comic section of the newspaper.

My dear...friends...I love you with all my heart.

2 Corinthians 6:11 (TLB)

Dear God,

Thank You for being my heavenly Father.
Thank You for all my friends.

God is amazing. Every single star has a name. He takes such good care of the universe, and He takes good care of you!

Color these stars. Make a beautiful pattern by coloring each star the same color, each diamond the same color, and so on.

He has decided the number of the stars and calls each one by name.

Psalm 147:4

Dear God,

When I look up into the sky at night and see all the stars that You made, I am amazed. Thank You for making such an incredible universe, and thank You for making me.

When you want something, you usually want it right away...right? But sometimes we have to wait for good things. God knows the right time for everything to happen, and we must learn to be patient. And you will find that when you wait for God's perfect timing, it is always worth it! To become good at something, like a sport, takes lots of practice and patience. The first time you try a new sport, you may not be too good at it... but practice makes perfect!

You need to be patient, in order to do the will of God and receive what he promises.
Hebrews 10:36

Dear God,

I know You have good things planned for my life. Help me to wait patiently for Your perfect timing.

•

Have you ever thought about doing something, but decided it was just too hard or even impossible to do? Well, guess what? God's specialty is the impossible! Impossible things are what God does best. So, try praying and asking God for help the next time you are facing a hard situation. God can make it happen!

In the space below, draw a picture of YOUR OWN invention. Make up something new that can help you in wonderful ways. You invent it! Write a few words about what your marvelous invention does. What do you call it?

For with God nothing will be impossible.

Luke 1:37 (NKJV)

•

Dear God,

I'm glad that You can do anything! Help me to always do the things that make You happy.

February 25

A bad temper will make you unhappy, and it will make everyone around you unhappy, too. There is always a better way to handle any situation: calm down, think before you speak, and ask God to take the anger away. Then you won't say or do things you will be sorry for.

Circle the times when it is okay to shout and scream and yell in anger:

1. You lose a game.
2. Your brother or sister messes up your room.
3. Someone calls you a name.
4. You don't get your way.
5. You can't find your overdue library book.
6. You don't like what is being served for dinner.
7. The dog ripped your favorite pair of shoes.

Guess what? You shouldn't have circled any of the sentences. Yes, things will happen that will make you feel upset. But make up your mind that you will not have a bad temper, and ask God to help you stay calm. Then you and everybody around you will have a happier, healthier life.

Hot tempers cause arguments, but patience brings peace.

Proverbs 15:18

Dear God,

Help me to stay peaceful no matter what is going on around me.

February 26

•

Do you know what the Bible means when it says that God has counted all the hairs of your head? It means that He knows everything about you...even the things that no one else could ever know. It also means God watches out for you and cares about you very, very much.

Give these people hair—pretty hair, silly hair, funny hair—any hair.

Even the hairs of your head have all been counted.

Matthew 10:30

•

Dear God,

I am glad You care so much about me. It gives me such a great feeling.

Have you ever noticed that sometimes the people around you seem to have no time to listen to you? Well, there is someone who is never too busy to listen and who lets you take all the time you want. Do you know who that is? Color the puzzle below to find the answer.

Color each space that has a dot in it. Make sure you use a nice, bright color. Remember, God always listens and always cares about you.

I love the LORD, because he hears me; he listens to my prayers.

Psalm 116:1

Dear God,

Thank You for hearing my prayers. I am glad You are never too busy for me.

FEBRUARY FEBRUARY FEB

February 28

•

What memorable moment did you enjoy in February? Did something unusual happen? Did something nice happen? Did you do something sweet...or funny? Now is your chance to tell all about it.

Glue or tape a photograph or draw a picture of February's memorable moment. Write (or have someone help you write) all about what you did.

What I say is the truth.

Proverbs 8:7

•

Dear God,

Thank You for all the special things that happen in my life.

MARCH

March 1

God made everything in the world. Do you love the feeling of wind in your face? God makes that wind blow. You can't see the wind, but you know when it is near. You can't see God, but you know when He is near...because you feel wonderful!

Have you ever flown a kite on a windy day?
Was it fun? What happened?

Follow the arrow and go through the maze.

God is the one who...created the winds.

Amos 4:13

Dear God,

You are awesome! You made the whole world, and you also know all about me and love me.

March 2

Once Jesus was in a boat with His friends when a fierce storm hit the lake. His friends begged Jesus to help them. Jesus stood up and told the wind to stop, and it did. When you have problems, Jesus wants to help you, just like He helped His friends that day.

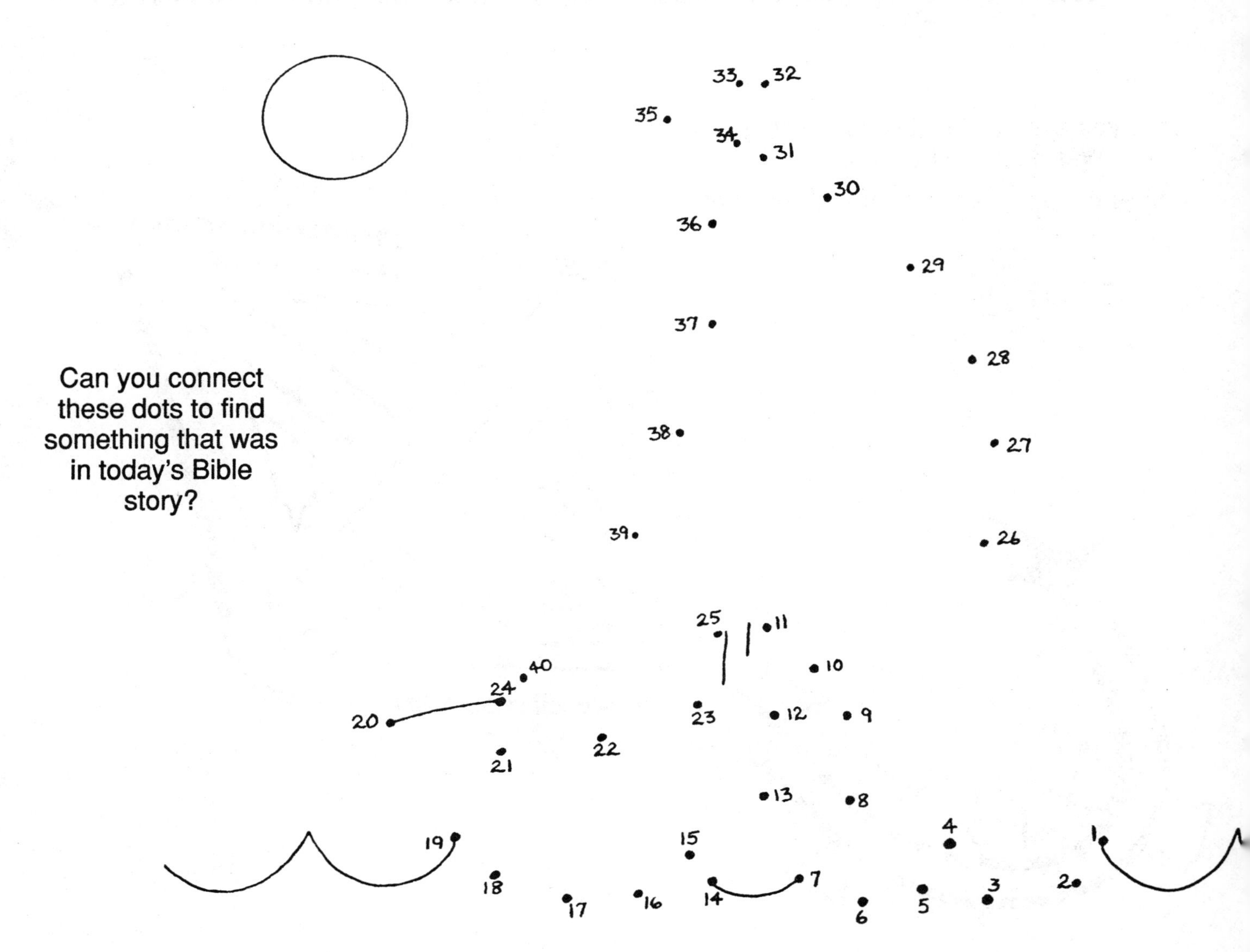

Can you connect these dots to find something that was in today's Bible story?

"What kind of man is this?" They said, "Even the winds and the waves obey him!"

Matthew 8:27

Dear God,

Thank You for Your love. Thank You for caring so much about me.

Can you imagine how beautiful the sky must have looked when God filled it with birds for the very first time? The air was full of sweet chirping and singing, and has been ever since.

Let the skies be filled with birds of every kind.

Genesis 1:20 (TLB)

Dear God,

Thank You for making such a beautiful world. Thank You for the sweet music of birds.

Can you think of something you would like to get as a present? You can probably think of many things! God loves to give you presents, and He gives you things that are good for you.

Draw what present you would like most in the world.

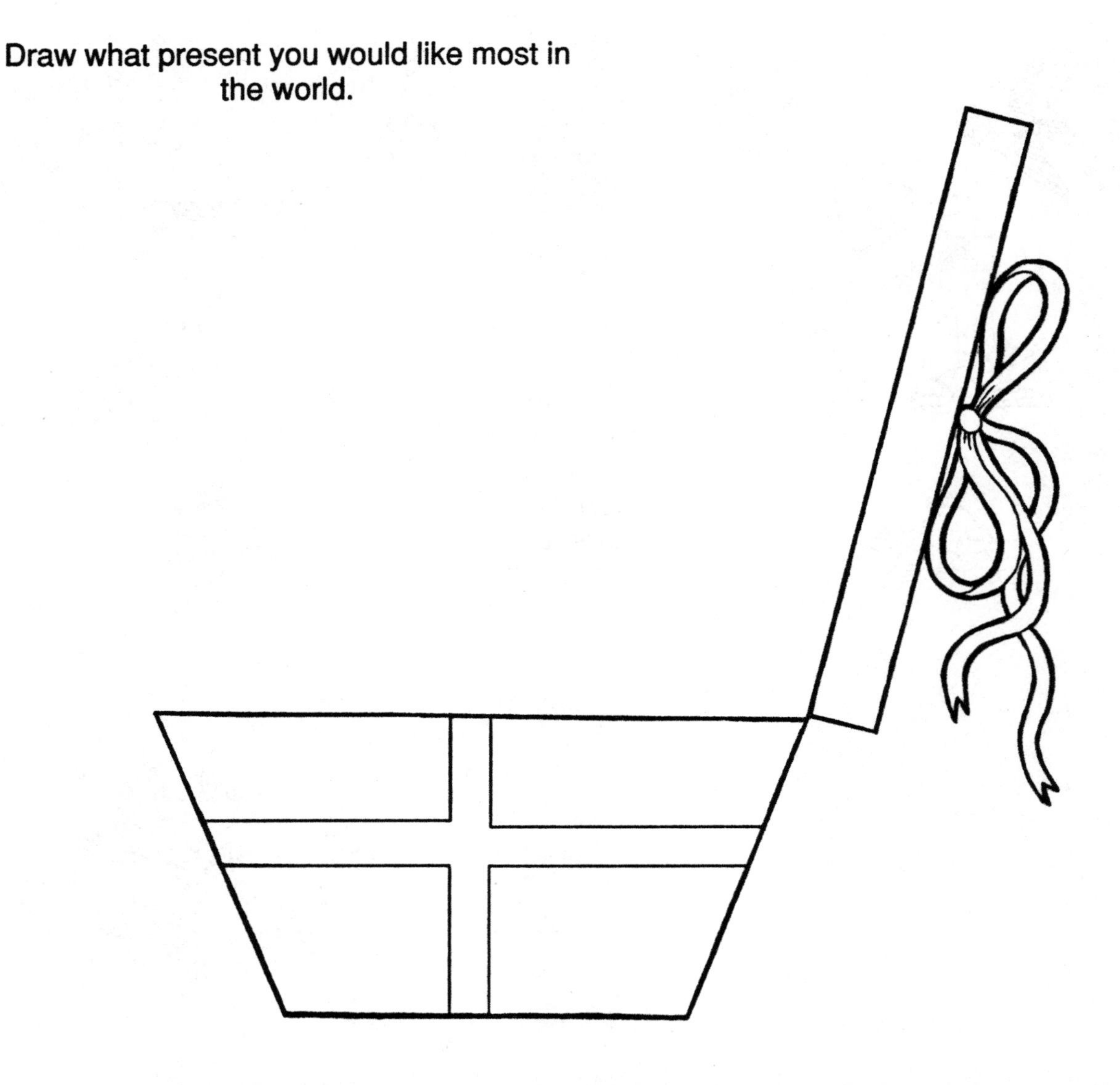

Every good gift and every perfect present comes from heaven.

James 1:17

Dear God,

Thank You for giving me so many wonderful things. Your presents don't break or fall apart like some of my toys do. Thank You for giving me the very best!

March 5

•

Noah was a good man who loved and obeyed God. The rest of the people on earth had forgotten about God and were very bad. God decided to flood the whole earth with water, but He wanted Noah and his family to be safe, so He told them to build a big boat — an ark.

Can you find the name "Noah" in this picture?

Noah had no faults and was the only good man of his time.

Genesis 6:9,10

•

Dear God,

I am glad that You take care of people who love You.

March 6

Noah and his family were safe during the flood because Noah had obeyed God. While he was building the ark, his neighbors had made fun of him. Noah didn't care; he decided to obey God. Don't you think Noah was glad he had done what God told him to do?

Can you find 10 differences between these two pictures?

So Noah went out of the boat with his wife, his sons, and their wives. All the animals and birds went out of the boat in groups of their own kind.

Genesis 8:18,19

Dear God,

Help me to always obey You even if other children make fun of me. Let me do what makes You happy; I want You to be proud of me.

God wanted to save Noah and his family, but He wanted to save the animals, too. Noah brought two of each kind of animal into the ark. Aren't you glad God saved the animals so we could have them in our world today?

Finally the day came when the Lord said to Noah, "Go into the boat with all your family, for among all the people of the earth, I consider you alone to be righteous. Bring in the animals, too."

Genesis 7:1 (TLB)

Dear God,

It is good to know that no matter what is going on in the world, You will take care of me and keep me safe...because I love You.

God promised Noah that He would never again destroy the whole world with a big flood. Did you know that God always keeps His promises?

Draw a rainbow in the sky.

When the rainbow appears in the clouds, I will see it and remember the everlasting covenant between me and all living beings on earth.

Genesis 9:16

Dear God,

Thank You for keeping Your promises. Help me to keep my promises, too.

Have you ever tried to take a walk on a very windy day? God controls the wind, and God controls where His Holy Spirit goes, too. Another name for the Holy Spirit is the "Spirit of the Lord" or the "Spirit of God."

Connect the dots to find out what kind of building uses the wind for power.

The wind blows wherever it wishes; you hear the sound it makes, but you do not know where it comes from or where it is going. It is like that with everyone who is born of the Spirit.

John 3:8

Dear God,

Thank You for the Holy Spirit, who helps make me brave, strong, and obedient.

March 10

•

You can't always know what is going on inside someone just by looking at him. The person who you think is unfriendly may just be shy, and the person you think is mean might really be hurt or afraid. If you take the time to get to know someone, you might end up with a new friend!

Give each girl below a different hat. Each hat must be different from the others: one can be beautiful, one can be silly, and one can be strange or funny.

When you finish drawing the hats, look at each girl and say what you think she is like. See why it is important to get to know people instead of judging people by how they look.

Do not judge others, so that God will not judge you.

Matthew 7:1

•

Dear God,

Help me not to judge people. Help me to see something good in everyone.

God wants you to obey your parents. Your parents know what is best for you and what will keep you safe and out of trouble.

These children were told to stay out of their neighbor's field. One day on the way home from school, some of the children decided to go into the field. They told the others, "If you don't come with us, you are afraid!" What would you do? What would make your parents happy? What would make God happy? What might happen to the children who go into the field?

Children, obey your parents in all things, for this is well pleasing to the Lord.
Colossians 3:20 (NKJV)

Dear God,

Help me to obey my parents all the time so that all will go well with me.

March 12

If you had to choose a place on which to build your house, would you build it on rock or sand? When Jesus spoke of building your house, He was saying that if you love and trust God, you will be like a house built on the strongest of rocks. Nothing will be able to bother or hurt you.

Draw a picture of where you live. No matter where you live, if the people in your house love God, you will have a happy home.

Anyone who hears these words of mine and obeys them is like a wise man who built his house on rock. The rain poured down, the rivers flooded over, and the wind blew hard against that house. But it did not fall, because it was built on rock.

Matthew 7:24

Dear God,

I am glad that if I trust in You, You will always take good care of me.

When Jesus was 30 years old, He left His home in Nazareth and went to see John the Baptist at the Jordan River. John knew that Jesus was the Messiah, the Son of God. In obedience to God, Jesus had come to be baptized.

Connect the dots to see what happened next.

To find out what John the Baptist said to Jesus, use the following guide:

A	B	C	D	E	F	G	H	I	J	K	L	M	N	O	P	Q	R	S	T	U	V	W	X	Y	Z
1	2	3	4	5	6	7	8	9	10	11	12	13	14	15	16	17	18	19	20	21	22	23	24	25	26

"__ __"

9 15 21 7 8 20 20 15 2 5 2 1 16 20 9 26 5 4 2 25 25 15 21

At that time Jesus arrived from Galilee and came to John at the Jordan to be baptized by him.

Matthew 3:13

Dear God,

Help me to always do the things You want me to do.

A dove is white and gentle, and is often used as a picture of peace and purity. A dove brought Noah an olive branch to let him know the flood was over. A dove descended from heaven after Jesus was baptized, showing that God's Spirit was upon Him.

Hand shadows are lots of fun! All you need is a light and a flat surface like a screen or wall.

To make your dove fly, just move your hand across the screen or wall. You can raise and lower your hand to imitate the movement of a real bird.

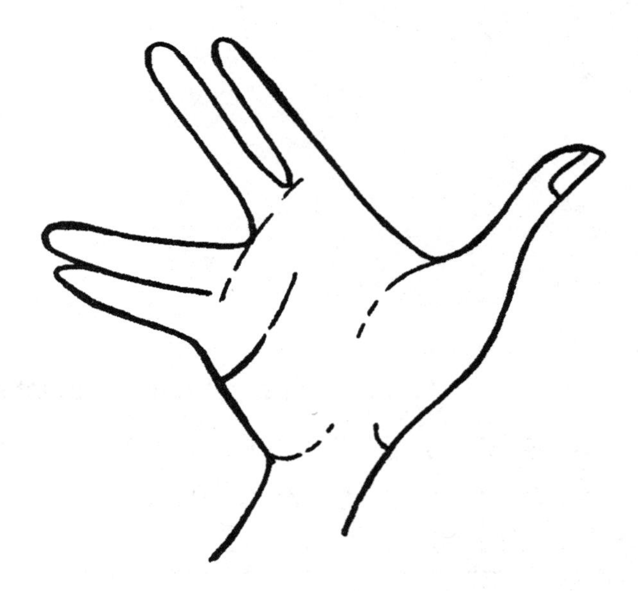

As soon as Jesus was baptized, he came up out of the water. Then heaven was open to him, and he saw the Spirit of God coming down like a dove and lighting on him.

Matthew 3:16

Dear God,

Thank You for Your Holy Spirit. Thank You that I can be a part of Your family. I love You!

It's so much fun to fly a kite on a windy day! It is fun to watch your kite dip and swirl in the wind. God's Holy Spirit is like that wind—He lifts us up into exciting new places.

Draw yourself flying these kites. Hold on tight! Design and draw your own kites on the ends of the three empty strings.

The wind blows wherever it wishes; you hear the sound it makes, but you do not know where it comes from or where it is going. It is like that with everyone who is born of the Spirit.

John 3:8

Dear God,

Just like a kite in the wind, I always want to go where Your Holy Spirit wants me to go.

March 16

In Bible times, people had wonderful parties called "feasts"! At a feast they served lots and lots of food for hours and hours. That was their way of celebrating a special event. Today's Bible verse is saying that life can be a wonderful celebration!

Draw your idea of the perfect birthday party. Who is there with you? What are you doing?

He who is of a merry heart has a continual feast.

Proverbs 15:15 (NKJV)

Dear God,

Thank You for birthdays; they are fun. Thank You that every day with You can be like a happy party.

March 17

God has good plans for His people. Sometimes those plans include moving from one place to another. The people of Israel moved from Egypt to a new country. What country did your ancestors come from?

Draw a picture of yourself in the country of your ancestors. What does it look like around you? What are you wearing? What is the weather like? Do you like it there?

Bring them up from that land to a good and spacious land, to a land flowing with milk and honey.

Exodus 3:8 (NASB)

Dear God,

Thank You for making sure that I was born in exactly the right place to exactly the right parents.

Did you ever notice how much better you feel when your room is all picked up and your toys are where they belong? God wants us to be neat and organized in every part of our lives. He wants us to take good care of everything He gives us. Being organized helps us feel more peaceful.

Put these toys neatly on the shelves. Draw each toy on the shelf where it belongs.

Everything must be done in a proper and orderly way.

1 Corinthians 14:40

Dear God,

Help me to be neat and orderly in everything I do.

Jesus taught us to love one another. He said that real love is always there and never ends.

Write the name of someone you love on each petal of the flower. Under each name, write one thing you love about that person.

The message you heard from the very beginning is this: we must love one another.

1 John 3:11

Dear God,

Thank You for loving me. Help me to always be kind and loving to others.

We should love everyone...especially our family!

Draw a picture or glue a recent photograph of your family in this space.

Love one another warmly as Christian brothers, and be eager to show respect for one another.

Romans 12:20

Dear God,

Thank You for my family, and help me to be kind and show respect to them!

Look up into the night sky and you will see hundreds of stars! The universe is so big, but God is even bigger than the universe because He made it all.

Draw yourself traveling through outer space in an interesting spaceship.

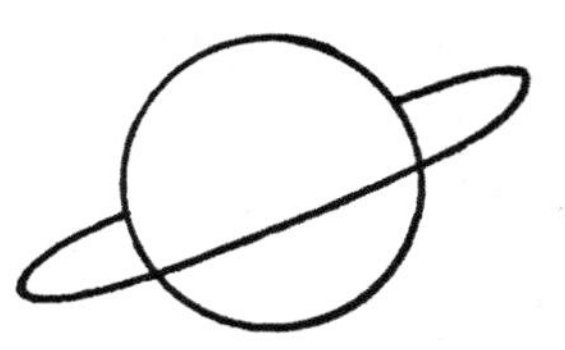

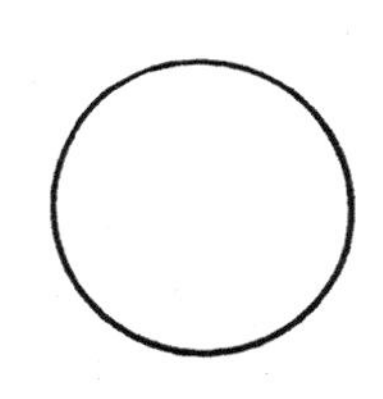

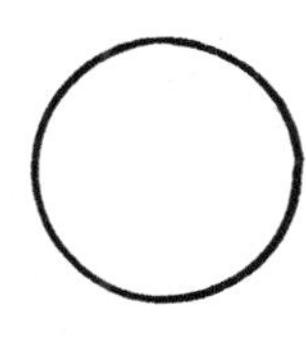

The heavens declare the glory of God.

Psalm 19:1 (NKJV)

Dear God,

You sure do have a big world and universe to look after. At the same time, You are interested in every part of my life. Thank You for loving me so much.

How wonderful is our God! He wants you to love Him and thank Him for all the good things He does for you. God is right there with you! Let's join all the angels in heaven and shout, "Hallelujah!"

Draw yourself with the angels singing praise to God.

Glory to God in the highest heaven.

Luke 2:14

Dear God,

You are the greatest! You are wonderful! Thank You for loving me.

God has promised that if we obey Him, He will bless us wherever we are, give us good food to eat, keep us safe, and help us be successful. God is very good! Remember that wherever you are, God is with you.

To color this picture, use the following code:

1-red	3-yellow	5-green
2-blue	4-orange	6-brown

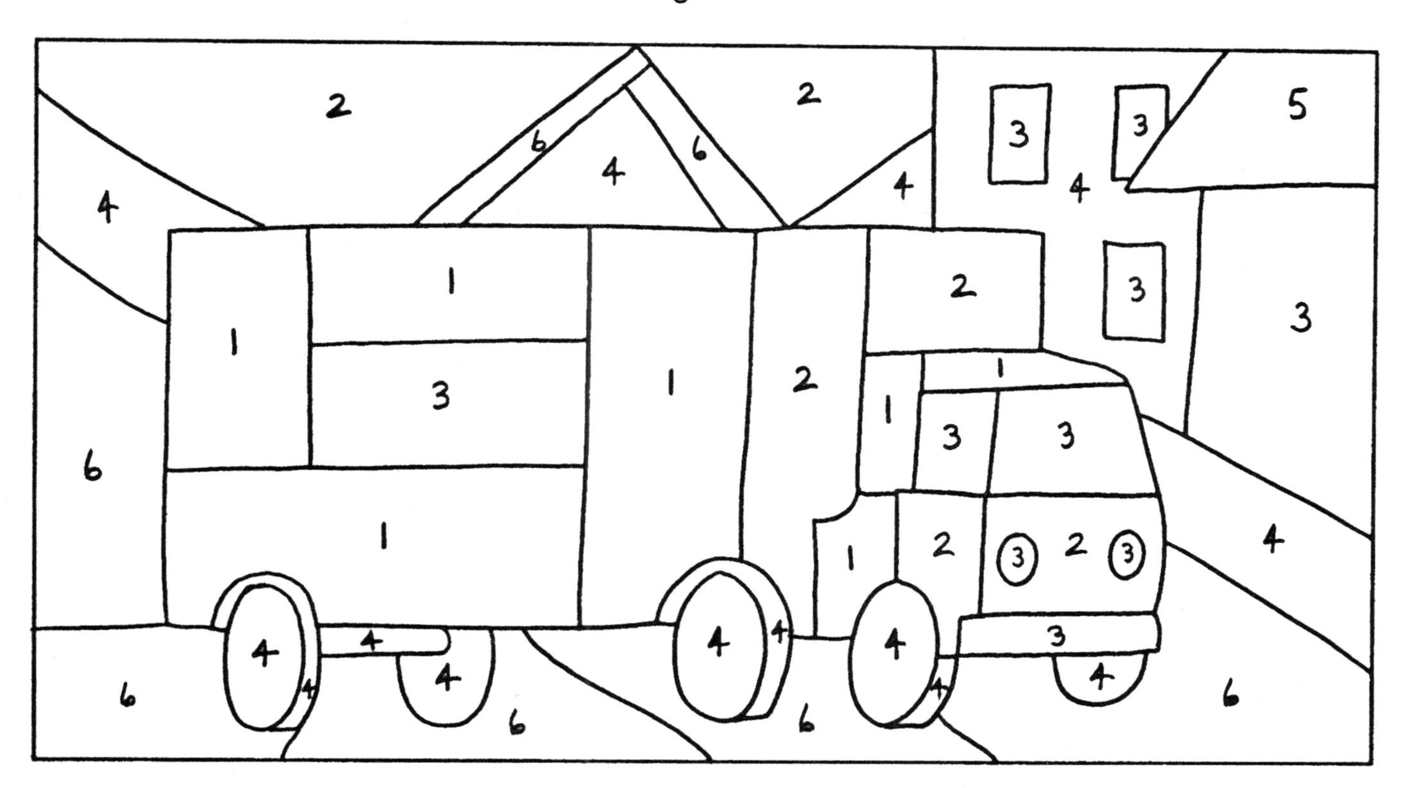

List three things you would like about living in...

The City	The Country
1.	1.
2.	2.
3.	3.

Blessed shall you be in the city, and blessed shall you be in the country.

Deuteronomy 28:3 (NASB)

Dear God,

Help me to obey You. Thank You for all Your good gifts.

Sometimes it is nice to be alone. You can be alone up in a tree, in a garden or in your room. You can dream, read, draw, or just rest. But you are never really alone...God is with you always.

Design what you think would be the perfect bedroom for you.

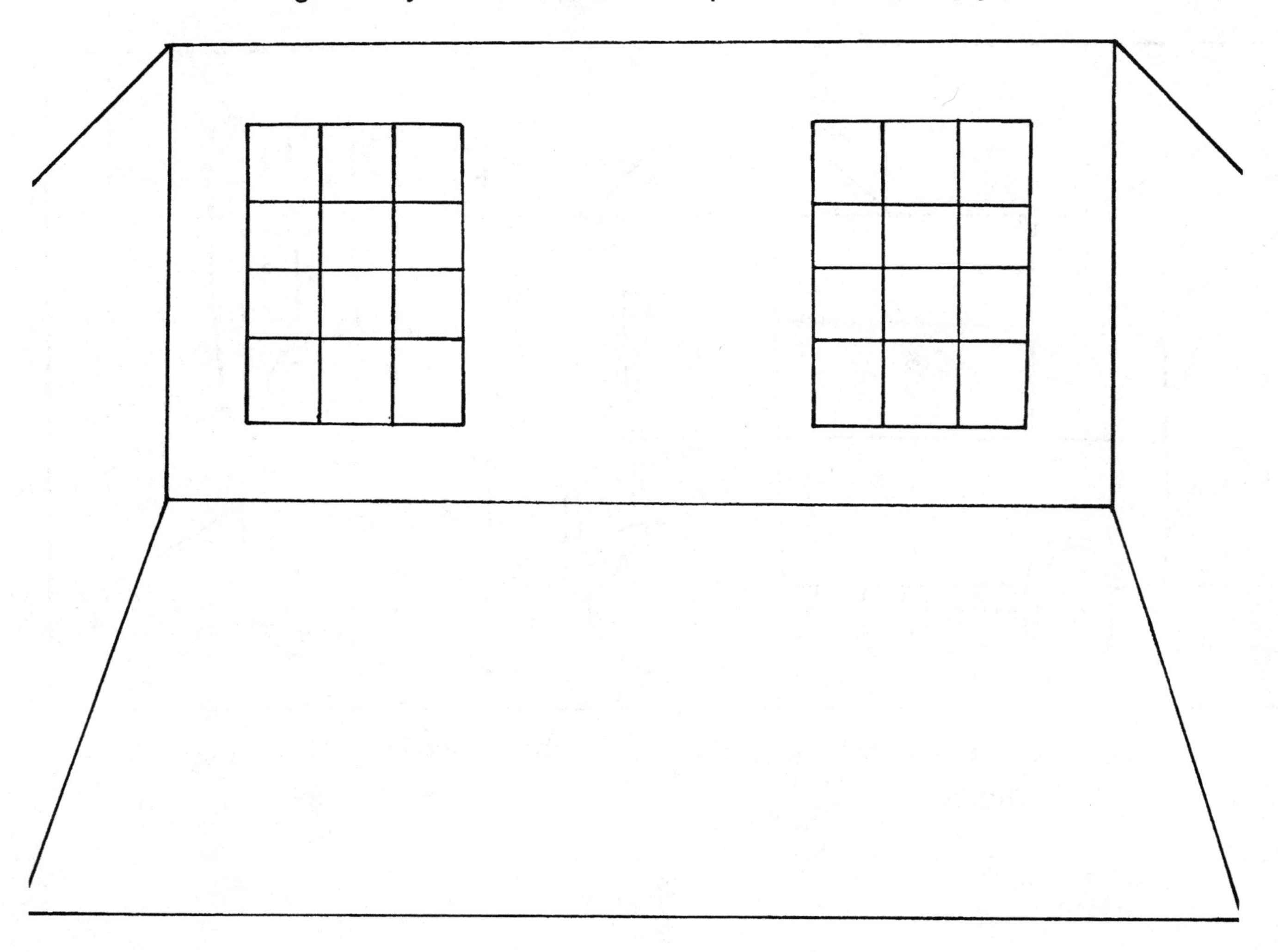

Let us go off by ourselves.

Mark 6:31

Dear God,

Thank You for the peace I feel when I think of You.

•

Being kind to others means doing and saying nice things that make them happy. Think about what that person would really like—a flower, a kind word, or a trip to the park. Little acts of kindness often mean a lot!

In the vase below, draw a flower for each time you did something nice for your family and friends today.

If you did something nice for Dad, put in a daisy.

If you did something nice for Mom, a rose.

If you did something nice for your brothers or sisters, put in a tulip (one for each of them)!

Did you do something nice for a friend? Put in a daffodil.

Did you do something nice for somebody you didn't know? Put in an azalea.

Be kind.

Ephesians 4:32

•

Dear God,

I like it when people are kind to me. Help me to be kind to other people.

Be careful of what you say. Your words can get you into a lot of trouble. Always stop and think before you speak. The tongue is little, but it can get us into BIG trouble!

WATCH YOUR WORDS GAME

Two or more people can play this game. Take turns flipping a coin. Heads means you move forward two spaces, and tails means you move forward one space.

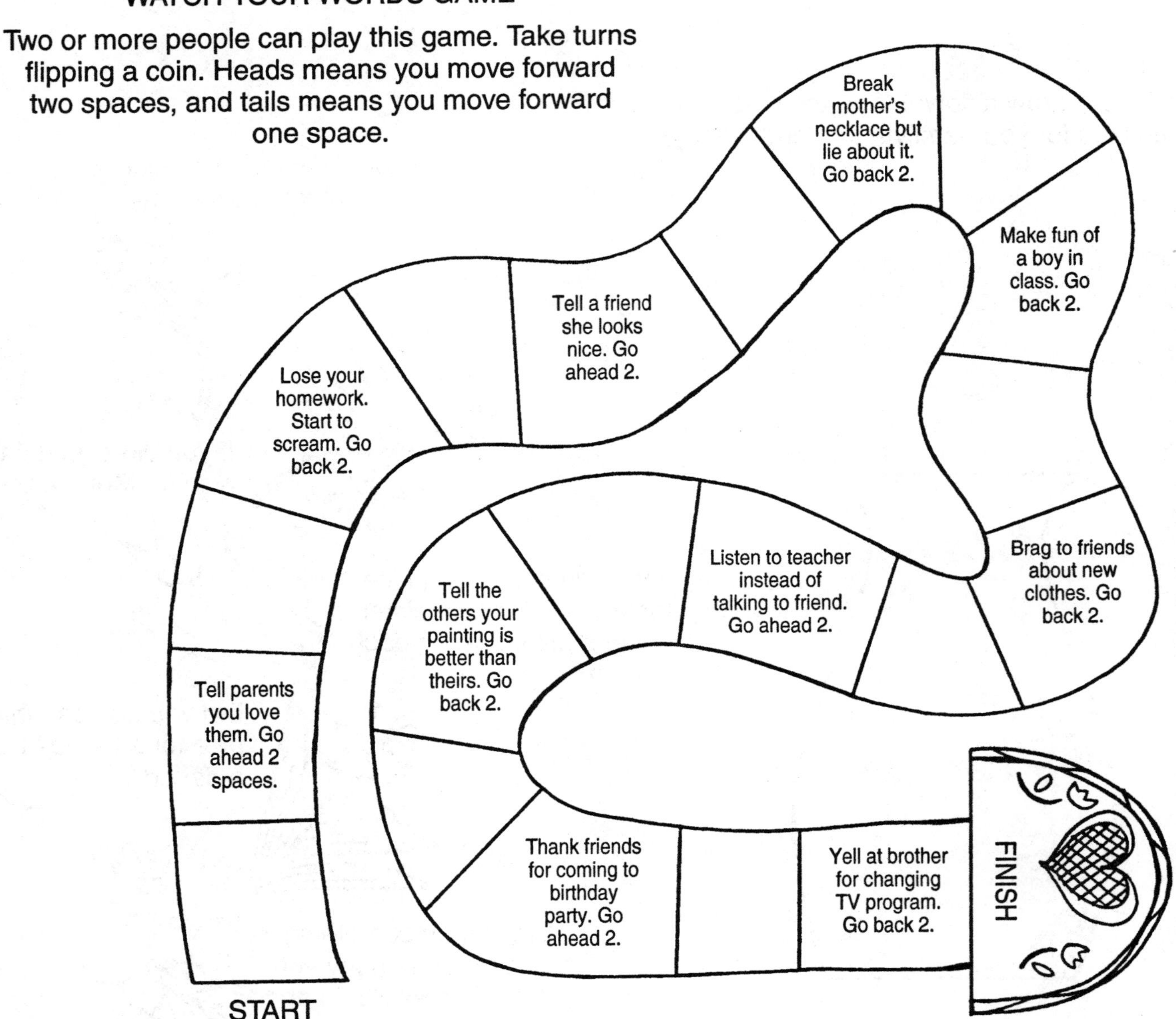

The tongue, small as it is...can boast about great things.

James 3:5

Dear God,

Help me to always watch my words and speak in the kindest way.

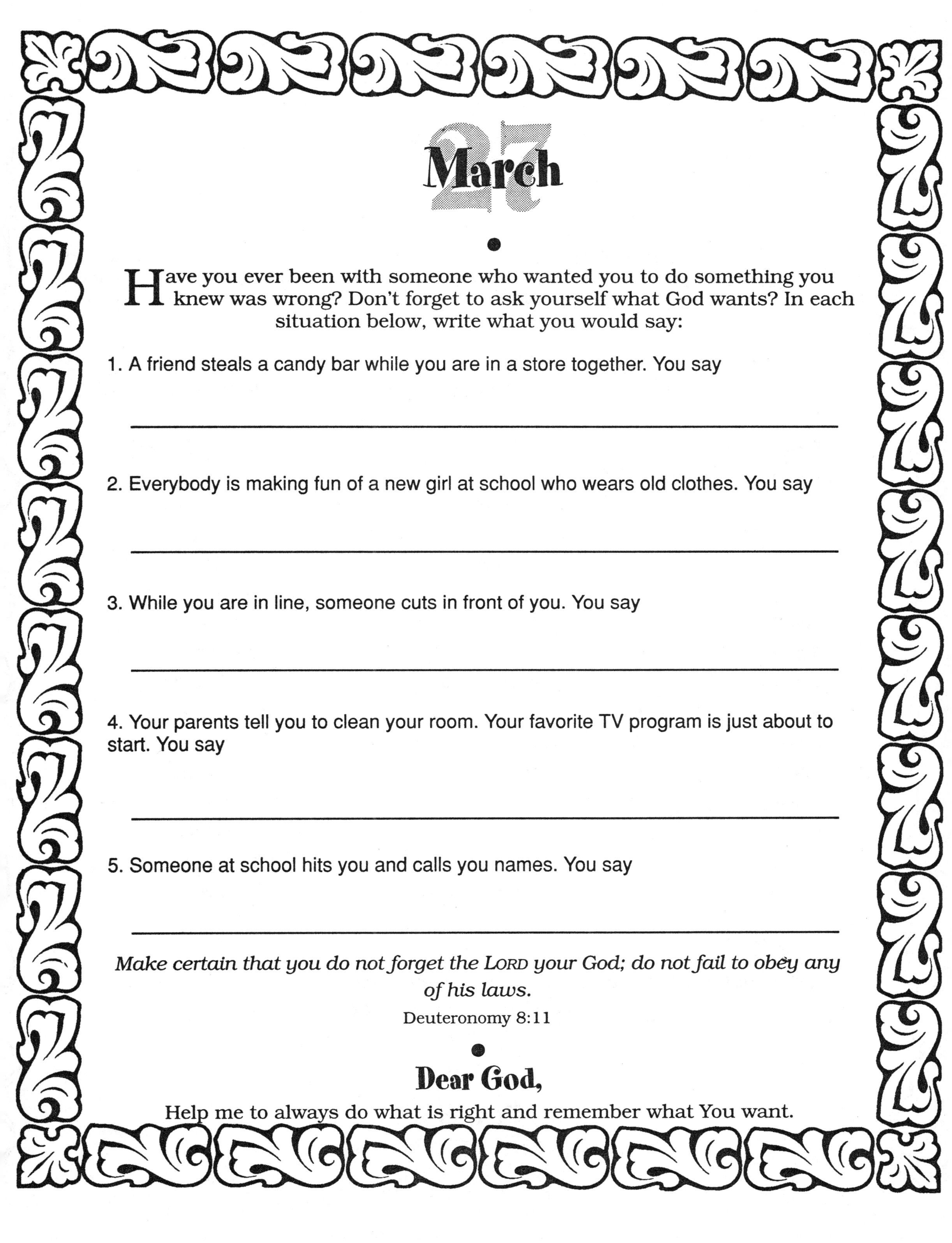

March 27

Have you ever been with someone who wanted you to do something you knew was wrong? Don't forget to ask yourself what God wants? In each situation below, write what you would say:

1. A friend steals a candy bar while you are in a store together. You say

____

2. Everybody is making fun of a new girl at school who wears old clothes. You say

____

3. While you are in line, someone cuts in front of you. You say

____

4. Your parents tell you to clean your room. Your favorite TV program is just about to start. You say

____

5. Someone at school hits you and calls you names. You say

____

Make certain that you do not forget the LORD your God; do not fail to obey any of his laws.

Deuteronomy 8:11

Dear God,

Help me to always do what is right and remember what You want.

•

When Jesus went back to heaven to be with His Father, He said that He would send the Holy Spirit to help and comfort us. God's Spirit helps us to be good. He gives us the power to stand up and say no to what is bad. The Holy Spirit helps us to live God's way instead of our own way.

Circle all the words that describe the fruit or results of the Holy Spirit.

love
peace
joy
obedience
truthfulness
patience
happiness
anger
goodness
selfishness
lying
neatness
sharing
screaming
punching
kicking

hatefulness
kindness
stealing
friendliness
pouting
jealousy
crying
helpfulness
faithfulness
bossiness
gentleness
self-control
listening
misery
mean words
ignoring people

thoughtfulness
honesty
pushiness
sharing
helping the poor
disobedience
gratefulness
cheating
kind words
forgiveness
caring
hopefulness
sadness
loneliness
bragging
complimenting

But the Spirit produces love, joy, peace, patience, kindness, goodness, faithfulness, humility, and self-control.

Galatians 5:22

•

Dear God,

Thank You for Your Holy Spirit.

Actions speak louder than words! It is easy to say the words, "I love you." But real love is more than just words. People will know if we love them by the way we treat them.

Design your own pizza. Put all your favorite toppings on it. Think about what other people want on their pizza instead of just what you want. That is love in action.

If you love me, you will obey my commandments.

John 14:15

Dear God,

Help me to show love to others by my actions.

Have you ever run in a race? Did you win or lose? In the "race of faith," you can wake up every day and decide to believe that God loves you and wants the best for you. In the race of faith, you choose to believe everything Jesus has taught you.

Connect these dots to see what you need in a race.

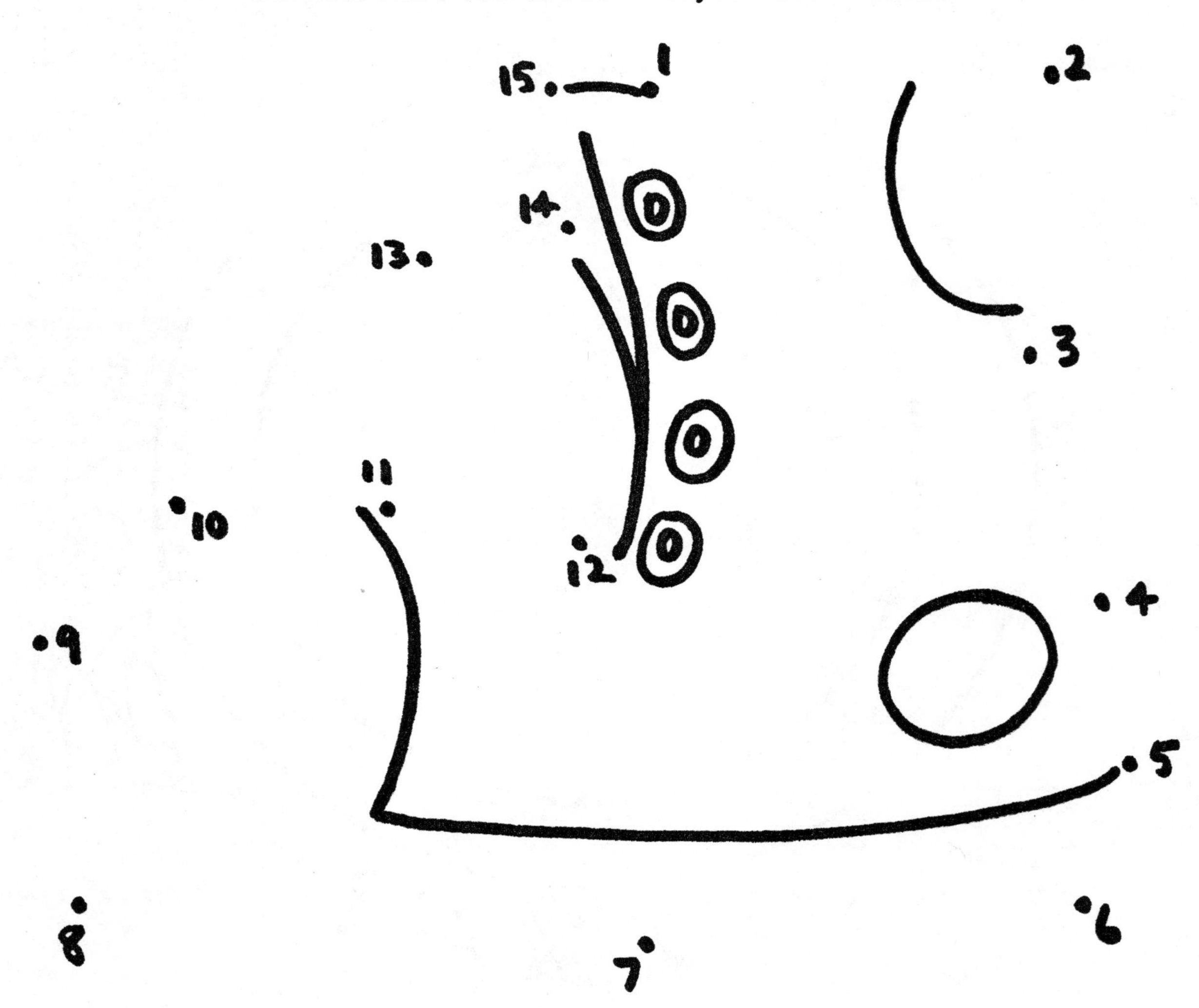

Run your best in the race of faith, and win eternal life for yourself.

1 Timothy 6:12

Dear God,

I'm glad there is one race I *know* I can win...the race that leads to heaven!

31 March

Something special happened this month. Tell all about it! Someday you will read this page again and be glad you wrote about March's memorable moment!

Glue or tape a photograph or draw a picture of the special event in the space below. Then write (or have someone help you write) about what happened.

The road the righteous travel is like the sunrise.

Proverbs 4:18

Dear God,

Thank You for all the special moments in my life.

APRIL
5

April 1

Do you love spring? It is a time of new beginnings. The snow melts and green grass starts to appear. And everywhere, birds start to sing and flowers start to bloom. Spring is in the air! God makes sure spring always follows winter...and He always will.

Find 15 little hearts hidden on this page. Color all these beautiful flowers.

The winter is over.

Song of Songs 2:11

Dear God,

Flowers are so beautiful! How did You ever come up with so many different designs?

April 2

•

From the beginning of time to the end of time, the earth and all the people on it have belonged and will belong to God. That is because He made everything. Even though our world is always changing, one thing is always true: People need God.

One hundred years ago children dressed differently than you dress today. Their bicycles looked different, too. Draw a picture of what you think a bike will look like 100 years in the future. How do you think children will dress in 100 years?

The world and all that is in it belong to the LORD; the earth and all who live on it are His.

Psalm 24:1

•

Dear God,

I'm glad You are in charge of everything...now and forever!

God made this world an amazing place, didn't He? He made beautiful trees, hills, and flowers. He made the four seasons so that the outdoors is always changing. Have you noticed how the same place looks different in spring, summer, fall, and winter? Do you have a favorite season? Which is it?

Turn this cold winter landscape into a warm summer scene.

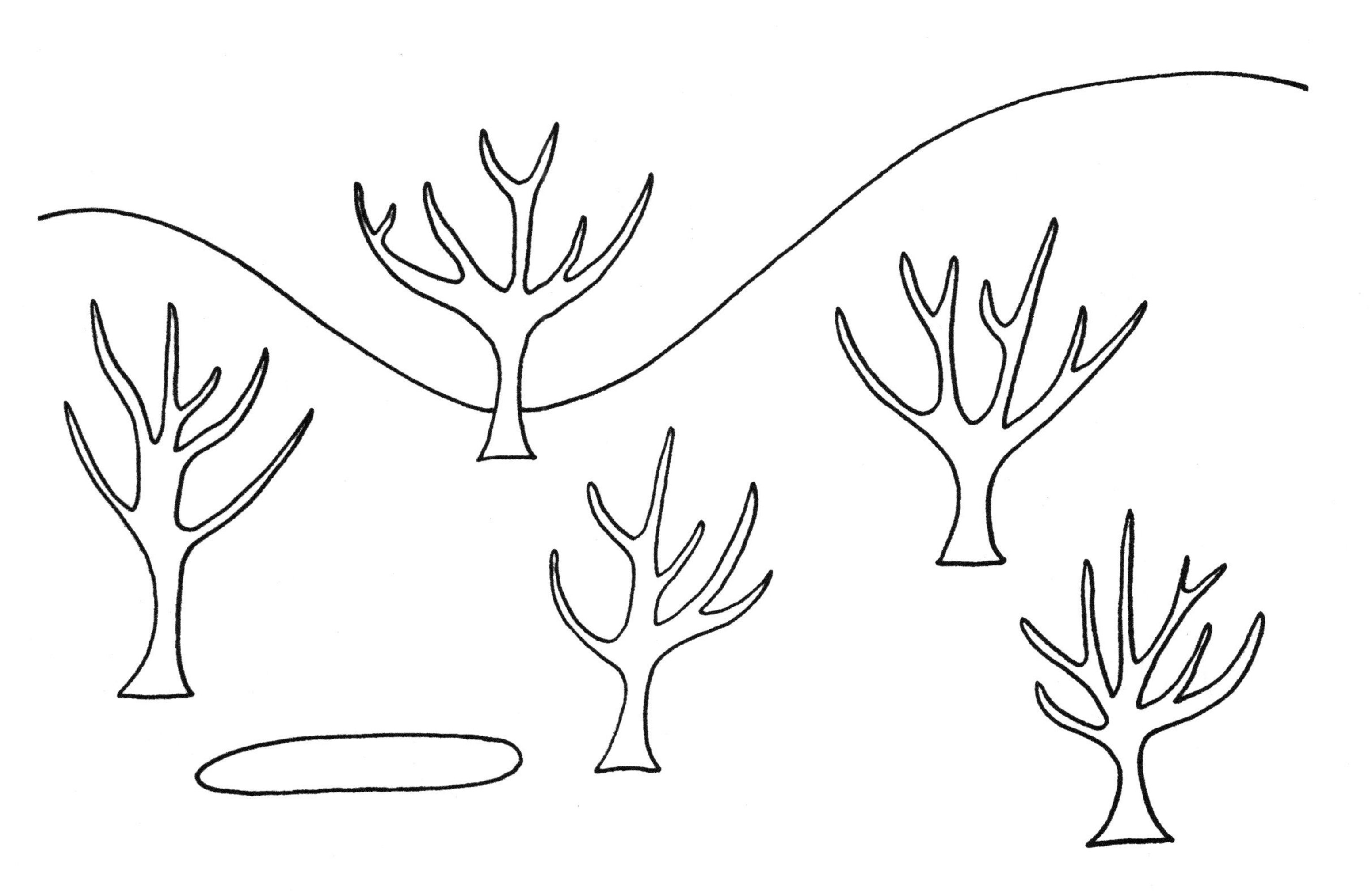

You made summer and winter.

Psalm 74:17

Dear God,

Thank You for this beautiful world. You are truly awesome!

April 4

Going to church is a very important part of life. Just as your body cannot grow without food, your spirit needs the Word of God to stay healthy. Reading the Bible, praying, and talking about God with other Christians is just as important as eating breakfast, lunch, and dinner.

Draw a picture of your church. Draw you and your family going to church.

Let us not give up the habit of meeting together.

Hebrews 10:25

Dear God,

I always seem to find time to watch television, play with my toys, and eat. Help me to also spend some time each day with You.

April 5

Worry is a big waste of time. Worry does not change what will happen now or in the future. Remember—God is in charge of everything and will never forget you. He will always take good care of you.

Draw some baby birds in the nest.

Look at the birds! They don't worry about what to eat...for your heavenly Father feeds them. And you are far more valuable to Him than they are.

Matthew 6:26 (TLB)

Dear God,

Thank You for taking such good care of me. Help me to always remember to say Thank You.

Don't you love flowers...especially when you have planted the seeds yourself! There are so many different kinds of flowers, and each one is beautiful and special.

Draw your own flowers. You can even make up a brand-new kind of flower!

The flowers are springing up.
Song of Solomon 2:12 (TLB)

Dear God,

You know how to make beautiful things...especially flowers! They make the world such a beautiful place.

Have you ever planted a seed? If you water it every day and keep it in the sun, you will have a little sprout in a few days. Before long, you will have a big plant. You may be little like the sprout, but God has big plans for your life. With God's love and care, your life can grow into something beautiful.

Draw yourself planting the little seed below. Don't forget your shovel!

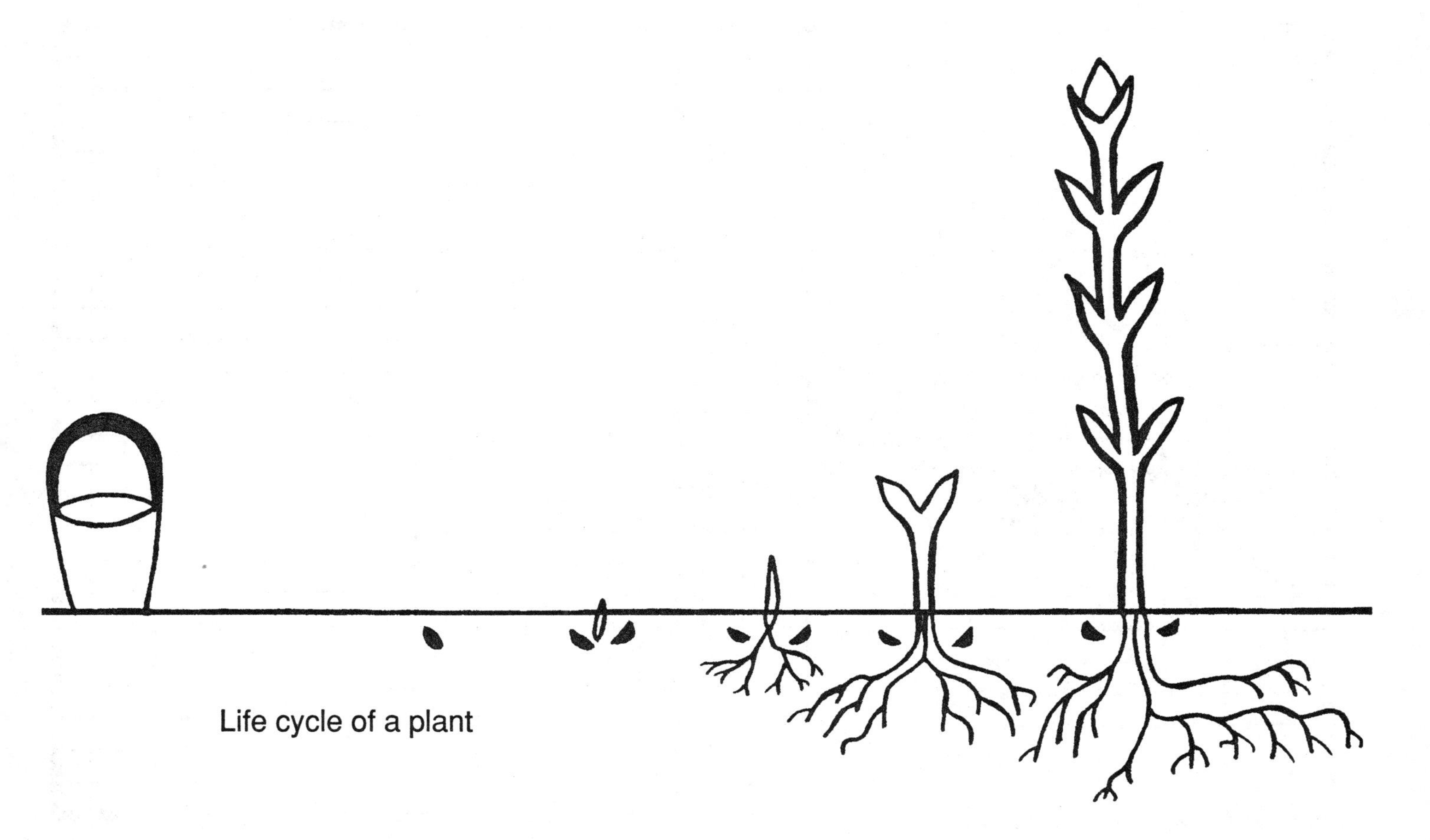

Life cycle of a plant

A grain of wheat remains no more than a single grain unless it is dropped into the ground and dies. If it does die, then it produces many grains.

John 12:24

Dear God,

Even though I am small, help me to trust You every day. Then I can grow into someone strong who can do great things for Your glory!

If you ever get upset with someone, or if a person is upset with you, make up right away. Don't let the day end without getting rid of all the bad feelings between you. And remember, it's not hard to tell a friend that you are sorry. A real friend can't wait to give you a big hug and tell you he or she loves you!

Copy the picture on the left onto the grid on the right side.

Do not let the sun go down on your anger.

Ephesians 4:26 (NASB)

Dear God,

Thank You for always forgiving me when I do something wrong. Help me to forgive others in the same way.

After a long, cold winter, it is wonderful to feel the warm spring sun shining down on you. But God's love *always* shines down on us...rain or shine, cloudy or sunny. God's love and glory shines on those who love Him. Name five ways that you can tell when spring has arrived.

Draw yourself jumping this rope.

The glory of the LORD is shining on you.

Isaiah 60:1

Dear God,

Thank you for the warm spring days. Thank You for Your love that always shines down on me.

Only God can make the rain fall and the sun shine. Plants need rain so they can grow and make beautiful blossoms. Remember, April showers bring May flowers.

Here is a fun game to play with a friend: Take turns crossing out one, two, or three raindrops in each umbrella. Whoever crosses out the last raindrop wins.

Who is wise enough to count the clouds and tilt them over to pour out the rain?
Job 38:37

Dear God,
Thank You for rain.

Ever since Adam and Eve sinned in the garden of Eden, people have been separated from God. God loved you so much that He was willing to have His Son Jesus die so that you could be with Him in heaven forever. On the cross, Jesus made things right again between people and God.

He went out, carrying his cross.

John 19:17

Dear God,

Thank You for Your love for me.

•

Three days after Jesus died, His friends came to the tomb. They were shocked to see that the tomb was empty, and that an angel was sitting there at the entrance. The angel told them that Jesus was alive and that they would see Him soon!

Count how many times you can find the number "3" in this picture.

He is risen!

Mark 16:6 (NKJV)

•

Dear God,

Jesus is alive today and forever. I'm glad, because that means I can live forever in heaven, too.

After Jesus came back from the dead, He visited many of His friends. One man named Thomas had not yet seen Jesus in person, and didn't believe that He was really alive. So Jesus went to see Thomas, and Thomas finally believed!

Someday you will see Jesus and His arms will be opened wide for you. Make sure that you run into His arms!

Stop your doubting and believe!

John 20:27

Dear God,

I believe in Jesus, even though I haven't seen Him. When I do see Him, I will run into His arms!

Jesus told His friends to tell other people that He had risen from the dead. He told them that when people believe, they should be baptized and follow Him. That was 2,000 years ago. Today people are still telling the good news of Jesus and His gift of eternal life.

When you meet people who don't know anything about Jesus, what will you tell them? Write (or have someone help you write) what you would say in the space above.

Go, then, to all peoples everywhere and make them my disciples.

Matthew 28:19

Dear God,

Help me to tell others about the good news of Your love.

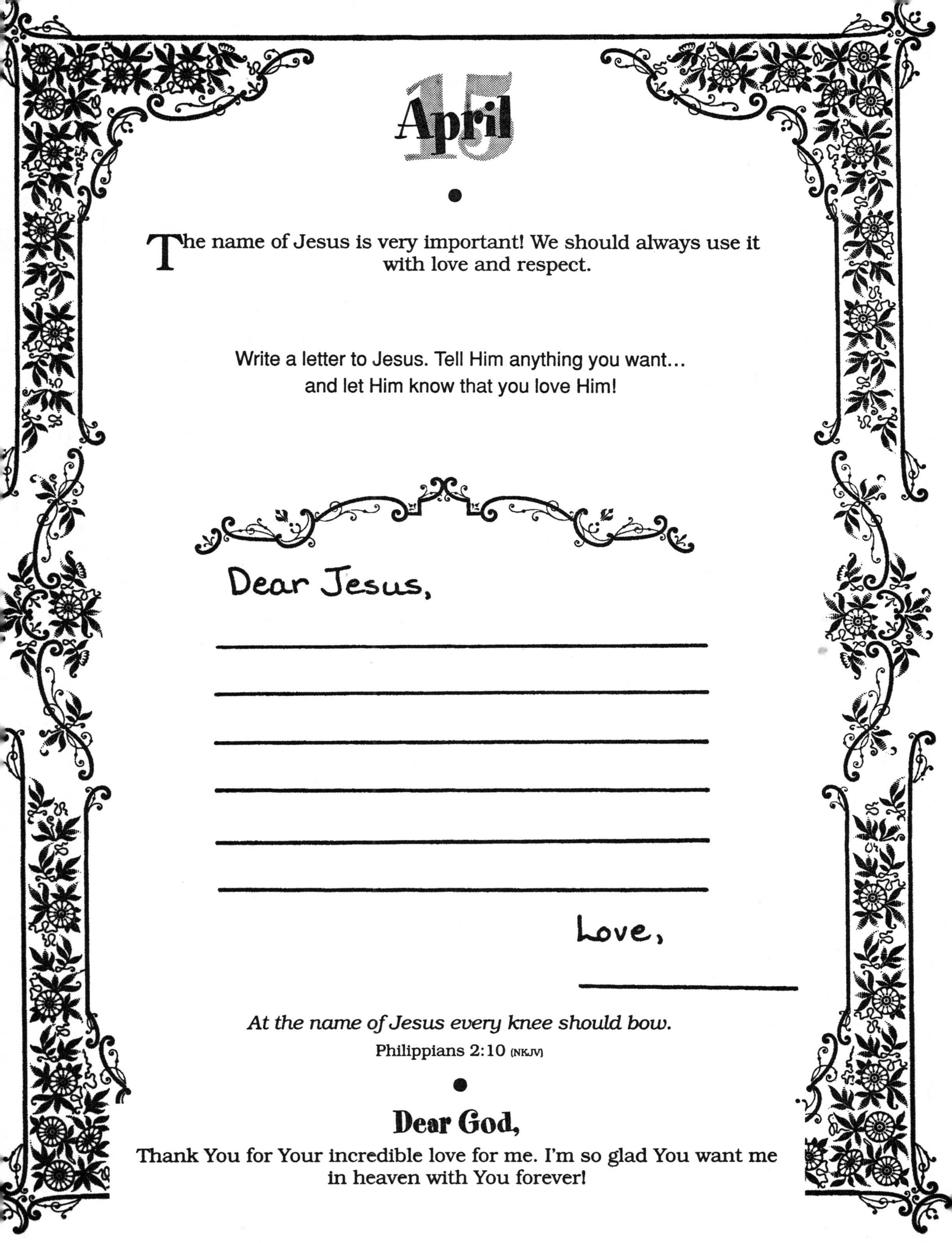

April 15

The name of Jesus is very important! We should always use it with love and respect.

Write a letter to Jesus. Tell Him anything you want... and let Him know that you love Him!

Dear Jesus,

Love,

At the name of Jesus every knee should bow.

Philippians 2:10 (NKJV)

Dear God,

Thank You for Your incredible love for me. I'm so glad You want me in heaven with You forever!

When you love Jesus and want to do everything He asks, your whole life will blossom like a beautiful flower in the spring. A life without Jesus is like a picture that isn't colored in...something is missing!

Finish these animal shapes by drawing their faces, spots and stripes. Then color them!

For what is life? To me, it is Christ.

Philippians 1:21

Dear God,

I am so thankful that because of Jesus I can be forgiven when I do things that I shouldn't. Someday I will live with You in heaven forever.

Do you know what it means to do something diligently? It means to work very hard at it ...you practice. When you practice hard at music, baseball, or art you get good results. When you work hard at finding God you will get the best result of all: friendship with God.

Would you like to learn how to draw a house the way artists draw? You can draw an object so that it looks more lifelike. To do this, get a ruler and a pencil. Draw your house in the empty box. Follow these directions: 1. First draw a square, then put a triangle on top. 2. Now, using a ruler, draw a straight line from each of the corners to the dot in the upper right-hand corner. 3. Finish drawing your house, erasing the lines you don't need. Add the flowers and trees.

[God] is a rewarder of those who diligently seek Him.

Hebrews 11:6 (NKJV)

Dear God,

I want to know more and more about You my whole life long!

Jesus lives forever! And we will live forever, too, in heaven with Jesus. Wouldn't you like to let everyone know how wonderful Jesus is and how much He loves them?

Make up your own television commercial telling everyone about Jesus. Write the words for the commercial and draw a picture from your commercial in the television below.

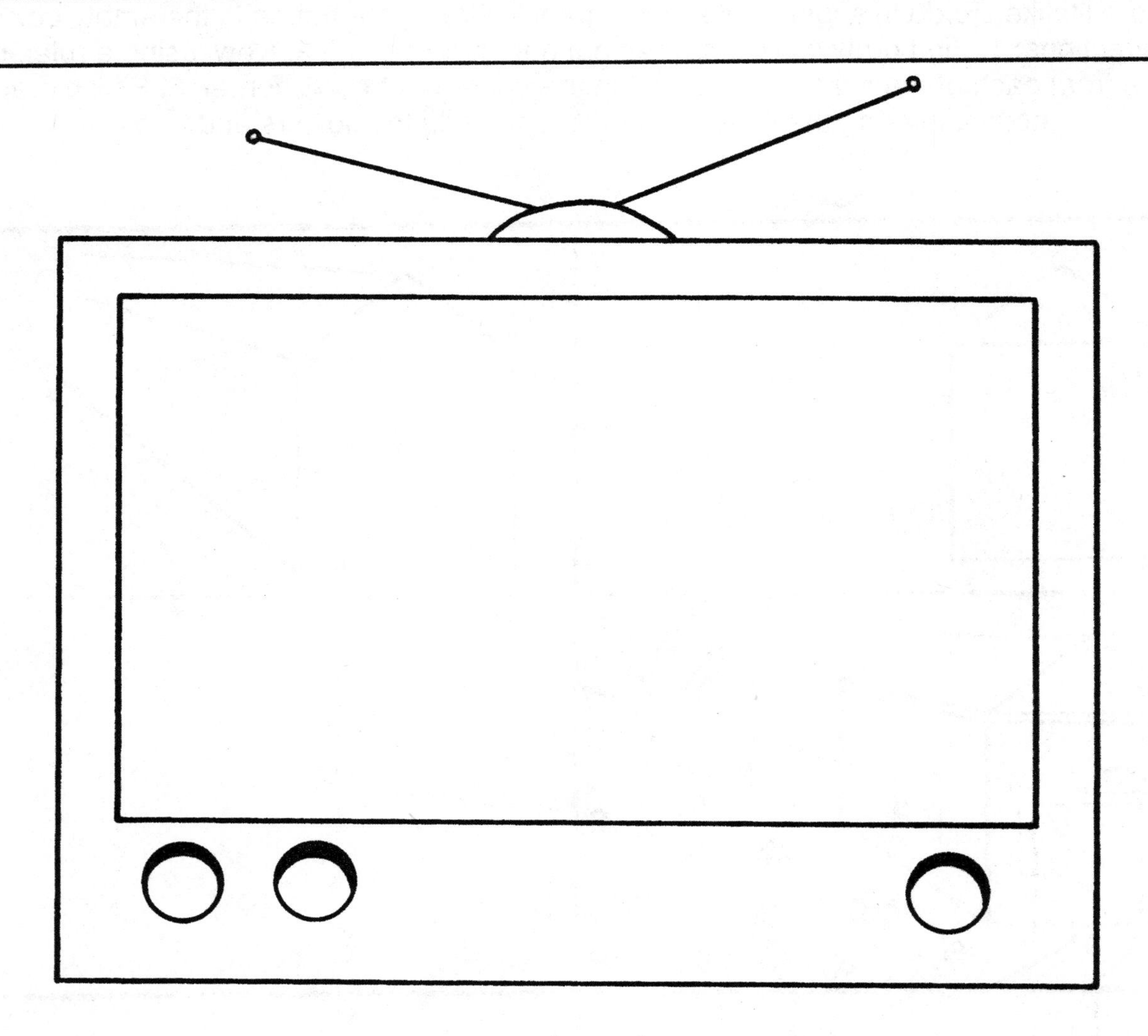

Jesus lives forever...

Hebrews 7:24

Dear God,

Every day I see many things on television that I don't really need, such as toys. Help me to always remember what *is* important and what I really need.

Sometimes it is good to keep your mouth zipped. God doesn't want you to gossip because it can hurt other people's feelings. How would you like people saying bad things about you? Good friends can trust each other not to gossip.

Read the sentences below, and circle the times you should keep your mouth zipped.

1. The kids at school are making fun of a boy who can't catch the ball.
2. Your teacher asks you a question in class.
3. You answer the telephone.
4. All the kids are saying someone is mean.
5. Your best friend just won the art contest. You wish you had won.
6. Your father asks if you have seen his glasses.

Gossip is spread by wicked people;
they stir up trouble and break up friendships.
Proverbs 16:28

Dear God,
Help me to be kind and loving to everybody.

April 20

•

When you trust God to take care of you, all kinds of exciting things can happen. Knowing that God has lots of great ideas for your life is a great feeling. It is like being able to run for a long time without getting tired, or flying up in the air like an eagle.

People have always wanted to fly. First they flew in hot air balloons. Today we fly in supersonic jets anywhere in the world. In the future our airplanes may seem old-fashioned. Draw a picture of what you think airplanes will look like in the future.

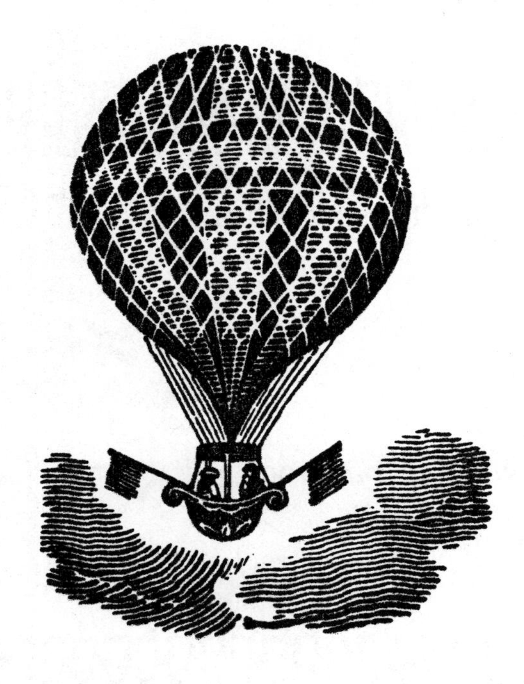

But those who trust in the LORD for help will...rise on wings like eagles.

Isaiah 40:31

•

Dear God,

I'm glad You care about every part of my life and want only the very best for me.

•

Did you know that God really hears your prayers? There are many people in the Bible who prayed and received miraculous answers from God. They prayed because God can do things that people can't. God can make blind people see, crippled people walk, and much more.

Write three prayer requests that you have right now. Check off the boxes when they are answered.

I pray to you, O God, because you answer me.

Psalm 17:6

•

Dear God,

I want to know more and more about You my whole life long!

God wants only what is best for His children. Even if something bad happens, He will make sure there is a good ending!

Sometimes people say "a picture is worth a thousand words." Glue or tape a photo here that has a story behind it.

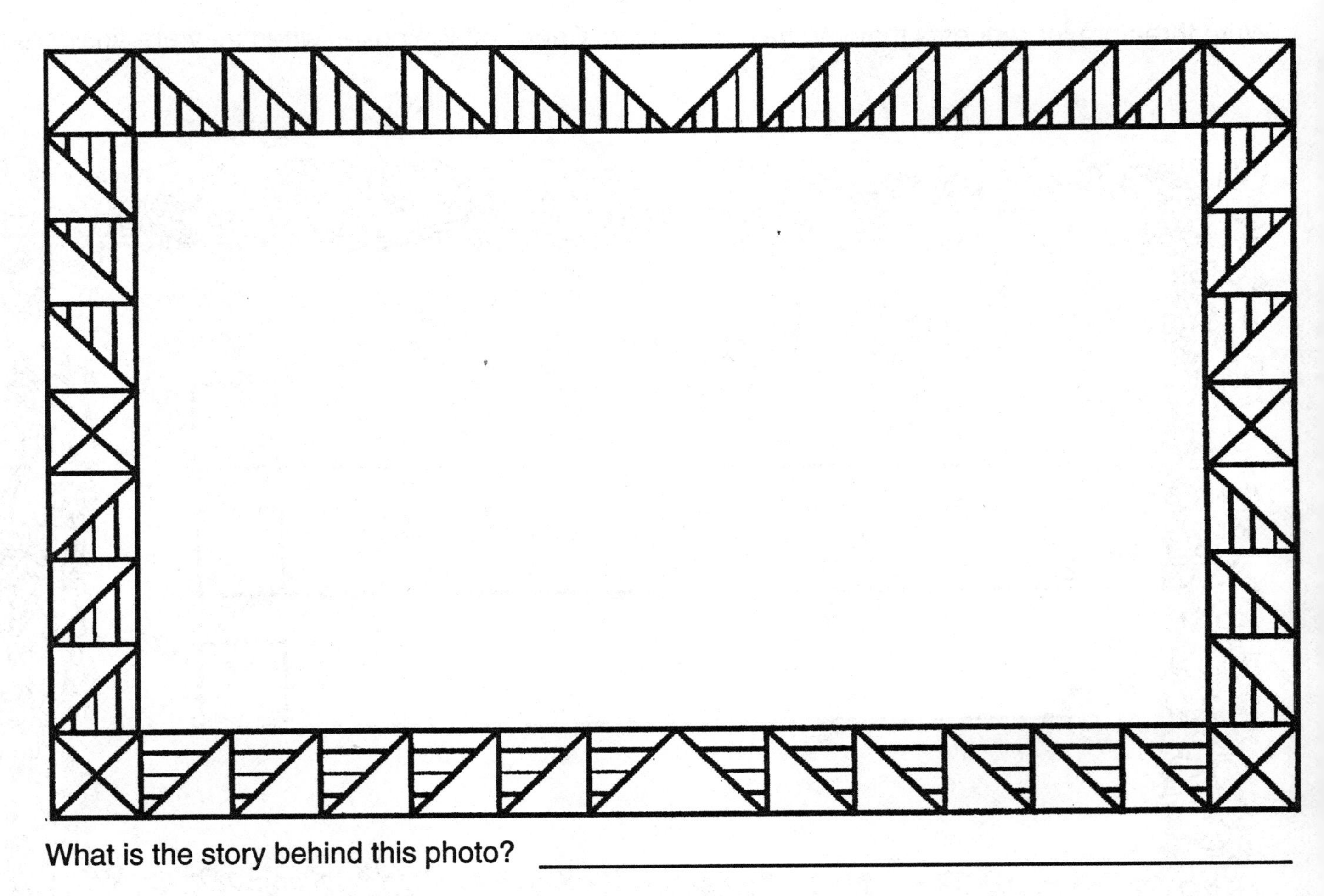

What is the story behind this photo? ______________________________

____

____

And we know that all things work together for good to those who love God.

Romans 8:28 (NKJV)

Dear God,

Thank You for wanting the best for my life. I love You!

Abraham married Sarah and they grew very old without ever having a child. This made them sad. One day God told Abraham that he and Sarah would have a son. Abraham began to laugh, since he was almost 100 years old. But God always keeps His promises. The next year, Sarah had a son and they named him Isaac.

Connect the dots to find out why Abraham and Sarah are so happy.

I am the Almighty God. Obey me and always do what is right.

Genesis 17:1,2

Dear God,

You can do anything; nothing is too hard for You!

•

Abraham sent one of the servants to find a wife for his son, Isaac. Abraham's servant prayed that when he asked for a drink of water at the well, the right girl would answer. Rebekah answered.

To find out how Rebekah answered Abraham's servant, cross out every third letter. Then cross out every B, F and Z. Print the remaining letters in the spaces below.

_ _ _ _ _   _ _ _   _   _ _ _ _   _ _ _ _

_ _ _ _   _ _ _ _   _ _ _ _ _ _   _   _ _ _ _ _.

You must go back to the country where I was born and get a wife for my son Isaac.

Genesis 24:4

•

Dear God,

I am thankful that I can know what You want for my life...even the right person to marry.

April 25

A long time ago, a man named Jacob had a dream that came from God. Do you remember any of your dreams? If you pray for a peaceful sleep each night, God will give you very sweet dreams.

Draw a picture of a dream you had. If it was a long dream, draw a picture of one part of the dream.

He dreamed that he saw a stairway reaching from earth to heaven, with angels going up and coming down on it.

Genesis 28:12

Dear God,

Thank You for happy, sweet dreams. Good night!

April 26

Joseph's coat of many colors was a gift from his father, but it made his brothers jealous. One day the brothers took Joseph's coat and sold him to traders from Egypt. In Egypt God was with Joseph, and when he grew up the Pharaoh made Joseph governor of Egypt.

Jacob loved Joseph more than all his children, because he was the son of his old age. He made him a tunic of many colors.

Genesis 37:3 (NKJV)

Dear God,

Help me to never be jealous, especially of my brothers and sisters. Please be with me at all times, just like You were with Joseph.

•

Joseph was an important man in Egypt. When a famine began all over the earth, Joseph's brothers came to buy grain because they had nothing to eat. They didn't recognize Joseph, their brother. But Joseph forgave them for the wrong they had done to him. God had worked through their bad deeds so that Joseph could later save their lives and be a blessing to them. What lesson can you learn from Joseph? Joseph trusted God no matter what happened to him.

Look up and down to find the hidden words

God
Jacob
Brothers
Joseph
Egypt
Canaan
Famine
Grain
Dreams
Benjamin
Goshen

V X A K L J A C O B E H B I L
J G L B R O T H E R S B E M T
D R E A M S B C G R A I N P O
F A M I N E N O Y Q Y A J G Z
K I N G A P V W P H A R A O H
X N G O S H E N T G F C M D S
G T P J I O J A K F D C I R D
H C A N A A N U S B X Z N E F

Now hurry back to my father and tell him that this is what his son Joseph says: "God has made me ruler of all Egypt; come to me without delay."

Genesis 45:9,10

•

Dear God,

I'm glad I can read about people like Joseph. Help me to trust You like Joseph did.

Isn't it wonderful that God has promised that we don't have to be afraid of death! If we love Jesus and live for Him, we will be with Him in heaven forever.

Draw a picture of what you think heaven looks like. Don't forget to draw your special house that Jesus is getting ready just for you!

God will have a house in heaven for us to live in, a home he himself has made, which will last forever.

2 Corinthians 5:1

Dear God,

Thank You that You have promised me a beautiful home in heaven, where I will live with You forever. Help me live to serve Jesus.

Some things in life are simply impossible to do. But did you know that God's specialty is the impossible? It's a snap for Him! These things are impossible to do—give them a try.

Put your hand flat on a table with your middle finger bent under. Now try to lift your ring finger. It's impossible!

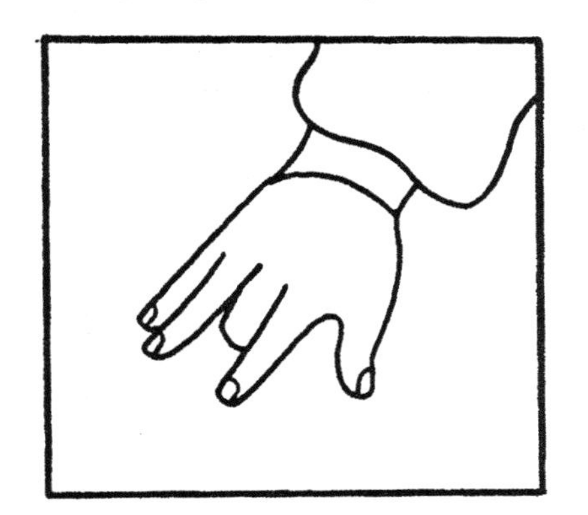

Bend your knees, just a little, and hold your toes with both hands. Now try to jump forward like a bunny, without letting go of your feet. It's impossible!

Stand with your feet and back against a wall. Have someone put a coin on the floor right in front of your toes. Now see if you can pick up the coin without bending your knees. It's impossible!

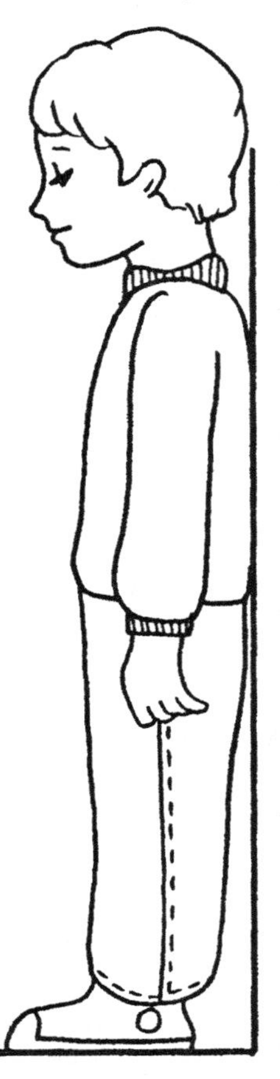

Place one hand tightly on the top of your head. Keep your arm out to the side and your elbow raised the whole time. Now have someone hold on to your arm, and try to lift your hand from your head. It's impossible!

This is impossible for man, but for God everything is possible.

Matthew 19:26

Dear God,

There are many things that are impossible for me to do. But nothing is impossible for You!

April 30

Can you believe this is the last day in April? Remember, if you enjoyed a special event or activity any time during this month, you can turn to this page and write about it so you don't forget! What was that special moment in April that you would like to remember?

Glue or tape a photograph or draw a picture of April's memorable moment in the space below. Write (or have someone help you write) about what happened.

Everything I say is true.

Proverbs 8:8

Dear God,

Thank you for all the wonderful things You are doing in my life.

MAY

It is important to learn about God's way when you are young; then you will know how to live all of your life. Whenever people try to point you the wrong way and make you do something bad, ignore them and go God's way instead. God's way is always the right way!

Color these arrows that are pointing in every direction.

Train up a child in the way he should go, and when he is old he will not depart from it.

Proverbs 22:6

Dear God,

I know that all my life I will have choices to make. Thank You for letting me know the right way to live—Your way!

What happens when you spend more and more time with a friend? You get to know him or her better and better. And guess what happens when you spend time praying to God and reading the Bible? You will learn more and more about Jesus—how kind and loving He is. Best of all, you will learn that Jesus has promised to always be with you. He wants to be your best friend!

Fill in the blank with your name.

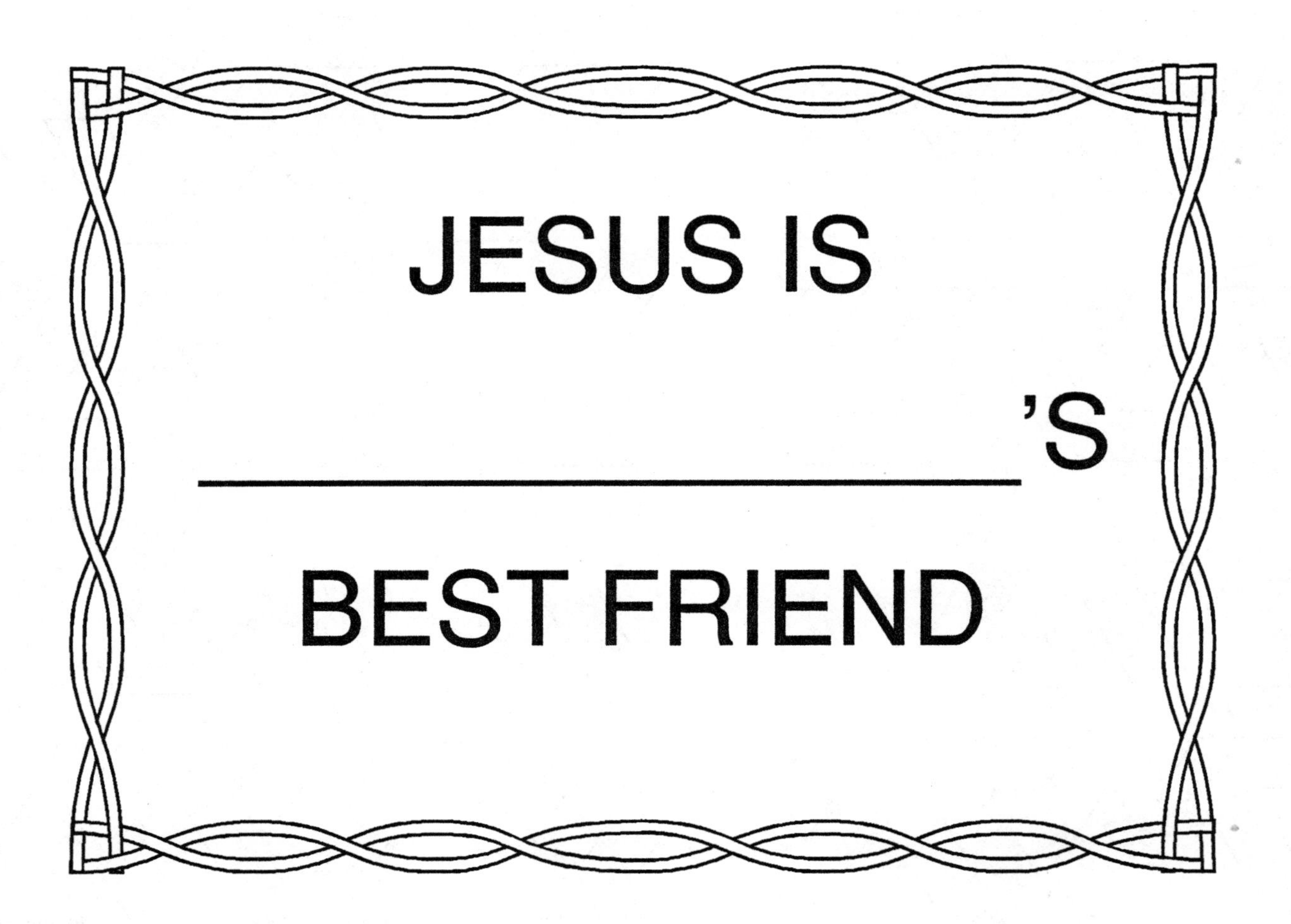

Grow in the grace and knowledge of our Lord and Savior Jesus Christ.

2 Peter 3:18 (NKJV)

Dear God,

Thank You for loving me so much. Thank You for making me Your child.

May 3

Jesus was born in Bethlehem, then as a young child He went to Egypt. His family later returned to Nazareth, where He grew up. His first miracle was at a wedding in Cana, and He was baptized in the Jordan River by John the Baptist. He spent a lot of time in Capernaum, where He performed many miracles and walked on water on the Sea of Galilee. He was arrested, crucified, and buried in Jerusalem. Three days later, He rose from the dead.

Draw a line from city to city to show where Jesus walked.

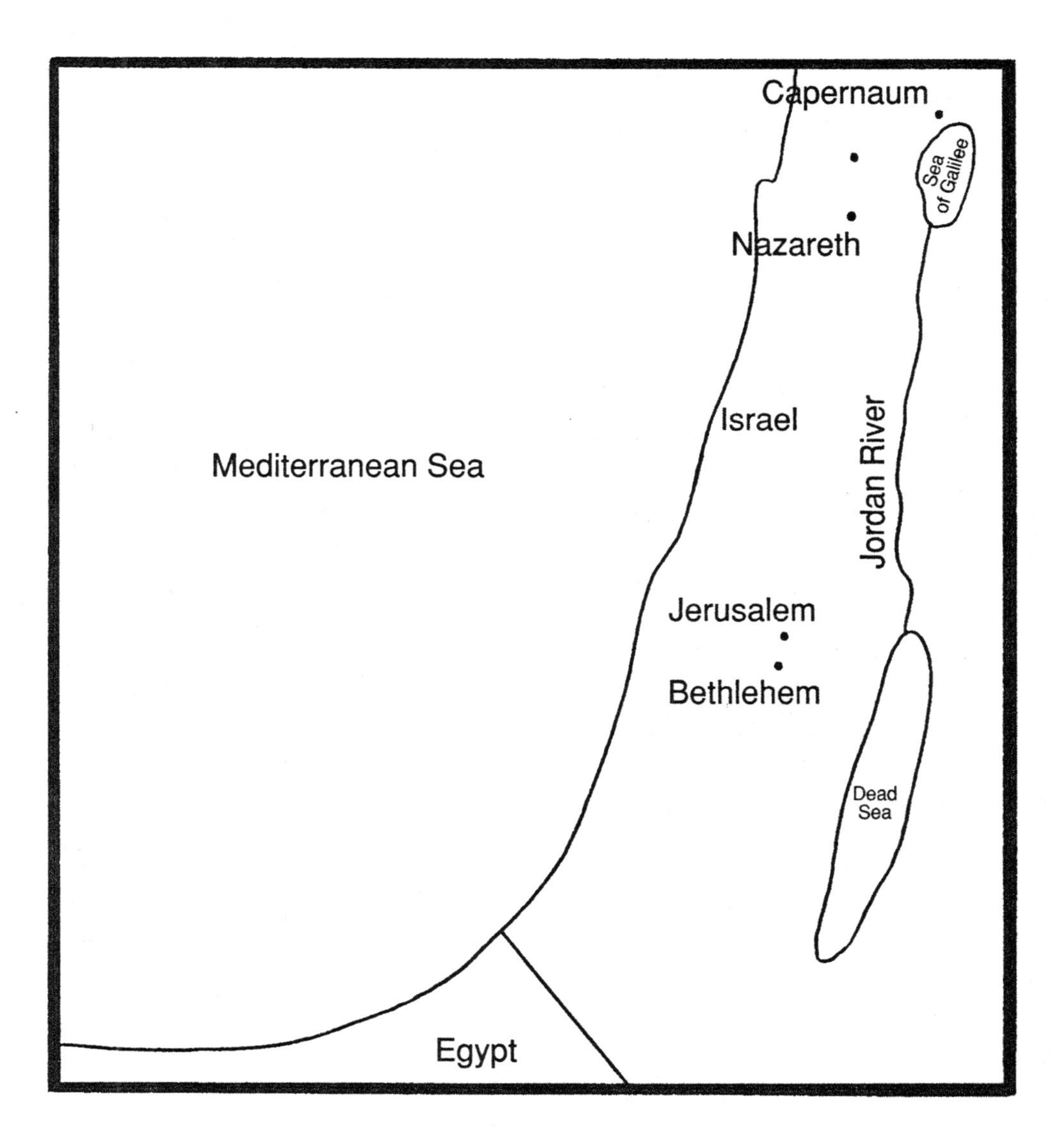

Jesus went all over Galilee...

Matthew 4:23

Dear God,

Thank You for the incredible love You show me through Jesus.

Jesus performed many miracles—healing the sick, raising the dead, and multiplying loaves and fishes. When the disciples saw Jesus walking on water across the Sea of Galilee during a bad storm, they fell down and worshiped Him. They knew Jesus was the Son of God.

Draw the path that Jesus took to the boat in the storm.

Jesus came to the disciples, walking on the water.

Matthew 14:25

Dear God,

I know that nothing is impossible for You. Help me to always remember and depend on Your power and ability.

Jesus healed people of many different sicknesses. People who were crippled could walk, those who were unable to speak could talk, and even blind people could now see! Can you imagine how excited those blind people must have been when suddenly they could see? What do you think was the first thing they wanted to see? Draw it in the glasses.

Then Jesus touched their eyes and...their sight was restored.

Matthew 9:29,30

Dear God,

Thank You for all the beauty I see around me every day.

YES, MOM!

You can show love to all the people in your life in many different ways. Speaking kind words to your friends, obeying your parents, and sharing with your brothers and sisters are all ways of showing love.

In each box below, draw a cartoon that shows how you can love others. Draw a balloon that shows what each person is saying. Try to think of four different ways to show love.

Keep on loving one another.

Hebrews 13:1

Dear God,

Help me to be kind, patient, and obedient so I can show love.

May 7

Isn't God amazing? He takes such good care of all the animals, birds, and insects!

Today's scripture is from the book of Psalms, which starts with the letter p. Can you find eight p's hiding in this picture? Color the whole page after you find all the p's. Make these creatures of God look beautiful!

Countless creatures live.

Psalm 104:25

Dear God,

Thank You that even the small insects You made are beautiful.

Your can show your mother how much you love her by picking up after yourself (so she has less work to do), obeying her (so she doesn't have to say something ten times), and getting along with your brothers and sisters (so she doesn't have to play referee). You can show your appreciation by telling her, "I love you" (every mom loves to hear that).

In the space below, write and color a beautiful card for mom.

When your mother is old, show her your appreciation.

Proverbs 23:22

Dear God,

Thank You for my mom. She is special, and I love her a lot!

How do you know if you are loved? One way to know is when people say, "I love you." Another way you can know is by what people do for you and how they treat you.

Everyday, in every situation, ask yourself, "What is the loving thing to do?" How can I show the love of God to others?" Fill out this chart by writing how you could show love to others.

THE PROBLEM	WHAT I WOULD DO	HOW I WOULD DO IT
Mom is tired and the kitchen is a mess.		
The baby fell down and is crying.		
Dad is sick in bed with a bad cold.		
The new boy at school feels lonely and left out.		

My children, our love should not be just word and talk; it must be true love, which shows itself in action.

1 John 3:18

Dear God,

You show Your love for me by all the things You do for me. Help me to show love to others by what I say and do.

Jesus said that even after He returned to heaven, we would be able to feel a very special gift from Him—His peace. Even on crazy, busy days, the peace of Jesus can be with us!

Is there a special way you like to relax? Draw yourself resting in this nice, cozy chair.

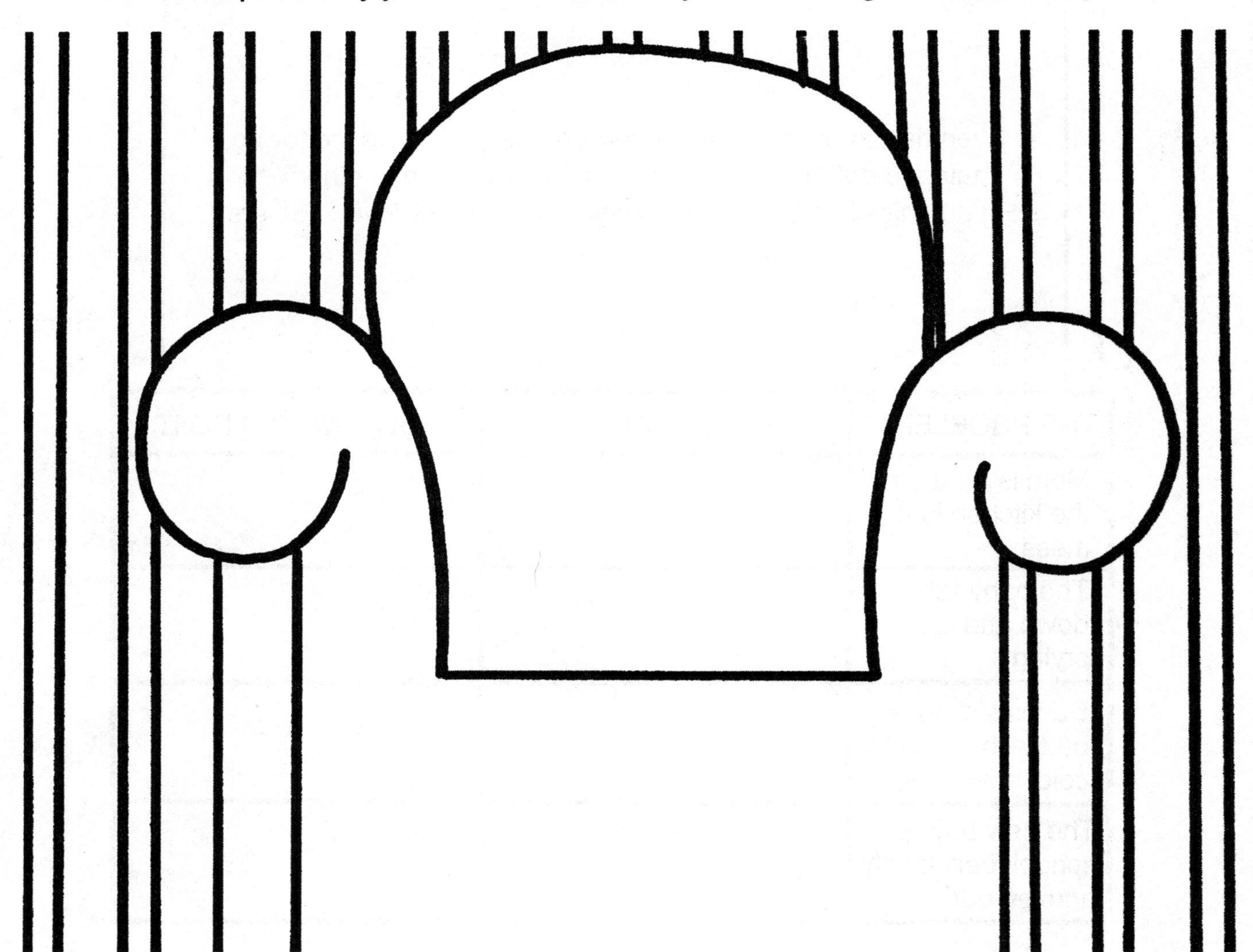

Peace is what I leave with you; it is my own peace that I give you.

John 14:27

Dear God,

I am glad that I can feel peaceful no matter what is going on around me.

Have you ever done something wrong and been afraid to tell your parents? Always tell them right away, even if it was an accident. The faster they know what went wrong, the faster they can help make things better.

Molly was told to stay out of the kitchen. She went in anyway and made a mess. She spilled her drink, broke a cup, and got paper towels and bread all over the floor. What should Molly do? What would you do?

Your sin will catch up with you.

Numbers 32:23 (TLB)

Dear God,

Thank You for always forgiving me when I tell You that I am sorry.

•

Isn't it great to have good friends? A true friend sticks beside you in good times and bad. Even if everybody else gets mad at you, a real friend sticks by your side. And there is one Friend who sticks close by you all through your life; He will never let you down. Who is He?

Draw a picture of you and your friends doing something you enjoy.

There is a friend who sticks closer than a brother.

Proverbs 18:24

•

Dear God,

Thank You for friends, and thank You for promising to always stick close by me every day of my life.

You don't need to worry about anything. God will make sure you have clothes and food and everything else you need. Look at the beautiful flowers. Do you think they worry about anything? God takes care of all their needs!

Connect the dots to see who is smelling this flower.

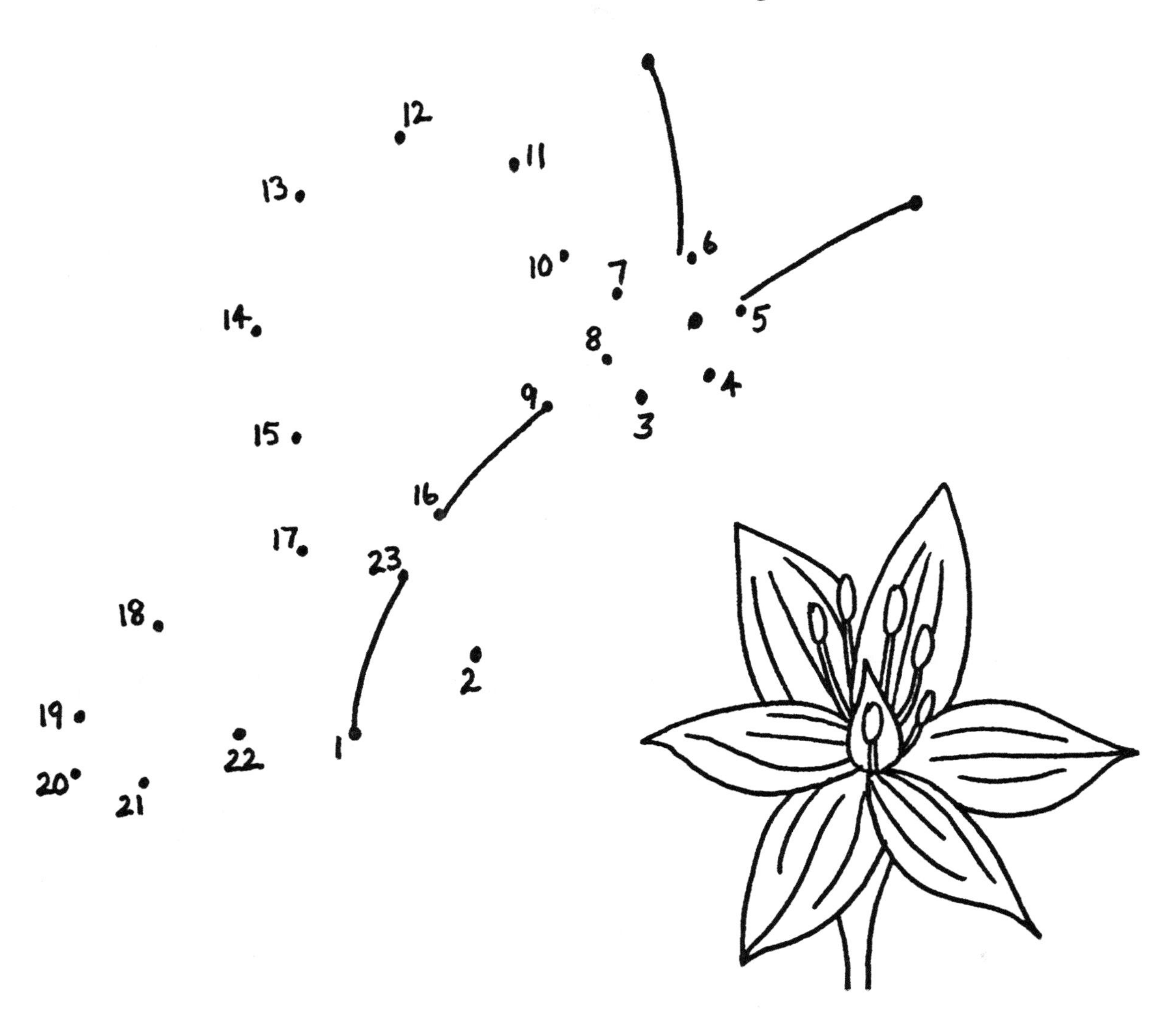

Why worry about your clothes? Look at the field lilies! They don't worry about theirs.

Matthew 6:28 (TLB)

Dear God,

Help me to trust You for all my needs.

•

When a caterpillar is born, it has a busy life crawling around on the ground. Then one day the fuzzy caterpillar turns into a beautiful butterfly! Now he can fly through the air and visit trees and birds. Did you know that our lives change just as much when we become a part of God's family? Everything becomes beautiful and brighter!

Draw a pretty design on this butterfly's wings.

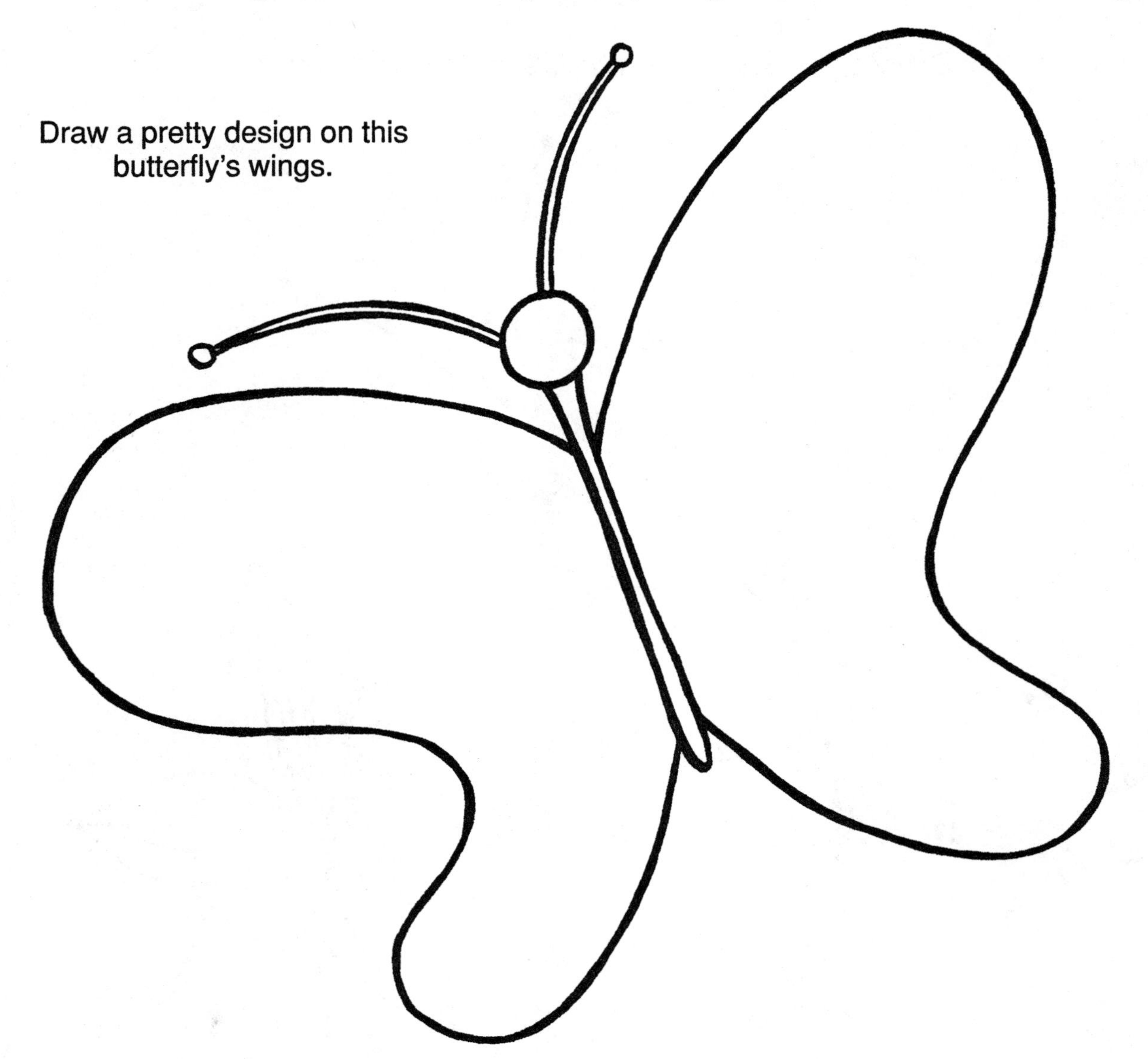

Do not be surprised because I tell you that you must be born again.

John 3:7

•

Dear God,

Thank You that I can be a part of Your family. I'm glad I can live with You in heaven someday

•

When you truly love God, you will also love and care about others and have nothing to hide from them. Don't say you love God unless you also show love for people.

Showing kindness is an important part of being a Christian. Read this story, then think of a way to end it with an act of kindness.

THE FIRST MOVE

Eddie was having fun playing ball with his friends. He noticed a new boy who had just moved next door. Eddie had been too busy to introduce himself. That night, Eddie's dad told the family they would soon be moving because he had a new job in a different state. Eddie felt afraid when he thought about making new friends. Then he thought about the new boy next door. The next day, ______________

____

____

____

____

____

Whoever loves his brother lives in the light.

1 John 2:10

•

Dear God,

Thank You for Your love for me. Help me to be friendly to others.

What happens when the sun is shining its light? Flowers grow, and children can run outside and play. In the Bible, the word "light" is used to describe the goodness and love of God. Love and light makes flowers grow, and they make you grow, too!

Draw a beautiful flower garden...put flowers everywhere!

Whoever loves his brother lives in the light.

1 John 2:10

Dear God,

Thank You for Your love, which shines down on me like the sun.

•

Do you know how to make new friends? The best way to start is to be a good friend yourself. A good friend is kind. A good friend is thoughtful. A good friend tells only the truth, even if it isn't easy. A good friend is quick to forgive.

Write about a fun time you had with a friend.

Never forget to be truthful and kind.

Proverbs 3:3

•

Dear God,

Thank You for my friends. They make life extra special!

Jesus loved to talk to people and answer all their questions. Pretend you have gone back in time to when Jesus was on earth and that you are interviewing Him for the newspaper. What do you think that He would say?

The Good News

Jesus from Nazareth was seen healing sick people, walking on water, and even raising the dead! Here's our exclusive interview with Him:

Reporter: Hello, Jesus! What do You have to say to our readers?

Jesus: ______________________________

____

____

____

____

____

Exclusive interview by ______________

He will teach the ways that are right and best to those who humbly turn to him.

Psalm 25:9 (TLB)

Dear God,

Thank You for the Bible because it tells me the truth about Jesus.

Be strong in the Lord! God's protection is like armor—just like the knights used to wear long ago. We must put on God's armor to protect us from all the bad things in the world.

Make this person look like you. Then draw onto your picture all the parts of the armor of God.

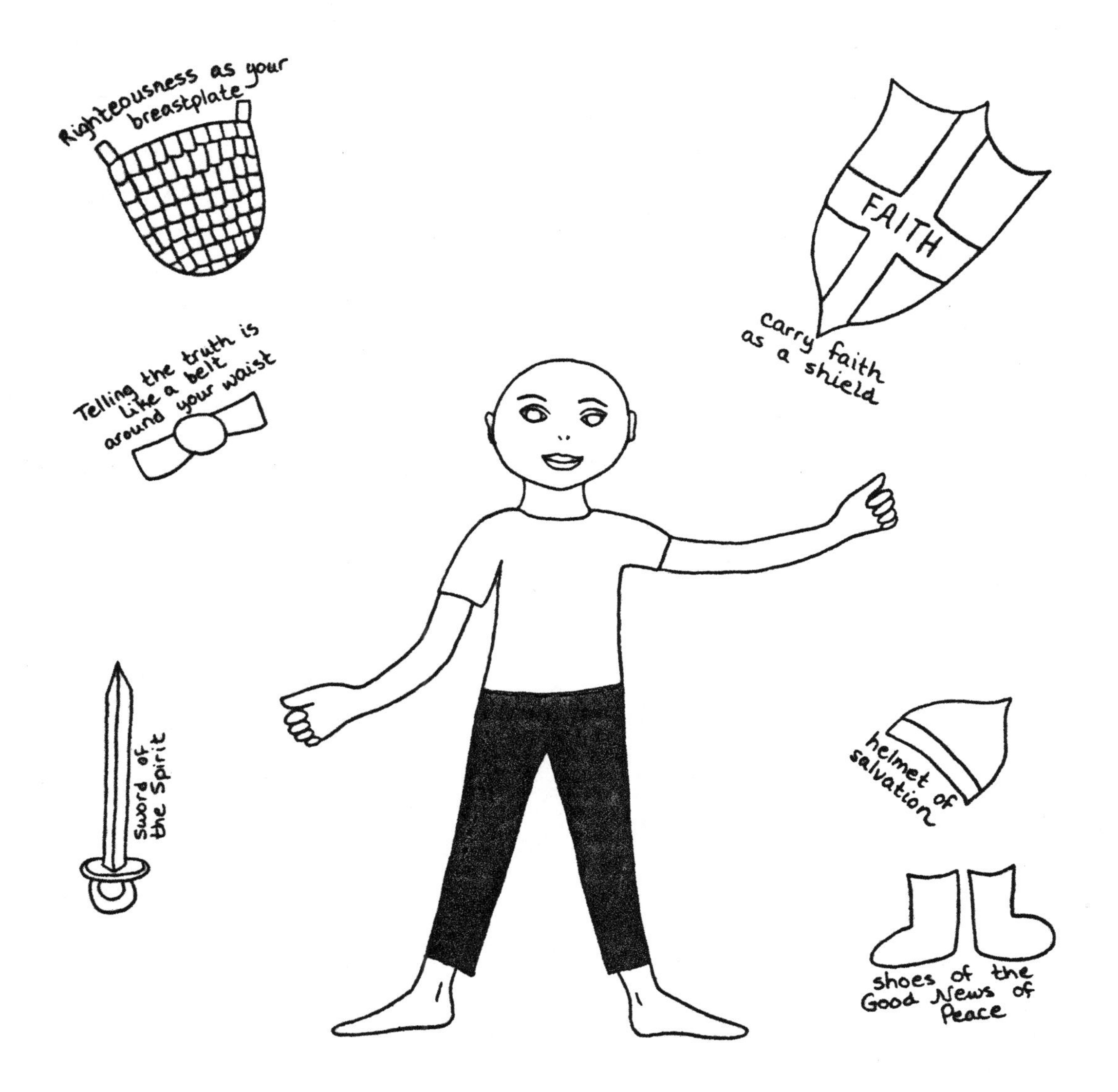

Put on all the armor that God gives you, so that you will be able to stand up against the Devil's evil tricks.

Ephesians 6:11

Dear God,

I am glad that I can be protected from evil as long as I believe in You.

Birds are singing, flowers are sprouting, leaves are appearing...it must be spring! Even after the coldest winter, we know that God will always make sure the earth blossoms again with new life.

Draw a picture of something you love to do in the spring.

For the winter is past ...the flowers are springing up and the time of the singing of birds has come.

Song of Solomon 2:11,12

Dear God,

Thank you for spring. Thank you for baby birds in their nests and beautiful plants and flowers. Thank You for brand-new beginnings.

•

You can make God happy by doing what He wants you to do—keep on living a good life day after day. Be kind, tell the truth, and read the Bible daily so you can know how God wants you to live.

Design your own bookmark. It can be really fancy or very simple.

Do you love to read? Name a good book you read recently:______________________________

God wants us to...live good...lives day after day.

Titus 2:12 (TLB)

•

Dear God,

Thank You for the most important book of all—the Bible!

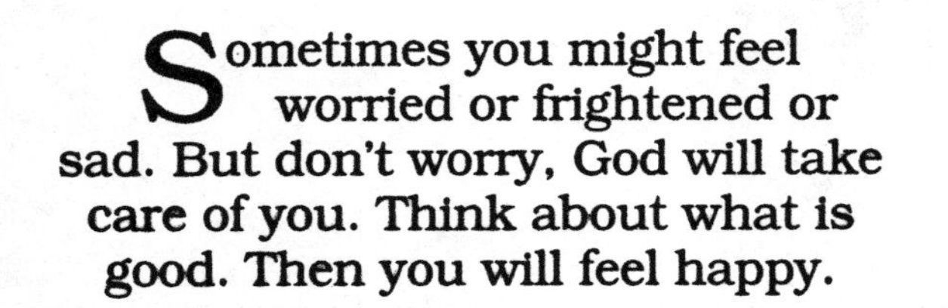

Sometimes you might feel worried or frightened or sad. But don't worry, God will take care of you. Think about what is good. Then you will feel happy.

Glue a photograph or draw a picture of you and your family having fun on a really happy day...a day to remember!

Fill your minds with those things that are good.

Philippians 4:8

Dear God,

Thank You for giving me so many good things to think about.

Work is a part of life! By working, grown-ups can earn money to buy things. Some people work in offices, some work in fields, and others work in stores. But more important than *where* we work is *how* we work. We should work with love for God! Every job is important

What kinds of jobs do your parents have? Perhaps both of your parents go to work every day. Or maybe one parent goes to work and one stays at home to watch the children and take care of the housework. In the spaces below, draw pictures of your dad and mom working.

This is my dad working. This is my mom working.

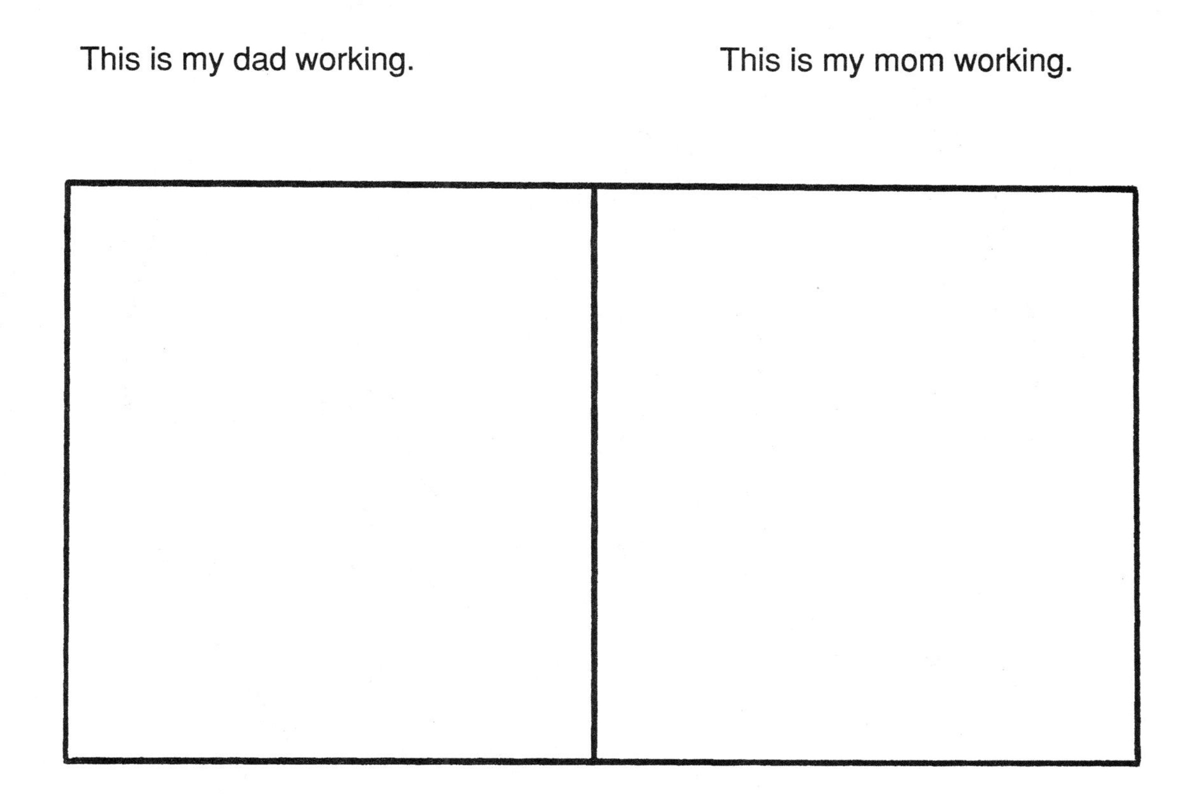

Work hard and do not be lazy. Serve the Lord with a heart full of devotion.

Romans 12:11

Dear God,

Thank You for giving me so many chances to do good each day!

This Bible verse says that no matter how hard you try to be good, you will still make mistakes and do wrong—we all do. The Bible calls this "sin" and the Hebrew word for sin means "missing the mark"...like missing the bull's-eye in archery. Only Jesus never missed the bull's-eye!

Lay this book on the floor. Make a tiny ball from a piece of paper and throw it at the target. Try to get the ball to hit the bull's-eye in the middle. If you are with someone, take turns. Good luck!

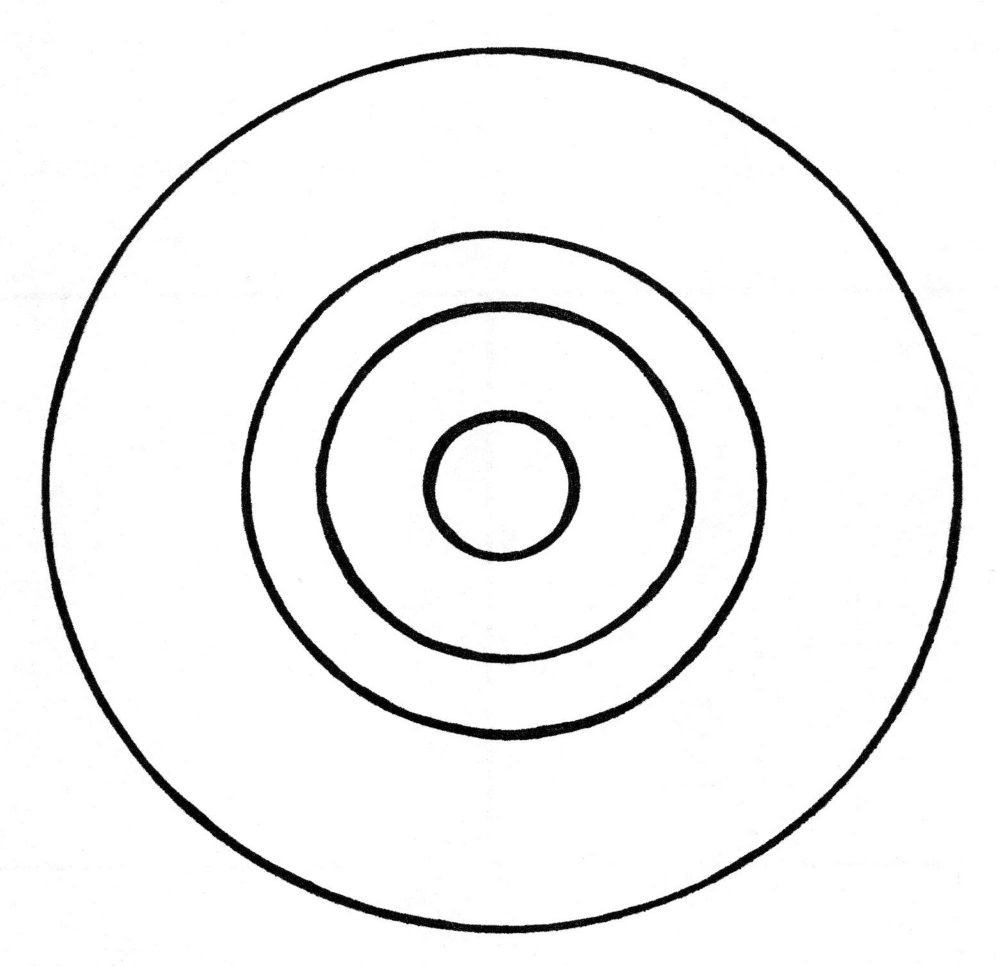

Yes, all have sinned; all fall short of God's glorious ideal...

Romans 3:23 (TLB)

Dear God,

Thank You for forgiving me. Thank You that I can get to heaven by trusting Jesus.

May 25

The pharaoh of Egypt had ordered that all the Hebrew baby boys must be killed. The pharaoh's daughter was bathing in the Nile River and saw baby Moses in a basket. She felt much love for the little boy, and decided to keep him and raise him as her own son. So Moses grew up as a prince of Egypt!

Color this picture.

When the baby's mother saw that he was an unusually beautiful baby, she hid him at home for three months.

Exodus 2:2 (TLB)

Dear God,

Help me to be kind to others when they are in need.

Moses held his rod over the Red Sea, and God opened the sea. The people crossed over and escaped from the Egyptian army.

Start at the arrow, and find the path that leads to the other arrow.

Moses told the people, "Don't be afraid. Just stand where you are and watch, and you will see the wonderful way the Lord will rescue you today."

Exodus 14:13 (TLB)

Dear God,

You can do amazing things for Your people. In fact, You can do even the impossible!

The Israelites wandered in the desert for 40 years. During that time, God took care of them. He had a cloud cover them during the day to protect them from the burning sun. A pillar of fire led the way at night.

Imagine a fluffy cloud protecting you from the hot sun. Now imagine God's love covering you like the cloud. Lots of nice things can cover you…like a warm, cozy quilt on your bed at night. Color in this quilt—square by square—with colors, designs, and pictures that you love.

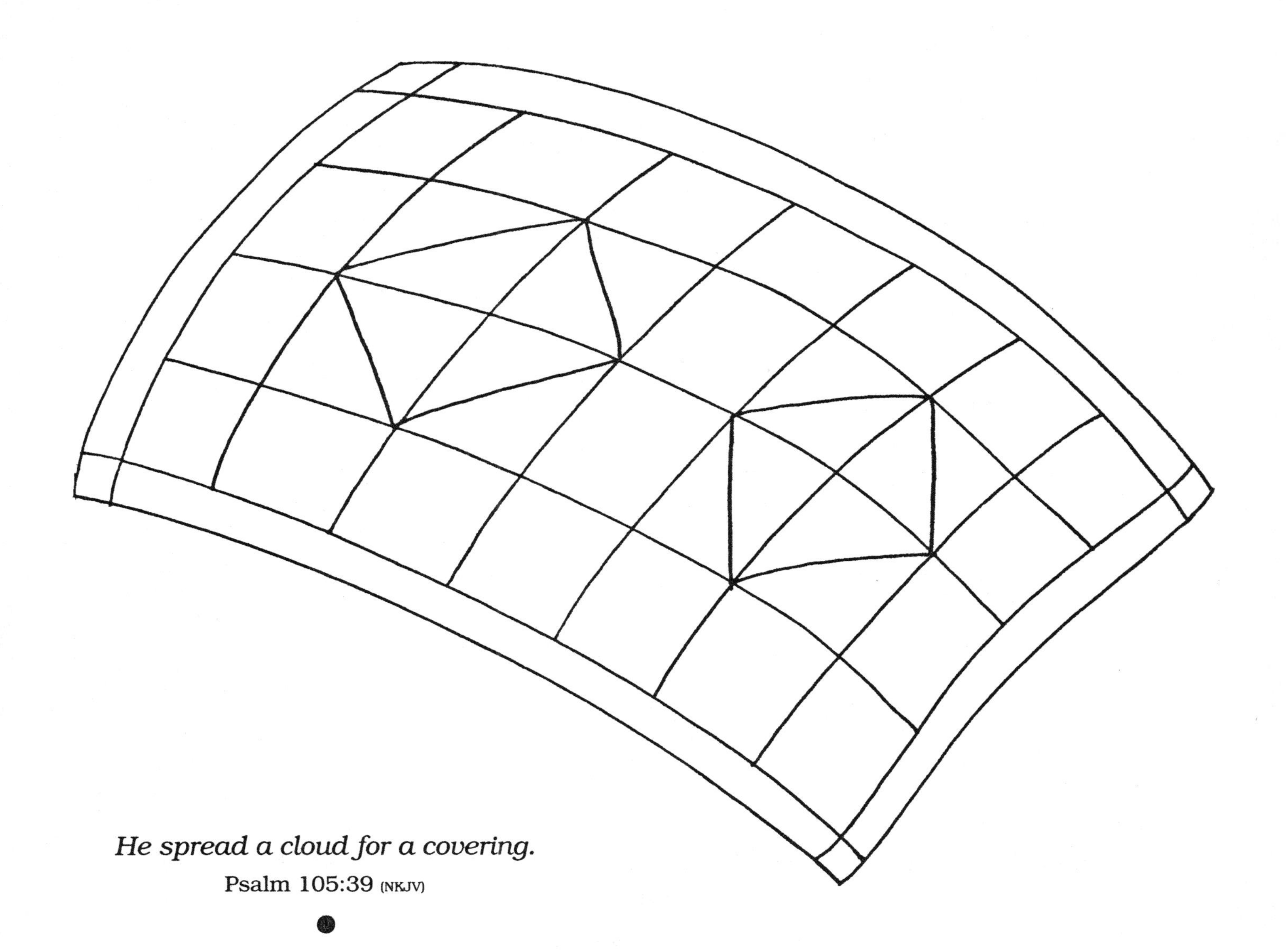

He spread a cloud for a covering.
Psalm 105:39 (NKJV)

Dear God,

I am glad Your love covers me like a cozy quilt on a cold winter's night.

•

The Bible tells us that there was a thick cloud on top of Mount Sinai, along with thunder, lightning, and the sound of a trumpet. Moses went up the mountain to talk to God, who gave Moses the Ten Commandments carved into two stone tablets.

Draw a picture of Moses receiving the Ten Commandments from God on Mount Sinai that day.

And the LORD called Moses to the top of the mountain, and Moses went up.

Exodus 19:20

•

Dear God,

Your commandments tell me the right way to live. Help me to do what is right.

What an amazing life Moses had! His mother put him in a basket in the Nile River and he was found by pharaoh's daughter and became a prince of Egypt. When Moses became a man, God spoke to him from a burning bush and told him that he would lead the Israelites out of Egypt and into the Promised Land. God opened the Red Sea so the Israelites could escape the Egyptian army. After that, God gave Moses the Ten Commandments.

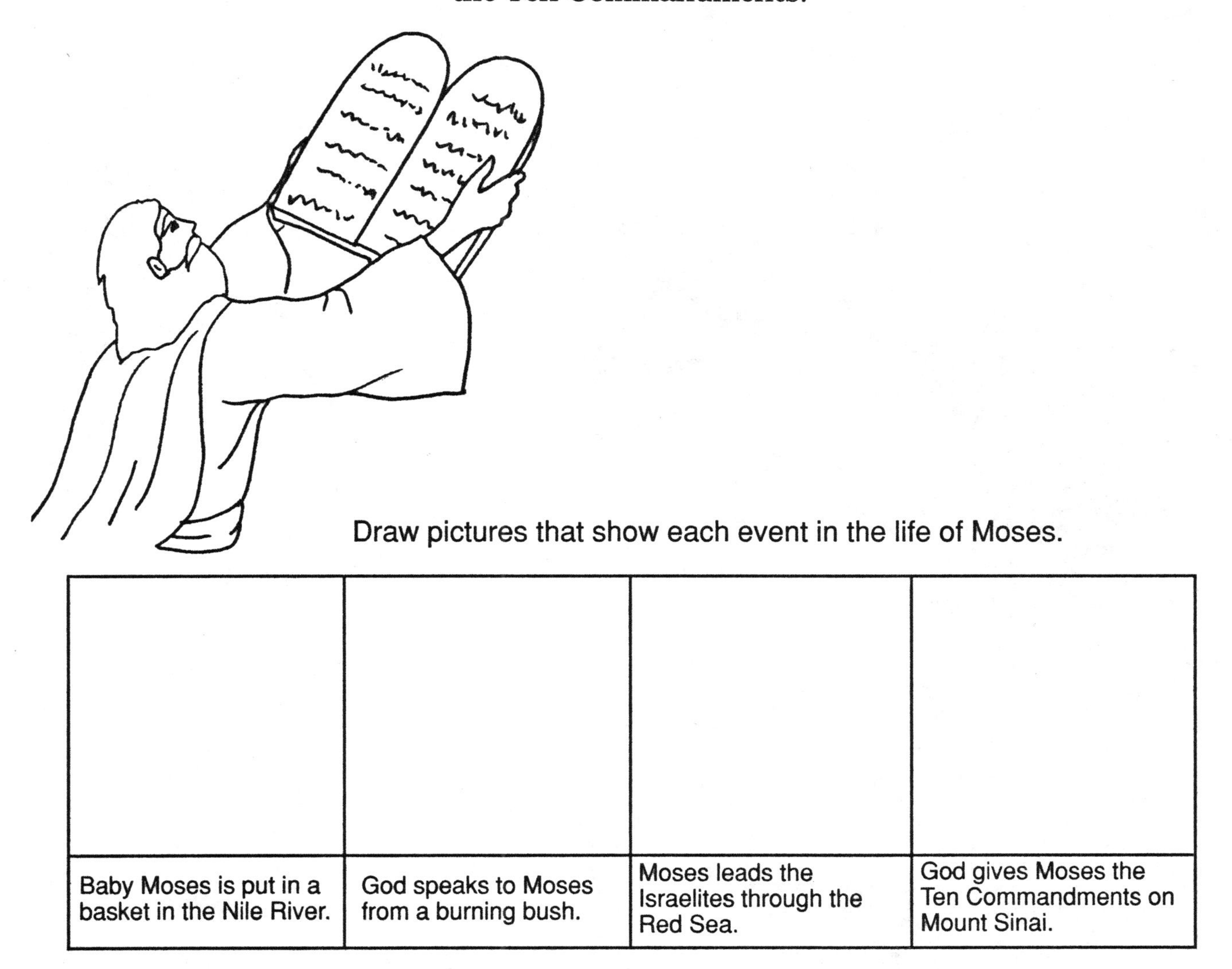

Draw pictures that show each event in the life of Moses.

Baby Moses is put in a basket in the Nile River.	God speaks to Moses from a burning bush.	Moses leads the Israelites through the Red Sea.	God gives Moses the Ten Commandments on Mount Sinai.

Moses, the man of God...No other prophet has been able to do the great...things that Moses did in the sight of all Israel.

Deuteronomy 33:1; 34:12

Dear God,

Help me to love and obey You like Moses did.

•

Some of us are good at singing. Some of us are fast runners. Some of us are able to talk easily with people. God made each one of us special. When another boy or girl is better at doing something than you are, that is God's plan for his or her life. We all have our special gifts. Let's be happy for each other when good things happen, and praise God!

Color this picture of four different friends having a great time.

Where there is jealousy and selfishness, there is also disorder and every kind of evil.

James 3:16

•

Dear God,

Thank You for the good gifts You give to each of us.

MAY MAY MAY MAY M

31 May

•

What a great month you had! Spring is here, and you had lots of fun. What was that memorable moment you would like to tell about? Did something special happen to you? Did you do something that made everybody proud of you? Did you do something you had never done before? Did you get a great surprise?

Capture May's memorable moment in the space below. Then write (or have someone help you write) the story of what happened.

A good man will receive blessings.

Proverbs 10:5

Dear God,

Thank You for all Your blessings.

JUNE

June 1

•

God created many wonderful animals in our world. Have you ever visited a farm or a zoo? Then you have seen, close up, some of God's amazing creations!

Draw some of the animals you would find on this farm.

Praise him...all animals.

Psalm 148:9,10

•

Dear God,

I love all the animals You have made.

June 2

Did you know that every good gift you have comes from God? He made everything, and He gives everything. He even gave you all your talents and abilities. Can you sing? Thank God! Can you dance? Thank God! Are you doing well in school? Thank God! The best way to thank God is to use what He has given you to praise Him.

In each of these boxes, write a special talent or ability you have, and thank God for it.

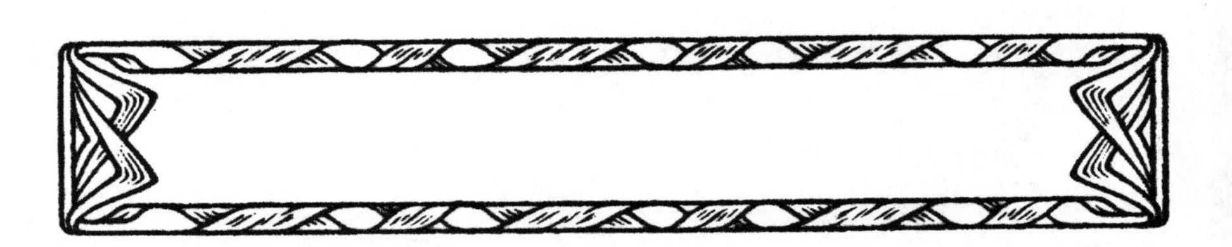

I will take pleasure in doing good things for them.
Jeremiah 32:41

Dear God,

Help me to always ask You what You would like me to do with the gifts You give me.

It's easy to love people when they are nice. It's not so easy to love them when they are mean or are bothering you. But, with God's help, you can be nice to everyone, no matter how they treat you. God loves everyone, and He wants us to love them, too!

Fill in the chart below with the names of different people you know. Check the box that best describes how you treat that person. Decide how to show kindness to difficult people.

I AM NICE TO:	Always	Usually	Sometimes	Never

Since God so loved us, we also ought to love one another.

1 John 4:11 (NIV)

Dear God,

Help me to be kinder to everyone.

•

Did you know that each country in the world has its own flag? Every flag has symbols and colors on it that tell us something about the country. In heaven there will be people from all around the world. Even though we may look and act differently and have different languages here on earth, we will all be one big happy family in heaven. We will all praise God together!

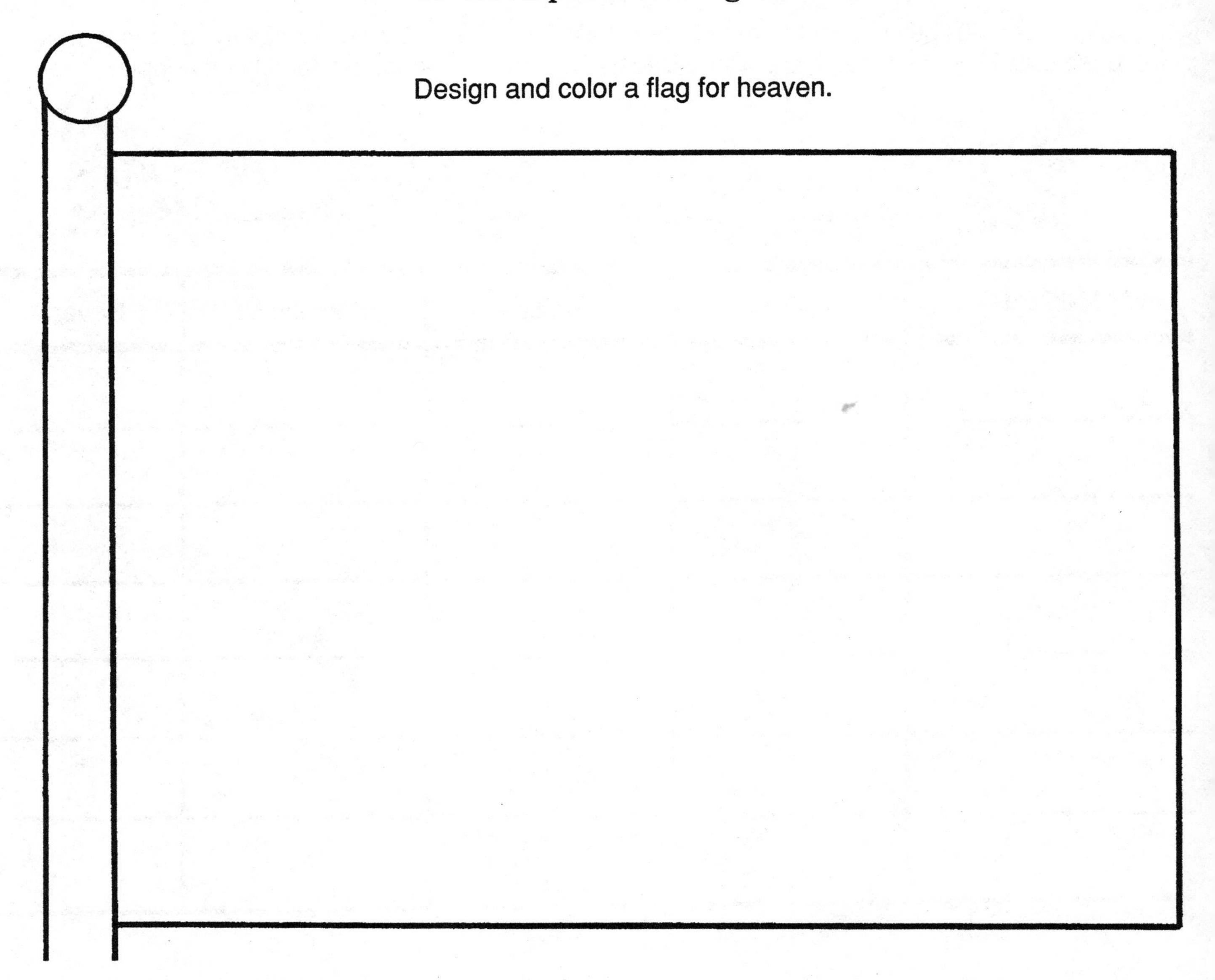

The world and all that is in it belong to the LORD; the earth and all who live on it are his.

Psalm 24:1

•

Dear God,

Thank You for loving me here on earth...and in heaven, too!

•

Good manners are important; being polite is a way of letting people know that you care about them. But did you know that every country has a different way of showing good manners?

In Japan, it is polite to greet someone with a deep bow.
In Chile, a handshake and a kiss on the cheek shows good manners.
In France, you say hello by kissing both cheeks.
In Fiji, a smile and upward movement of your eyebrows is the polite way to greet people.
Make a list of good manners you know: good table manners, telephone manners, manners with guests, and so on.

Try to do good to each other.

1 Thessalonians 5:15 (TLB)

•

Dear God,

Help me remember to always be polite and show respect to others.

•

Jesus wants you to always obey your parents and tell the truth. Sometimes that is not easy to do.

This little boy's parents told him not to climb the ladder. What should he tell his dad and mom when they find everyone hurt and crying? How could things have been different? Did you obey your parents today? What did you do?

You are my friends if you obey me.

John 15:14 (TLB)

•

Dear God,

Help me to obey and always tell the truth. I know I will enjoy a happier life if I do.

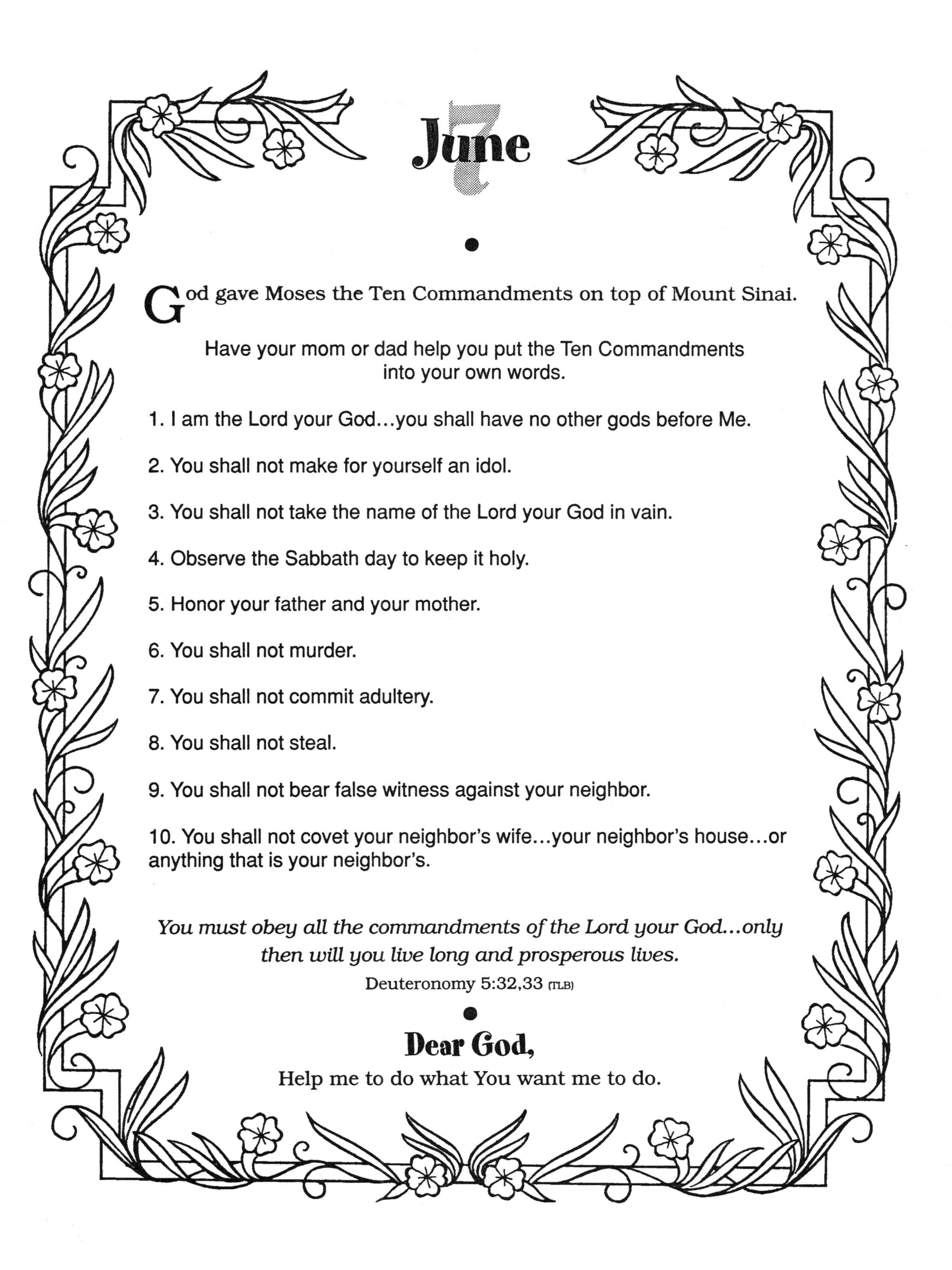

June 7

God gave Moses the Ten Commandments on top of Mount Sinai.

Have your mom or dad help you put the Ten Commandments into your own words.

1. I am the Lord your God...you shall have no other gods before Me.
2. You shall not make for yourself an idol.
3. You shall not take the name of the Lord your God in vain.
4. Observe the Sabbath day to keep it holy.
5. Honor your father and your mother.
6. You shall not murder.
7. You shall not commit adultery.
8. You shall not steal.
9. You shall not bear false witness against your neighbor.
10. You shall not covet your neighbor's wife...your neighbor's house...or anything that is your neighbor's.

You must obey all the commandments of the Lord your God...only then will you live long and prosperous lives.

Deuteronomy 5:32,33 (TLB)

Dear God,

Help me to do what You want me to do.

•

We have so many reasons to be happy and thankful, don't we? God has given us so many wonderful gifts, talents, and characteristics that make each of us special!

Decorate this T-shirt for yourself any way you like…with bows, butterflies, or baseballs. Then think about something you really like about yourself, and write it on the blank line.

Always be full of joy in the Lord; I say it again, rejoice!

Philippians 4:4

•

Dear God,

Thank You for the way You made me. Thank You for all that I can do, think, and say.

•

God knows and cares about every part of your life. He has made you a special and unique creation; there is no one else on earth exactly like you—there never was and never will be.

Tell a little about yourself by filling in the blanks.

ALL ABOUT ME

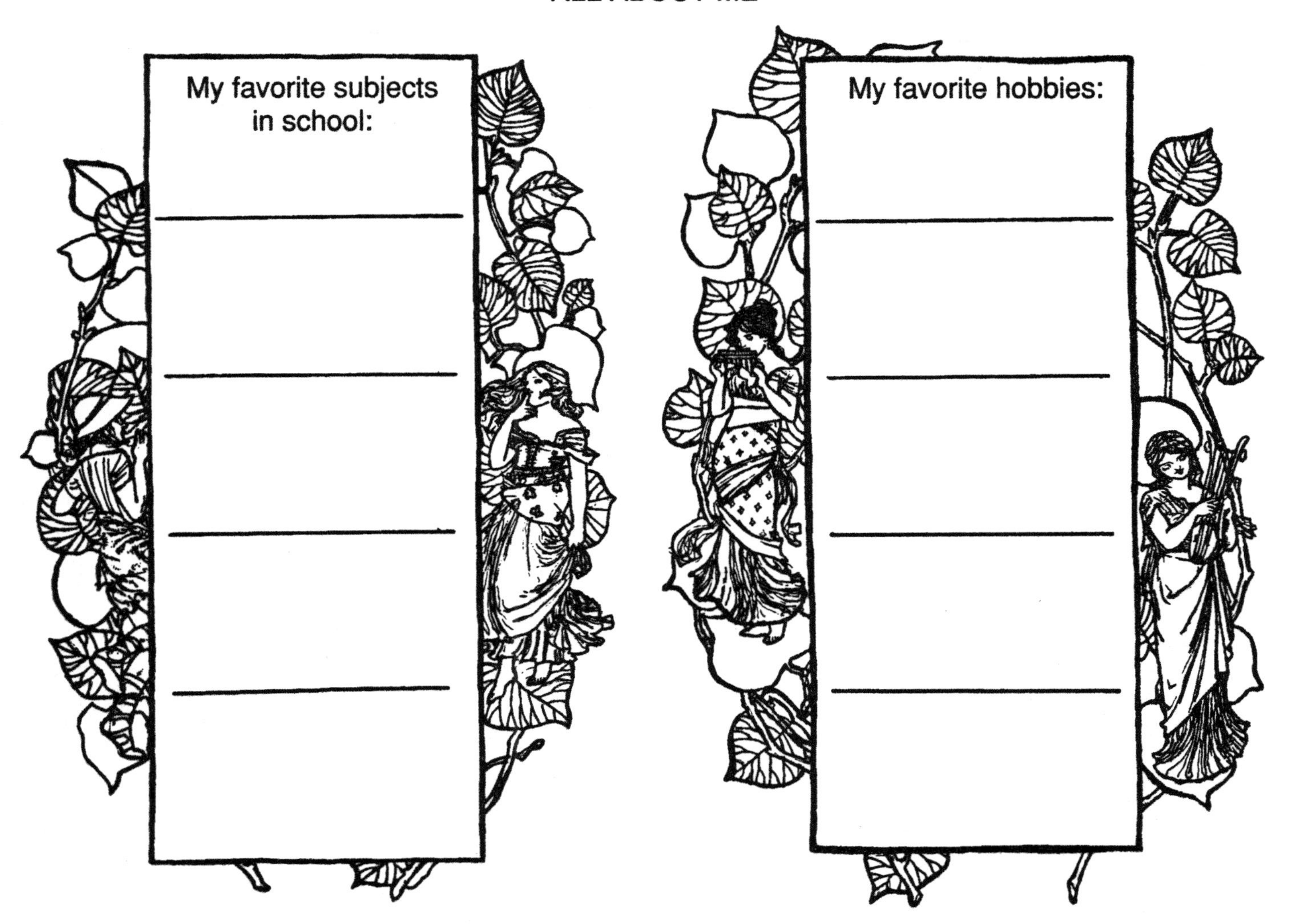

O LORD, You have searched me and known me. You know my sitting down and my rising up.

Psalm 139:1,2 (NKJV)

•

Dear God,

Thank You for all the special talents and abilities You have given me.

What are the signs that summer is coming? The days get longer and hotter, the leaves on the trees are big and green, and their branches are full of ripe fruit. But the sign you probably notice most is that school is out and you are on vacation!

What do you enjoy doing in the summer? Draw a picture of it.

You made summer.

Psalm 74:17

Dear God,

Thank You for summer. I love running outside in bare feet. I also enjoy playing and swimming. Thank You for happy summer days!

Did you know that the sun sets at a different time every night? In the summer, the sun sets later than in the winter. That's why you can go outside in the summer for hours after dinner and it is still light. Every day of the year the sun sets right on time... God makes sure it does!

Follow the path through this maze that takes you to the center of the sun.

The sun knows the time to set.

Psalm 104:19

Dear God,

I may not understand how You run the universe, but You sure do a great job!

•

You should show kindness to other people every single day—to your friends, your family, and even to people you don't know. By showing kindness, you will show them that you understand the love of God.

Starting today, give yourself a heart for each kind deed you do during this next week.

♡ Kindness Chart ♡

Deed	Sun.	Mon.	Tues.	Wed.	Thurs.	Fri.	Sat.
played nicely							
helped somebody							
was friendly							
said nice things							
gave a hug							

Remember, you must demonstrate the love and kindness of the Lord.

1 Samuel 20:14 (TLB)

•

Dear God,

Thank You for being so kind to me. Help me to share that kindness with others.

It's so much fun to be a child! You can run, play, and do all kinds of fun and even silly things. Remember that God loves you and wants you to enjoy the life He has given to you.

Write (or have someone help you write) about a time when you did something silly. Save this page for later if you haven't done something silly lately.

Young people, enjoy your youth. Be happy while you are still young.

Ecclesiastes 11:9

Dear God,

Thank You for all the fun times in my life.

•

Don't you love to look up at the night sky and see all the countless stars? Did you know that our sun is a star? It looks bigger than all the other stars because it is the closest to our earth—just 93 million miles away! God's universe is a very, very big place.

Color this pattern, and make all the stars bright yellow.

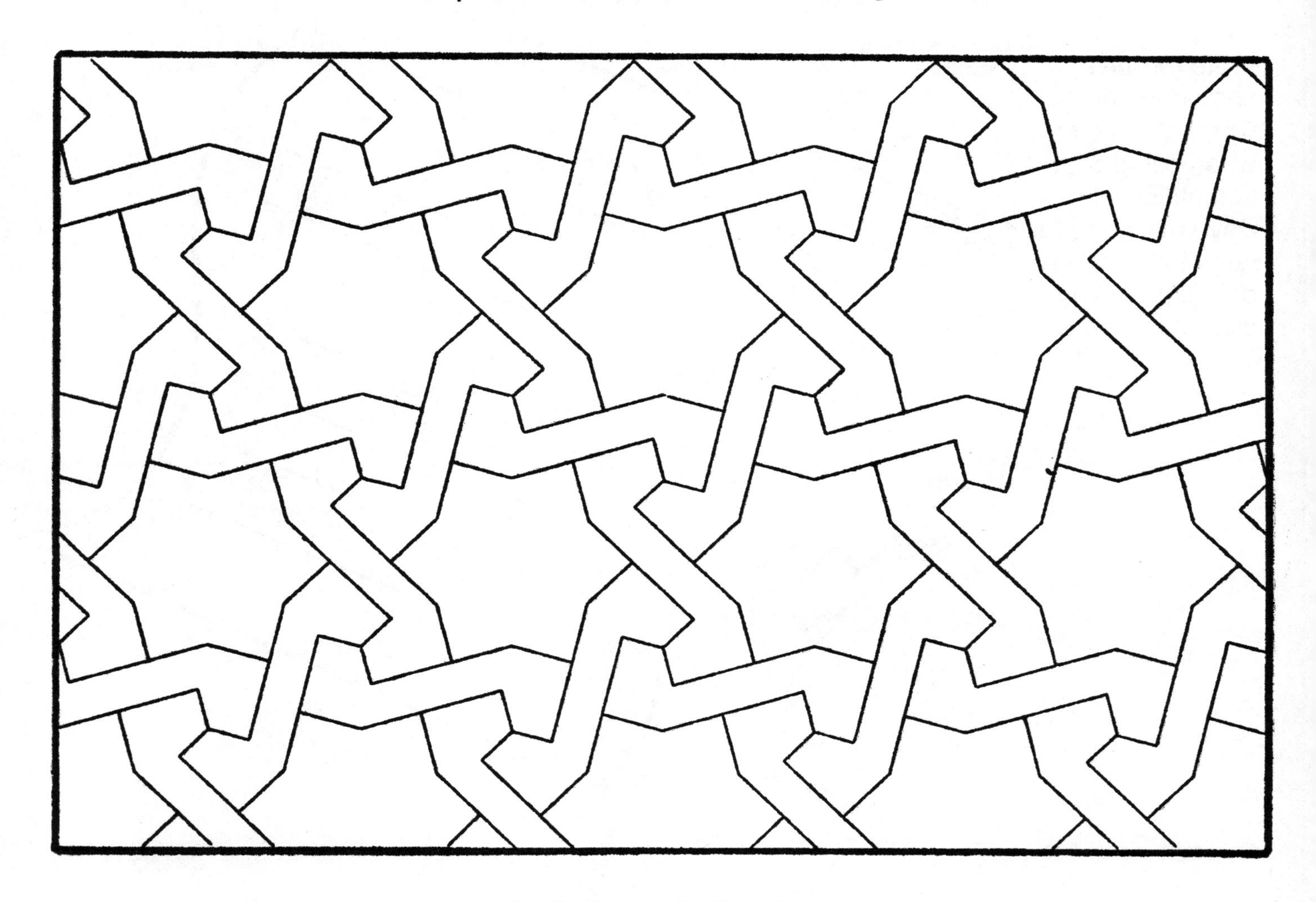

So God...made the stars.

Genesis 1:16

•

Dear God,

I am glad that even though You are a big God, You always have time for me.

•

Isn't it wonderful to have good friends? True friends love you, no matter what you do. They might get upset over something you have done, but true friends always make up. Real friendship is forever!

Draw a picture of your best friend in this frame. Under the picture, write your best friend's name and the reasons that you are good friends.

A friend loves at all times.

Proverbs 17:17 (NASB)

•

Dear God,

Thank You for the gift of good friends. Help me to always look for the good in others.

June 16

No matter what happens to you, God is always ready to help you. He wants to keep you safe and take care of your needs.

The word "help" starts with the letter H. Can you find ten H's on this page? When you are done, color the page.

God is my helper.

Psalm 54:4

Dear God,

I am so glad that I can always count on You for help. I don't have to be afraid as long as I trust in You.

Isn't it wonderful to know that God loves you and wants to give you good gifts? Every day you should count your blessings—you should thank God for the good things He has given you. Don't worry about what you want; instead, thank God for what you have.

Name five things you want to thank God for giving to you:

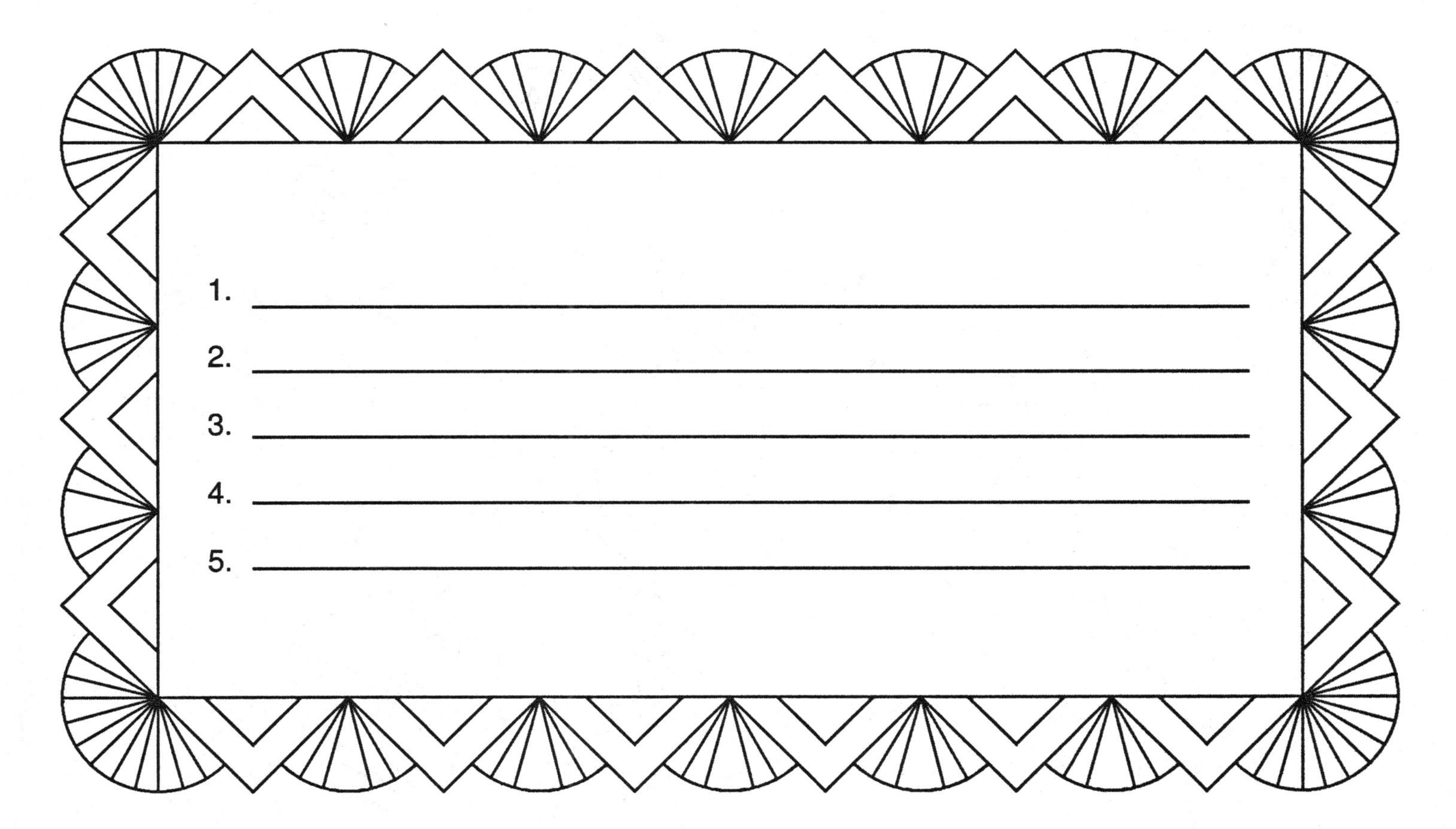

God has been kind to me.

Genesis 33:11

Dear God,

Thank You for all that You have given me. You are so good to me! I love You so much!

God gave us the Ten Commandments because He knows what is best for us. He knows what we need to do to be happy and to get along with others. God's laws are based on love!

Can you find the numbers 1-10 in this picture? When you are done, color Mama Bunny and Baby Bunny in their garden. How many of the Ten Commandments can you remember? (If you need help, see June 9.)

Listen to all the laws that I am giving you today. Learn them and be sure that you obey them.

Deuteronomy 5:1

Dear God,

You know what is best for me and how I need to live to be happy and peaceful. Thank You

If a tree gets lots of sun and water, it will become big and strong and grow good fruit. If you do everything God says, you will grow strong and be a blessing to the people you love.

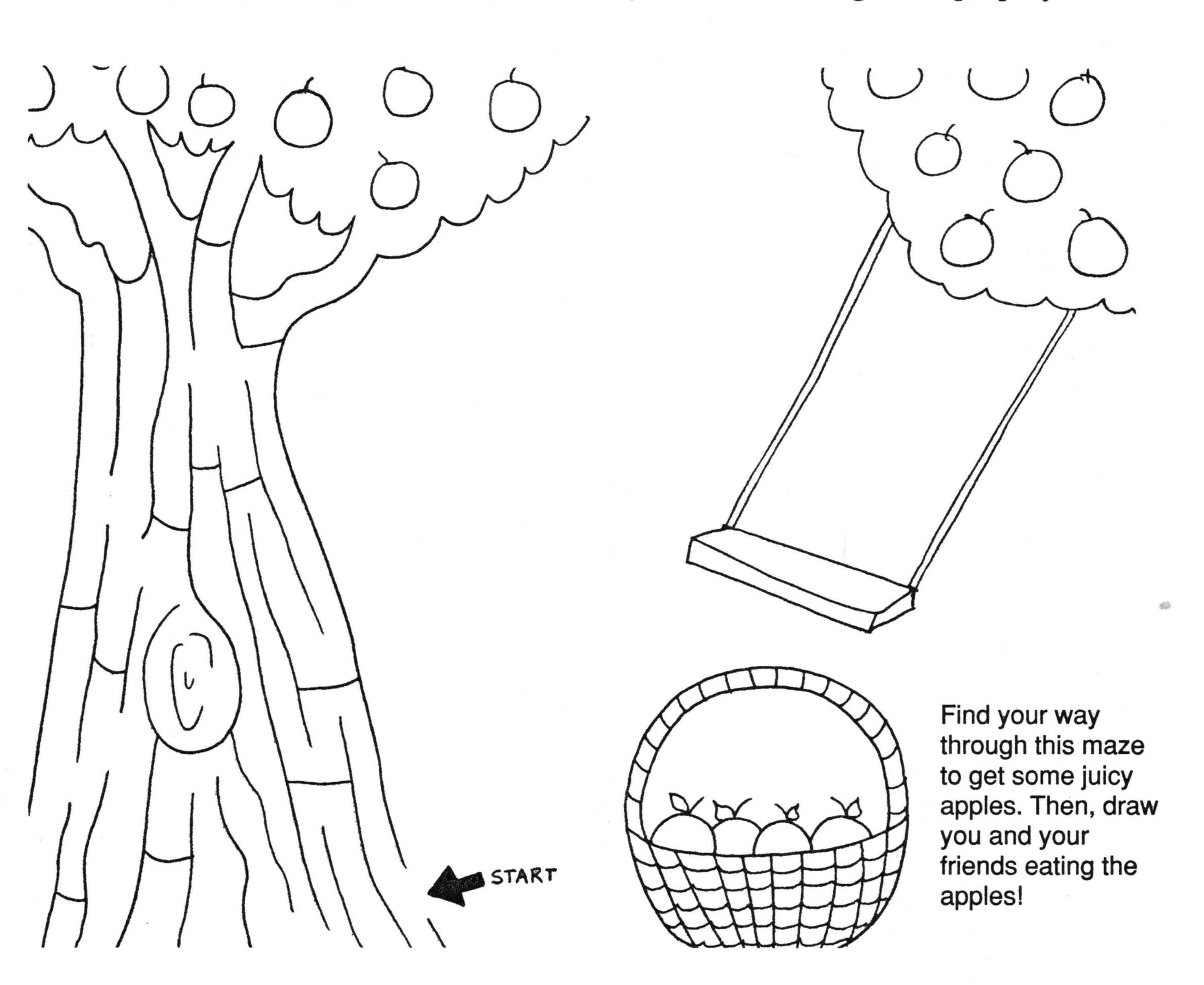

Find your way through this maze to get some juicy apples. Then, draw you and your friends eating the apples!

To have good fruit you must have a healthy tree.

Matthew 12:33

Dear God,

Thank You for all the delicious fruit we enjoy. Help me to grow up strong and healthy and be a good example to others.

•

How can you tell your parents how much they mean to you? One way is by doing what they tell you to do. Another way is to thank them for all the things they do for you. Best of all, you can say, "I love you!"

Draw a picture and write a special message to your dad.

Respect your father and your mother.

Deuteronomy 5:16

•

Dear God,

Thank You for my father.

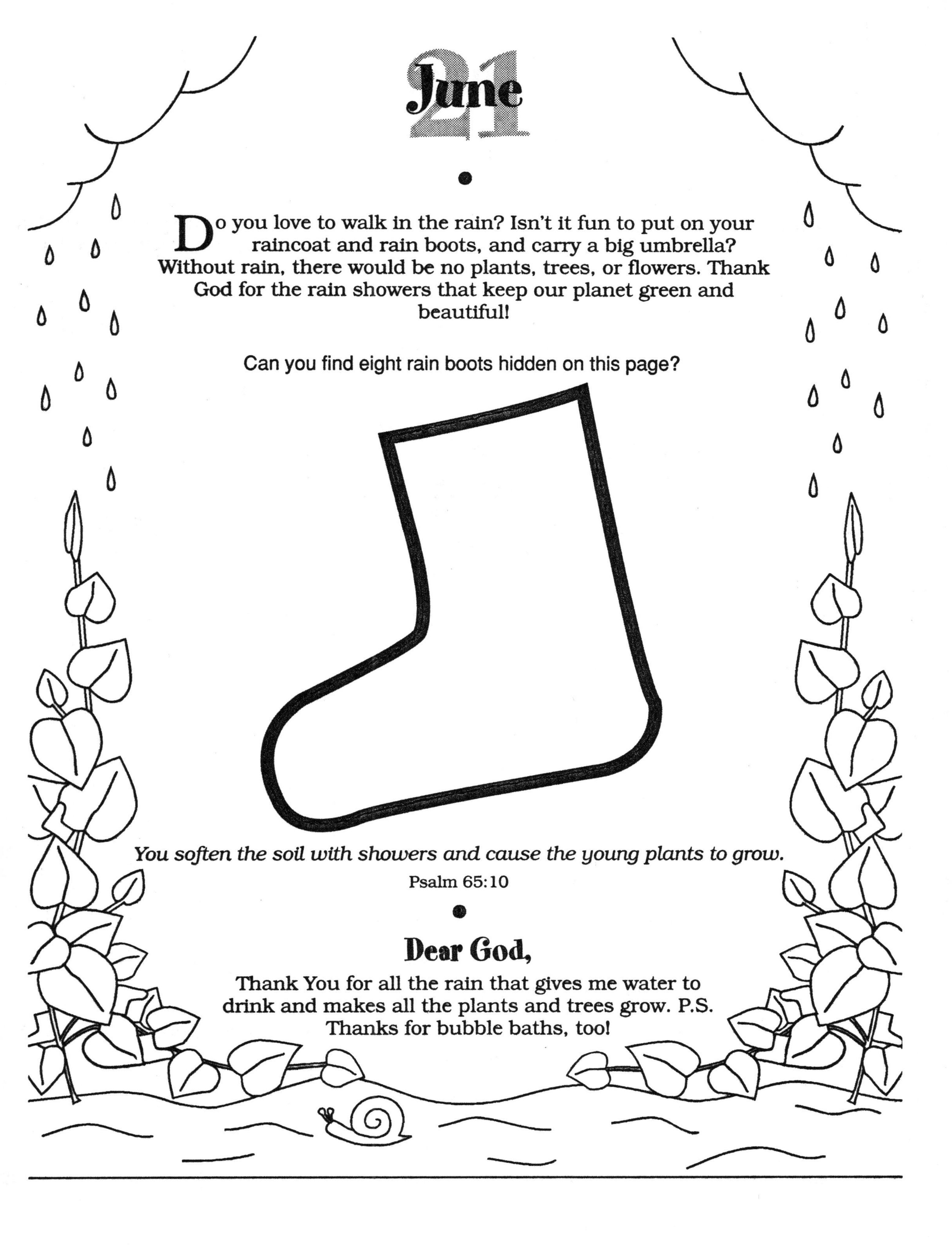

June 21

Do you love to walk in the rain? Isn't it fun to put on your raincoat and rain boots, and carry a big umbrella? Without rain, there would be no plants, trees, or flowers. Thank God for the rain showers that keep our planet green and beautiful!

Can you find eight rain boots hidden on this page?

You soften the soil with showers and cause the young plants to grow.

Psalm 65:10

Dear God,

Thank You for all the rain that gives me water to drink and makes all the plants and trees grow. P.S. Thanks for bubble baths, too!

June 22

There are many people all over the world who love and praise God. Have you ever mailed a letter to someone in a different country, or even in your own country? You put a stamp on the envelope so it could be delivered, didn't you?

Design your own postage stamps in the spaces below. Write the name of the country below each stamp. How about drawing a stamp for heaven?

Praise with one voice the God and Father of our Lord Jesus Christ.

Romans 15:6

Dear God,

I am so glad it is easy to talk to You! You always hear me, and I don't even need to use a stamp

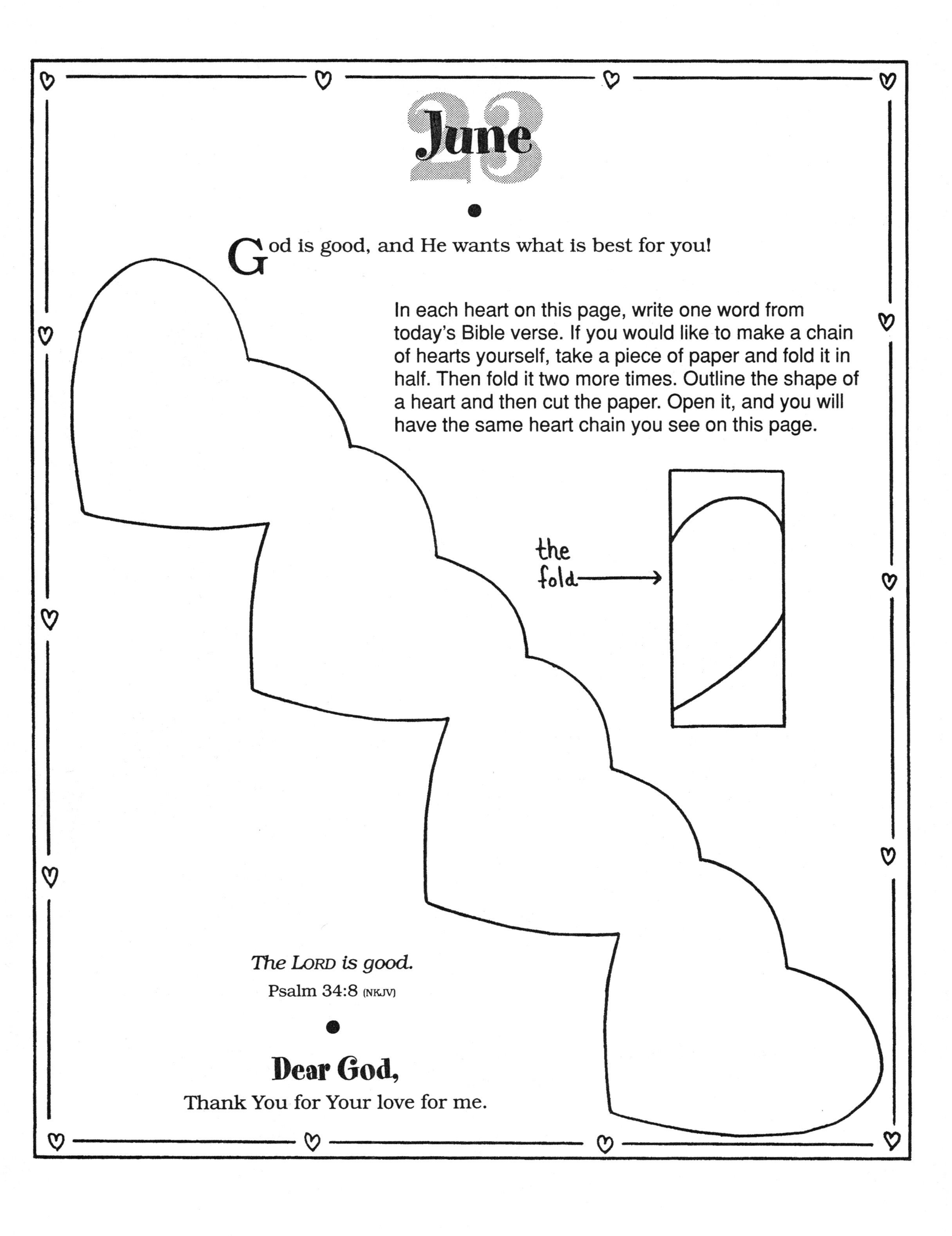

June 23

God is good, and He wants what is best for you!

In each heart on this page, write one word from today's Bible verse. If you would like to make a chain of hearts yourself, take a piece of paper and fold it in half. Then fold it two more times. Outline the shape of a heart and then cut the paper. Open it, and you will have the same heart chain you see on this page.

The LORD is good.
Psalm 34:8 (NKJV)

Dear God,
Thank You for Your love for me.

June 24

If you really want to know God, you will!

Can you find 30 hearts hidden in this picture?

You shall find Him when you search for Him with all your hearts and souls.

Deuteronomy 4:29 (TLB)

Dear God,

I want to be very close to You all of my life.

Did you know that it is silly to worry about anything? No matter how much you worry, it will not change your problems. Always remember that God promises to take good care of you. Trust God; He will never let you down.

Fill in the blanks.

My favorite bird is a ______________________________

because ______________________________________

Now draw a picture of your favorite bird.

You are worth so much more than birds!

Luke 12:24

Dear God,

You take care of all the birds in our world. I know I can trust You to take care of me.

•

Even Jesus and His disciples had to take time to rest. Do you have a special place you like to go to relax and think—a place where you can have some quiet time? Everybody needs that.

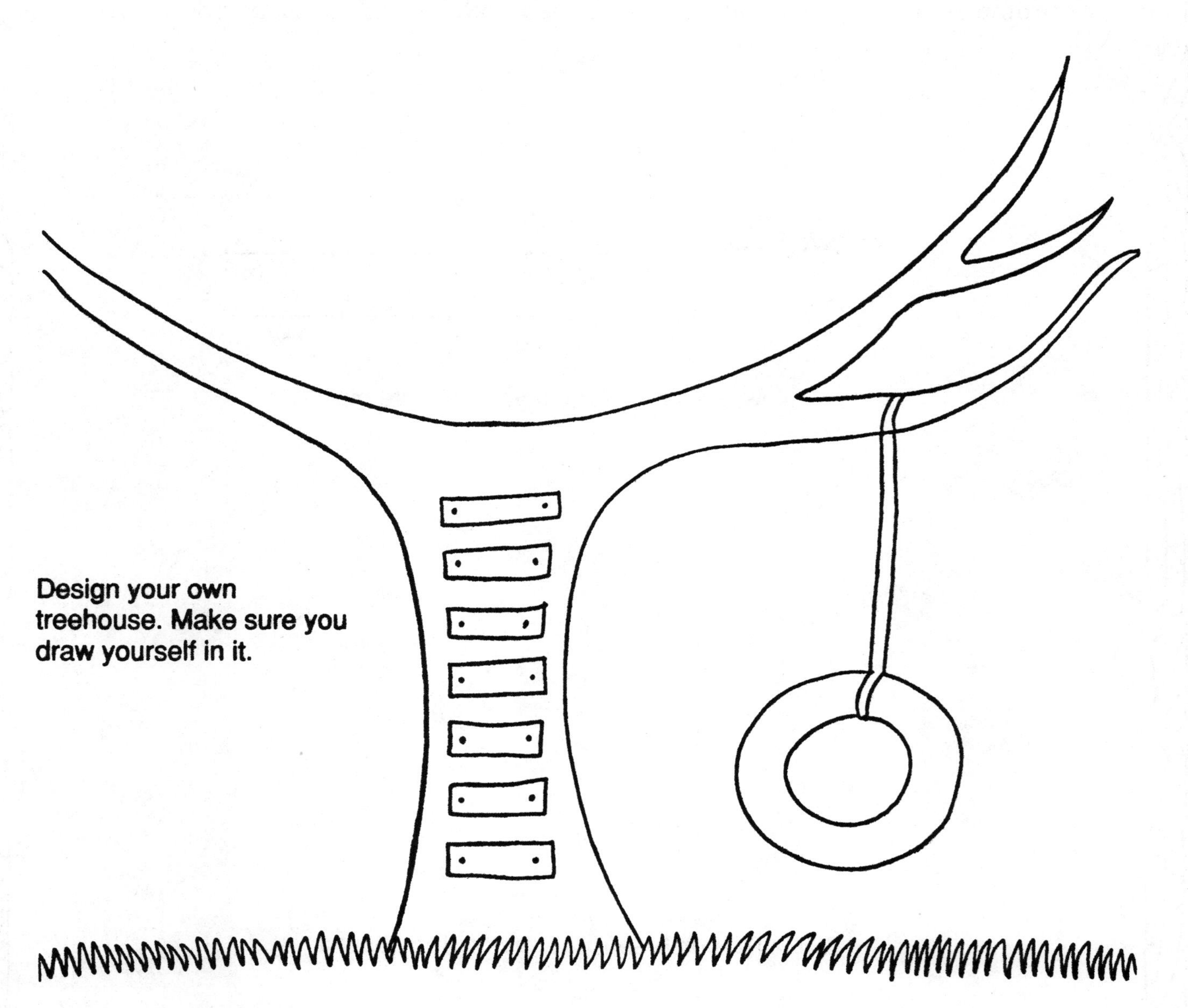

Let us go off by ourselves to some place where we will be alone and you can rest a while.

Mark 6:31

•

Dear God,

Thank You for peaceful, quiet times. Those times make me feel closer to You.

June 27

•

Jesus said you can add brightness everywhere you go by showing love, kindness, peace, and patience. When you love Jesus, you will stand out in a crowd because you will be so happy!

There are no windows on the train or the house and there is no sun in the sky. Things must be dark in this picture. Can you give this picture some light? Now color in this new, happy scene. The world needs light, just like we need Jesus.

You are like light for the whole world.

Matthew 5:14

•

Dear God,

Help me to be a good example of Your love and to shine Your light everywhere I go.

God has promised that if we walk in His way and do what is right, we will have happy, peaceful lives. In the same way that God gives rest to our souls, we need to give rest to our bodies, too. That is why grown-ups like to take vacations...and kids, too!

Draw a picture of where you would like to take a vacation.
Where are you? What are you doing?

And you shall find rest for your souls.

Jeremiah 6:16 (NASB)

Dear God,

I am glad that even when everybody around me is very busy, I can feel peaceful when I think of Your love for me.

What do you think of when you think of treasure? Gold, diamonds, and rubies? Whatever kind of treasure you are imagining, nothing on this earth lasts forever. Treasures that last are kindness, good deeds, prayers, and praise, and every time you tell someone about Jesus. Store your treasures in heaven, where it counts!

There are at least 25 diamonds in this picture. See how many you can count.

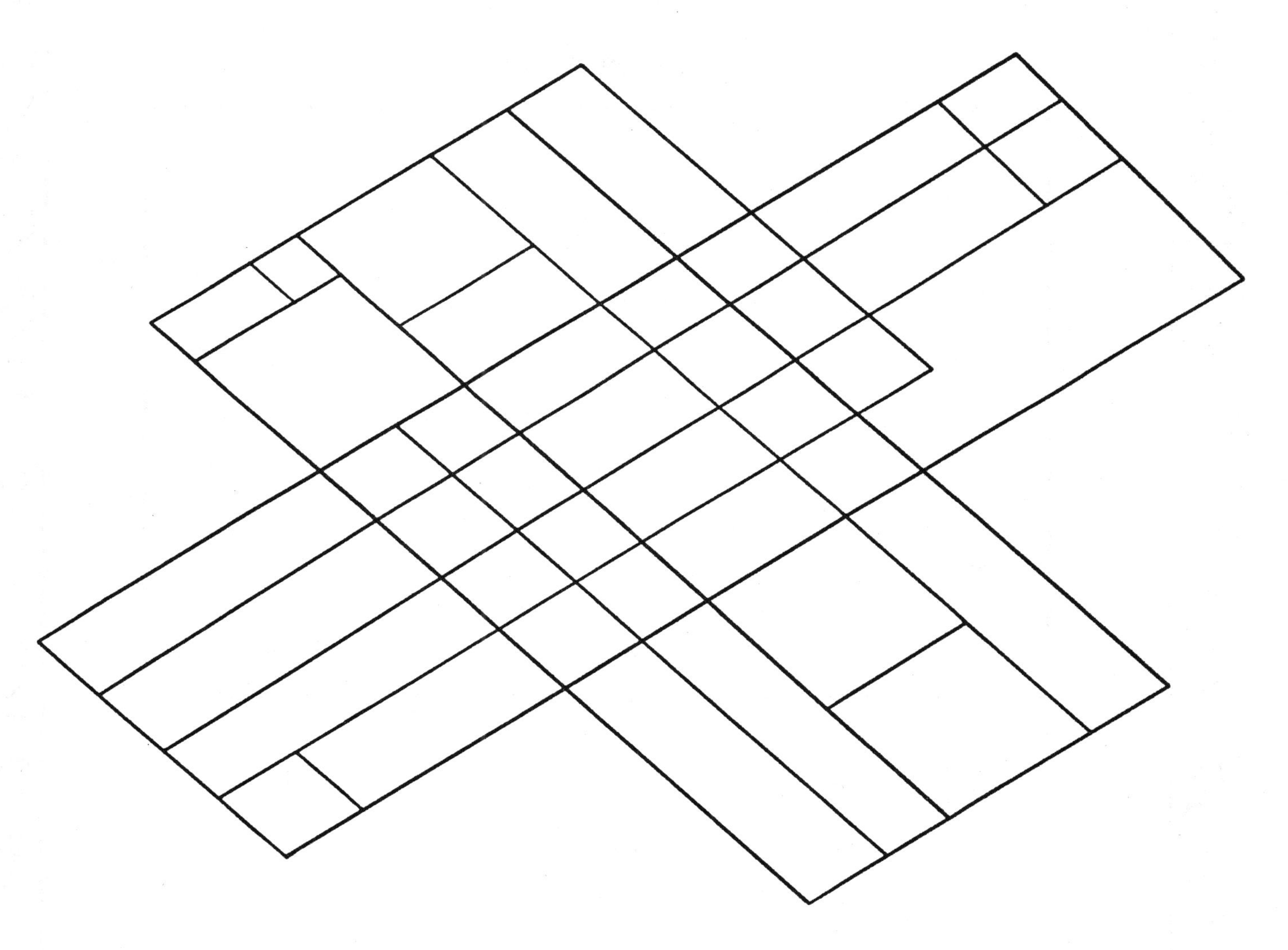

Lay up for yourselves treasures in heaven.

Matthew 6:20 (NKJV)

Dear God,

Help me to always remember what is really important in life: loving others and loving You.

JUNE JUNE JUNE JU

June 30

Summer is here and school is out. A lot has happened this month. What was the most memorable moment for you? What was something special that you said or did and that you never want to forget? Did you do something brave or kind or funny? Did God bless you in a wonderful way? Let's hear about it!

June's Memorable Moment

God has been kind to me.

Genesis 33:1

Dear God,

You are the greatest! Thank You for what You are doing in my life.

JULY

Some things are right, and some things are wrong...it's as simple as that! When you love God, you will find yourself wanting to do what is right—most of the time! When you make mistakes, it is your parents' job to help correct you and show you the right way. It is not always easy to do what is right, but with God's help, we can become more and more obedient.

Can you find 12 things that are wrong with this picture?

Never be tired of doing right.

2 Thessalonians 3:13 (TLB)

Dear God,

Help me to obey You and my parents so I will have a safe and happy life.

We can learn a lot about who God is by looking at the wonderful world He has created. He makes sure every fish and animal has the right kind of food to eat, the right kind of air to breathe, or the right kind of water to live in. God takes good care of you, too!

Draw some interesting fish and other sea creatures, and color them.

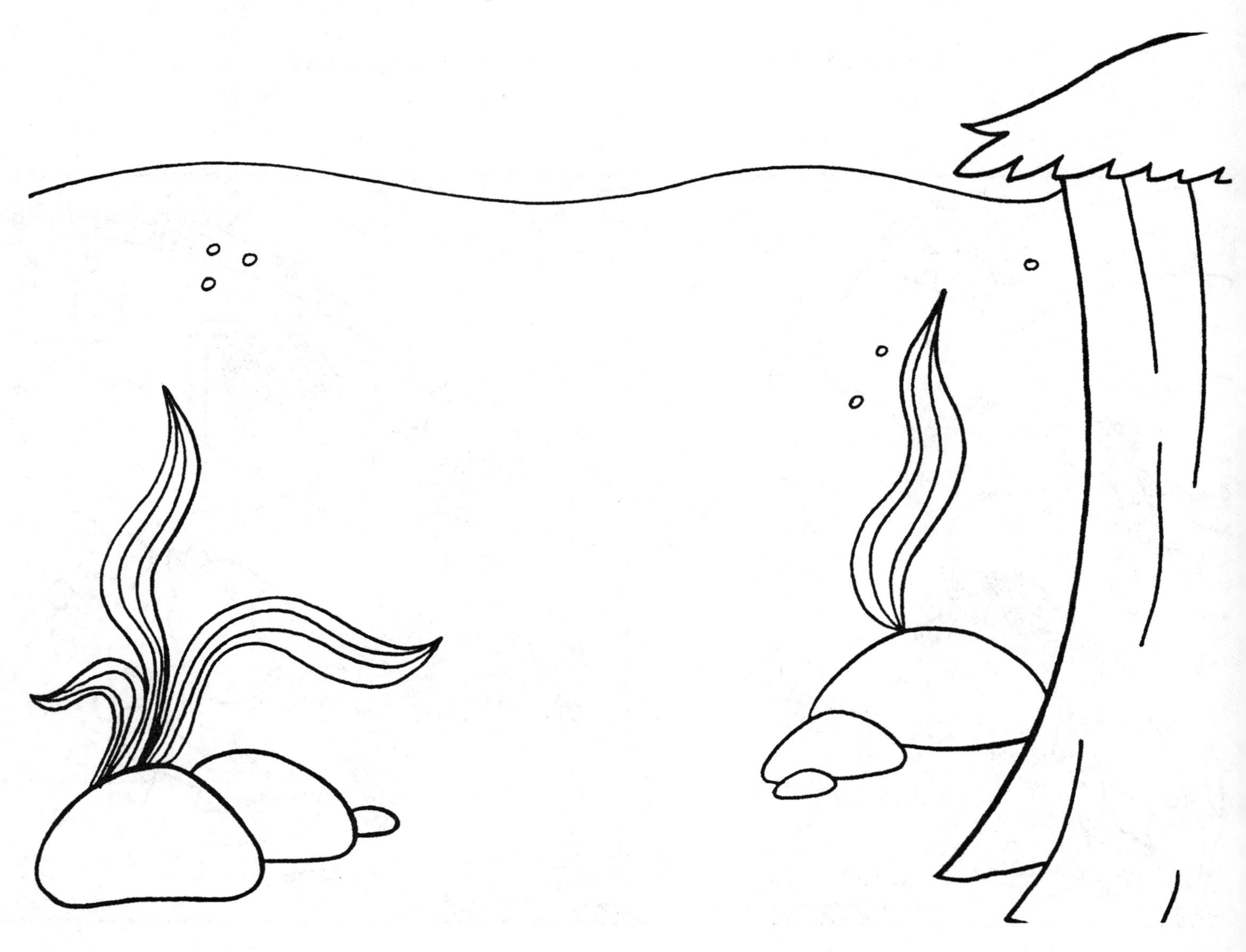

He rules over the sea, which he made.

Psalm 95:5

Dear God,

Thank You for the water, food, and air You made for us.

Someday, when Jesus returns, everyone will know about Him.
What a wonderful day that will be.

Did you know that this planet is mostly water? Have you ever seen one of the oceans? Have you ever gone swimming in a lake, stream, or pool? Write a story about a fun time you had in the water.

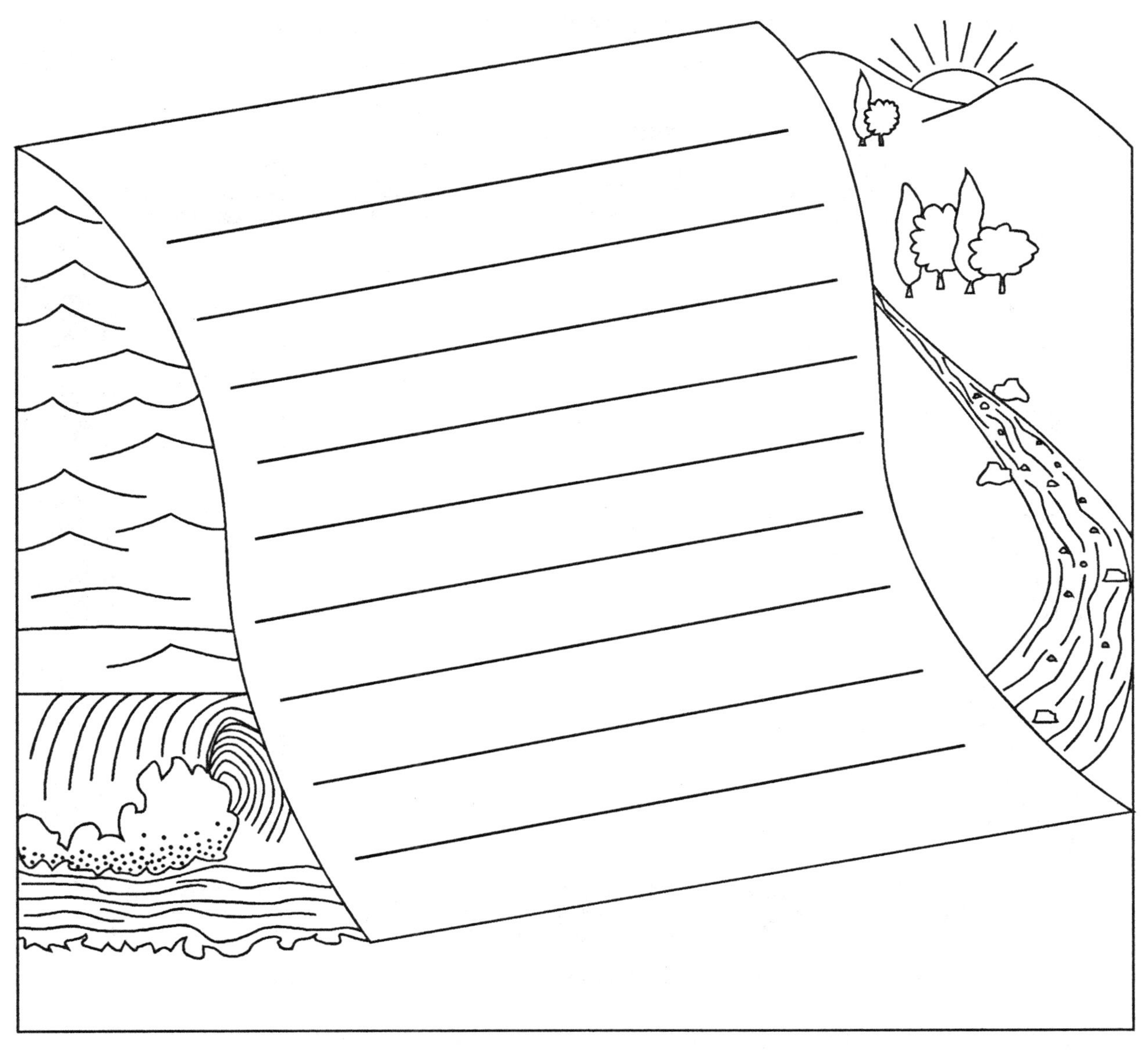

The land will be as full of knowledge of the LORD as the seas are full of water.

Isaiah 11:9

Thank You for cool water on hot summer days!

•

The Lord told Moses and his brother, Aaron, to say a blessing for the people of Israel. You can read that blessing below. When you say these words to someone, you are asking God to bless him and take good care of him. You are asking that God be kind to him and that good will happen to him. What could be better than that!

Make game pieces using buttons, pennies, or little pieces of paper. Play this game as if you were playing tic-tac-toe, but try to get four in a row. Take turns and use strategy to win the game.

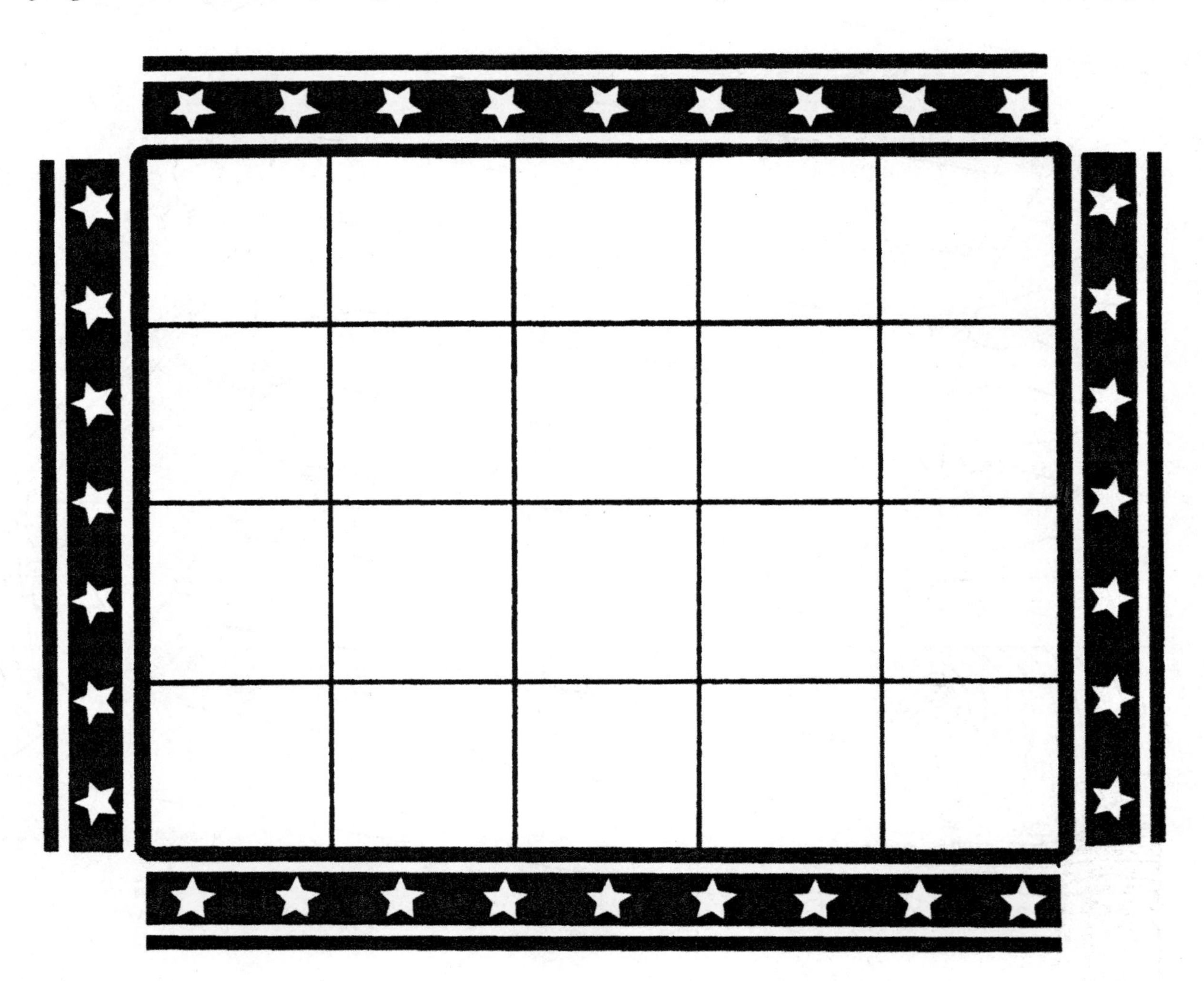

The LORD bless you and keep you; the LORD make his face shine upon you and be gracious to you; the LORD turn his face toward you and give you peace.

Numbers 6:24-26 (NIV)

•

Dear God,

Thank You for Your blessing on me.

Have you ever thought about how amazing it is that you can plant a seed and, before long, have something delicious to eat? Warm sunshine, lots of rain, and God's perfect plan turn that little seed into corn, or watermelon, or a big pumpkin. God's creations are incredible!

Can you get through this corn maze? What is your favorite way to eat corn?

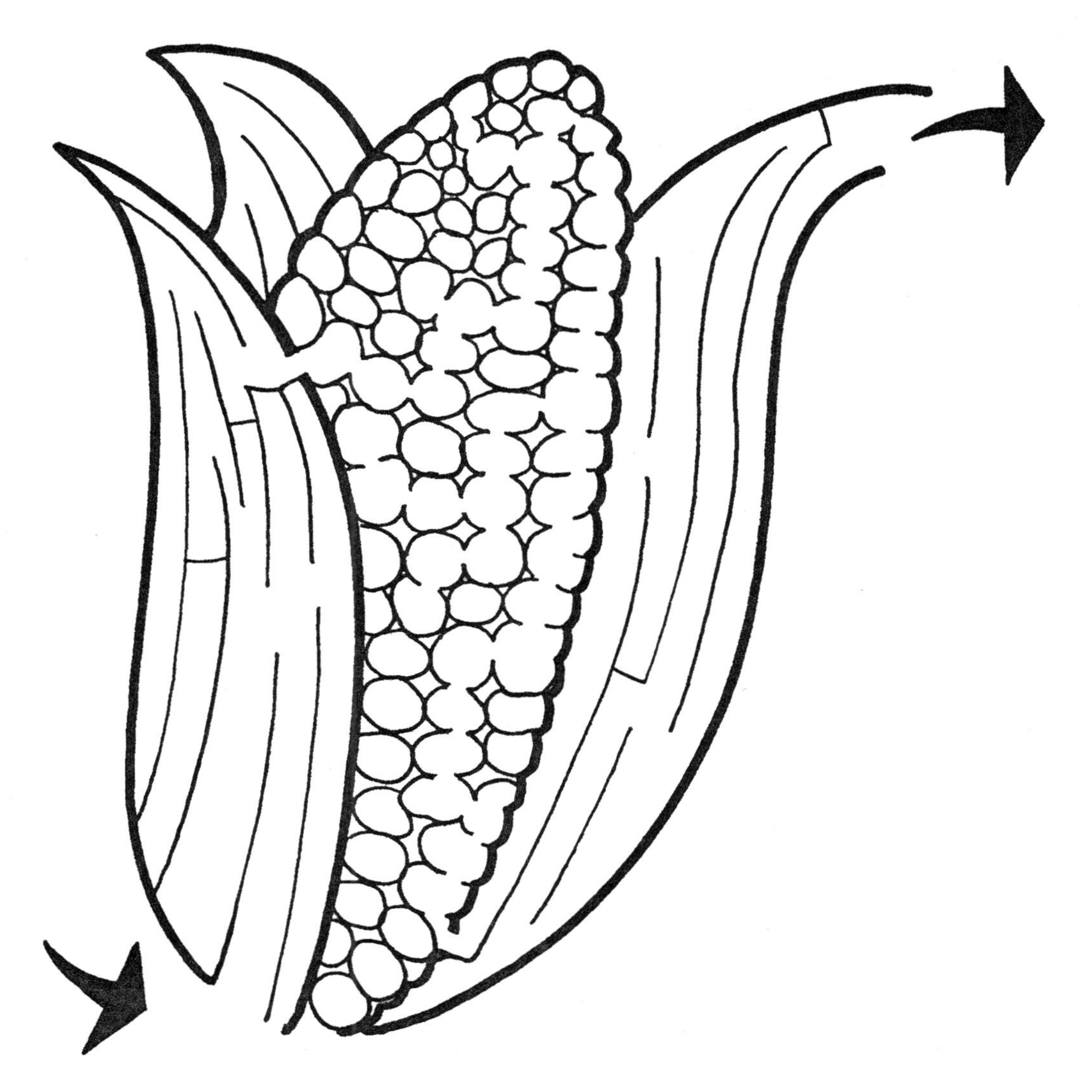

You provide the earth with crops.

Psalm 65:9

Dear God,

Thank You for all the delicious food You give me to eat. Thank You for the wonderful way seeds turn into flowers, trees, and food.

God always knows exactly where you are and what you need. He has promised to give you everything you need, and His supply never ends!

Draw yourself at the beach. Draw everything you need to have a fun day.

With all his abundant wealth through Christ Jesus, my God will supply all your needs.

Philippians 4:19

Dear God,

You know exactly what I need every day, and I am so glad You will always take care of me.

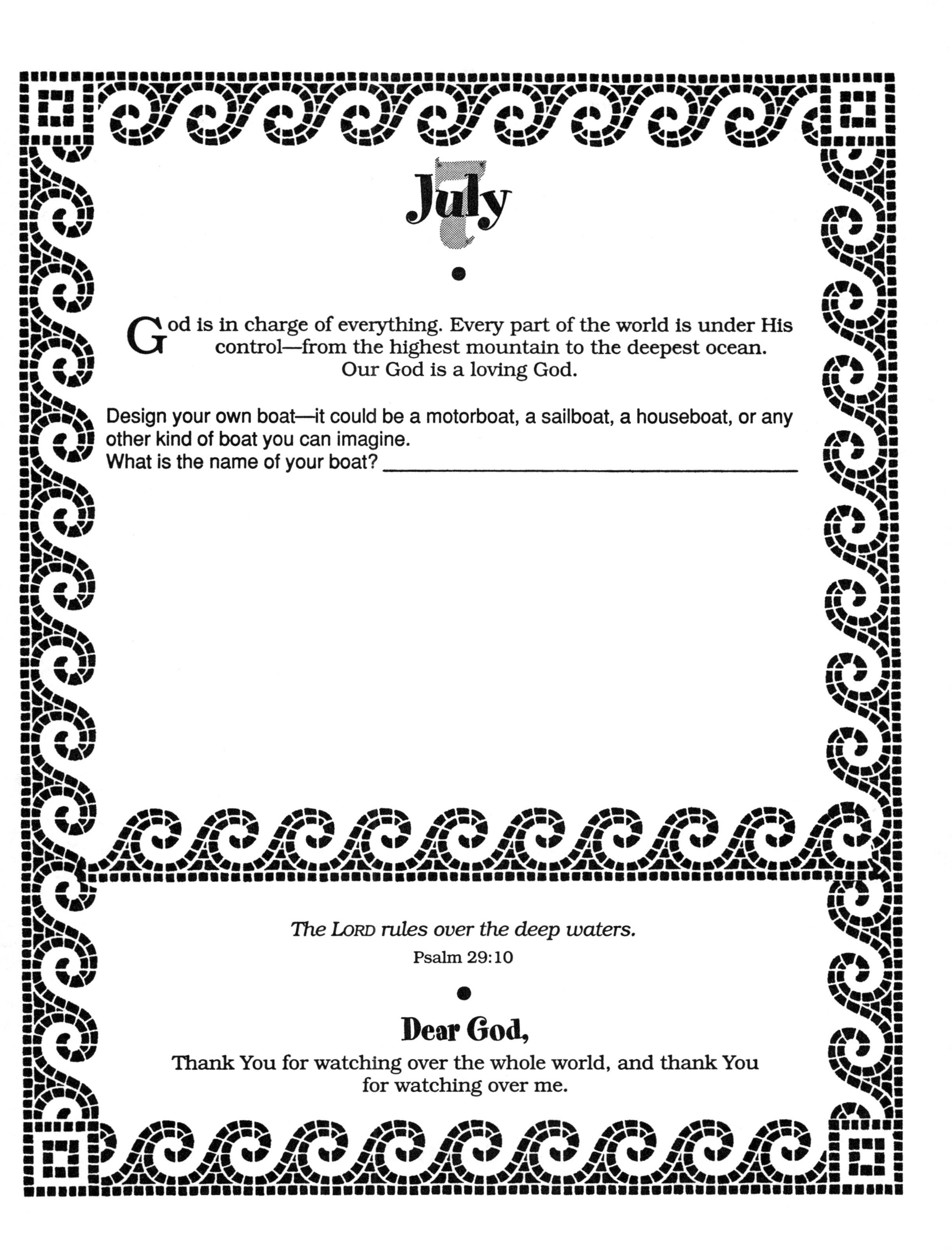

July 7

God is in charge of everything. Every part of the world is under His control—from the highest mountain to the deepest ocean. Our God is a loving God.

Design your own boat—it could be a motorboat, a sailboat, a houseboat, or any other kind of boat you can imagine.
What is the name of your boat? ________________________________

The LORD rules over the deep waters.
Psalm 29:10

Dear God,

Thank You for watching over the whole world, and thank You for watching over me.

It is fun to watch the sun rise in the morning. Each day is a wonderful gift from God. Wake up every day and expect something great to happen!

Color the sky and water all the beautiful colors that you see when the sun is rising or setting.

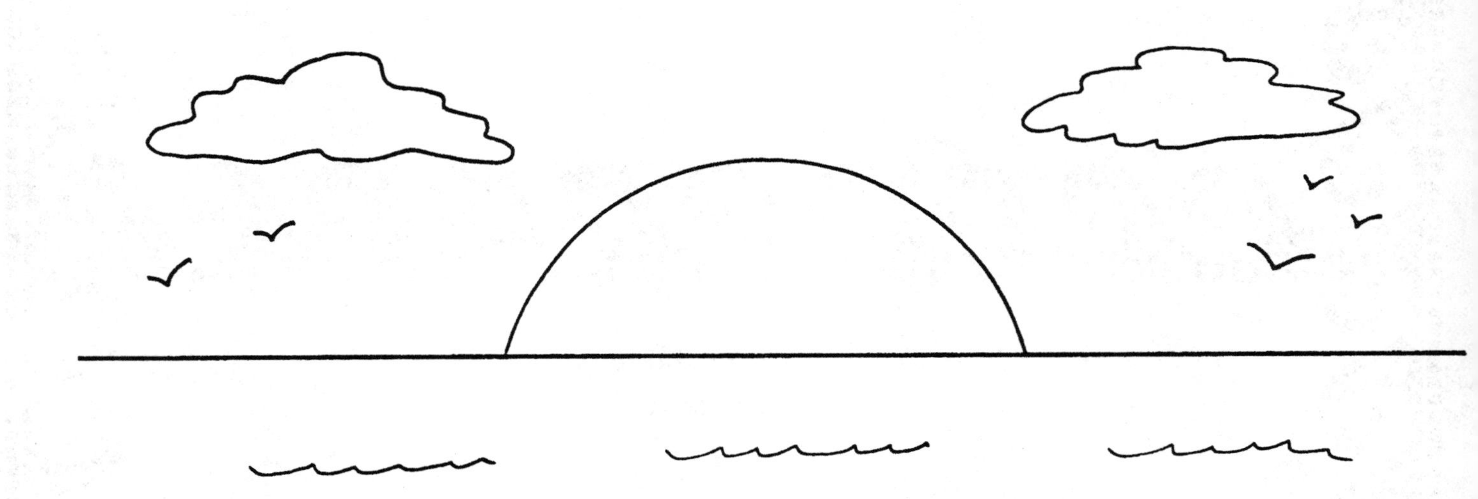

This is the day that the Lord has made. We will rejoice and be glad in it.

Psalm 118:24 (TLB)

Dear God,

Thank You for each day You give to me. I am glad I can always count on You.

What makes you like someone? There may be many different reasons. But if you had to describe those reasons with just one word, it would probably be *love.*

Circle all the phrases below that best describe the kind of friend that you would like to have. Think about what kind of friend you are to others.

WHAT I LIKE IN A FRIEND

Makes a mess and doesn't help clean up.

Says nice things about people.

Gets angry when losing a game.

Always wants own way.

Plays fairly.

Tells others when they do a good job.

Hits, punches, and pushes.

Shares with others.

Breaks other people's things.

Always wants to be first.

Says mean things about people.

Remembers your birthday.

Wants you to disobey your parents.

A friend loves at all times.

Proverbs 17:17 (NKJV)

Dear God,

Help me to be a good friend to others. Help me to love others at all times.

•

Being honest and telling the truth isn't always easy, but it is the way God wants us to live. If we tell the truth, we will be friends with God, and we will be very brave!

Color these brave lions.

An honest person is as brave as a lion.

Proverbs 28:1

•

Dear God,

Help me to tell the truth. When I tell the truth I know You will be right there with me to keep me safe.

July 11

Real love is shown by the way we treat the people around us. What happens when you show love to others? They will love you and want to be with you. The Bible teaches us about real love—the love of Jesus.

Give the story below a happy ending.

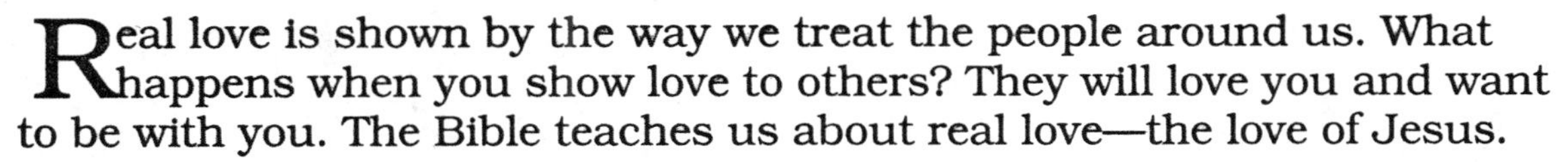

SELFISH SALLY

Sally was a pretty little girl but she didn't have any friends. She couldn't understand why the other children didn't want to play with her. They knew how talented and smart she was, because she told them all the time. She had the best toys in the neighborhood—but she never let anyone else play with them. One day, Sally saw a new boy in the neighborhood. She decided to try to become friends with him. ____

____

____

____

Love is patient and kind; it is not jealous or conceited or proud; love is not ill-mannered or selfish or irritable.

1 Corinthians 13:4,5

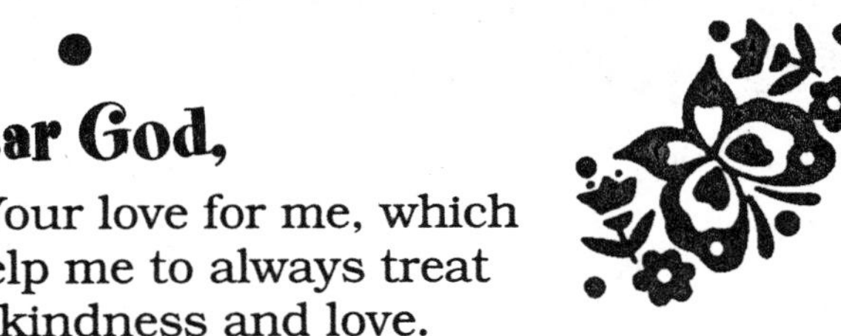

Dear God,

Thank You for Your love for me, which never ends. Help me to always treat others with kindness and love.

July 12

God has given us wonderful bodies. Let's make God proud of us by using them in ways that are healthy.

In this space, glue or tape a photograph of you doing one of your favorite sports.

You made all the...parts of my body.

Psalm 139:13 (TLB)

Dear God,

Help me to take good care of the body You have given me.

Samuel was a young boy who lived in the temple. One night Samuel heard God call to him, and he listened. Samuel listened for God's messages, and shared them with the people of Israel.

SP_ _K, L_RD, Y_ _R S_RV_NT _S L_ST_N_NG

✿ = A   ♡ = E   △ = I   ⍱ = O   ⊂ = U

The LORD came and stood there, and called as he had before, "Samuel! Samuel!"

1 Samuel 3:10

Dear God,

Let me always hear Your voice of love in my heart.

The best way to learn and grow wise is to talk to people who are older and have lived longer than you. Older people can also answer your questions about the Bible. Isn't it wonderful to have parents and grandparents who can help you learn?

In this box, glue or tape a photograph of your grandparents or some friends who are like grandparents to you.

Get wisdom and insight!

Proverbs 4:5

Dear God,

Thank You for the wise people in my life who love me—especially my parents and grandparents.

When King David was a small boy, he knew that God was very, very big. With just a sling and a stone, David defeated the giant Goliath! With God on your side, you don't need to fear anything.

Follow the line from each letter on top and fill in the box on the bottom with the same letter to discover the secret message.

David answered, "You are coming against me with a sword...but I come against you in the name of the LORD Almighty."

1 Samuel 17:45

Dear God,

Thank You for promising to always be with me. I am glad I never need to be afraid.

When David grew up, he became king of Israel. David was a good king who loved God very much. When he did wrong, he would tell God he was sorry. He loved music and wrote many of the psalms, or songs of praise to God.

King David needs to find two harps that are exactly the same. Circle them for him.

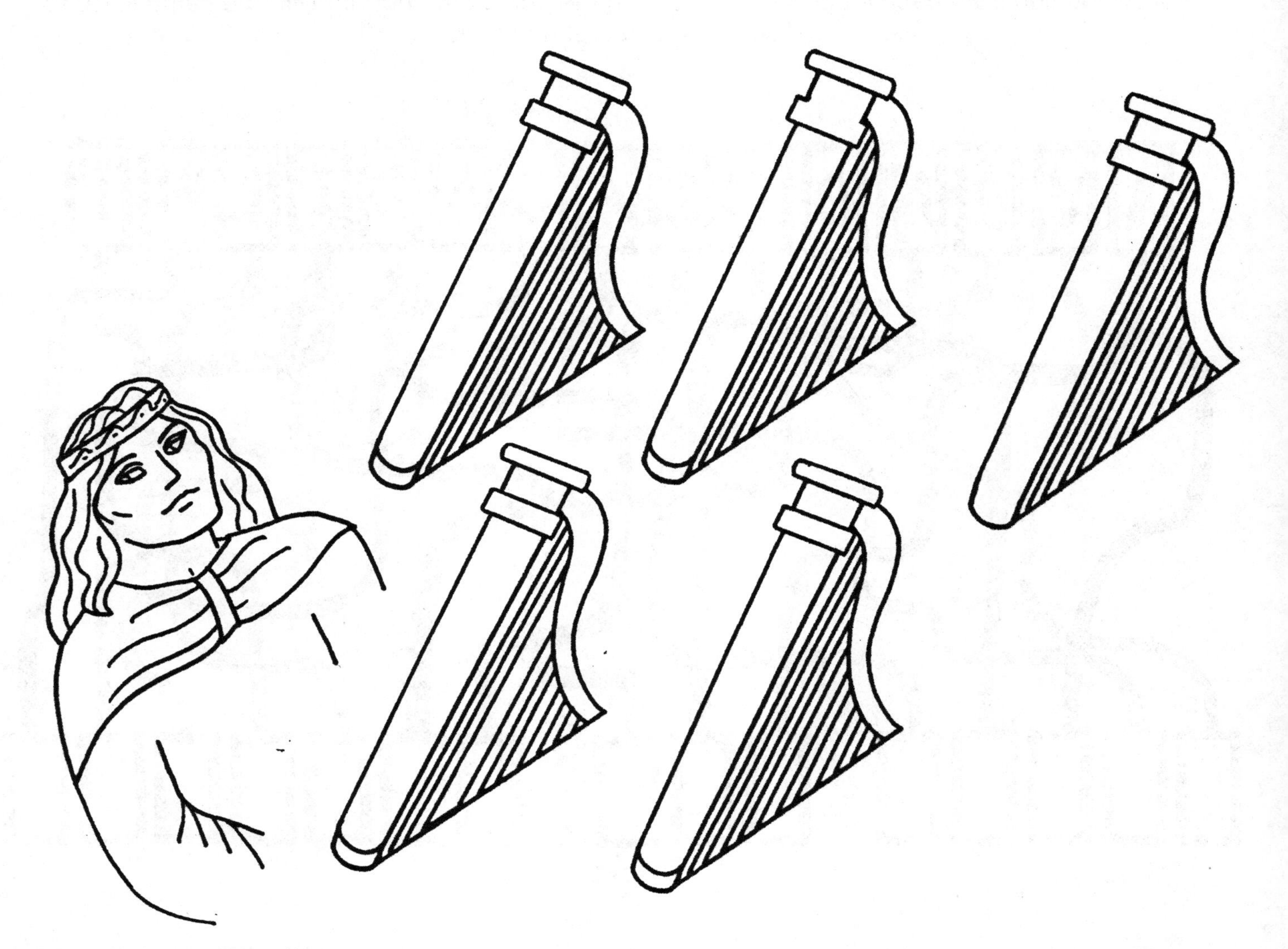

I took you from looking after sheep in the fields and made you the ruler of my people Israel.

2 Samuel 7:8

Dear God,

Help me to always love and praise You, just like King David. I know You will do exciting things with my life, too.

David, the little shepherd boy who killed the giant, Goliath, grew up to be king of Israel. He was a good king because he loved God very much.

Imagine yourself as a king or queen of this kingdom. What rules would you make for your people? Think of a fun holiday for your kingdom. Then color the castle.

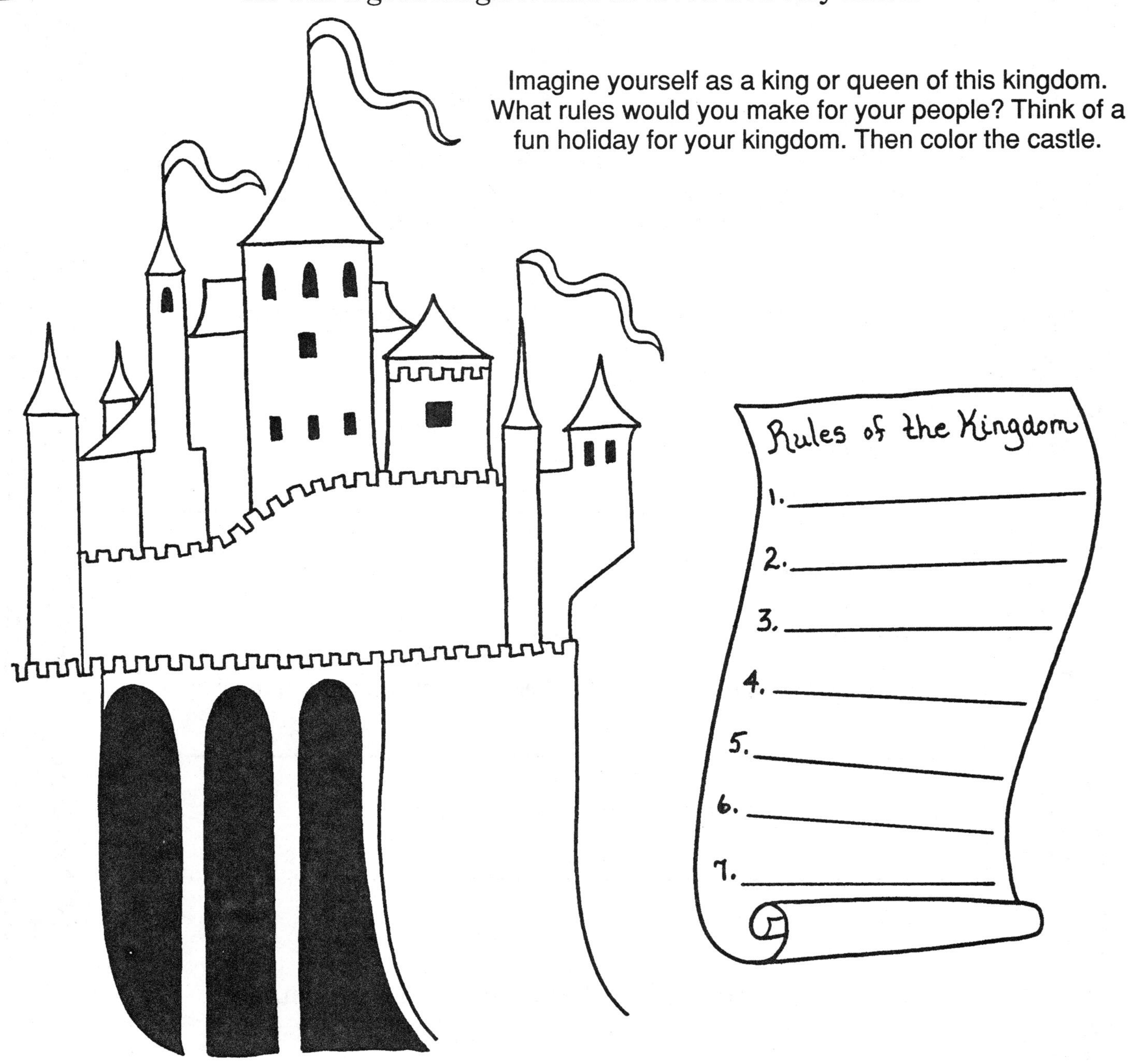

Then the leaders of Judah came to David and crowned him king.

2 Samuel 2:4 (TLB)

Dear God,

Help me to always make good decisions and do what is right.

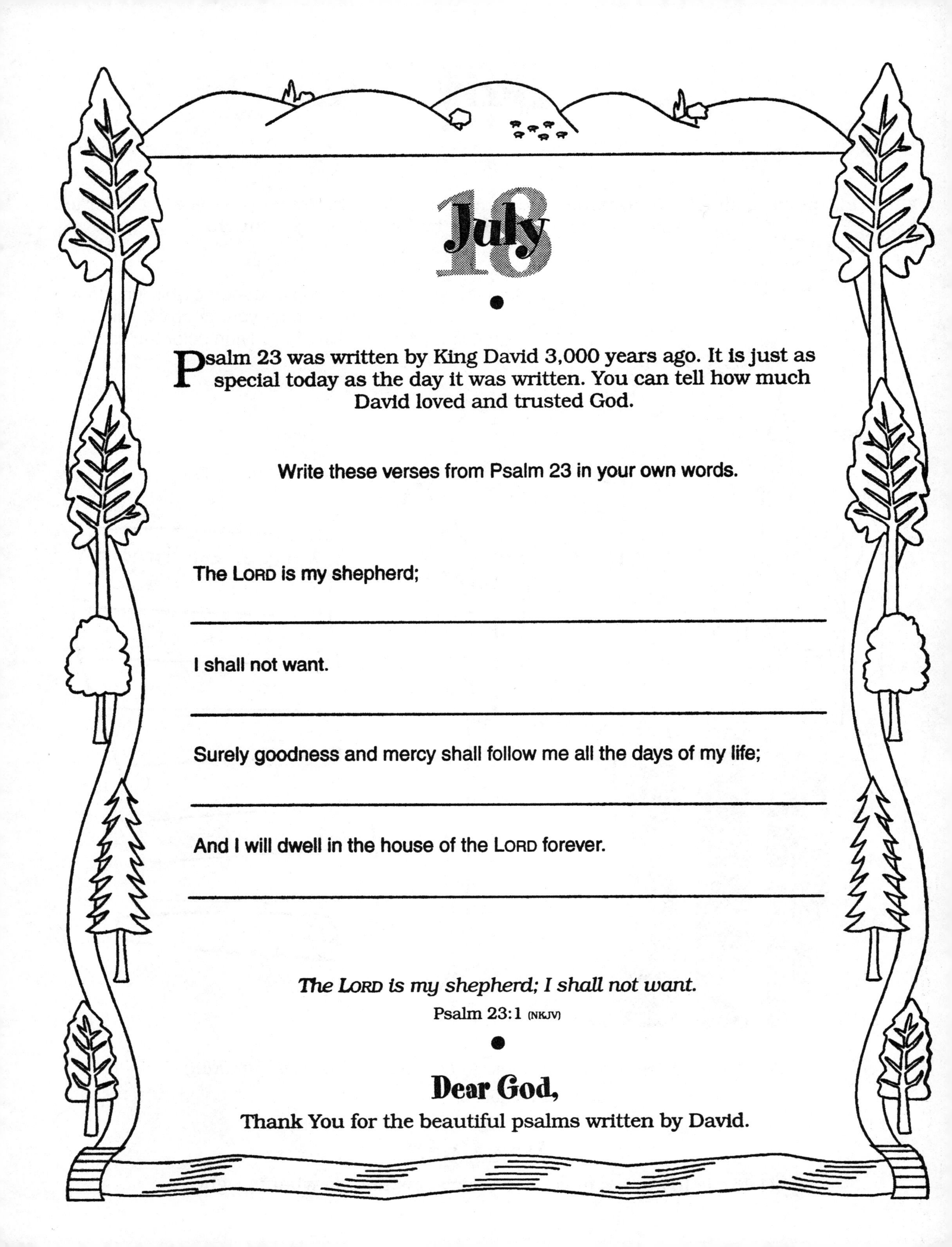

July 13

•

Psalm 23 was written by King David 3,000 years ago. It is just as special today as the day it was written. You can tell how much David loved and trusted God.

Write these verses from Psalm 23 in your own words.

The LORD is my shepherd;

___

I shall not want.

___

Surely goodness and mercy shall follow me all the days of my life;

___

And I will dwell in the house of the LORD forever.

___

The LORD is my shepherd; I shall not want.

Psalm 23:1 (NKJV)

•

Dear God,

Thank You for the beautiful psalms written by David.

We all need time once in a while to enjoy quiet and peace. God knows that. We can always know peace by spending time with God. Wherever you are, He can quiet your spirit and make you feel peaceful and calm.

Color this peaceful scene.

He makes me to lie down in green pastures: He leads me beside the still waters.

Psalm 23:2

Dear God,

Thank You that You give the gift of peace.

Some people came to Jesus with a question. They wanted to know which of the Ten Commandments was the most important. Jesus said that the most important commandment is to love God with all of your heart.

Which commandment was Jesus talking about? Color in the number of the most important commandment with blue. (Answer appears below.)

Answer: 1

Jesus answered, "Love the LORD your God with all your heart, with all your soul, and with al your mind."

Matthew 22:37

Dear God,

I want to love You with all my heart.

Jairus had a 12-year-old daughter who was very sick. He begged Jesus to come and pray for his little girl. When they got to Jairus's house, the little girl had already died. Jesus told Jairus not to be afraid, but believe. Jesus went into the girl's room, took her by the hand, and told her to get up. The girl got up right away and started walking!

Draw in the faces of Jairus, his wife, and his daughter as Jesus brings her back from the dead.

Jesus took her by the hand and said to her... "Little girl, I tell you to get up!"

Mark 5:41

Dear God,

You can do anything! What is impossible for us is easy for You!

The disciples were caught in a big storm. They were very frightened. But Jesus stood in the boat and told them not to fear.

T	Z	H	B	E	R	D	E
P	W	B	A	S	B	A	Z
G	Z	R	D	E	A	P	T
N	Y	C	P	A	N	L	M

_ _ _ _ _ _ _ _ _ _ _ _ _ _ _ _ _ _ _ _

"Why are you so frightened?" Jesus answered. "What little faith you have!" Then he got up and ordered the winds and the waves to stop.

Matthew 8:26

Dear God,

I am glad I never had to be afraid. You are stronger than anything in the world.

There are many stories about brothers and sisters in the Bible. When God decided to give you brothers and sisters, it meant He wanted to give you very special friends. The answer to the question in Genesis 4:9 is "yes," God wants you to help take good care of your brothers and sisters. Give each of your brothers and sisters a big hug today and tell them you love them.

Write (or have someone help you write) what you like about each one of your brothers and sisters:

Am I supposed to take care of my brother?

Genesis 4:9

Dear God,

Thank You for the special gift of brothers and sisters. Help me to be kind and loving to them all my life.

How many commercials do you see every day on television? Some of them are easy to remember because they have little songs, or jingles, that tell you about what they are selling and why it is so great. Make up a commercial telling people about God and why He is so great. Maybe a song will come to your mind. King David said to sing a new song to God!

MY COMMERCIAL

Draw a picture from your commercial in the television below.

Sing a new song to the LORD! Sing to the LORD, all the world!

Psalm 96:1

Dear God,

I want to tell the whole world how wonderful You are.

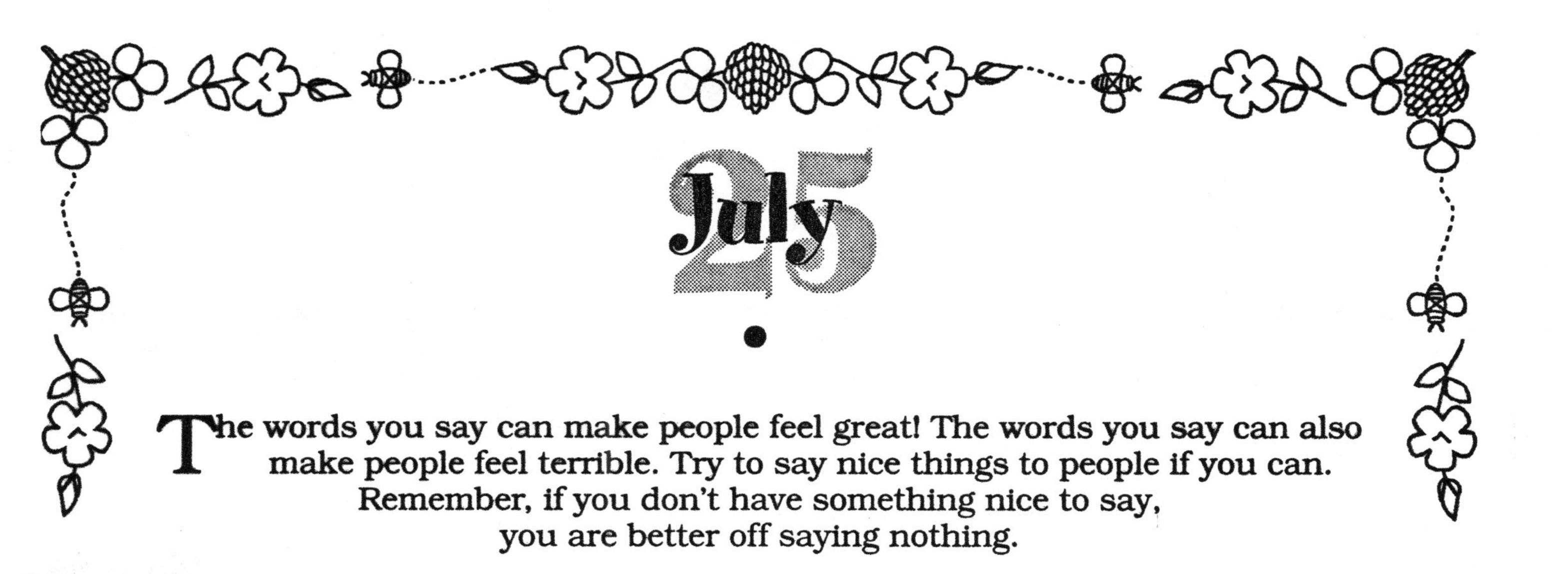

The words you say can make people feel great! The words you say can also make people feel terrible. Try to say nice things to people if you can. Remember, if you don't have something nice to say, you are better off saying nothing.

Finish this sentence.

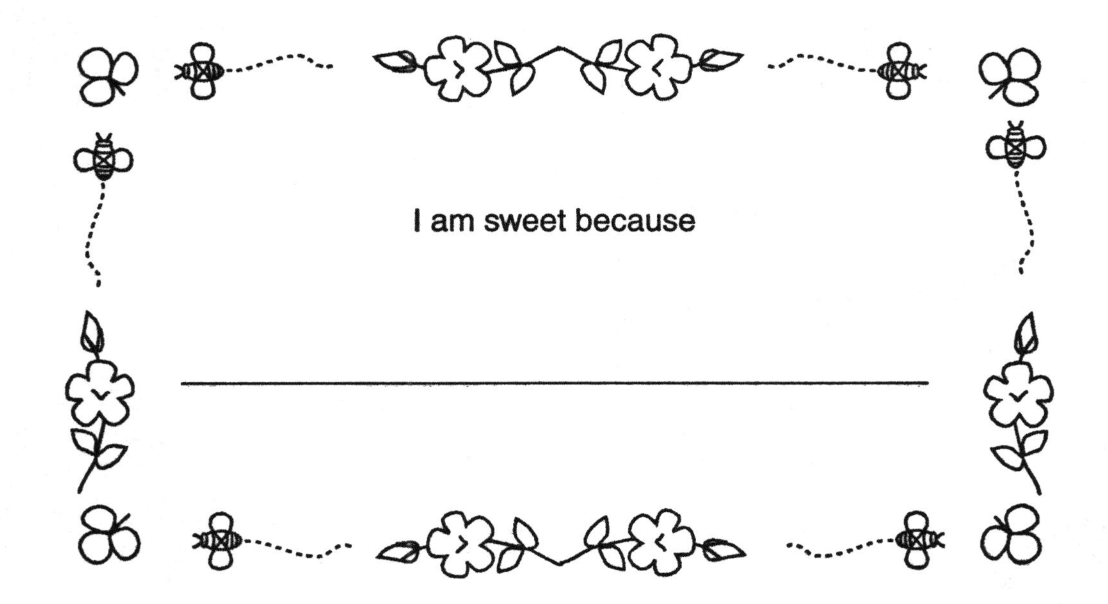

Kind words are like honey—sweet to the taste and good for your health.

Proverbs 16:24

Dear God,

Help me to be careful about what I say to other people. Help me to pay attention only to what is said with love.

Many thousands of people were listening to Jesus talk. He knew they were getting hungry, but there was no food to feed the people. A young boy had five loaves of bread and two fish. Jesus prayed, and the bread and fish multiplied so there was plenty to feed everybody!

Color this picture of Jesus and the boy with the bread and fish.

Jesus took the five loaves and the two fish, looked up to heaven, and gave thanks to God.
Matthew 14:19

Dear God,

I know that You will always take care of me, just like You took care of those five thousand peopl

I am sure you can think of many fun activities you would like to do and places you would like to go. When you make plans, always make sure you ask God to guide you, and He will take you in the right direction.

Draw yourself walking on this road.
Where are you going?

A man's heart plans his way, but the LORD directs his steps.

Proverbs 16:9

Dear God,

Help me to do what You want me to do. Help me to follow You every step of the way.

Since the time that Jesus was here on earth 2,000 years ago, people and their problems haven't changed. We still struggle with the same problems that people had when Jesus was here. That's why everything Jesus said 2,000 years ago is still important to hear today! The way to heaven hasn't changed.

Find where you live in the world. Draw a big star over your home, then draw lines to every place you have traveled.

There is nothing new in the whole world.

Ecclesiastes 1:9

Dear God,

I am so thankful You sent Jesus to this earth to teach us how to live.

Christians are our brothers and sisters. As brothers and sisters, we are to love each other! How do you show love for someone? One way is to think about what you can do to make that person happy, and then do it.

Pick one member of your family. Now pretend that you are designing this room just for him or her. Fill the room with all the things that person loves. Have fun!

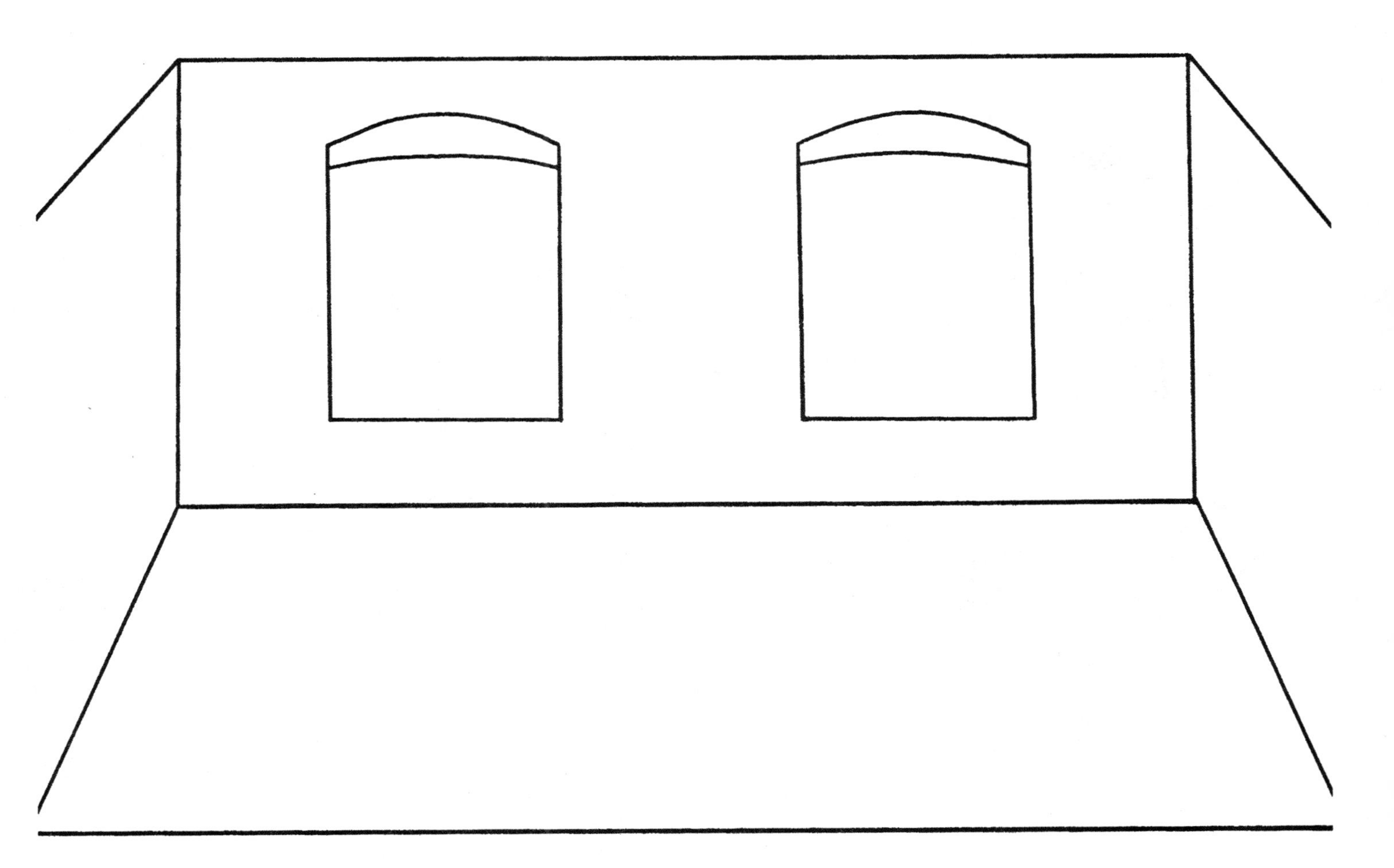

Love one another warmly as Christian brothers.

Romans 12:10

Dear God,

Thank You for my family, and help me to love my Christian brothers and sisters.

Gentle things are nice, aren't they! Gentle birds and animals are fun to pet, and gentle words make people feel good. The quickest way to get into a fight is to yell back at someone. If you meet someone who is angry, he or she will start to calm down if you answer gently.

Draw a gentle dove on this branch.

A gentle answer quiets anger, but a harsh one stirs it up.

Proverbs 15:1

Dear God,

Help me to not get into fights. Even if someone yells at me, help me to stay calm and gentle and give a quiet answer.

JULY JULY JULY JULY

July 31

Summer is in full swing, and you've been having a great time. Did you go somewhere exciting? Did you do something that was fun? Did you do a good deed? Let's hear about a memorable moment too good to forget!

Glue or tape a photograph or draw a picture of July's memorable moment in the space below. Then write (or have someone help you write) all about it.

When a good man speaks, he is worth listening to.

Proverbs 10:20 (TLB)

Dear God,

Thank You for always being with me, and thank You for all my great memories.

AUGUST

You may be small, but that doesn't mean you aren't important. God loves you very much; you are special!

Color the big bears brown, and color the small bears your favorite color!

Do not let anyone look down on you because you are young, but be an example for the believers in your speech, your conduct, your love, faith, and purity.

1 Timothy 4:12

Dear God,

Help me to remember that I am important because You love me. And even though I am little, help me to always set a good example to others.

The book of Psalms is made up of songs that King David wrote to God.

Can you make up a song about why you love God? While you are singing, have someone help you write down all the words.

WHY I LOVE GOD

by ____________

____

____

____

____

____

____

____

____

Sing a new song to him, play the harp with skill, and shout for joy!

Psalm 33:3

Dear God,

I want to tell You how much I love You every day. I hope You like my song.

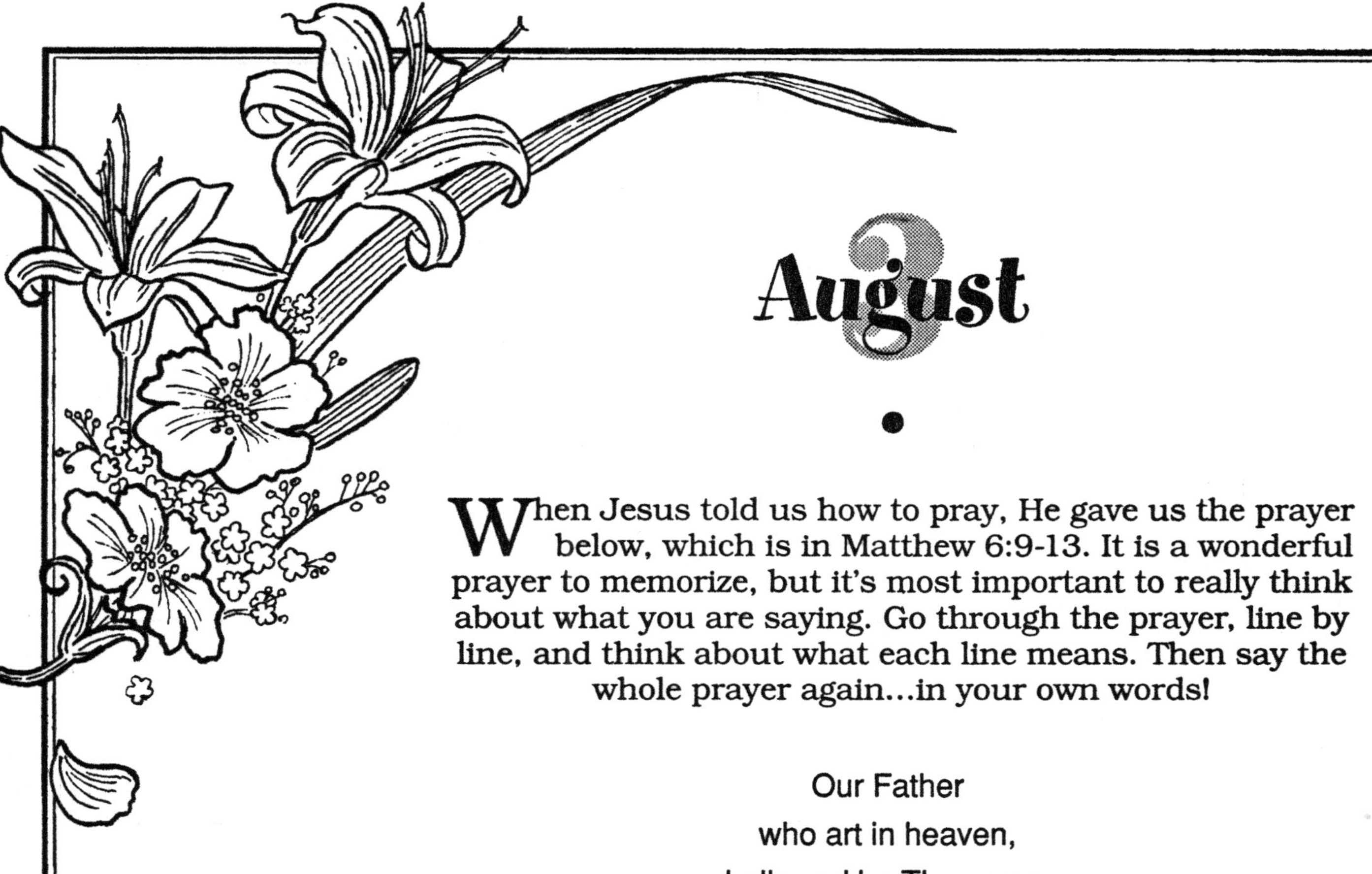

August 3

When Jesus told us how to pray, He gave us the prayer below, which is in Matthew 6:9-13. It is a wonderful prayer to memorize, but it's most important to really think about what you are saying. Go through the prayer, line by line, and think about what each line means. Then say the whole prayer again...in your own words!

Our Father
who art in heaven,
hallowed be Thy name.
Thy kingdom come.
Thy will be done,
on earth as it is in heaven.
Give us this day our daily bread.
And forgive us our trespasses,
as we forgive those who trespass against us.
And lead us not into temptation,
but deliver us from evil.
For Thine is the kingdom,
and the power, and the glory, forever.
Amen.

Pray along these lines...
Matthew 6:9 (TLB)

Dear God,

I want my prayers to always come from my heart. I am so glad I can call You my Father!

The words of God in the Bible are described as sweet. There are also many Scripture verses that make us think of sweet smells. Find the verses on the following list, then write what each verse describes.

Proverbs 27:9

___

Leviticus 2:4

___

2 Chronicles 9:27

___

Psalm 23:1

___

Song of Solomon 2:4

___

Matthew 2:11

___

John 12:3

___

Exodus 3:8

___

Exodus 30:34

___

How sweet are Your words to my taste,
sweeter than honey to my mouth!
Psalm 119:103 (NKJV)

Dear God,

Thank You for giving us lots of nice scents.

It's a great feeling to be in a warm, cozy bed and have a nice, peaceful sleep. But what if your room is so messy you can hardly get to your bed? Show God that you can take good care of your room and all the wonderful things He has given you. When you take care of what you have, God wil give you more.

Tonight, before you go to bed, take time to clean your room. After your room is all cleaned, you can fill out this certificate.

When I lie down, I go to sleep in peace.

Psalm 4:8

Dear God,

Thank You for all my toys, books, and other fun things. Help me to take good care of what You have given me.

Jesus was talking to some young fishermen who spent every day catching fish. Jesus told them that if they followed Him and told people about God, they would become fishers of people! They would help people to know God and get "hooked" on His love.

Can you find the path through this maze from one arrow to the other?

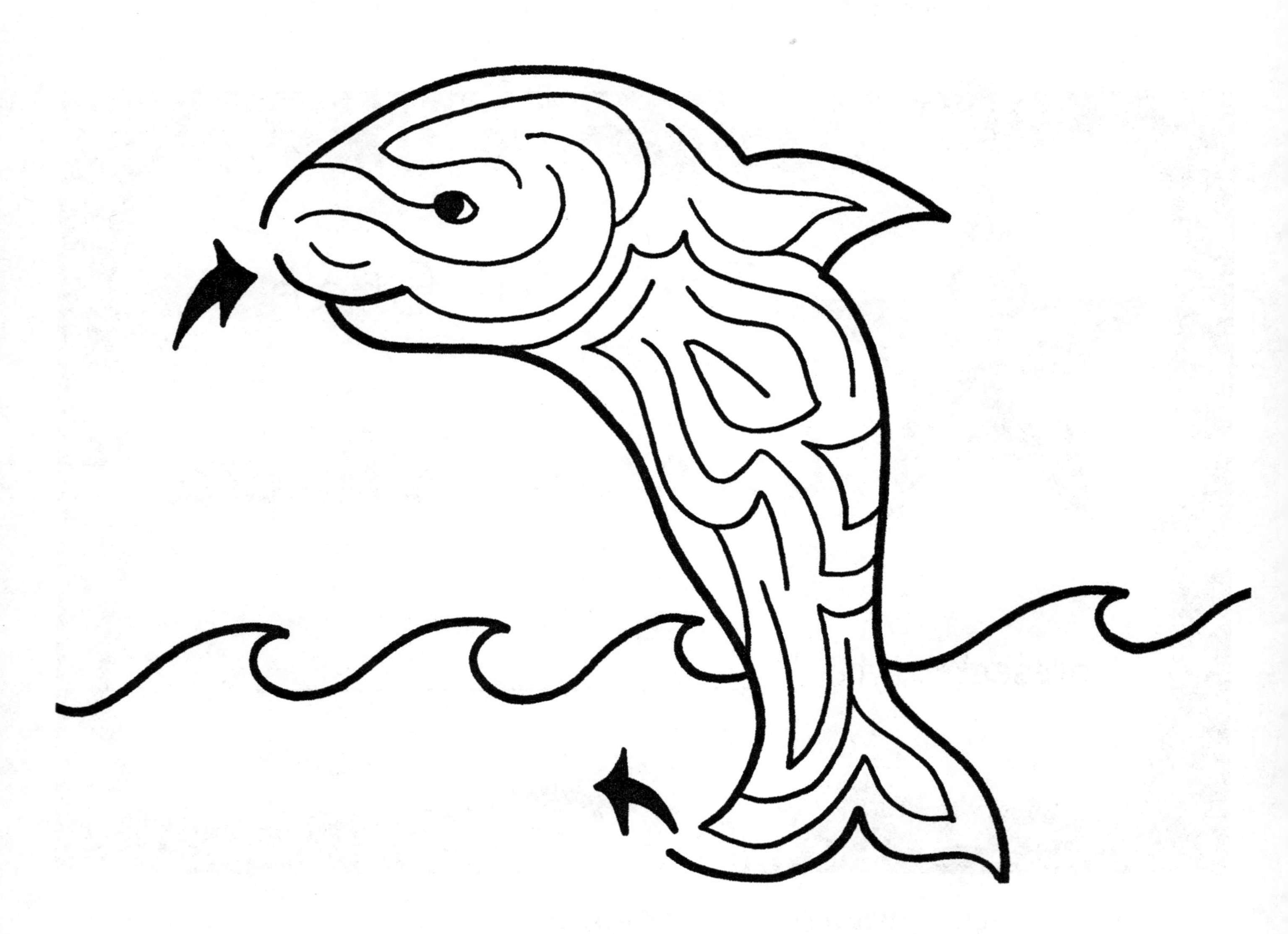

Follow me...and I will make you fishers of men.

Mark 1:17 (NIV)

Dear God,

Help me to always set a good example to others. Let them see Your love in me.

Jesus said that if we listen to His teachings and follow Him, we are like His sheep and He is like our shepherd. Sheep listen to the voice of their master because they trust him. If someone comes along and tries to get us to believe something that is wrong, we need to stick close to Jesus, our Good Shepherd.

You can draw a sheep. Draw your sheep in box 4, following the steps shown in boxes 1, 2, and 3. Now color in your picture.

My sheep listen to my voice; I know them, and they follow me.

John 10:27

Dear God,

Thank You for making me a sheep in Your flock. Help me to always do what is right.

•

Did you know that while we are here on earth we can be so close to God every day that it seems we are living in the same house? That's because we can ask Him for advice and ask Him to take care of us every day. Someday we will live in God's house...in heaven!

Draw a picture of you in God's house.

I have asked the LORD for one thing...to live in the LORD's house all my life.

Psalm 27:4

•

Dear God,

I feel good every day just knowing You love and care for me. Thank You for wanting to be so close to me.

Jesus was born as a tiny baby in a stable in the little town of Bethlehem...a far cry from His home in heaven. But He came because He loved you very much and wanted to make a way for you to live with Him in heaven—forever!

Connect these dots so you can read this special message.

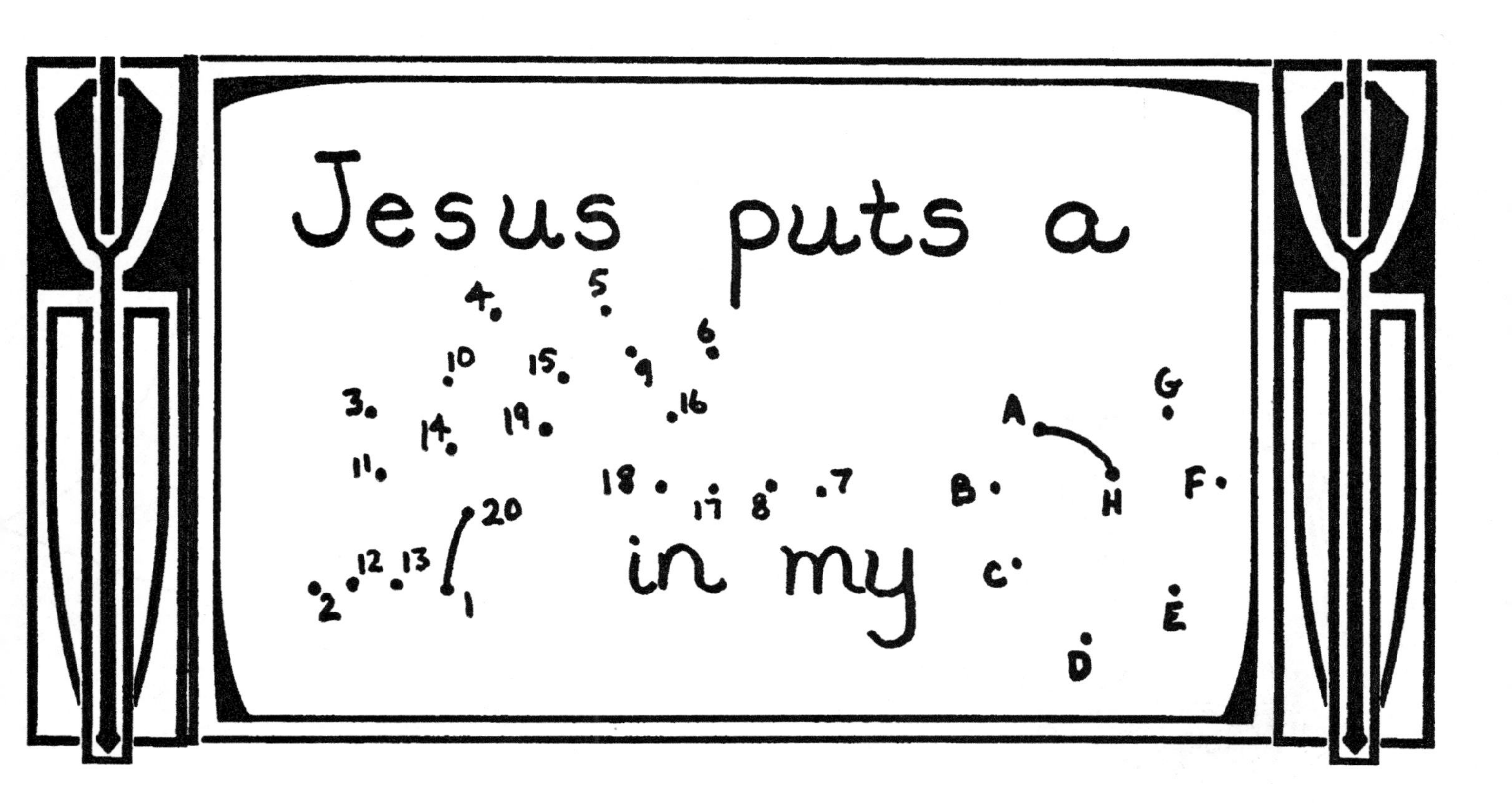

He has provided for us a mighty Savior.

Luke 1:69

Dear God,

Thank You for loving me so much!

August 10

•

It's nice to know that wherever we go, God is with us. God is with you in school, in a museum, in the grocery store, at Grandma and Grandpa's house, in the park, on a train, in the car, and in an airplane.

Write (or have someone help you write) a story about a fun trip you took. Who did you see? What did you do?

And I will always guide you and satisfy you with good things.

Isaiah 58:11

•

Dear God,

I'm glad that I am never alone. You are always watching over me.

August 11

People fight because they want their own way. But God's way is love, peace, and happiness. In every problem, there is always a way to find a solution without fighting.

This boy stole some eggs from his friend. Now they are fighting. How could things have been different? What if they had talked to each other? What would they be doing now? Talk about it.

Live in peace with one another.

Mark 9:50

Dear God,

Help me to stay out of fights and use kind words instead of angry words.

August 12

A young boy once asked his father for his share of money so he could travel and see the world. But in a short time, he had spent it all and was miserable. Finally, he decided to go home to his father. His father was so happy to see him, that he had a big feast and celebration!

Help the prodigal son find his way back home.

But the father called to his servants. "Hurry!" he said... "For this son of mine was dead, but now he is alive; he was lost, but now he has been found."

Luke 15:22-24

Dear God,

I am glad that even if I do something wrong, Your love and forgiveness is there for me.

Isn't the sky amazing? It is always changing. It can be bright blue, full of fluffy white clouds, or stormy with big thunder clouds. Sometimes cloud shapes remind you of animals, plants, and even people!

Draw some interesting cloud shapes in the sky.

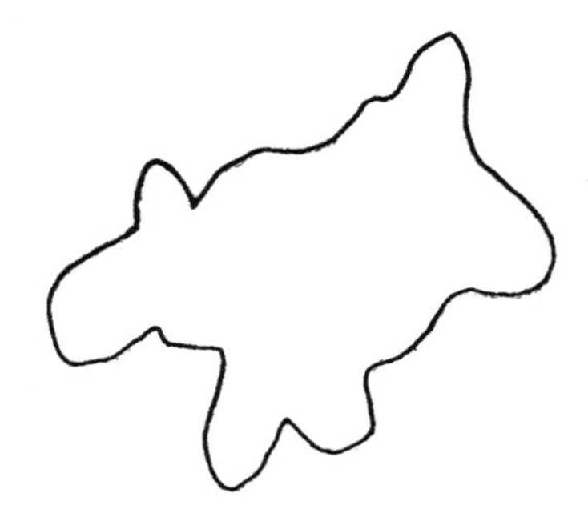

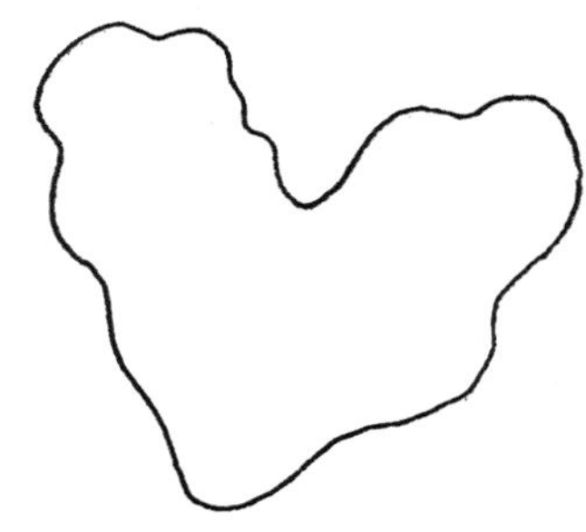

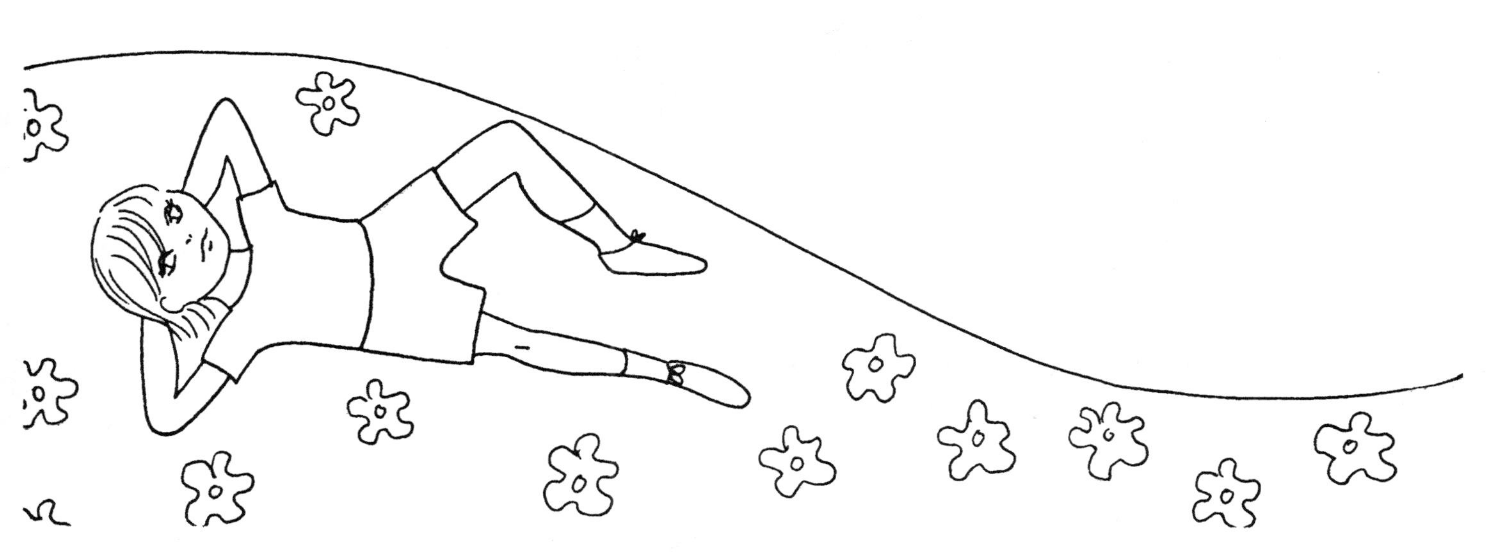

When I look at the sky, which you have made.

Psalm 8:3

Dear God,

Thank You for so much beauty in this world.

August 14

Life is full of wonderful moments that remind us of the goodness of God: a hug or kiss from a loved one, a beautiful sky full of sunshine, a brand-new baby coming into the world. God is so good and His love for us is so real!

Draw a picture of yourself on a picnic. Who is with you? What kind of food did you bring? Draw it in the picture.

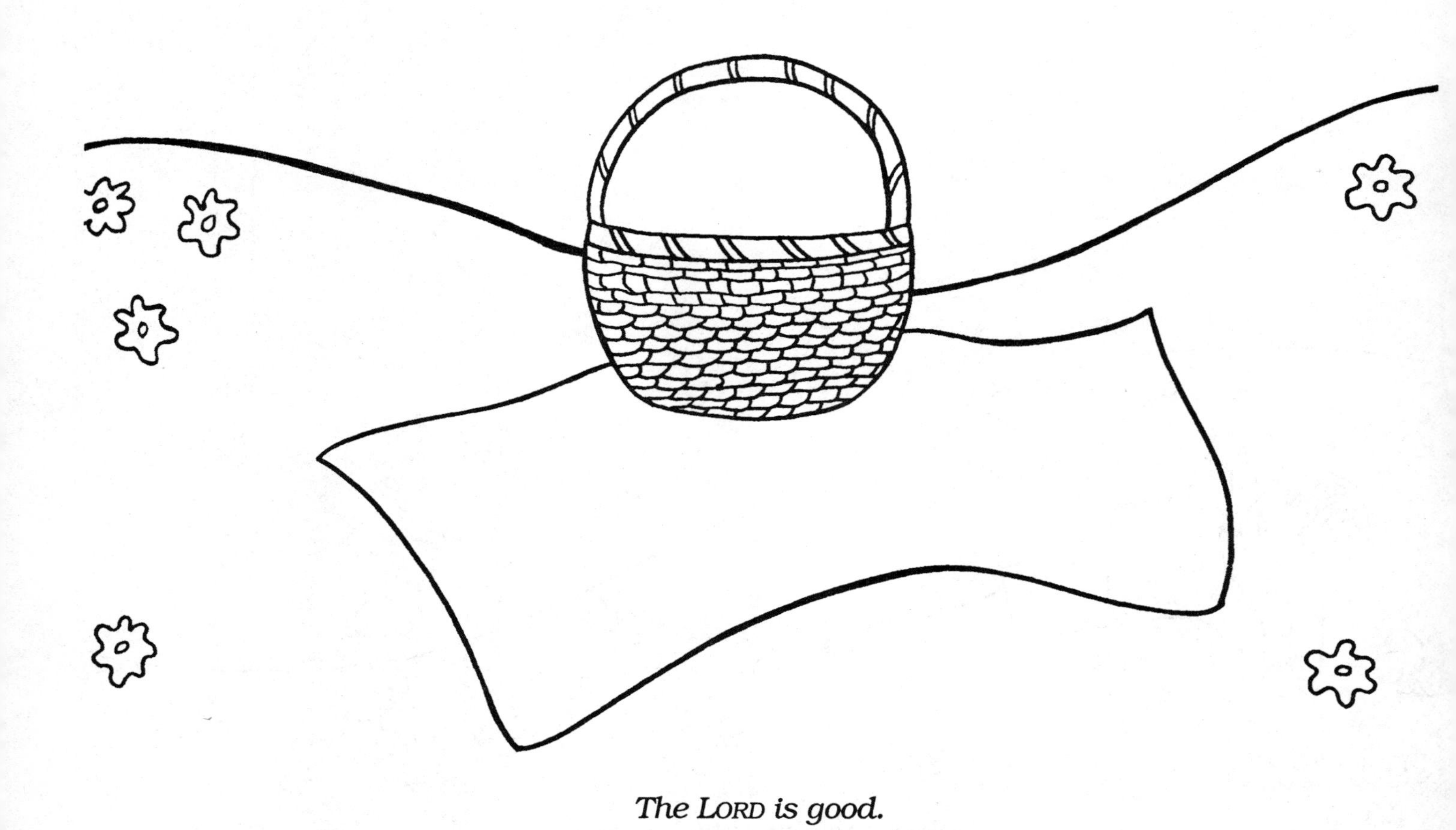

The LORD is good.
Psalm 100:5

Dear God,

Thank You for all the happy moments in my life that remind me how good You are to us.

August 15

The Bible is God's word for us, and it tells us everything we need to know to live a happy life here on earth as well as a happy life in heaven forever. The Bible is our guide book that tells us how to keep our lives running well.

What is your favorite Bible verse? Write it in the space below.

My favorite Bible verse is

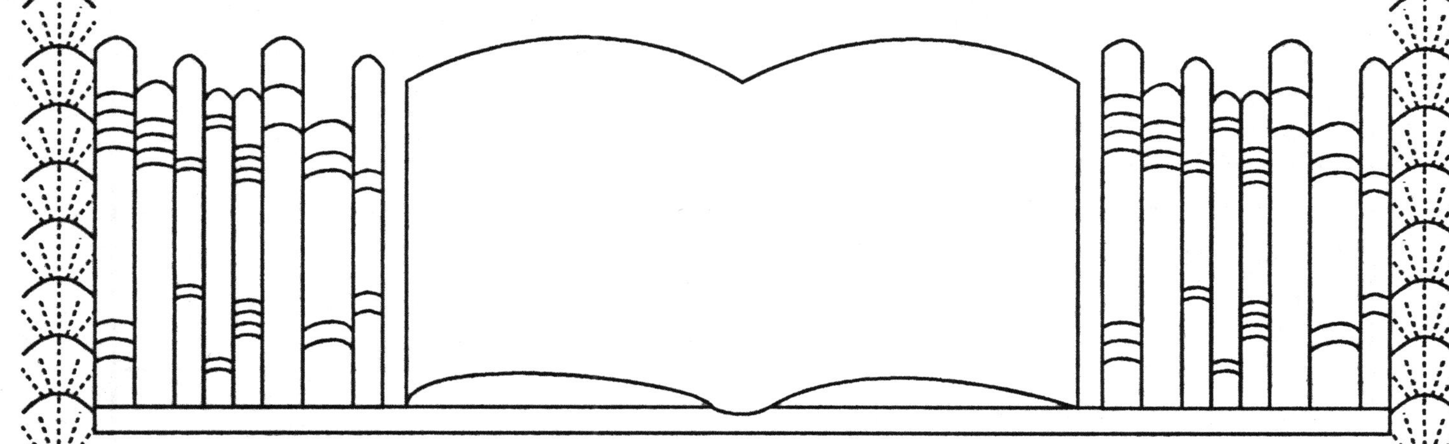

Your word is a lamp to guide me and a light for my path.
Psalm 119:105

Dear God,

Thank You for the Bible. It is like Your love letter to me.

Serving one another means helping one another. That is a way of showing people that we love them. Give everyone in your family a big hug and kiss, right now!

Give yourself a star or a colorful sticker for every helpful activity you do the rest of the week. Your parents can fill in the square on the bottom with a special activity they would like you to do each day.

Helper Chart

Activity	Sun.	Mon.	Tues.	Wed.	Thurs.	Fri.	Sat.
Clean your room							
Make your bed							
Set the table							
Do something your parents ask							

Let love make you serve one another.

Galatians 5:13

Dear God,

Thank You for Your love for me, and help me to show love to my family by serving them.

August 17

Can you think of some different ways to cheer up a friend? You could bring him or her flowers, a gift, or write a nice note. You could tickle your friend or tell a funny joke. Whatever way you choose, your friend will feel much better!

TRY THESE JOKES FROM THE BIBLE

1. Did you know that Adam was a great runner?

   He was the first in the human race.

2. Did you know that Adam and Eve had a car?

   God drove them out of the garden.

3. Did you know that Joseph was a tennis player?

   He served in the pharaoh's court.

4. Now let's test you on books of the Bible. What's at the beginning of Nehemiah and at the end of the book of John?

   The letter 'n.'

5. What's at the end of the Bible?

   The letter 'e.'

Worry can rob you of happiness, but kind words will cheer you up.

Proverbs 12:25

Dear God,

I am glad You want me to be happy. Thank You for all the things that make me smile.

August 18

What is better than finding a cool, shady place on a hot summer day? Walking with God is like that...He protects us from danger and lets us relax.

Draw yourself relaxing in this shade-covered hammock.

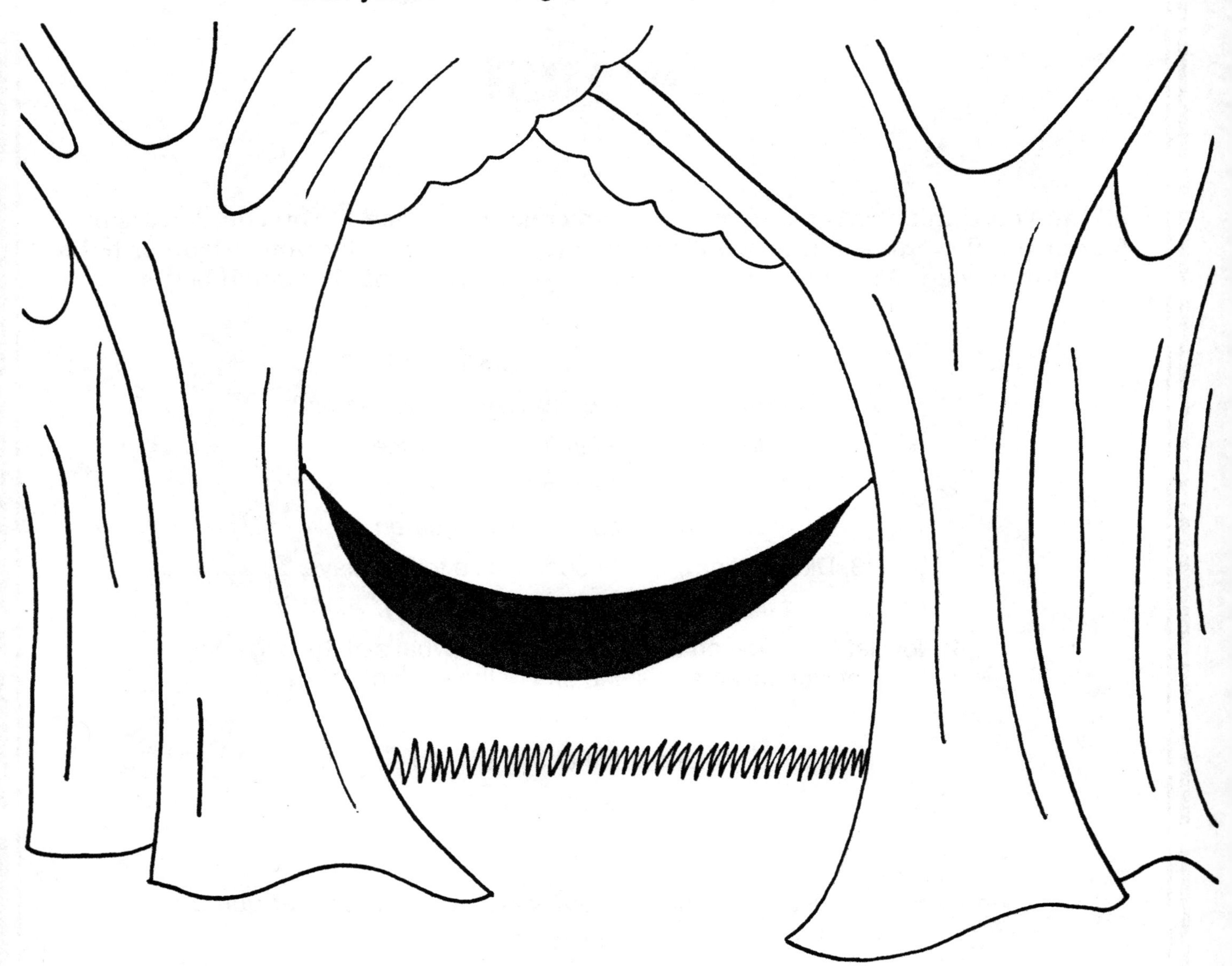

He who dwells in the secret place of the Most High shall abide under the shadow of the Almighty.

Psalm 91:1 (NKJV)

Dear God,

Help me to remember that You are bigger than any problem and that You will protect me.

We can be friendly to all kinds of people...those from our neighborhood, school, or church, for example. If someone needs a meal, a place to stay, or even just to talk, you should welcome them. We love others because Jesus loves us.

How many words can you make using the letters in the word "hospitality"?

♡ HOSPITALITY ♡

______	______	______
______	______	______
______	______	______
______	______	______
______	______	______
______	______	______
______	______	______
______	______	______
______	______	______
______	______	______

0-10 Try again! 11-20 Good! 21-30 Very Good!
Over 30 - Fantastic!

Open your homes to each other without complaining.

1 Peter 4:9

Dear God,

Help me to be a good friend to others, especially when they are in need.

Jesus finished everything He had to do here on earth. We should finish whatever we begin, too.

This is the land of "Nothing is finished." Can you finish this picture? Here's one hint: Should a rainbow have only one stripe?

It is finished!

John 19:30

Dear God,

Help me to finish what I begin. Thank You for always finishing the things You start...including Your plan for my life!

In the Bible, Jesus is known as the King of kings. He is greater than any earthly king; His Kingdom will never end! Here on earth and forever in heaven, He will be known and loved as the King of kings.

Find something in the box below that belongs to Jesus, the King of kings. If a shape is marked "B," color it blue. If it is marked "P," color it purple. If it is marked "Y," color it yellow.

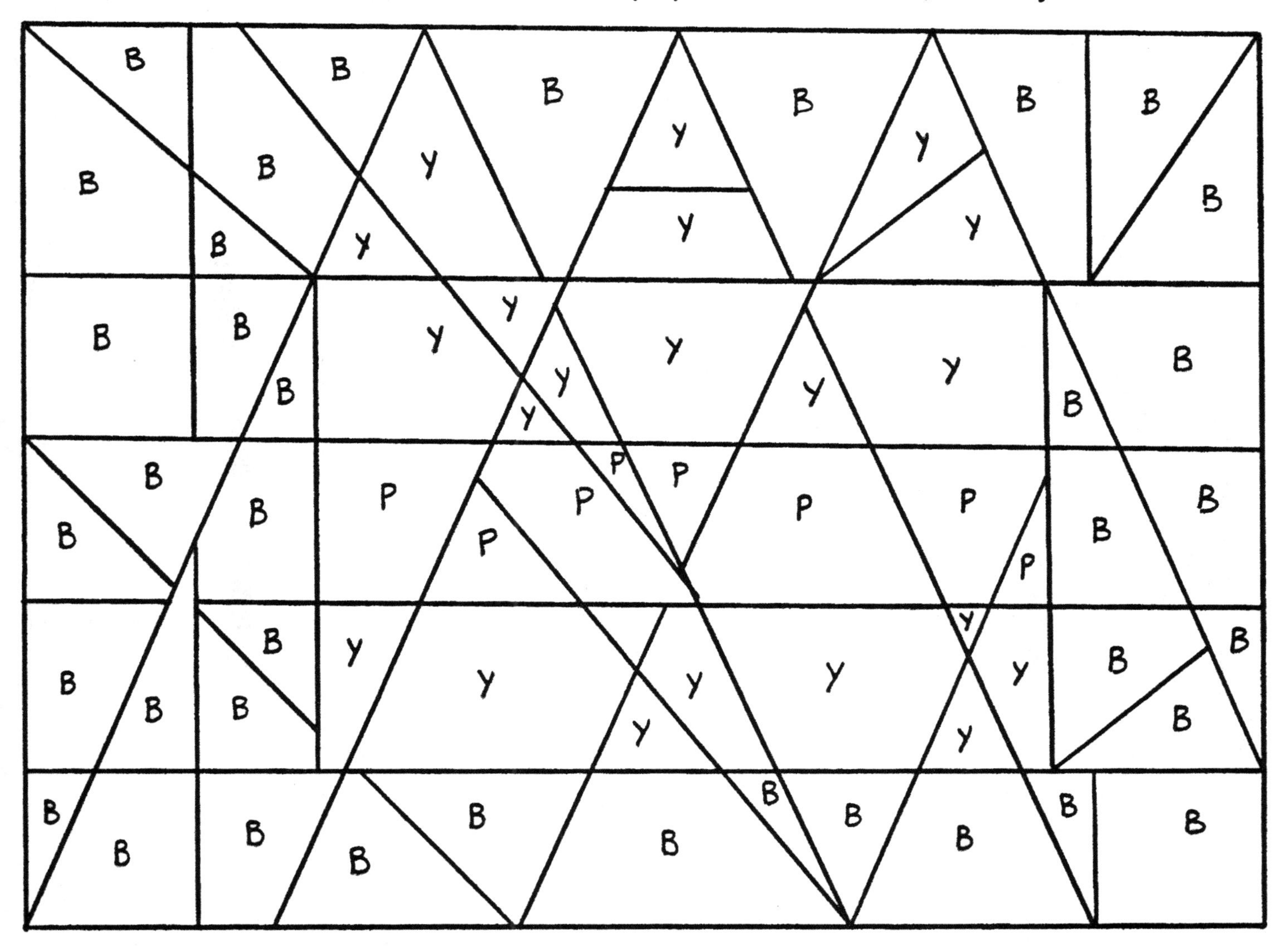

King of kings and Lord of lords.

Revelation 19:16

Dear God,

It will be great to see Jesus in person someday in heaven!

Did you know that if you love Jesus you are royalty? That's right! The Bible says we are kings and priests for God. How did that happen? Jesus is King of kings, and He calls us His brothers. Someday we will rule with Him.

Draw a picture of how you would look, as a king or priest who helps Jesus rule in heaven.

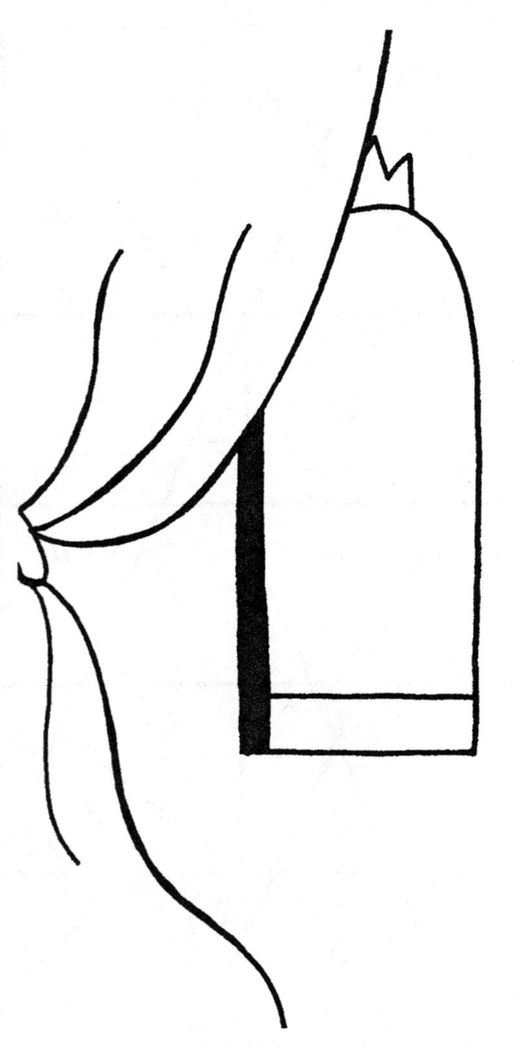

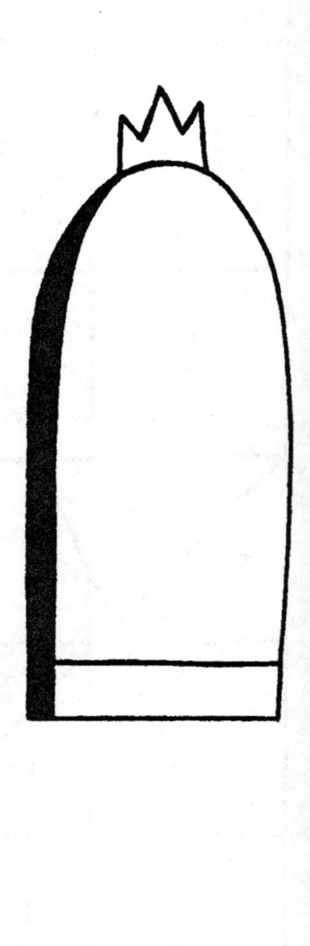

To Him who loved us...and has made us kings and priests...be glory...forever and ever.
Revelation 1:5,6 (NKJV)

Dear God,

Thanks for making me part of Your royal family.

Every day you have many opportunities to do good. You can obey your parents quickly, you can be good in school, and you can be kind to others. Sometimes you will see other children doing something that is wrong, and they might want you to join them. Remember to just say no and walk away. Then you will be doing what is good!

Connect these dots to see today's important message.

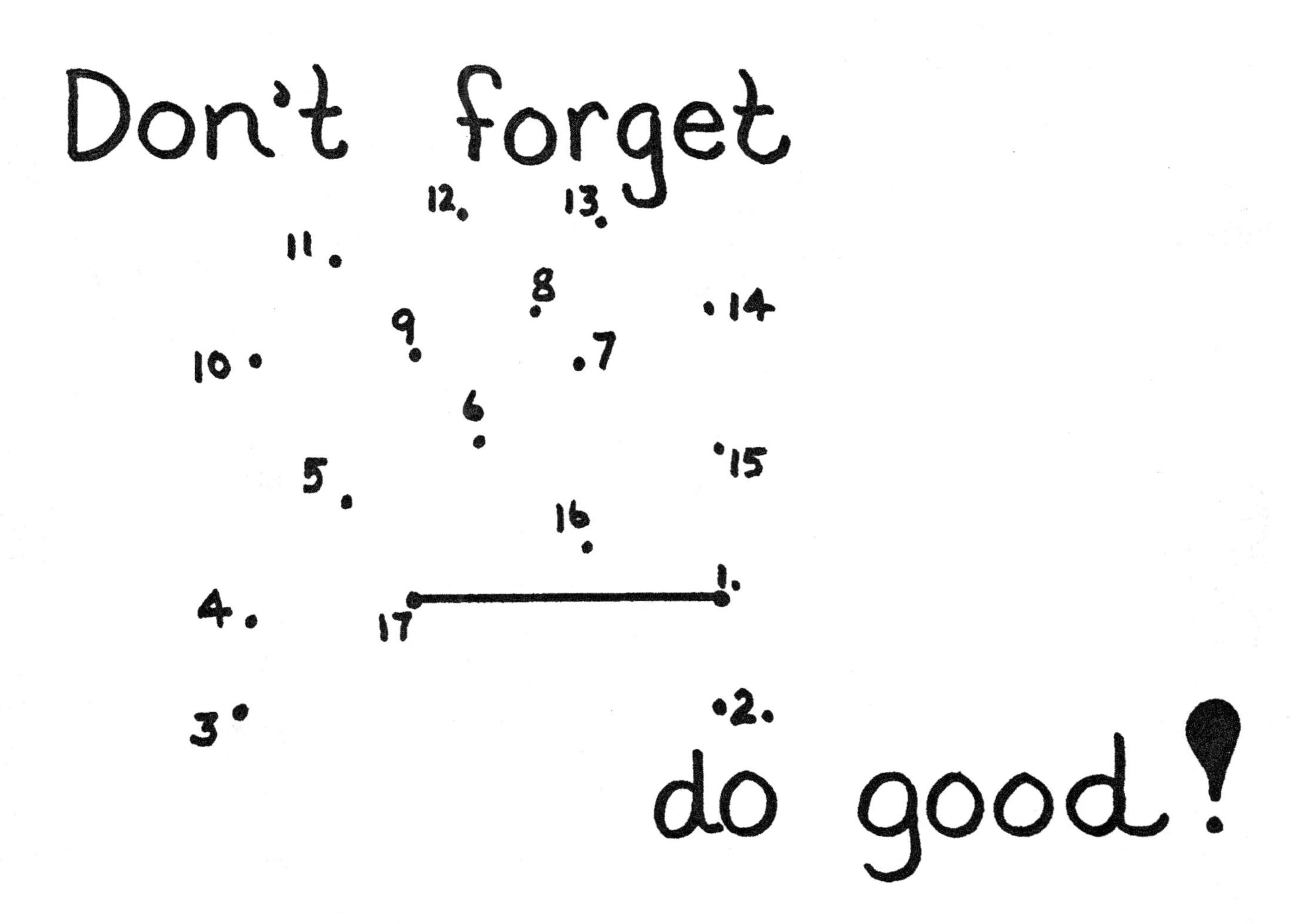

Do not forget to do good.

Hebrews 13:16

Dear God,

Help me to always do what will make You proud of me.

24 August

It is good to tell God how much we love Him and how wonderful He is. You can praise Him with words, with a song, or even with a musical instrument.

Think of three words that describe God, and write them next to each musical note.

My favorite instrument is the

___________________________.

Praise the LORD's glorious name.
Psalm 29:2

Dear God,

Thank You for all that You do for me every single day.

I'm sure your parents often tell you stories about funny things you said when you were little, and I'm sure you are still saying funny things now! Children have a special view of the world; they say the funniest things!

Write (or have someone help you write) some of the funny things you have said. You can add to this during the year.

There is...a time to weep and a time to laugh.

Ecclesiastes 3:1,4 (NIV)

Dear God,

I am glad You have given me five senses: the senses of sight, hearing, touch, taste, and smell. And I'm glad for another sense...the sense of humor.

Telling the truth is important; it's worth more than anything money can buy.

Design your own downtown. First, on the blank space above the door of each store, write the name of that store. Make sure to include all your favorite stores. Then color in your town.

Buy the truth, and do not sell it.

Proverbs 23:23 (NKJV)

Dear God,

Nothing is more valuable than Your love. Nothing is more important than telling the truth.

August 27

As a child, your body is growing faster than it will at any other time in your life. You are also growing and learning how to be the kind of person Jesus wants you to be.

Look at the words below. What kind of person does Jesus want you to be? Circle those words. Cross out the words that describe what kind of person you don't want to be.

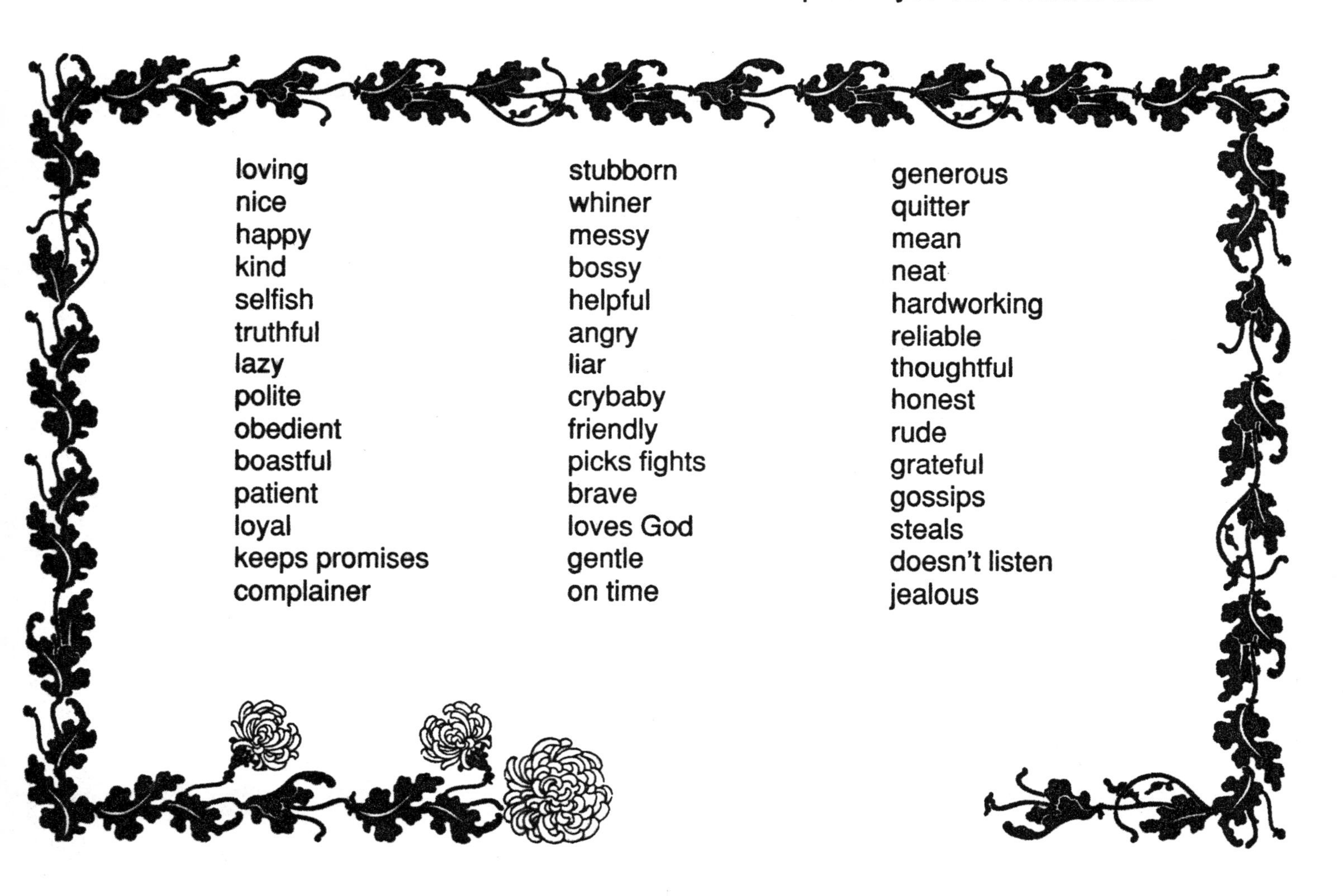

loving
nice
happy
kind
selfish
truthful
lazy
polite
obedient
boastful
patient
loyal
keeps promises
complainer

stubborn
whiner
messy
bossy
helpful
angry
liar
crybaby
friendly
picks fights
brave
loves God
gentle
on time

generous
quitter
mean
neat
hardworking
reliable
thoughtful
honest
rude
grateful
gossips
steals
doesn't listen
jealous

Continue to grow in the grace and knowledge of...Jesus Christ.

2 Peter 3:18

Dear God,

I want to know more about You. Show me Your love every day.

Did you know that God loves to give you what you need? He is your heavenly Father and you are His child. It's okay to ask God for what you need when you pray. If it's good for you, He would love to give it to you.

Draw a picture of something you need that you would like God to give to you.

Ask, and you will receive; seek, and you will find; knock, and the door will be opened to you.

Matthew 7:7

Dear God,

Thank You for hearing my prayers, and thank You for caring for me so much.

God is in charge of the whole earth. Even the oceans are under His control. How many fish do you think there are in the ocean? God knows how many!

There are seven fish hidden on this page. Can you find them? Then, draw some fish of your own and color in all the beautiful sea shells.

The Lord rules over the deep waters.

Psalm 29:10

Dear God,

Nothing is hidden from You. You know everything!

What is an ignorant person? Someone who doesn't know the truth. When you know the truth about who God is and how much He loves you, you will be wise, happy, kind, and considerate.

Help these explorers find their way through the jungle river to "Home Sweet Home." Then color the picture.

So be careful how you live. Don't live like ignorant people, but like wise people.

Ephesians 5:15

Dear God,

Help me to stay peaceful by remembering how much You love me.

Boy, it's hot in August! What is this month's memorable moment for you? Did you try something new that you thought you couldn't do? Did you remember that God is always with you, taking care of you? Did you do a fun activity or take a vacation? What did you do on the hottest day of the year?

Glue or tape a photograph or draw a picture of August's memorable moment in the space below. Then write (or have someone help you write) about what happened.

Trust in the LORD and you will be happy.

Proverbs 16:20

Dear God,

Thank You for August's memorable moment!

SEPTEMBER

September 1

You don't need a phone to call God; He hears your every prayer. He loves you very much.

If you could call God and ask Him any question, what would you ask?

____

____

Can you fill in all the squares on this telephone with the right letters and numbers? If you need help, look at a real phone in your house.

He hears me when I call to him.

Psalm 4:3

Dear God,

I'm glad You hear me whenever I call You.

When you begin to feel mad, the best thing to do is not say anything until you've had a chance to think carefully and relax. You will be glad you did, and so will everybody else.

What is the best way to handle each of these situations? Write your answers.

1. Your best friend has been saying mean things about you. The next time you are together, you say

____

2. Somebody pushes you at school and calls you names. You say

____

3. Your brother or sister ruins the project you have been working on for a long time. You say

____

4. You are late for school and can't find your shoes. You say

____

People with quick tempers cause a lot of quarreling and trouble.

Proverbs 29:22

Dear God,

Help me to control my temper.

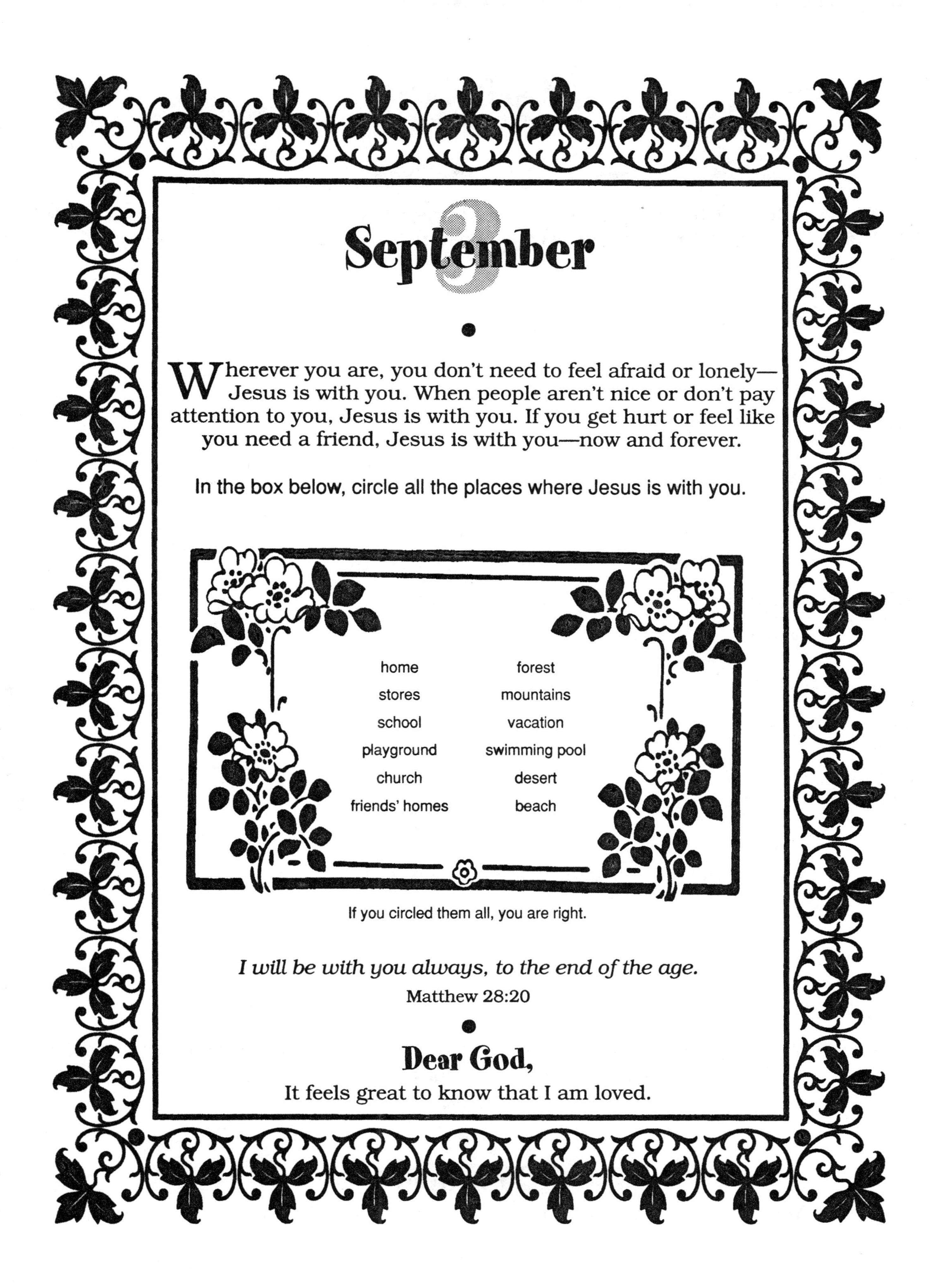

September 3

Wherever you are, you don't need to feel afraid or lonely—Jesus is with you. When people aren't nice or don't pay attention to you, Jesus is with you. If you get hurt or feel like you need a friend, Jesus is with you—now and forever.

In the box below, circle all the places where Jesus is with you.

home	forest
stores	mountains
school	vacation
playground	swimming pool
church	desert
friends' homes	beach

If you circled them all, you are right.

I will be with you always, to the end of the age.

Matthew 28:20

Dear God,

It feels great to know that I am loved.

Do you know what happens when you do good to other people? Everybody's happy! Try to think of nice ways you can help the people you love every day.

Draw you and your family doing an activity you love to do together.

So then, as often as we have the chance, we should do good to everyone, and especially to those who belong to our family in the faith.

Galatians 6:10

Dear God,

Thank You for my family. Help me to show my love for them by doing good to them.

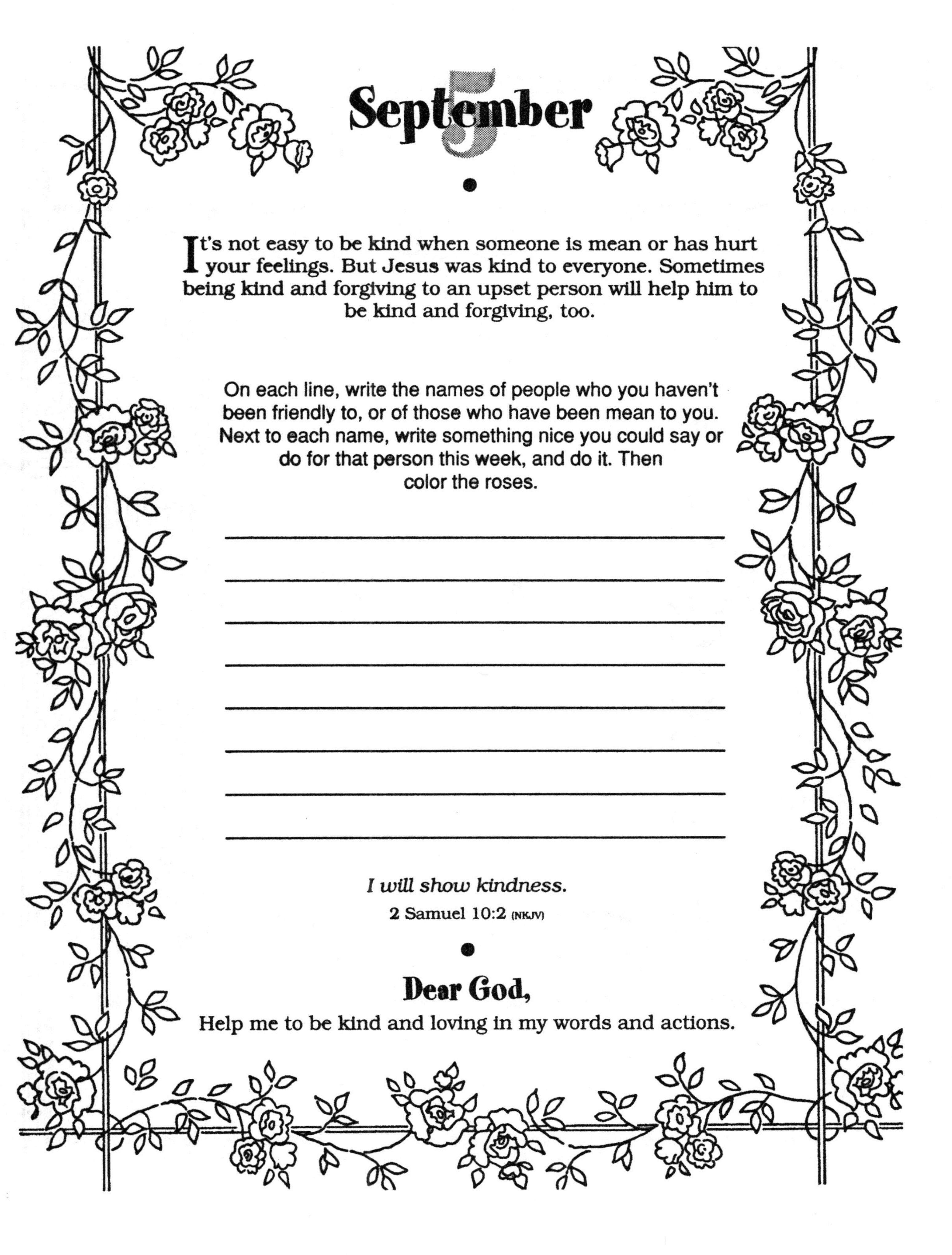

September 5

It's not easy to be kind when someone is mean or has hurt your feelings. But Jesus was kind to everyone. Sometimes being kind and forgiving to an upset person will help him to be kind and forgiving, too.

On each line, write the names of people who you haven't been friendly to, or of those who have been mean to you. Next to each name, write something nice you could say or do for that person this week, and do it. Then color the roses.

____

____

____

____

____

____

____

____

I will show kindness.

2 Samuel 10:2 (NKJV)

Dear God,

Help me to be kind and loving in my words and actions.

September 6

We have a lot to be glad about, don't we? Every day, God gives us incredible blessings. He is wonderful!

In this space, glue or tape a photograph of you celebrating a special day.

Rejoice, and be glad.

Matthew 5:12 (NASB)

Dear God,

Every day with You is a special day.

September 7

•

Doing something new can be scary...like the first day of school or going to a new church for the first time. But you are never alone, because God is always with you. He will help you.

Draw yourself walking into your classroom on the first day of school. What clothes are you wearing? What are you bringing with you? What is your teacher's name? What grade are you in?

My teacher is ______________________________

I'm in grade ______________________________

I will trust in you.

Psalm 55:23

•

Dear God,

Thank You for being with me every step of every day.

The Bible tells us the stories of many different people. The Old Testament tells us of God's people and prophets, and the New Testament tells what Jesus did on earth.

Keep a record or diary of what you do for a week. Start today, and write what you do during each day of next week.

Weekly Diary

Sun.	Today I
Mon.	Today I
Tues.	Today I
Wed.	Today I
Thurs.	Today I
Fri.	Today I
Sat.	Today I

These are the records of...

Genesis 11:10 (NASB)

Dear God,

When people read my life story, I want them to know about all the wonderful works You did in my life.

People were surprised when they saw Jesus spending time with poor and sick people. They wondered why He didn't just spend time with the rich, healthy, and important people. Jesus never worried about being popular with people, He just did what would please God.

Have you been to the doctor lately?

Tell a story about a visit to your doctor.

My Trip to the Doctor

____

____

____

____

____

____

____

____

____

____

____

My doctor's name is:

Jesus heard them and answered, "People who are well do not need a doctor, but only those who are sick."

Matthew 9:12

Dear God,

We need You when we're sick or when we're healthy. We need You all the time.

•

Jesus told the story of the lost sheep. He is like the shepherd who went out to find his lost sheep, because He does not want any one of us to miss out on heaven.

There is a lost sheep hiding in this picture. Color all the shapes that have a dot to find the sheep. Use one dark color, like green, to color.

He leaves the other ninety-nine sheep in the pasture and goes looking for the one that got lost until he finds it.

Luke 15:4

•

Dear God,

Thank You for caring so much for me. Help me to always stay close to You.

September 11

When you spend time with wise people, you can learn a lot from them.

Tell a story you have heard from your grandparents or another older friend about their childhood.

____

____

____

____

____

____

____

____

____

Be with wise men and become wise.

Proverbs 13:20 (TLB)

Dear God,

Thank You for my grandparents and their special love.

•

The entire world and all that is in it belongs to God because He made it all. He did a great job, didn't He? We should always take good care of everything He gives to us.

Draw everything this dog needs to be taken care of.

The world and all that is in it belong to the LORD.

Psalm 24:1

•

Dear God,

Thank You for Your gift of creation. Help us to care for what You give us.

Shepherds take good care of their sheep. They make sure the sheep have lots of grass to eat and water to drink. They make sure they are safe. God is like our shepherd. He will make sure we are safe and have everything we need.

Draw some sheep for this shepherd.

The LORD is my shepherd, I shall not want.

Psalm 23:1 (NASB)

Dear God,

Thank You for taking such good care of me. Thank You for making sure I have everything I need.

September 14

•

Daniel worshiped the God of Israel; so the king had to put Daniel in a pit filled with lions. The next morning, Daniel was safe! The king made a new law that commanded everyone to worship Daniel's God...the one real God!

Find the eight D's in this picture.

May your God, whom you serve so loyally, rescue you.

Daniel 6:16

•

Dear God,

Help me to always be brave, like Daniel, and trust You with every problem.

No matter what is happening around you, you can feel joy. Do you know why? Because God is always with you!

Finish this story. You can write it yourself, or have someone else write down what you say.

It makes me happy when

____

____

____

____

____

____

____

But the righteous are glad and rejoice in his presence; they are happy and shout for joy.

Psalm 68:3

Dear God,

Knowing You makes me happy. Thank You for loving me so much.

•

What is the biggest animal you can think of? What is the smallest? Do you have a favorite animal? Aren't you glad God decided to make all kinds of animals?

Draw a cow. Make your cow inside the blank square by copying what you see in squares 1, 2, and 3. Now color it. Good job!

Then God commanded, "Let the earth produce all kinds of animal life: domestic and wild, large and small."

Genesis 1:24

•

Dear God,

Thank You for all the wonderful animals.

September 17

Isn't it wonderful how God takes care of all the wild animals? He made sure that they have everything they need!

This little squirrel is getting ready to store food for the long winter. Fill his basket with food that is good for a squirrel. Only give animals food that is good for them!

Men and animals are in your care.

Psalm 36:6

Dear God,

Thank You for giving me only what is good for me.

•

Isn't it exciting to think that Jesus is busy right now preparing a beautiful place for you in heaven?

Think of a person you love a lot. Now get this house ready for that person. Fill and surround it with all the things that person loves. Make the house perfect just for him or her.

This special house is for ______________________________.

In my Father's house are many mansions...I go to prepare a place for you.

John 14:2 (NKJV)

•

Dear God,

I am glad You want me to live with You in heaven forever.

Did you know that God is always on time? He makes sure the fruits and vegetables ripen on the vines at exactly the right time. That is why we have plums and peaches in the summer and pumpkins just in time for fall hayrides.

Did you know that a raisin is just a grape that has been sitting out in the sun?
Find your way through this maze.

It was the season when grapes were beginning to ripen.

Numbers 13:20

Dear God,

Thank You for all the good foods that make each season special.

Jesus never forces Himself into anyone's life. He waits to be invited in...like when someone knocks at your door. When you do invite Jesus into your life, you will have found the "key" to happiness.

Connect these dots to find out what this is.

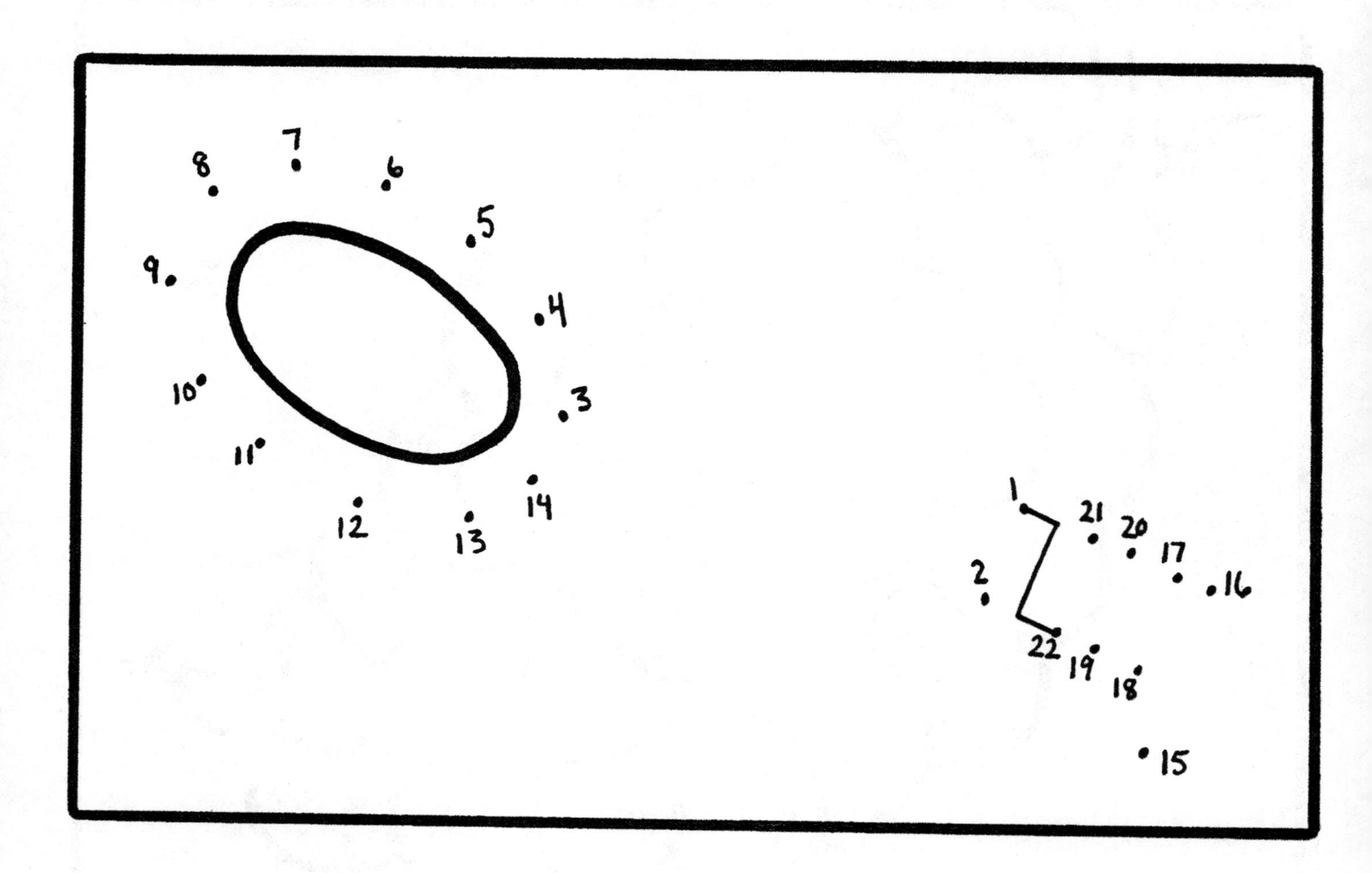

Behold, I stand at the door and knock.

Revelation 3:20 (NKJV)

Dear God,

Thank You for Jesus—I know He is my friend in good times and bad—my whole life long.

Did you know that worrying about your problems will not change them? Worrying just makes you feel awful. Give all your worries to God. He will take care of you.

Are you worried about anything?
Write each of your worries inside these balloons. Now draw yourself letting go of the worries—the balloons—to God!

Let him have all your worries and cares, for he is always thinking about you and watching everything that concerns you.

1 Peter 5:7

Dear God,

Help me to always remember to send all my worries off to You.

Won't it be exciting when we see Jesus come from heaven? He will be coming to bring us home, because heaven is our real home!

We, however, are citizens of heaven.

Philippians 3:20

Dear God,

I'm glad heaven is my real home, forever. It must be awesome!

September 23

•

There is much we can learn in school. But besides reading, writing, and arithmetic, we must also learn what is right and wrong. This we can do by learning about God.

In the space below, write the names or draw the faces of your best friends in school.

Teach a child how he should live.

Proverbs 22:6

•

Dear God,

Help me to be a good learner. Help me to listen and obey.

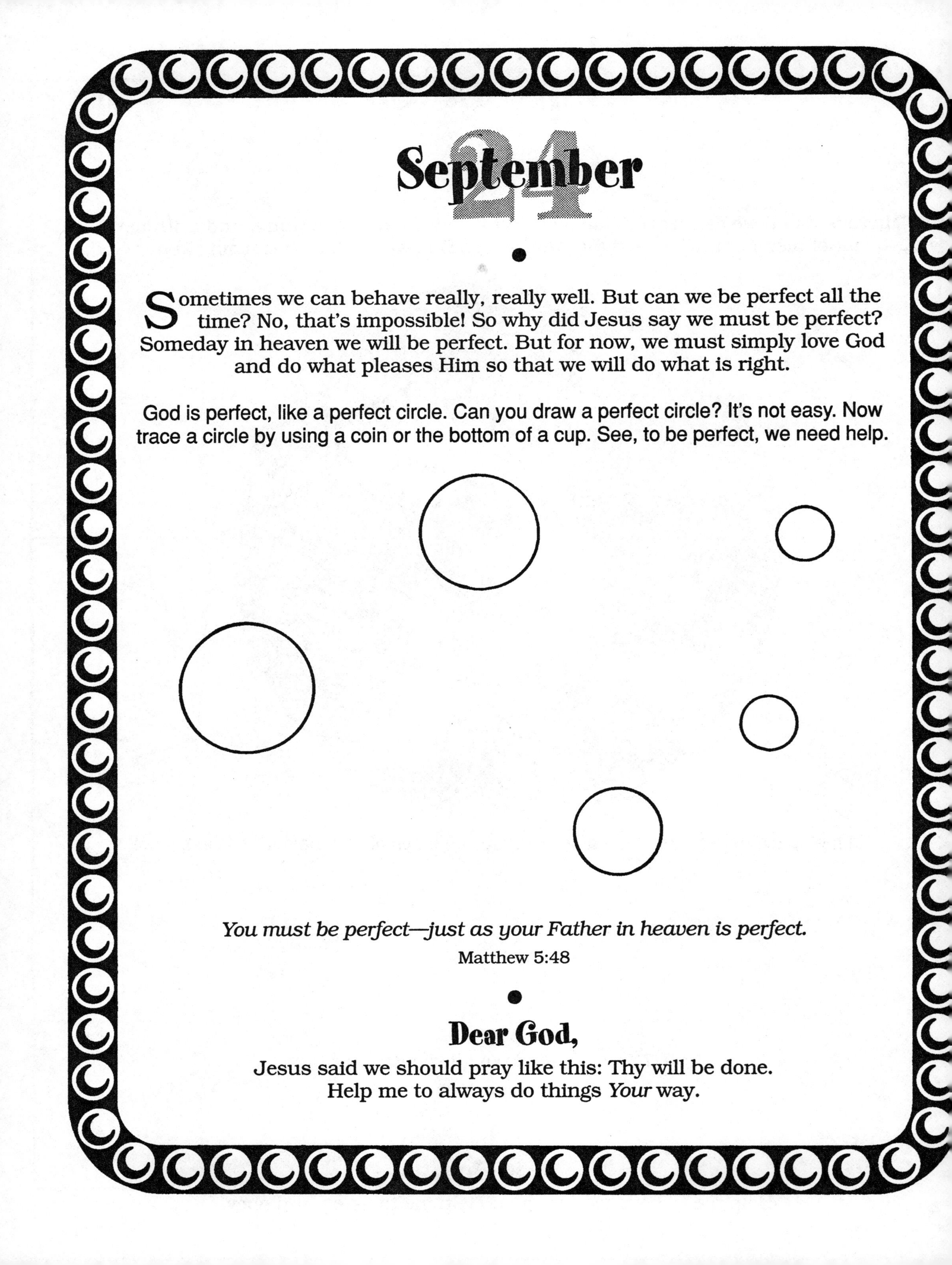

September 24

Sometimes we can behave really, really well. But can we be perfect all the time? No, that's impossible! So why did Jesus say we must be perfect? Someday in heaven we will be perfect. But for now, we must simply love God and do what pleases Him so that we will do what is right.

God is perfect, like a perfect circle. Can you draw a perfect circle? It's not easy. Now trace a circle by using a coin or the bottom of a cup. See, to be perfect, we need help.

You must be perfect—just as your Father in heaven is perfect.

Matthew 5:48

Dear God,

Jesus said we should pray like this: Thy will be done.
Help me to always do things *Your* way.

September 25

•

Everything God created tells how wonderful He is: beautiful flowers with their sweet perfume, shade trees with green leaves, oceans with their mighty waves, and the heavens filled with stars.

Put yellow in every shape that has a dot. Color every blank shape dark blue.

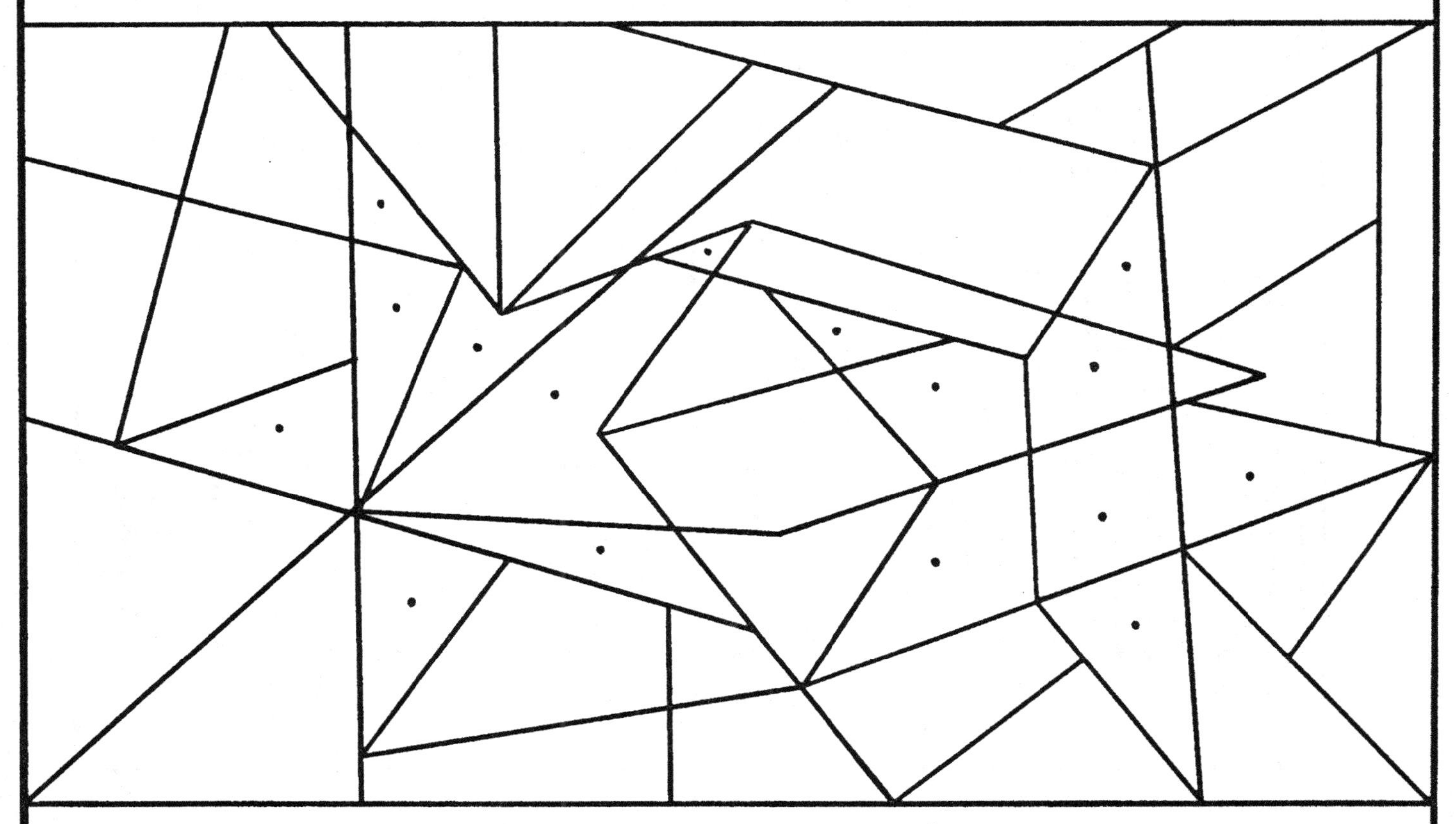

The morning stars sang together.

Job 38:7 (NASB)

•

Dear God,

You are so wonderful! I am glad that You made such a beautiful world for me to live in.

God wants us to be kind to each other, especially when people are in need. Kindness is thinking about and doing what would help another person. Even the smallest acts of kindness can make a person feel loved. What are some ways you can show kindness today?

Color each shape that has a dot • to find out today's important message.

Show kindness.

Genesis 24:12 (NKJV)

Dear God,

Thank You for Your kindness. Help me to always be kind to others.

When you are really thirsty, you don't want a tiny drop of water; you want to fill your cup to the top! Well, God wants to fill your life to the top with His blessings.

See this drawing? Using the squares for help, copy the cup and pitcher onto the blank squares then color your picture.

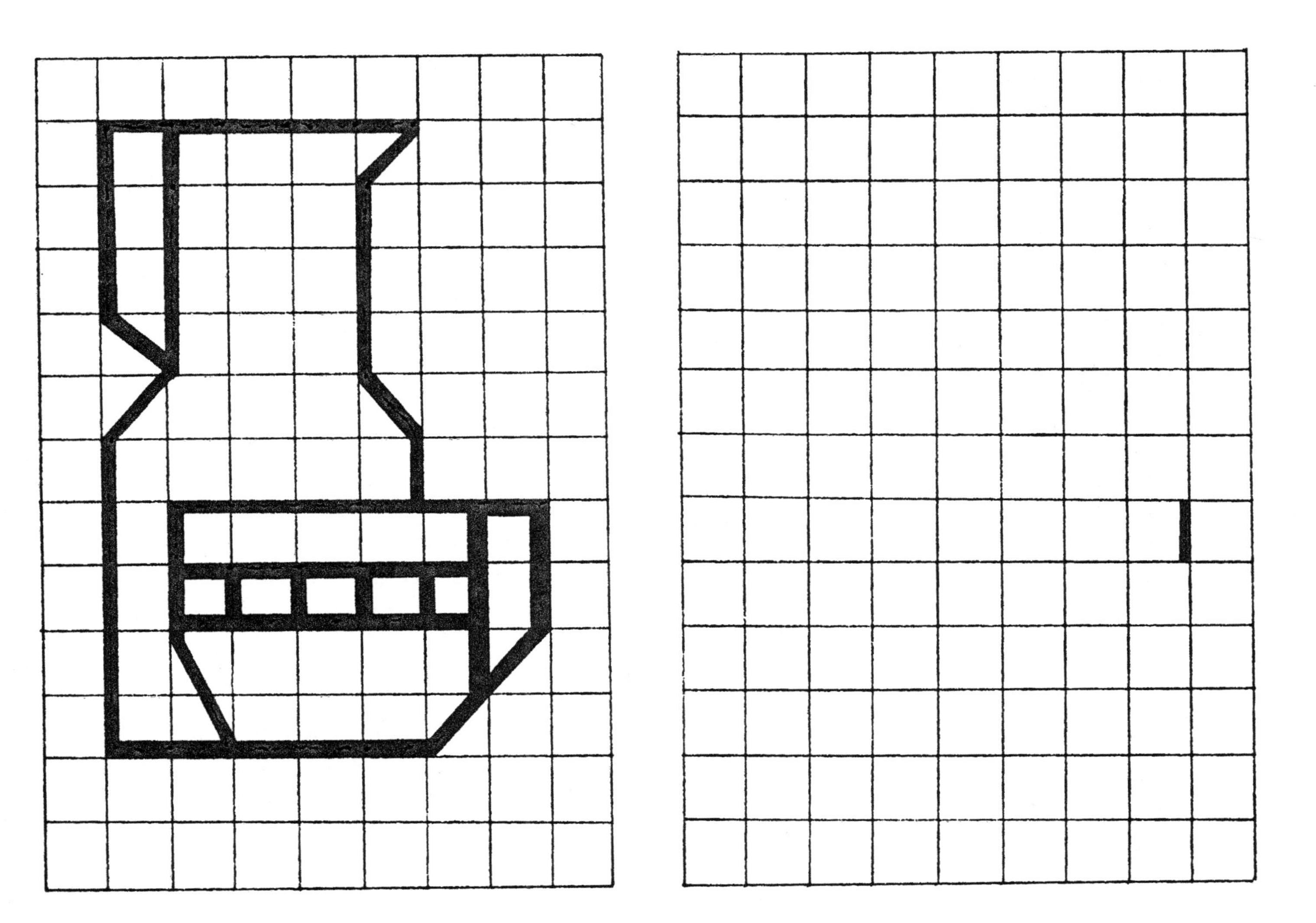

My cup overflows.

Psalm 23:5 (NASB)

Dear God,

Thank You for loving me so much. Thank You for knowing what I need. Thank You that Your love never changes.

September 28

•

Did you know that Jesus is coming again? But next time, He won't come as a tiny baby in a stable. He will come as King of kings and Lord of lords. His return will be so exciting!

Draw a picture of the Second Coming of Jesus.

There will be the shout of command, the archangel's voice, the sound of God's trumpet, and the Lord himself will come down from heaven.

1 Thessalonians 4:16

•

Dear God,

What an exciting day that will be! I look foward to living with You in heaven.

September 29

Did you know that God protects us from all kinds of trouble and problems? His love is like a big umbrella over us.

How would you help this boy caught in a storm? Give him everything he needs to stay dry and be protected from the rain.

God is our shelter and strength, always ready to help in times of trouble.

Psalm 46:1

Dear God,

Thank You for always watching out for me. Help me to help others when they need something.

SEPTEMBER SEPTEMBER

SEPTEMBER SEPTEMBER SEPTEMBER

SEPTEMBER SEPTEMBER SEPTEMBER

September 30

How was your September? You probably started school in a new class with a new teacher. With God's help, you will have a great school year and make lots of new friends. Did you do or say something you always want to remember?

Glue or tape a photograph or draw a picture of September's memorable moment in the space below. Write (or have someone help you write) all about what happened.

____

____

____

You may make your plans, but God directs your actions.

Proverbs 16:9

Dear God,

Thank You for taking such good care of me wherever I go.

SEPTEMBER SEPTEMBER

OCTOBER

Ever notice how you feel when you are having a good time with your friends? You feel happy, don't you? That's probably because you are both being nice and sharing with one another.

How do the children in these pictures feel? Show how they feel by drawing their faces.

There is more happiness in giving than in receiving.
Acts 20:35

Dear God,

Help me to be a kind person who thinks of others. Help me to give instead of just receive.

October 2

Do your friends need to be exactly like you? Can a friend look different than you do? Can he or she speak and act differently? Of course! That's what makes life interesting. If you both love Jesus, then you have a lot in common.

Give each of these pumpkins a different face. It can be funny, silly, or pretty.

I call you friends.

John 15:15

Dear God,

Help me to realize that no matter what people look like, You love us all.

If you owned everything in the world but couldn't go to heaven, you would never be happy. God wants us to live in heaven forever and ever. There are many things in this world that seem nice, but nothing compares to knowing God. That's why Jesus came...so we could get to heaven!

Write (or have someone help you write) a story about a place you have been or would like to go in the world. What would you like to see and do there?

What profit is there if you gain the whole world—and lose eternal life?

Matthew 16:26

Dear God,

Thank You for this big and interesting world. Wherever I go, let me always remember that I belong to You.

October 4

•

Just when you thought you would melt from all the summer heat, along comes autumn Autumn is harvest time. Trees are turning beautiful colors, and there are big piles of leaves to jump in! Now the air feels cooler and you can start to wear sweaters again.

Draw a picture of you doing an activity you love to do in autumn.

What a rich harvest your goodness provides!

Psalm 65:11

•

Dear God,

Thank You for hayrides, pumpkins, and crunchy leaves under my feet. Thank You for autun

Esther, whose Hebrew name was Hadassah, was an orphan girl who was raised by her cousin, Mordecai. King Ahasuerus chose her to be his queen and they lived in his palace in Shushan.

WORD SQUARES

On each word square below, begin at the arrow and circle the first letter. Then circle every other letter. The circled letters will make a word that will answer the question.

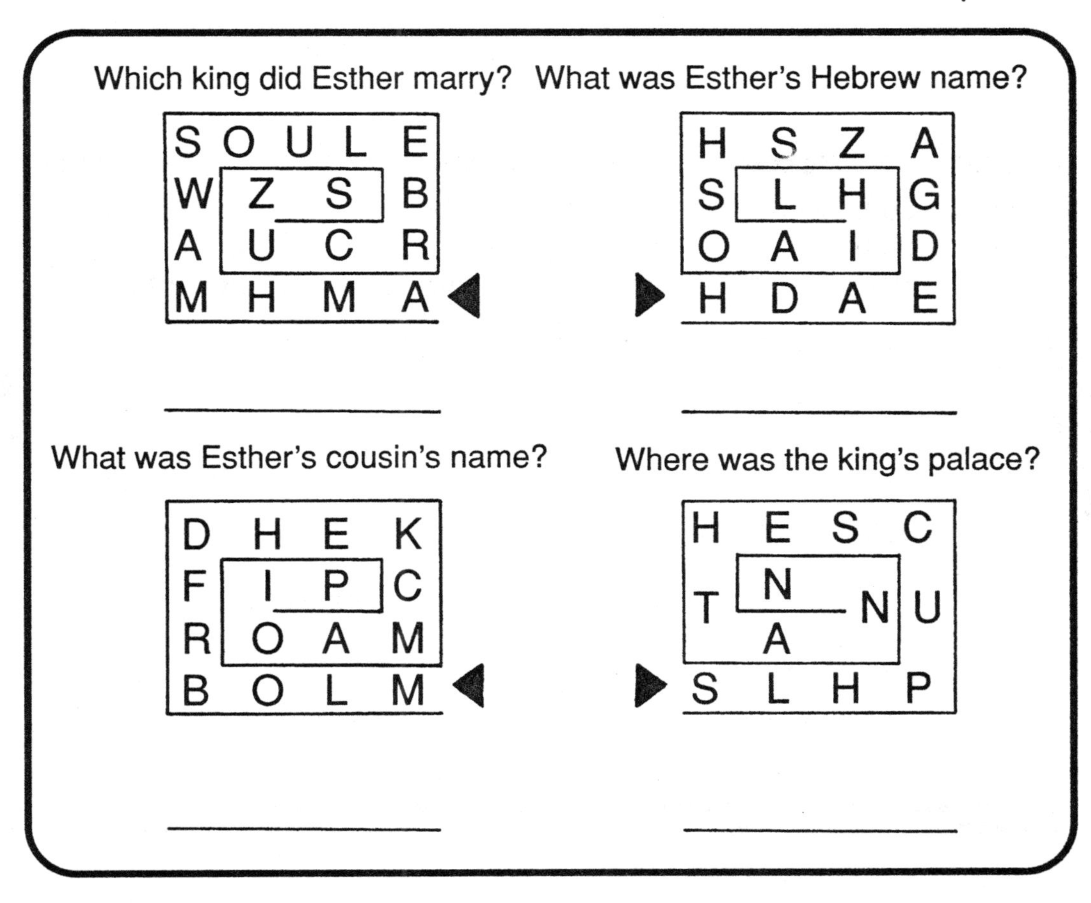

He set the royal crown on her head and declared her queen.

Esther 2:17

Dear God,

I like to hear Bible stories about people who loved You ... like Esther.

When an evil man convinced King Ahasuerus to kill all the Jews in the kingdom, Queen Esther bravely told the king that she was Jewish. She begged him not to kill the Jewish people. Esther realized that God had made her queen so that she could save her people.

Have you noticed that many of the people in the Bible were brave?
Can you name some of the people in the Bible who were brave?
Read the names below and circle them if they are in the story of Esther.

Mordecai	Daniel
Adam	Abraham
King Ahasuerus	Eve
Goliath	Herod
Noah	Joseph
Esther	Moses

Maybe it was for a time like this that you were made queen!
Esther 4:14

Dear God,

Help me to always be ready to stand up for what I believe.

October 7

•

You know that it is good to obey your parents, but did you know that you should obey them quickly? Finding something else to do first is a way of disobeying. The next time your parents ask you to help do something, take your mark, get set, then go!

HELP SUZY OBEY

Draw a line through the maze to show what Suzy should do when her mother asks her to make her bed. When should Suzy do the other activities?

Children, it is your Christian duty to obey your parents, for this is the right thing to do.

Ephesians 6:1

•

Dear God,

Help me to obey my parents right away! Then we will all be happy!

What does it mean to live in union with Jesus? It means that He is with us every moment of every day and that He touches every part of our lives.

In each section, write how Jesus can help you be more loving, truthful, and forgiving with your family, your friends, at school, and when you are playing.

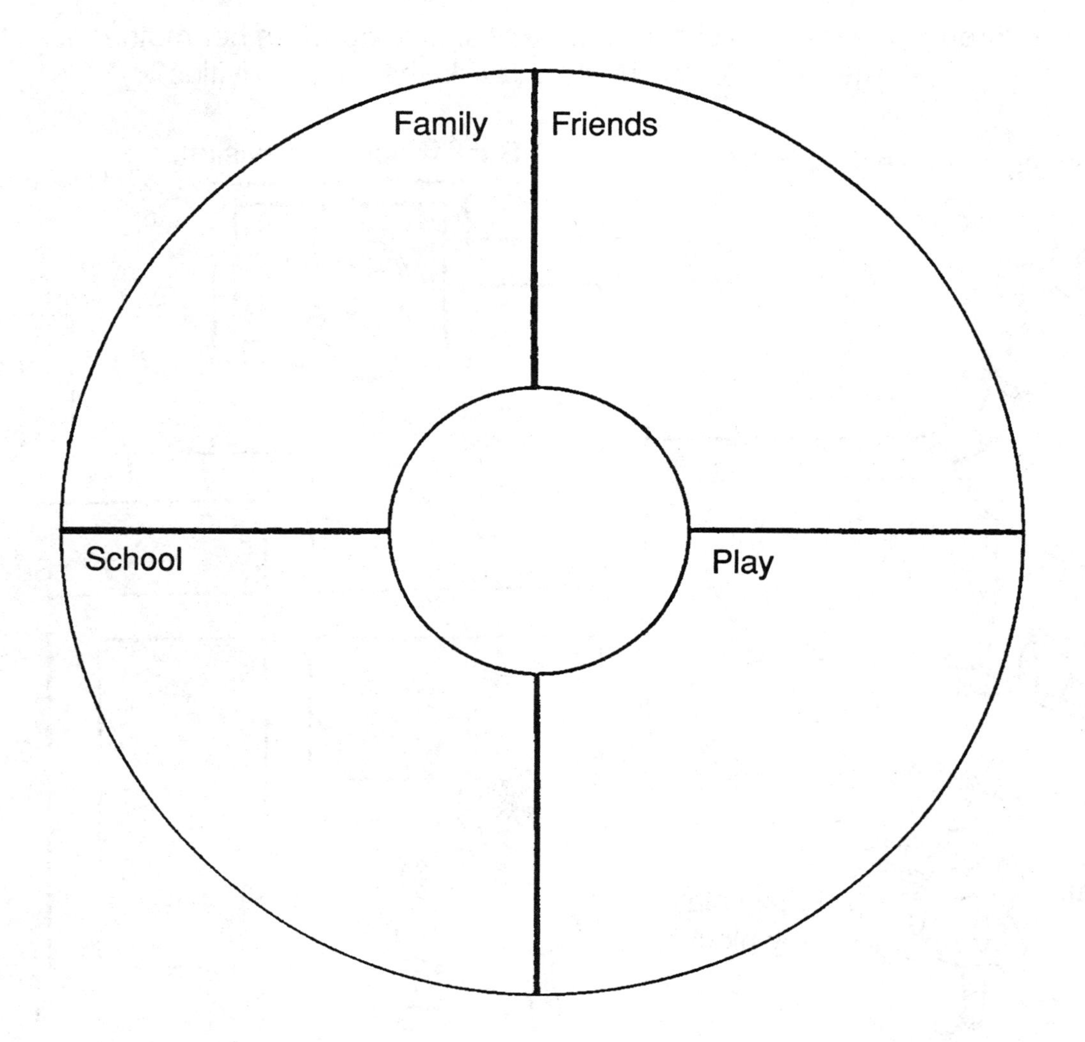

Since you have accepted Jesus Christ as Lord, live in union with Him.

Colossians 2:6

Dear God,

Help me to be like Jesus. Help me to be kind, loving, and forgiving.

Jesus spoke often about how important it is to love other people. Some people are not easy to love, but with God's help, we can treat everyone with love.

In each box below, draw yourself doing some of the things you love to do.

One of my many talents is	The food I love to eat most is
My absolute favorite sport is	This is how I like to relax

Love your neighbor as you love yourself.

Matthew 22:39

Dear God,

Help me to treat everybody with love, even when it's not easy.

Do you know how people can tell you are a Christian? They will know because they will see how you love other people.

How many words can you make from the letters in "Christianity"?

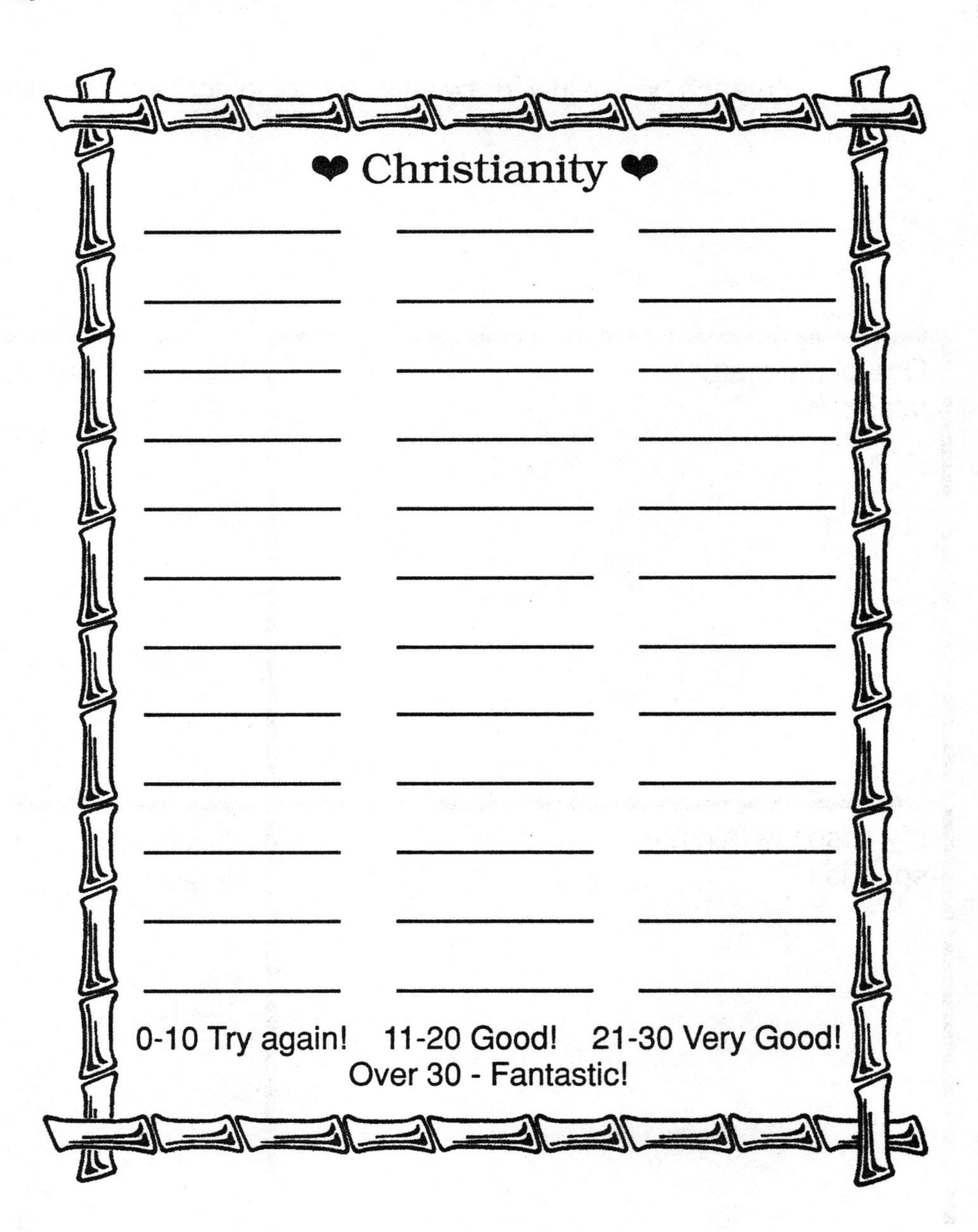

Love one another.

1 John 4:7

Dear God,

When people look at me, let them see Your love shining through.

October 11

What do you think it means to be rich? Did you know that learning about God makes you rich on the inside? The love of God in your heart is a treasure that can never be taken away.

There are different names for money in different parts of the world. Try to match the name of each country's money with the right country.

dinar	Albania
pound	China
yen	Ecuador
peso	India
krona	Iraq
lek	Ireland
yuan	Japan
sucre	Mexico
dollar	Sweden
rupee	Germany
deutsche mark	United States of America

Answers: Albania—lek; China—yuan; Ecuador—sucre; India—rupee; Iraq—dinar; Ireland—pound; Japan—yen; Mexico—peso; Sweden—krona; Germany—deutsche mark; United States of America—dollar.

Where your treasure is, there your heart will be also.

Matthew 6:21

Dear God,

Even if I had all the money in the world, without You, I would be sad.

October 12

Is God with us even when bad things happen? Yes! He is right there with you, giving you the help you need. He will take care of you! God hears your prayers. So talk to Him; He is waiting to hear from you.

Color this brother and sister who are thanking God before they eat their lunch.

In everything give thanks.

1 Thessalonians 5:18 (NASB)

Dear God,

Thank You for hearing my prayers, and thank You for answering them.

October 13

Think of all the places you go every day and all the chances you have to show God's love to people. A kind word, a helpful action, or even a smile will let others feel the love of God.

There are different ways to tell people "I love you." Fill in the blanks in the box below.

HERE'S HOW I CAN SHOW GOD'S LOVE

At home: ______________________________

At school: ______________________________

At play: ______________________________

At church: ______________________________

At the library: ______________________________

On the phone: ______________________________

At the movies: ______________________________

Beloved, let us love one another, for love is of God.

1 John 4:7 (NKJV)

Dear God,

Thank You for Your love. Help me to always show love to others.

•

Is there a special treat that someone in your family loves to eat? Even if it takes a long time to mix all the ingredients, you can show someone you love them by working extra hard to make something special.

Draw yourself and the grown-up who helps you baking something special. Draw all the ingredients you need for your special creation. Then color the picture.

Let love make you serve one another.

Galatians 5:13

•

Dear God,

Help me to think of others and think of ways to make them happy.

Have you ever tried to walk in someone's footsteps? Was it fun? When the Bible tells us to walk in Jesus' steps, it means we should try to act like Jesus. We should try to love like Him and forgive like Him.

Connect the dots to find out where the footprints are going.

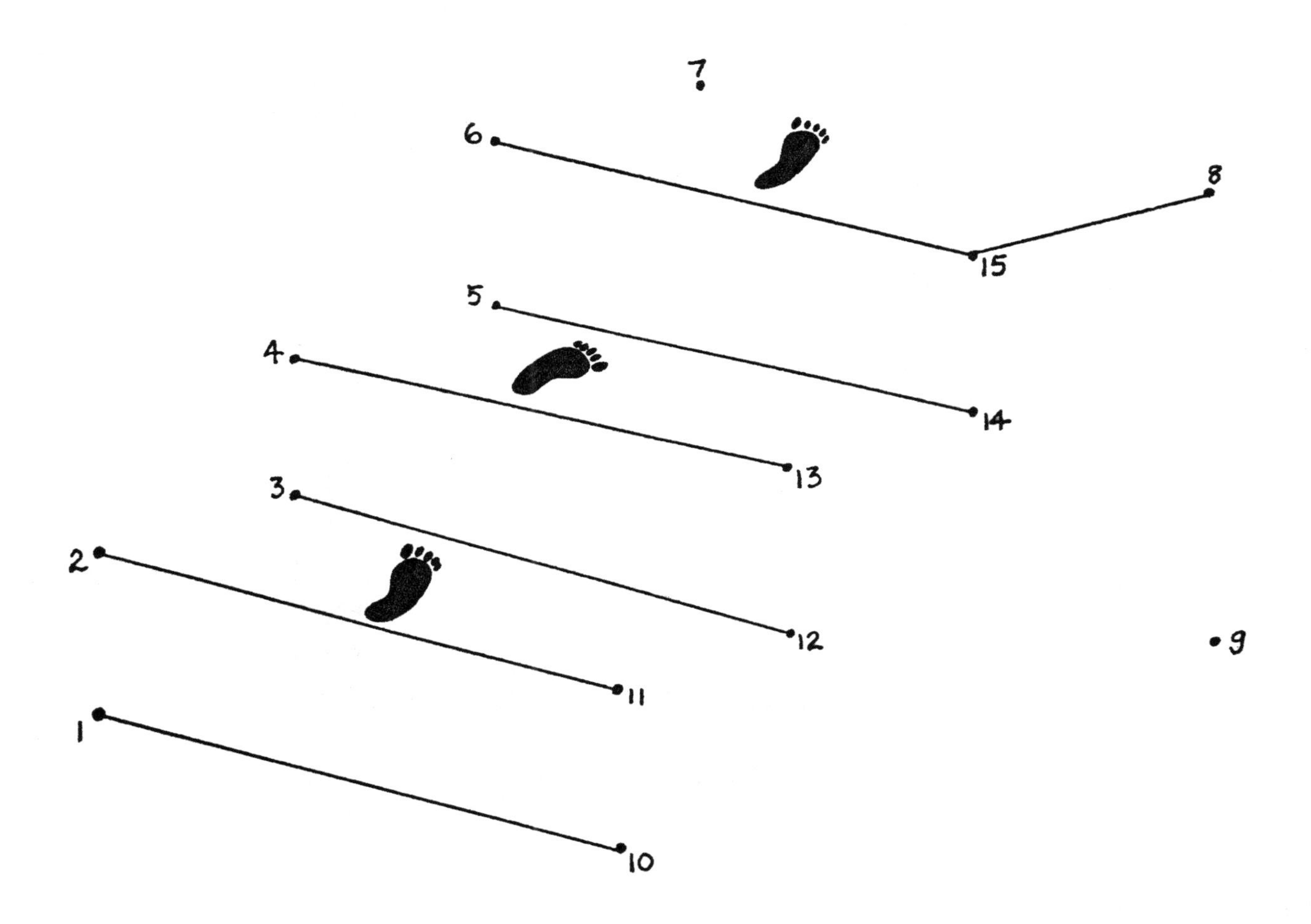

Christ himself suffered for you and left you an example, so that you would follow in his steps.

1 Peter 2:21

Dear God,

Help me to act like Jesus every day. Please help me love everyone—
even the people who are hard to love.

Jesus loves you, and He wants you to love other people. Tomorrow, do something kind for someone you don't know very well. Before you know it, you may have a new friend

Draw a picture of someone who you love very much.

This is a picture of ____________________, who I love because ______________________________.

I love you just as the Father loves me.

John 15:9

Dear God,

I'm glad I have so many people to love, and I'm especially glad You love me!

Anyone who has become a success will tell you he or she had to work hard. To play the piano well you must practice. To be a good baseball player you must play often. When you work around the house, it makes your parents happy, and you can learn to be a good worker!

Help clean the kitchen tonight. Sweep the floor, clear the table, and maybe you can even wash the dishes (if it's all right with your parents).

Work hard and become a leader; be lazy and never succeed.

Proverbs 12:24

Dear God,

Whatever I do, help me to do it well.

Your parents want you to grow up to love God. That's why we read the Bible. Moms and Dads also want you to know how to take care of yourself and others. That is why they give you work to do around the house. Even small work projects are important.

Make a list of all the work you do around the house each week.

Forgive the sins and errors of my youth.

Psalm 25:7

Dear God,

Help me to do what my parents ask me each week. Help me to do my work without grumbling.

•

To have good friends, you must be kind and loving. Try to speak nicely about your friends to other people. If your friend does something that bothers you, go to your friend right away and tell him or her…nicely!

On one line, write the name of a friend. On the next line, write why you like him or her very much.

Don't just pretend that you love others; really love them.

Romans 12:9

•

Dear God,

Thank You for the gift of good friends.

October 20

•

All that we say and think should be good and right—this pleases God. We should fill our minds and hearts with kind, loving thoughts and words.

Write a poem about something special to you. It can rhyme or not.

MY POEM

May my words and my thoughts be acceptable to you, O Lord.

Psalm 19:14

•

Dear God,

Help me to always say and think good things.

October 21

•

It's nice to settle into a cozy bed after a busy day. Are there special things you do before going to bed?

My favorite bedtime story is ______________________________

My favorite toy or blanket that I sleep with is ______________________

My favorite pajamas are ______________________________

Let us...rest awhile.

Mark 6:31

•

Dear God,

It feels great to get a good night's sleep after a busy day. Thank You for all my happy dreams.

When you love God and do what is right, your life will be a great joy to others.

Write the story of your life in a few sentences. Someone can help write it for you, if you just tell them all the highlights.

The memory of the righteous will be a blessing.

Proverbs 10:7 (NIV)

Dear God,

Thank You for what You have done in my life. Thank You for watching over me every single da

Have you ever put on a play? Everybody must do what the director says, then the play will be a success. The same is true in life: If you follow God's direction, you will know just what to do. He will guide your steps.

Do you like to dress up? Pretend you are able to dress up in any costume. Draw yourself in your favorite costume on this stage.

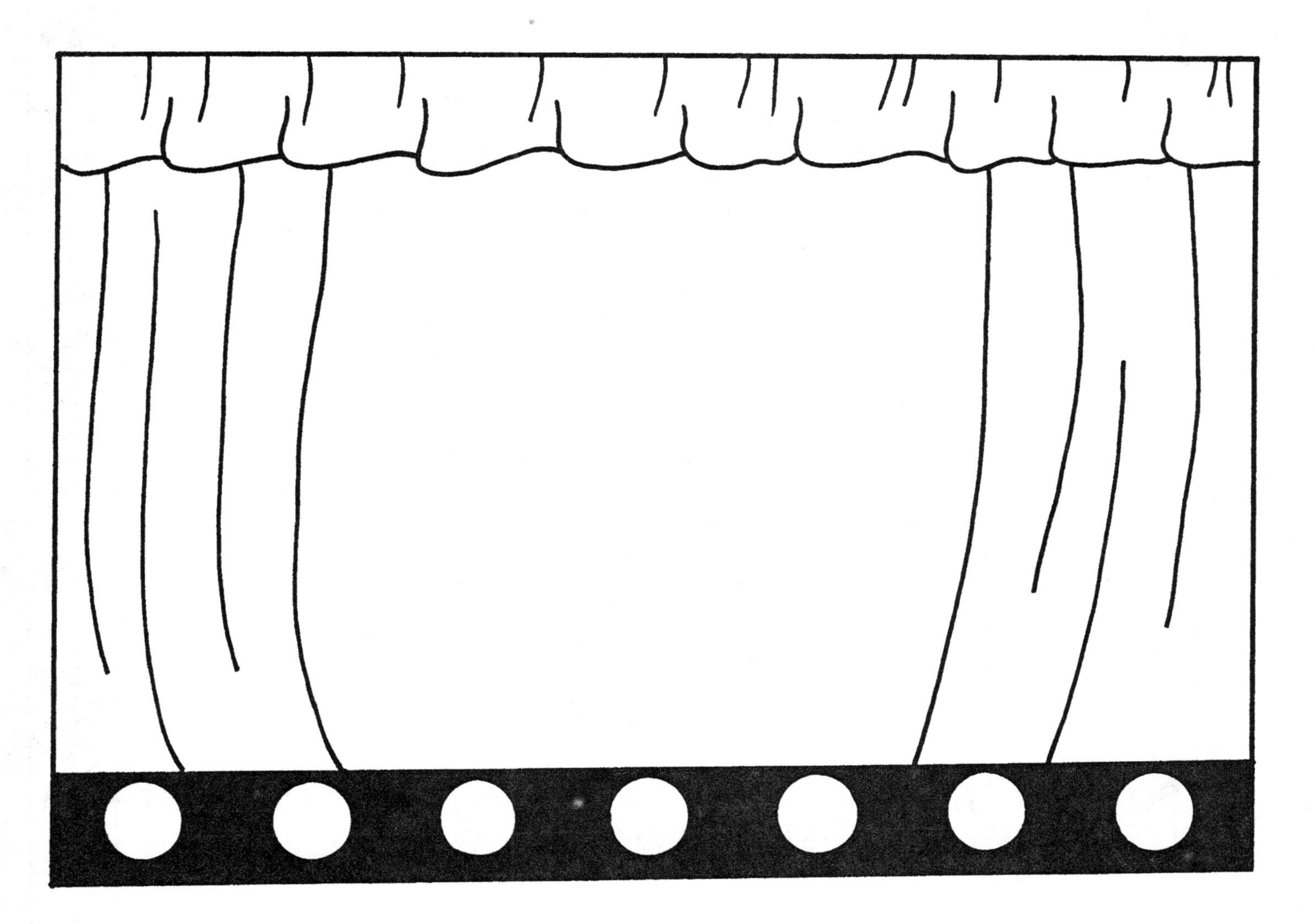

We will do everything that the LORD has said.

Exodus 19:8

Dear God,

I'm glad I don't have to act or pretend around You. You love me just the way I am.

October 24

God loves to hear you sing to Him! What is your favorite song from Sunday school? Sing it!

My favorite song from Sunday school:

____

____

Some of my other favorite songs:

____

____

____

____

____

____

Sing a new song to the LORD.

Psalm 98:1

Dear God,

I am glad You love music as much as I do.

Have you ever felt really tired? What if you were tired *and* had to carry something very heavy? You'd be happy if someone came along and offered to carry it for you! Jesus said He wants to carry all our problems, fears, and worries so that we can feel better.

Hundreds of years ago, people had donkeys and horses carry their loads. Draw a picture of what you think we will use for transportation in the future.

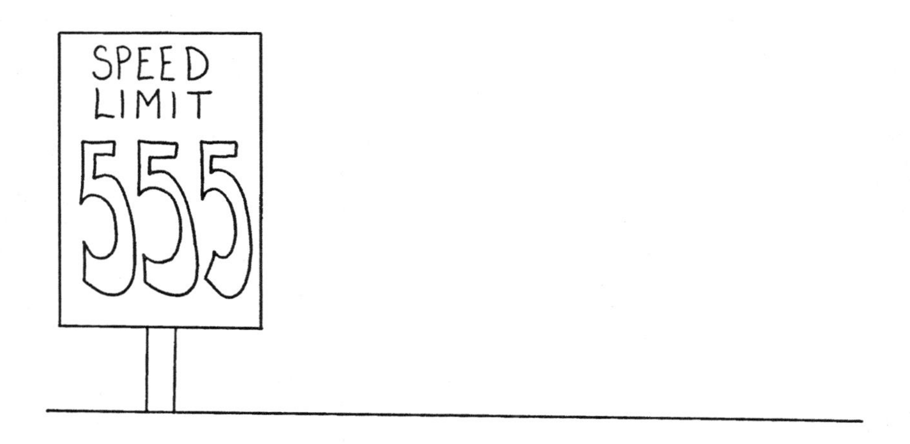

Come to me, all of you who are tired from carrying heavy loads, and I will give you rest.

Matthew 11:29

Dear God,

I am glad You want to carry my burdens. Thank You for being my "heavenly helper."

When a family decides to love and serve God, they will be blessed.

Pretend this is your house. Draw the furniture, paintings, rugs…everything. Which room is yours?

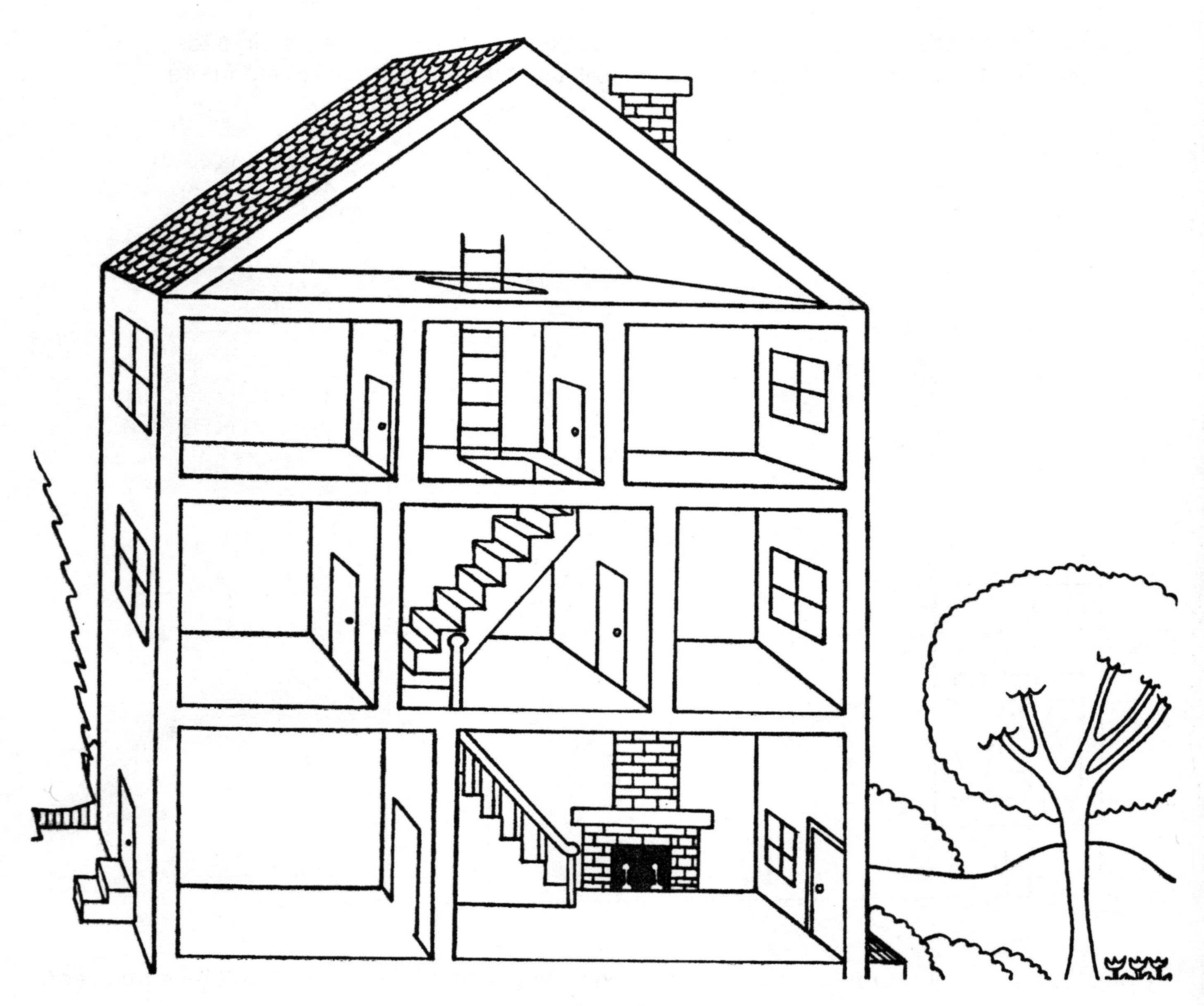

As for me and my house, we will serve the LORD.

Joshua 24:15 (NASB)

Dear God,

Thank You for letting me be born into a family that loves You.

In this life, sometimes you win and sometimes you lose. But no matter what happens, God is with you. He will never leave you alone. Sometimes you may face problems that make you want to give up, but faith in God will get you through even the toughest times.

You have a lot to offer! Have your family fill in the blanks with what they like about you!

Make sure that your endurance carries you all the way without failing, so that you may be perfect and complete, lacking nothing.

James 1:4

Dear God,

Help me to wake up every day expecting something wonderful to happen!

October 28

Did you know that helping others can be fun? Try raking a big pile of leaves. Then if it's okay with your parents, jump into it!

Leaf Rubbings

Put a leaf under this page and rub the paper lightly with a crayon. You will see an artistic design show up. Move the leaf around to make interesting designs. You can also make rubbings of tree bark, flat stones, or pine needles.

You children must always obey your fathers and mothers, for that pleases the Lord.

Colossians 3:20 (TLB)

Dear God,

Thank You for the beautiful autumn leaves.

October 29

•

What makes a person truly great? Some of the greatest people are not on television or in the newspapers. They live their lives quietly, loving God, doing good, loving others, and sharing. The world may not know who they are, but God does.

Tell about a person you would like to meet and why. Where would you meet? What would you say?

Let them do good, that they be rich in good works, ready to give, willing to share.

1 Timothy 6:18 (NKJV)

•

Dear God,

Help me to always put You first. You make people truly great.

October 30

Jesus loves us so we can love others. He fills your heart with love, kindness, and joy, so that you can be kind, helpful, and loving to others.

Finish these sentences.

1. If someone was crying, I would ____________________
2. If someone was hurt, I would ____________________
3. If someone was lonely, I would ____________________
4. If someone was sad, I would ____________________
5. If someone was afraid, I would ____________________

Everything you do or say, then, should be done in the name of the Lord Jesus, as you give thanks through him to God the Father.

Colossians 3:17

Dear God,

Help me to show love, kindness, and joy.

OCTOBER OCTOBER OCTOBER

October 31

•

Autumn leaves and brisk air...pumpkins and hayrides...October is such a beautiful month! Share the moment you would like to remember. Was it a beautiful sight? A special trip? Maybe you said the right word at the right time.

Glue or tape a photograph or draw a picture of October's memorable moment in the space below. Write (or have someone help you write) about what made it special.

Make it your aim to do what is right.

Amos 5:14

•

Dear God,

Help me to always aim to do what is right.

NOVEMBER

November 1

Isn't it fun to spend time with people who have been alive a long time? They always have interesting stories about life in the old days. Because they have lived many years, they have learned a lot.

Connect the dots to find out what grandma is doing.

Long life is the reward of the righteous; gray hair is a glorious crown.

Proverbs 16:31

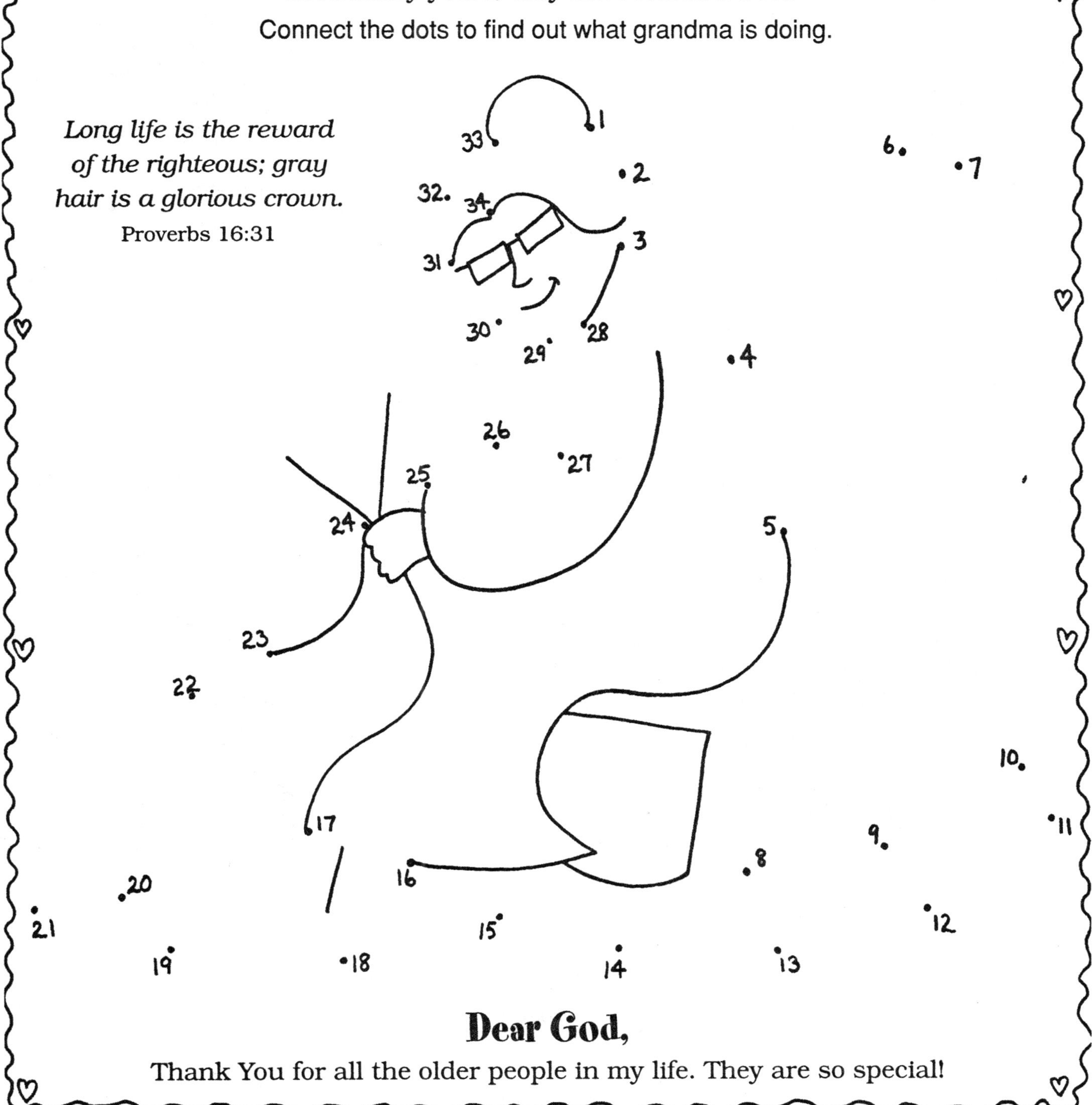

Dear God,

Thank You for all the older people in my life. They are so special!

After Jonah was swallowed by a whale, he prayed that God would save him. He was in the whale three days and three nights before he landed on dry land.

In my distress I called to the LORD, and he answered me.

Jonah 2:2

Dear God,

You heard Jonah's prayer, and I want to thank You for hearing mine.

Every person who has ever lived has gone through problems and difficult times when an important decision had to be made. The Bible is full of such stories. When you are a Christian, though, you don't have to face those moments alone. Jesus will stay with you always.

List these people according to when they lived: Adam, Eve, Noah, Abraham Lincoln, Matthew, John, Moses, Esther, King David, Mary, John the Baptist, George Wasington, you!

Before Jesus	During Jesus' time	After Jesus

Consider it pure joy, my brothers, whenever you face trials of many kinds.

James 1:2 (NIV)

Dear God,

I am glad that You are with me wherever I am. Please help me to make good decisions all my life.

November 4

•

Jesus said that when we love Him, we will be like bright, shining lights in this world. Don't be afraid to show everyone the light and love that is inside you. Don't be afraid to shine.

Do you have an award or certificate from school that is special to you? Glue or tape it to this page, and be proud of the good job you did at school. (Save this page for later if you don't have an award now.)

No one lights a lamp and puts it under a bowl; instead he puts it on the lampstand, where it gives light for everyone in the house.

Matthew 5:15

•

Dear God,

Thank You for all the talents and abilities You have given me.

November 5

•

The angels praise God, and so do all the other creatures in heaven. When you think about how wonderful God is, you just *have* to praise Him!

God has many interesting creatures. Which one is your favorite? Can you write a story about an animal you love and tell why you love it?

Praise the LORD, all his creatures.

Psalm 103:22

•

Dear God,

I love all of Your creatures, big and small.

When Jesus said you should love your neighbor as yourself, He meant you should love all people—not just your next-door neighbor. Treat other people kindly. Think of ways to make other people know you care about them.

Who would you like to visit? ______________________________ Follow the maze to that person's house. Every time you see a heart, stop and think of something nice you could say or do for your person. Even little things like giving a flower tells someone that you care!

Love your neighbor as you love yourself.

Matthew 19:19

Dear God,

Please help me love the people who aren't so easy to love.

November 7

Isn't it wonderful to read all the Bible stories about people who loved and trusted God? God took care of them...sometimes in absolutely amazing ways! He wants to take care of you, too.

Close your eyes, and point to a letter. Name someone from the Bible whose name begins with that letter. Tell something you know about that person. If it is a man, color the letter blue. If it is a woman, color the letter pink.

Happy are the people who know God is the LORD!

Psalm 144:15

Dear God,

I'm glad You are still taking care of people today, just like You did in Bible times. Thank You, Father.

We should always be sure we are doing what God wants us to do. With God helping us, we can do anything!

Connect the dots. Then draw a door, windows, flowers, and anything else that would make this the kind of place you want to visit.

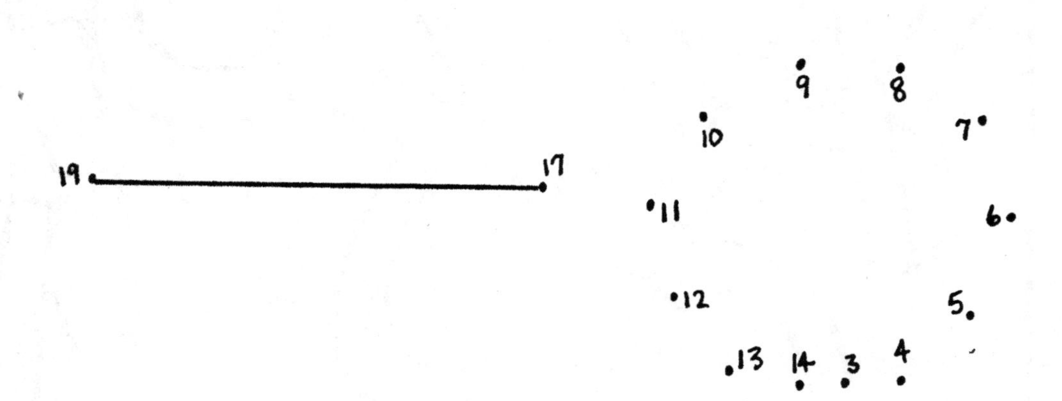

If the LORD does not build the house, the work of the builders is useless.

Psalm 127:1

Dear God,

Thank You for being so interested in every part of my life. Help me to do what pleases You.

God knew you before you were even born! He also knows all the days of your entire life. God knows everything!

Every day from God is special, isn't it? But holidays are extra special! Do you have a favorite holiday? Which is it? Can you guess the favorite holiday of everyone in your family? Ask them.

You saw me before I was born and scheduled each day of my life before I began to breathe.

Psalm 139:16

Dear God,

Thank You for the many wonderful memories of being together at holidays.

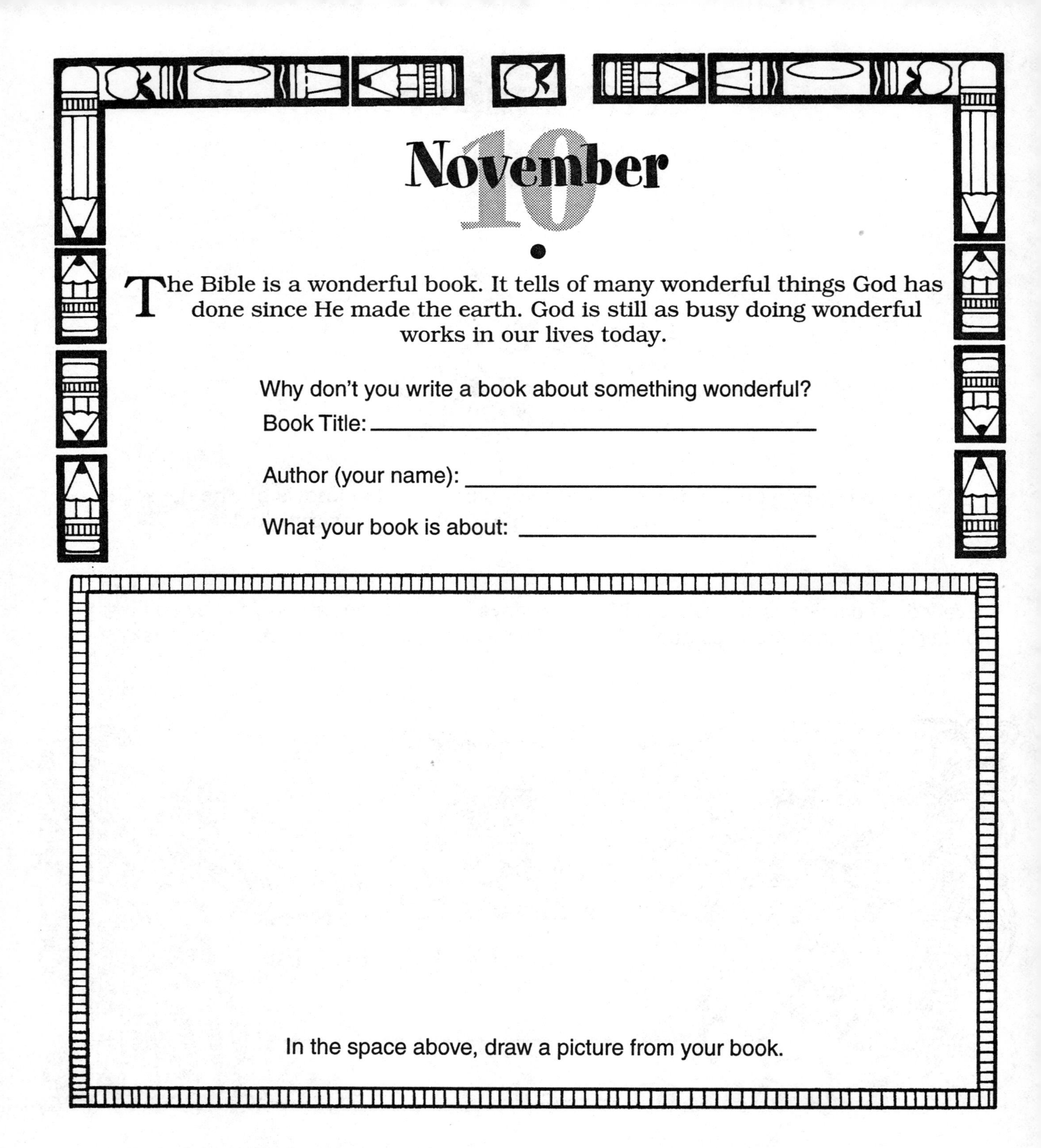

November 10

The Bible is a wonderful book. It tells of many wonderful things God has done since He made the earth. God is still as busy doing wonderful works in our lives today.

Why don't you write a book about something wonderful?

Book Title: ______________________________

Author (your name): ______________________

What your book is about: __________________

In the space above, draw a picture from your book.

We proclaim how great you are and tell of the wonderful things you have done.

Psalm 75:1

Dear God,

Thank You for the Bible. It is the greatest story of all, and best of all, it is true!

November

•

Our God is a loving God. The whole Bible tells story after story of God's love and care for all kinds of people. And God is just as busy today loving and caring for you!

Here's a fun game to play. Have someone tell you an answer below and then try to figure out what the question is. Remember all the Bible stories you have learned, and have fun!

Here are the answers:	What are the questions?
1. Adam	1.
2. Forty days and forty nights	2.
3. Jesus	3.
4. A whale	4.
5. Lions	5.
6. Esther	6.
7. Angels	7.
8. Red Sea	8.
9. Twelve	9.
10. A giant	10.

God is love.

1 John 4:16

•

Dear God,

Thank You for Your love that never ends.

November 12

Jesus said that any time we help people who are poor, hungry, sick, or in need, it is like we are doing it for Him.

Below, glue or tape a photograph of someone who has been kind to you.
Or, you can draw a picture of that person.

Whenever you did this for one of the least important of these brothers of mine, you did it for me

Matthew 25:40

Dear God,

Thank You for the people who are always kind to me. Help me to be kind to others.

November 13

It is important to learn what the Bible says because then you will know how to live your life.

BIBLE QUIZ

1. God's first words when He made the world were

a) Let there be heaven.

b) Let there be light.

c) Let there be earth.

2. Adam and Eve disobeyed God when they ate

a) forbidden fruit

b) pepperoni pizza

c) vegetables

3. One of the Ten Commandments is "You shall not ______________________."

a) skip

b) steal

c) smile

4. Jesus performed many miracles, including

a) walking to Jerusalem

b) walking on dirt roads

c) walking on water

5. King David loved to play

a) soccer

b) the piano

c) the harp

6. Esther was chosen to be queen because she was

a) Jewish

b) kind and beautiful

c) first in line

7. Abraham was 100 years old when

a) he died

b) Sarah gave him a surprise birthday party

c) he had a son

8. Daniel spent a night with some

a) lions

b) bears

c) tigers

9. Jesus was born in a

a) hospital

b) tent

c) manger

10. Jacob had

a) three sons

b) ten daughters

c) twelve sons

Teach them to your children.

Deuteronomy 6:7

Answers: 1. b 2. a
3. b 4. c 5. c 6. b
7. c 8. a 9. c 10. c

Dear God,

I want to read the Bible and learn about You all my life.

Jesus is a gentle, quiet visitor who waits to be invited into your life. Once you do, the best part of your life will begin!

Who or what would you like to see when you open the door? It could be a person you love or a place you want to visit. Draw what you see.

Listen! I stand at the door and knock.

Revelation 3:20

Dear God,

I am glad You are kind and gentle and that You are interested in my life.

Have you ever noticed how you feel after yelling at someone or being yelled at? Watch your words. Remember, some words help, and others definitely hurt.

Pretend you are at the grocery store. Fill your grocery cart with all kinds of healthy foods. Healthy bodies come from eating good food and healthy spirits come by praying and reading the Bible. Draw yourself pushing the cart, too.

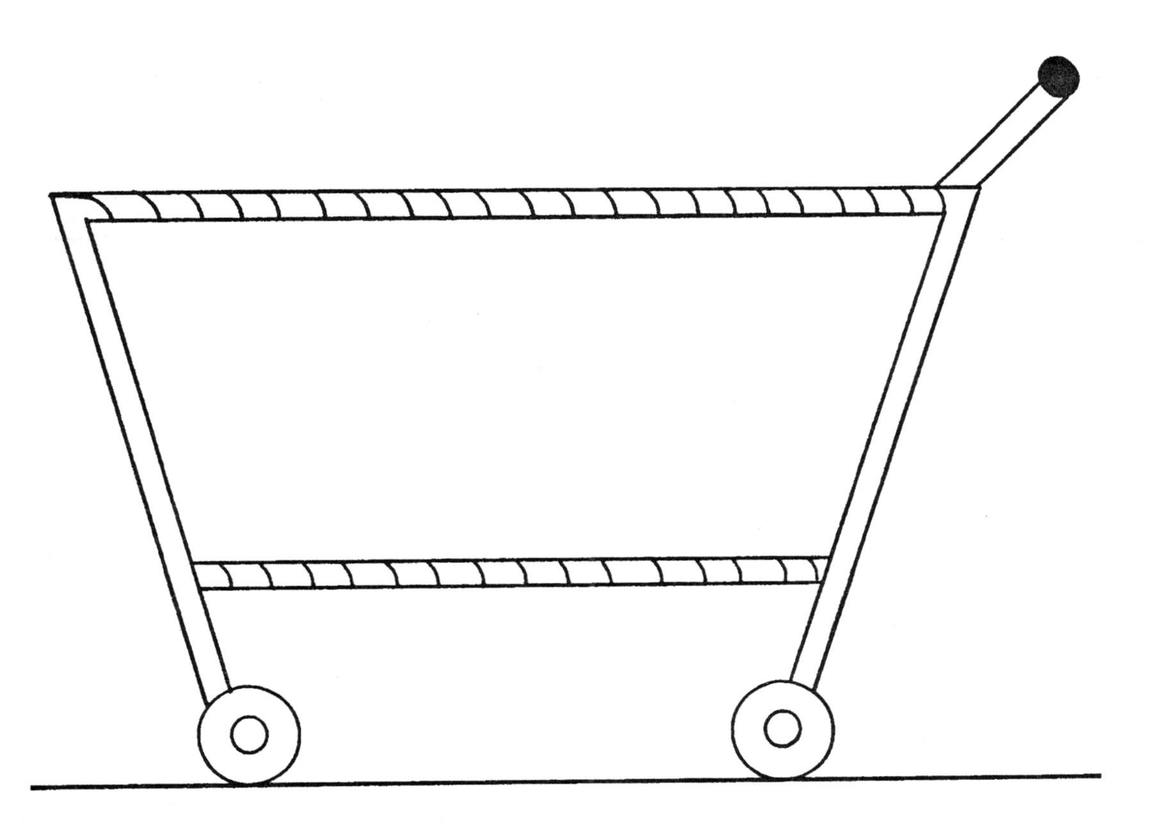

Kind words are like honey—sweet to the taste and good for your health.

Proverbs 16:24

Dear God,

Thank You for my healthy body. Help me to keep my spirit healthy by spending lots of time with You.

Every day you go lots of different places. Remember wherever you are, God is always with you because you belong to Him.

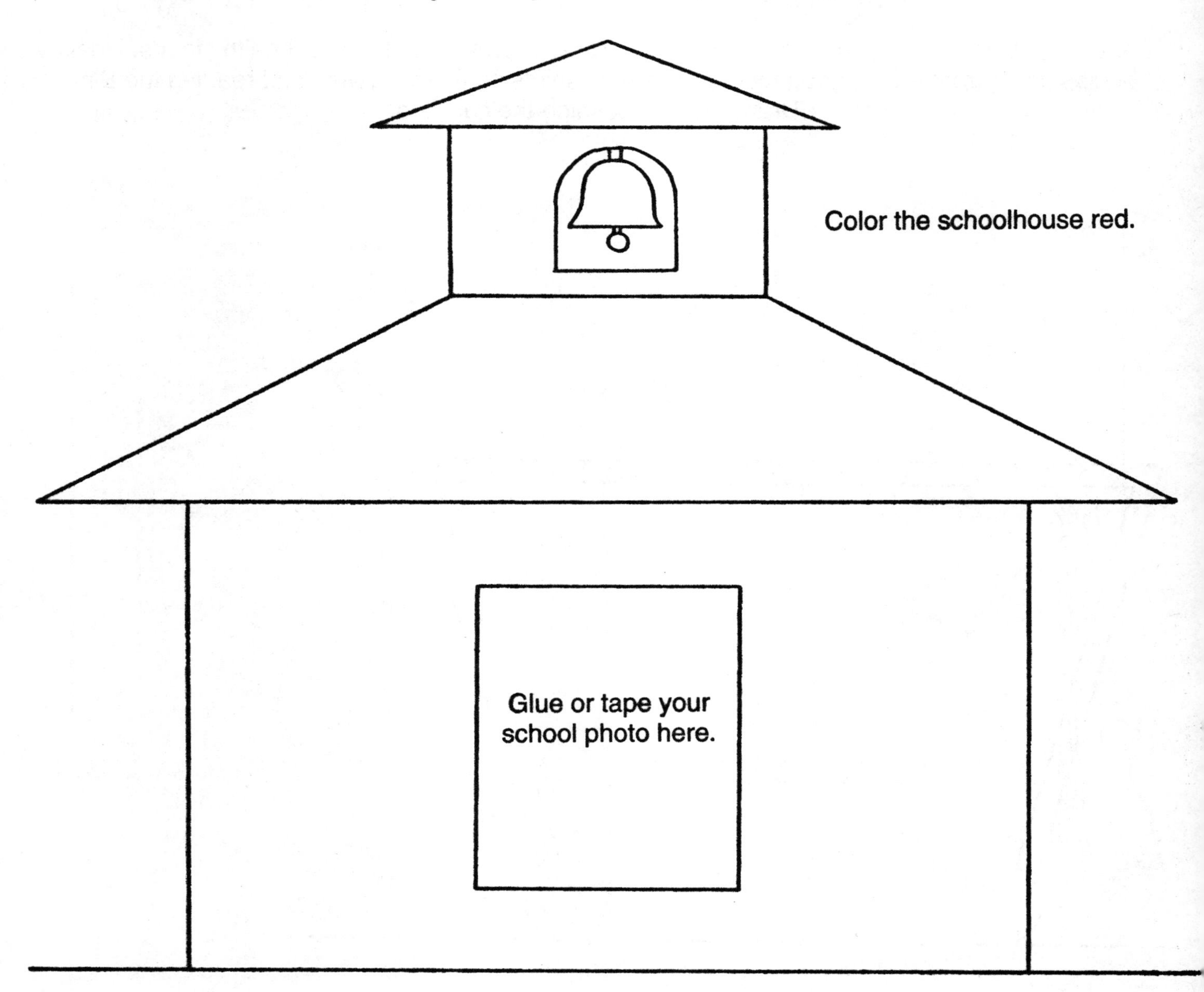

You belong to God.

1 John 4:4

Dear God,

Help me to always remember I am Your child. I belong to You!

God is loving, and since we are in His family, we should be, too. Give a kind word to everyone. Find nice things to say to other people.

Draw the pictures these two children are painting. Make one painting beautiful and make the other one not so great. Now imagine these two children talking. Will the child with the better painting brag about his painting or encourage the other child? How would the other child respond?

Love is patient and kind; it is not jealous or conceited or proud.

1 Corinthians 13:4

Dear God,

Help my words and actions to always be loving and kind.

God has given you a good mind, and He wants you to use it. Remember, the most important thing you can do with your mind is to love and obey God.

Here is a fun riddle that will test your ability to reason, or think.
Five friends live in this apartment building. Casey's apartment is the only one between Joe's and Sean's. Celeste's apartment has two windows. Joe's apartment is on one end. Alison's apartment does not have a circle for a window. Which apartment belongs to Alison?

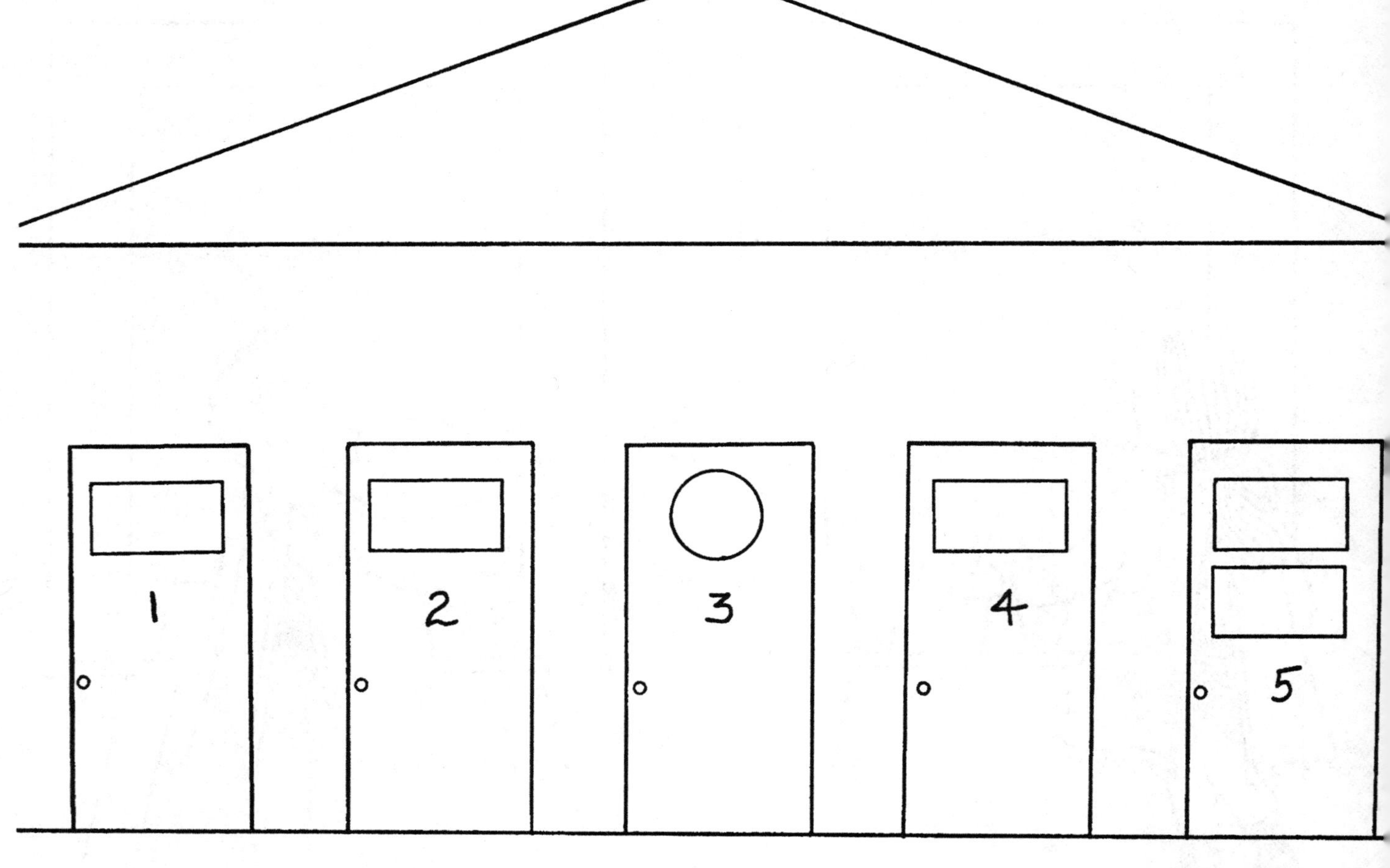

nswer: Apartment #4

Come now, and let us reason together.

Isaiah 1:18 (NASB)

Dear God,

Thank You for giving me a good mind. Help me to use it to make good decisions and do well in school.

If you want to be successful, you must work hard. Then God will open doors for you in life. But if you are lazy, you will not succeed.

I made my bed today!

your signature

Lazy people want much but get little, while the diligent are prospering.

Proverbs 13:4

Dear God,

Help me to be a good worker and helper.

When you depend on God for all your needs, you will be safe and protected—just like a house that is built on sturdy ground.

Design and color your dream house that you would like to live in someday.

A wise man...built his house on the rock.

Matthew 7:24 (NKJV)

Dear God,

It feels great to know that You will keep me safe, even through all kinds of storms. Thank You, Heavenly Father.

•

We need good food to eat every day, but that is not all we need. We also need to think about God, pray to Him, and read what He says to us in the Bible.

What is your favorite food? What would happen if that were the only food you were allowed to eat every day at every meal? How soon do you think you would get tired of eating the same food again and again? Name the four food groups:

1.

2.

3.

4.

Design a placement and decorate it with things you like.
Use your favorite colors!

Man must not depend on bread alone to sustain him, but on everything that the LORD says.
Deuteronomy 8:3

•

Dear God,

Thank You for all the good food I have to eat.

November 22

•

You can do many things with your hands, can't you? You can draw pictures, build with blocks, play musical instruments, and help your parents rake leaves. Whatever work we do with our hands, ask God to bless it.

Make a list of ways you could be helpful:

____

____

____

____

____

____

____

____

____

____

____

Establish the work of our hands.

Psalm 90:17 (NKJV)

•

Dear God,

I am thankful that You want good things to happen to me in life. I know that You and I together can be a winning team!

November 23

Do you know what it means to have reverence for God? It means you think God is very special and wonderful, and that you speak of Him with great respect.

On Thanksgiving pilgrims and Indians had a big feast together to thank God for the plentiful harvest. Do you know what the main dish was? Turkey, of course! Draw an outline of your hand. Now turn it into an Indian or a turkey!

He provides food for those who have reverence for him.

Psalm 111:5

Dear God,

Thank You for all the delicious food we eat every day, and especially on Thanksgiving Day.

We have so much to thank God for! What do you want to thank God for giving to you?

I'M THANKFUL FOR...
Draw outlines of your hands to give this turkey some feathers, then color your picture.
Write things you're thankful for on the feathers.

O give thanks to the LORD, *for He is good.*

1 Chronicles 16:34 (NASB)

Dear God,

Thank You for all Your many wonderful blessings!

November 25

Aren't you glad that God gives us delicious food to eat every day? He has made the earth so that it can give us all we need to be healthy and grow strong.

Draw a picture of you eating your favorite food. Who else would you like to have eating with you at the table?

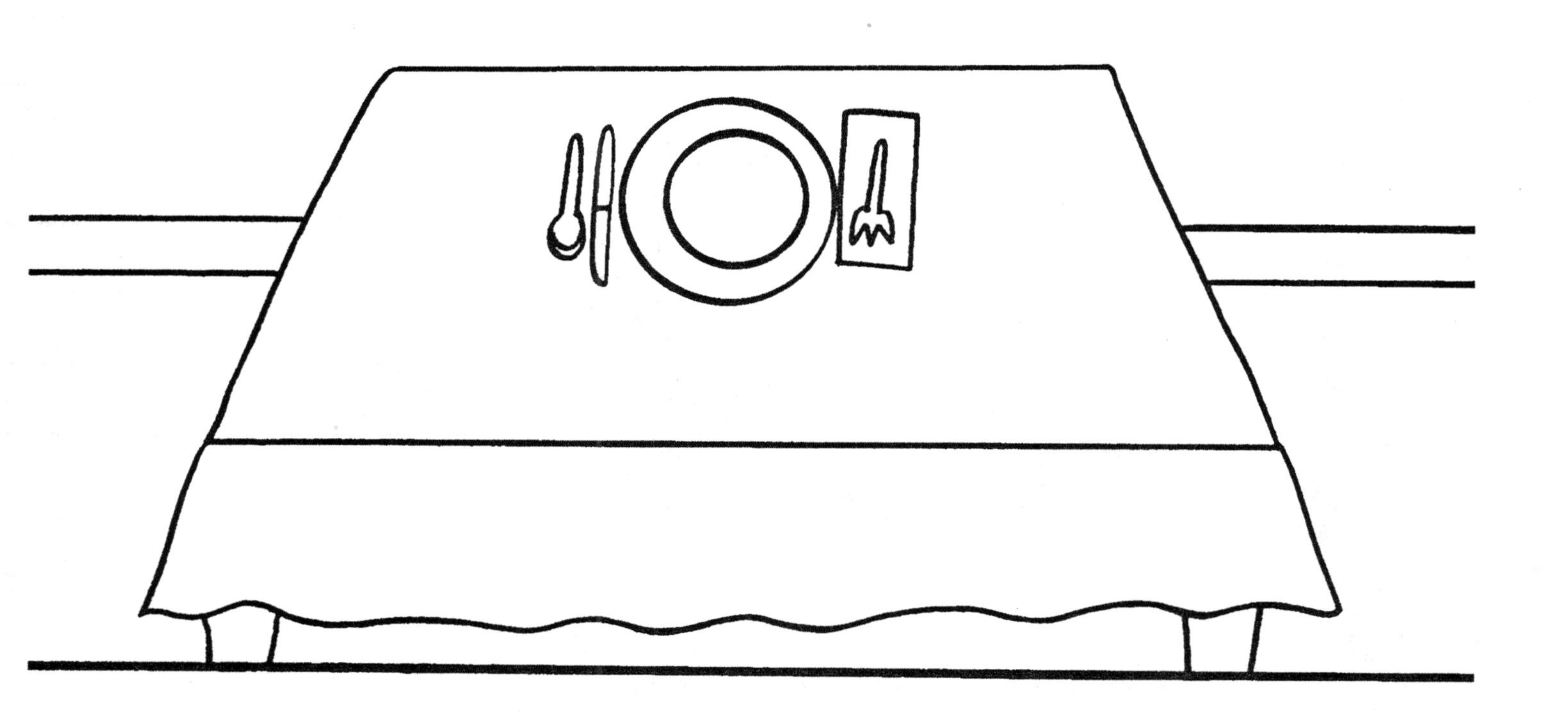

We feast on the abundant food you provide.

Psalm 36:8

Dear God,

Thank You for giving me good food every day. Thank You for taking care of all my needs.

We should always take the time to thank God for the food He gives to us.

Write a prayer to say before meals. Write it or have someone help write it for you:

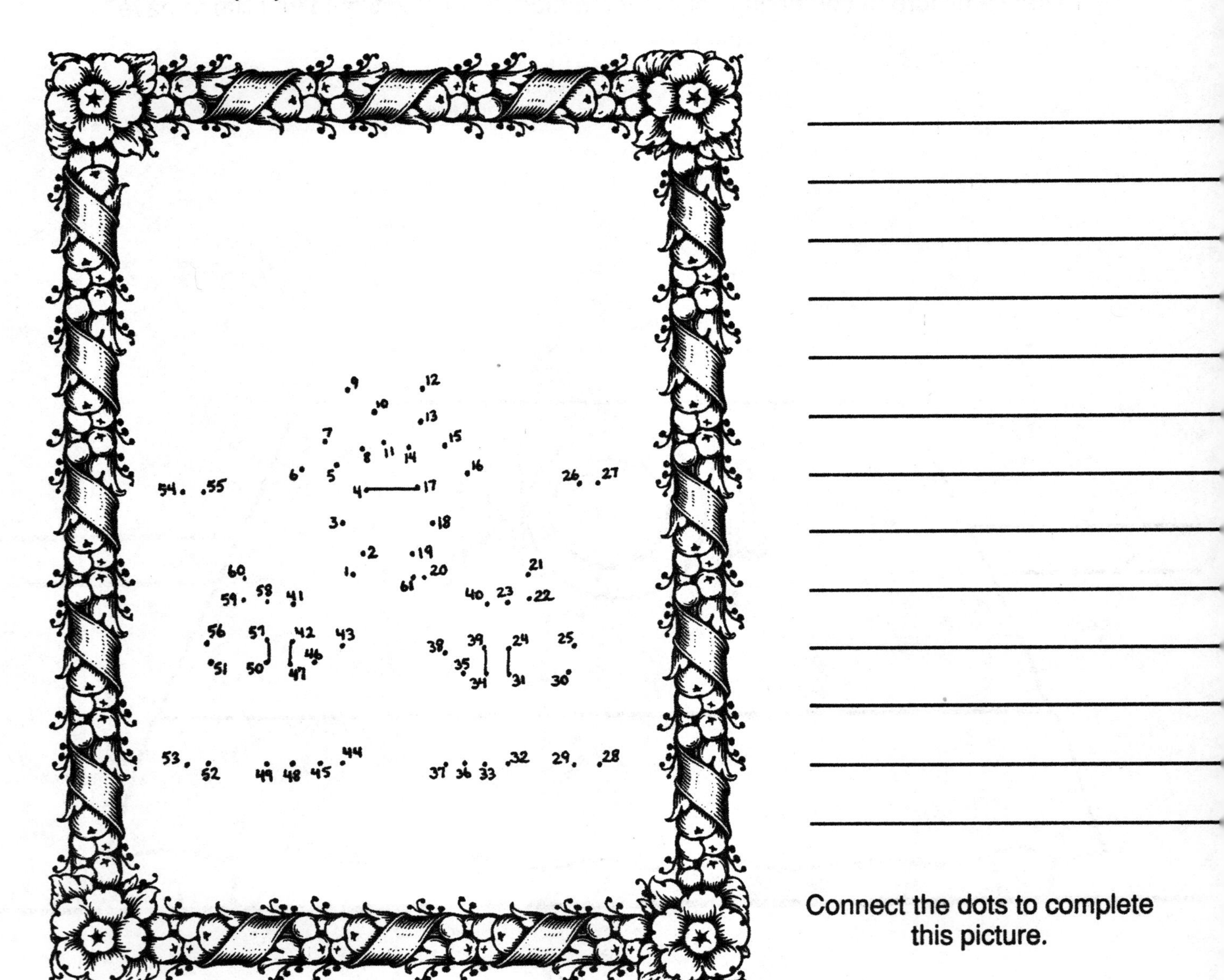

Connect the dots to complete this picture.

What a rich harvest your goodness provides!

Psalm 65:11

Dear God,

Thank You for the food that You provide every day.

From the tiniest ant to the biggest whale to the tallest giraffe, animals add a lot to this world. Aren't you glad God made so many animals?

Have you ever had fun with an animal, or has an animal you know ever done something really funny? Write (or ask someone to help you write) a story about that fun time.

LORD, you have made so many things!...The earth is filled with your creatures.

Psalm 104:24

Dear God,

Thank You for creating so many interesting and beautiful animals.

Tell the truth, and God will be pleased with you and other people will trust you. You might think that telling a lie will keep you out of trouble. But usually, it just gets you into more trouble! Wouldn't you like people to say that you are a truthful person?

Give this story a happy ending.

One day Paul was late for Sunday school. He told his teacher he was late because a big, purple rhinoceros had been chasing him. Finally he was able to climb a tree, and then he had to wait for a helicopter to rescue him. While Paul was talking, the other children started to giggle and Paul's teacher was not smiling.

No more lying, then! Everyone must tell the truth to his fellow believer, because we are all members together in the body of Christ.

Ephesians 4:25

Dear God,

Help me to obey You by always telling the truth.

God takes care of you all day long. He makes sure you are safe, that you have good food to eat, and gives you people who love you. We should always remember to thank God for the way He cares for us each day. Count your blessings!

Write on each finger something you can thank God for doing today.

How good it is to give thanks to you, O LORD.

Psalm 92:1

Dear God,

Thank You for taking such good care of me. Thank You for loving me so much.

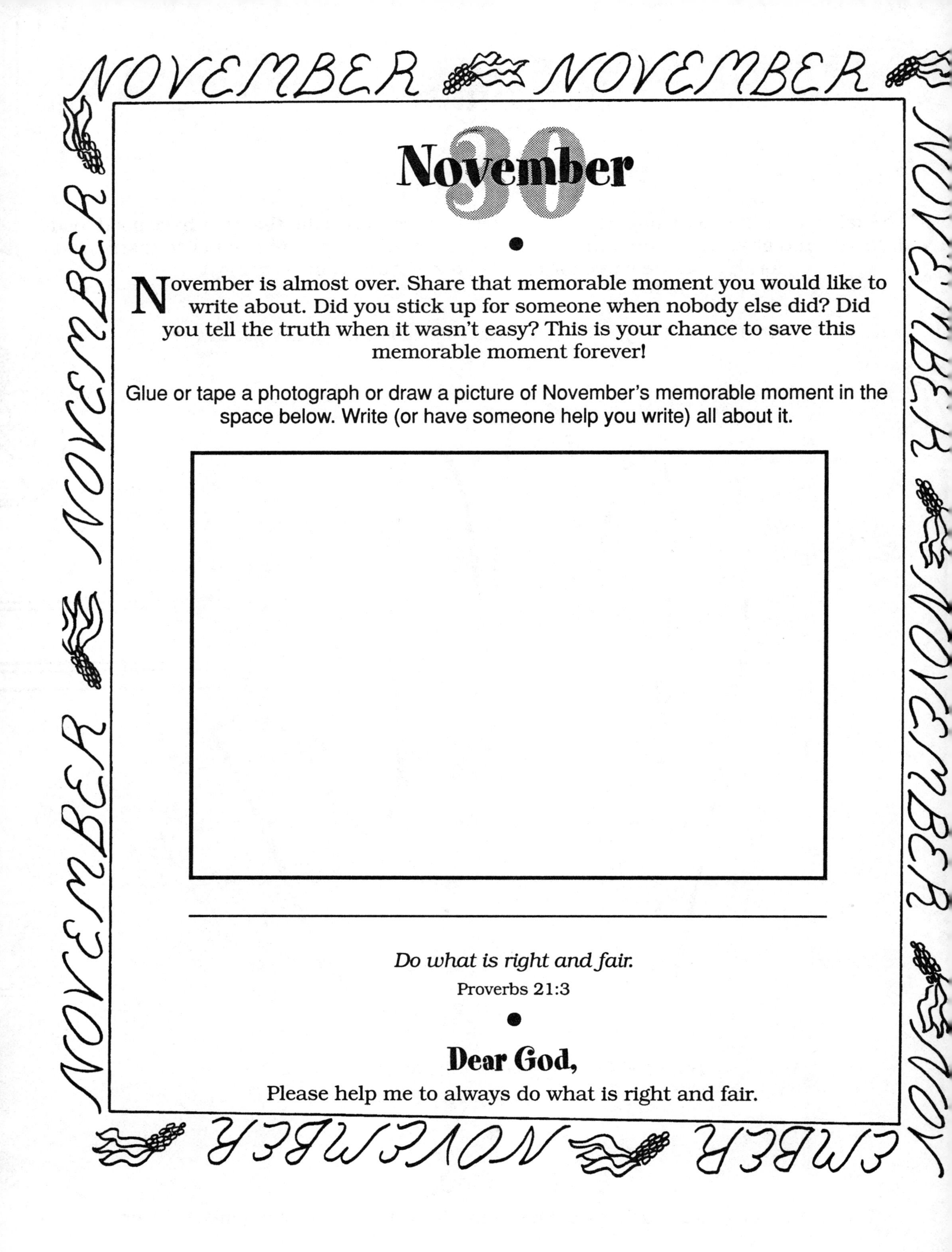

November 30

November is almost over. Share that memorable moment you would like to write about. Did you stick up for someone when nobody else did? Did you tell the truth when it wasn't easy? This is your chance to save this memorable moment forever!

Glue or tape a photograph or draw a picture of November's memorable moment in the space below. Write (or have someone help you write) all about it.

Do what is right and fair.

Proverbs 21:3

Dear God,

Please help me to always do what is right and fair.

DECEMBER

December 1

Jesus tells us that it is more blessed to give presents than get them. It is a way of showing love to others. So try giving. You'll feel great when you see the big smile on your friend's face!

Help these children find their presents, then color the picture.

It is more blessed to give than to receive.

Acts 20:35 (NKJV)

Dear God,

Help me to be a more giving, loving person. Thank You for Your gifts...they are the best of all!

December 2

Isn't it fun to sit in front of a warm fireplace and watch the snow fall outside? And it's even more fun to play in the snow! Snow makes everything look soft and sparkling-white. Snow is one of God's many great inventions!

Design your own snowmen. They can look funny, beautiful, or silly. Don't forget to add their faces, hats, arms, and mittens.

He spread snow like a blanket.

Psalm 147:16

Dear God,

Snow is fun to play in, ski on, and to watch as it falls. Snow makes winter a lot of fun!

December 3

The Bible tells us the truth about God. What it says is true now and will be true forever. Whenever you have a problem or question, you can find the answer in the Bible!

Your word, O LORD, will last forever; it is eternal in heaven.

Psalm 119:89

Dear God,

Thank You for all the great lessons I learn from reading the Bible.

December 4

•

Jerusalem is a very important city in the Bible. Jesus spent a lot of time there and did much of His work there. And it is where He will arrive when He comes back!

Color the city of Jerusalem.

May you see Jerusalem prosper all the days of your life!

Psalm 128:5

•

Dear God,

I pray for the peace of Jerusalem and look forward to the day when Jesus will enter through the city gates.

December 5

Jesus was always kind to people and made sure they had what they needed.

Talk about what's going on in this picture!

What is something nice you could do for somebody?

You should practice tenderhearted mercy and kindness to others.

Colossians 3:12

Dear God,

Thank You for taking good care of me. Help me to share Your love with others.

In today's Bible verse, Jesus was saying that your angel can talk to God, in person, anytime! What do you think they talk about? I'm sure your angel is helping to take good care of you.

Draw a picture of your angel.

See that you don't despise any of these little ones. Their angels in heaven, I tell you, are always in the presence of my Father in heaven.

Matthew 18:10

Dear God,

I know I don't ever have to be afraid. Thank You for providing angels to help watch over me.

December 7

When you give, what do you think of giving? Sometimes the best gift of all is to give yourself! When was the last time you offered to help someone? When you give of yourself, you will make that person happy, and you will make God happy, too.

Special activity: Look around the house right now. Is there something helpful you could do for someone? Do it now!

God loves a cheerful giver.

2 Corinthians 9:7 (NKJV)

Dear God,

Help me to be a cheerful, giving person.

December 8

Sometimes friends get into fights. Sometimes we do or say things that we shouldn't. If we are truly sorry and mean it from our hearts, our friendships can be okay again. Talking about problems and sharing forgiveness will make a friendship last a long time.

Help these children find each other so they can say they are sorry and become friends again.

Admit your faults to one another.

James 5:16 (TLB)

Dear God,

I am so glad that You have forgiven me.

December 9

When you go to bed at night, talk with God about anything that you did during the day that you shouldn't have done. Did you yell at someone? Did you tell a lie? Did you take something that didn't belong to you? Before you fall asleep, thank God for forgiving you, and ask Him to help you do better tomorrow.

Write a list of words or actions you did today that you know weren't loving. Did you know God will forgive you right away?

____

____

____

____

____

____

____

____

____

You must forgive one another just as the Lord has forgiven you.

Colossians 3:13

Dear God,

Help me to forgive others as You have forgiven me.

You may not be able to see your robe of righteousness, but it's on you! This Bible verse saying that you are acceptable to God and belong to His family.

Draw yourself wearing your robe of righteousness. Don't forget to decorate your robe.

My soul shall be joyful in my God; for He has clothed me with the garments of salvation, He has covered me with the robe of righteousness.

Isaiah 61:10 (NKJV)

Dear God,

I'm glad I belong to You. Thank You for making me righteous in Your sight.

December 11
Did you know that your prayers are important? God really hears them, and your prayers can help change things.
In each heart below, write a person's name and your prayer request for him or her.
We always give thanks to God ... when we pray for you.
Colossians 1:3, 4
Dear God,
I may be small, but I know that my prayers can do big things. Thank You for hearing my prayers.

God loves to hear His people praise Him. When you praise God, you show your love for Him. Can you think of some words right now that describe God?

In each box below, write a word that describes God. Make sure your word starts with the letter provided in the box.

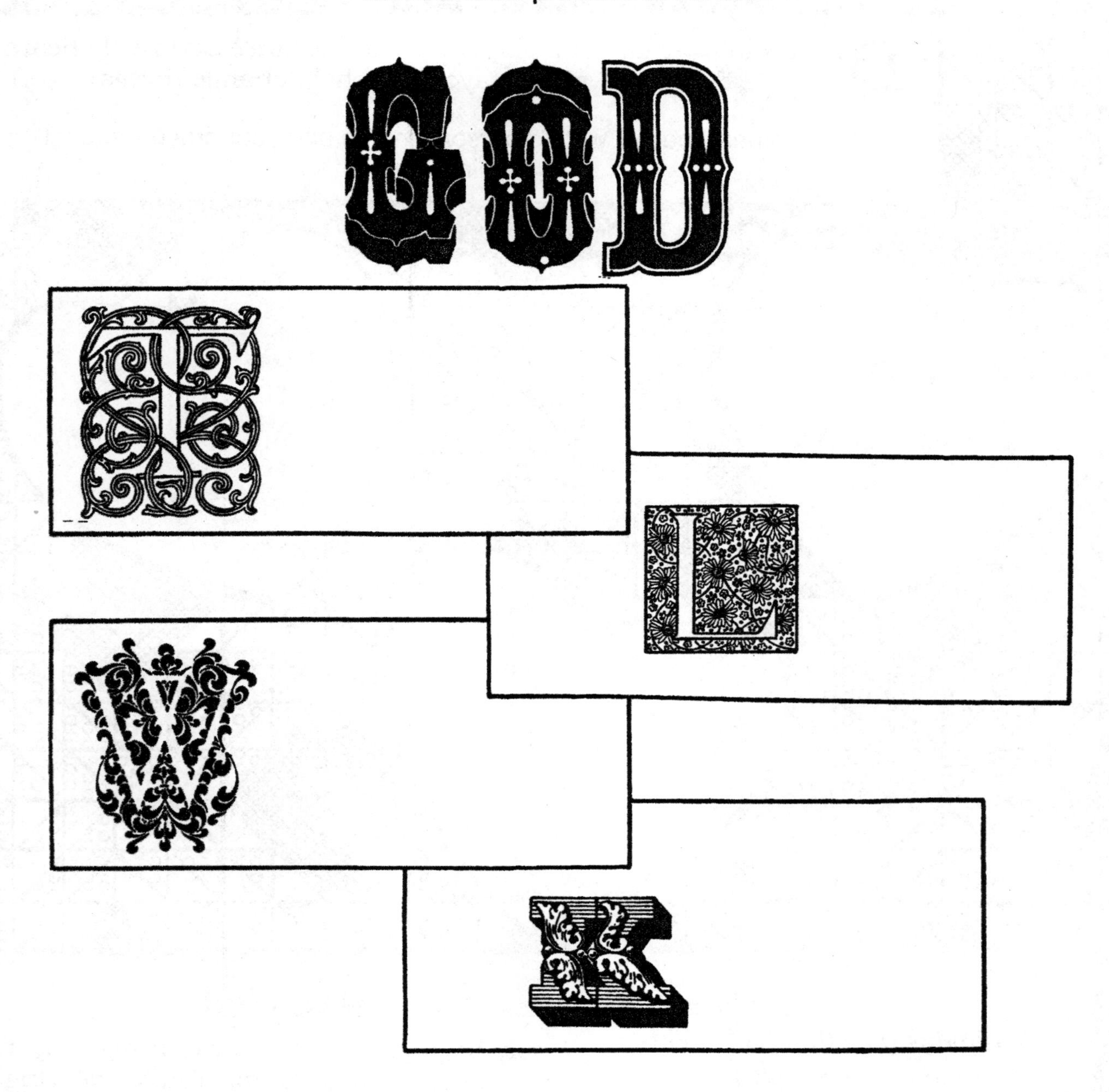

I will sing and give praise.

Psalm 108:1 (NKJV)

Dear God,

Your power is awesome. I know You can do anything. Thank You for loving me.

December 13

For thousands of years, God has chosen certain people to do His work on earth. And today, He still needs people. That is why it is important for you to obey your parents and God now, so that when you are older, God will know He can trust you to do His work.

Draw a line that matches the person on the left with what happened to him or her on the right.

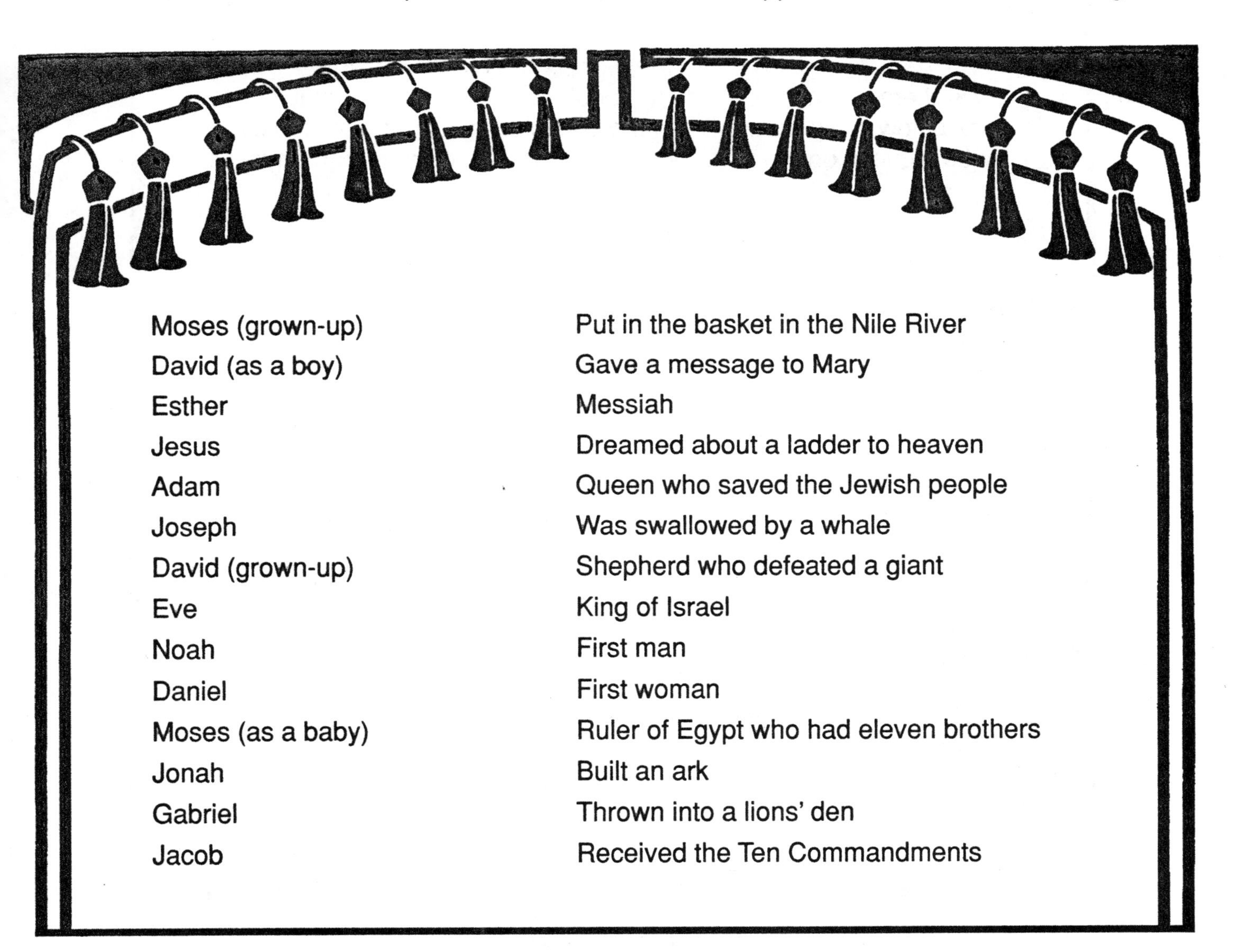

Moses (grown-up)	Put in the basket in the Nile River
David (as a boy)	Gave a message to Mary
Esther	Messiah
Jesus	Dreamed about a ladder to heaven
Adam	Queen who saved the Jewish people
Joseph	Was swallowed by a whale
David (grown-up)	Shepherd who defeated a giant
Eve	King of Israel
Noah	First man
Daniel	First woman
Moses (as a baby)	Ruler of Egypt who had eleven brothers
Jonah	Built an ark
Gabriel	Thrown into a lions' den
Jacob	Received the Ten Commandments

Happy are those whom you choose.

Psalm 65:4

Dear God,

Help me to always obey You, just like the people You chose in the Bible.

No matter what happens, God is always with you. He has promised that He will never leav you alone. There is nothing in the whole world that is stronger than the love of God.

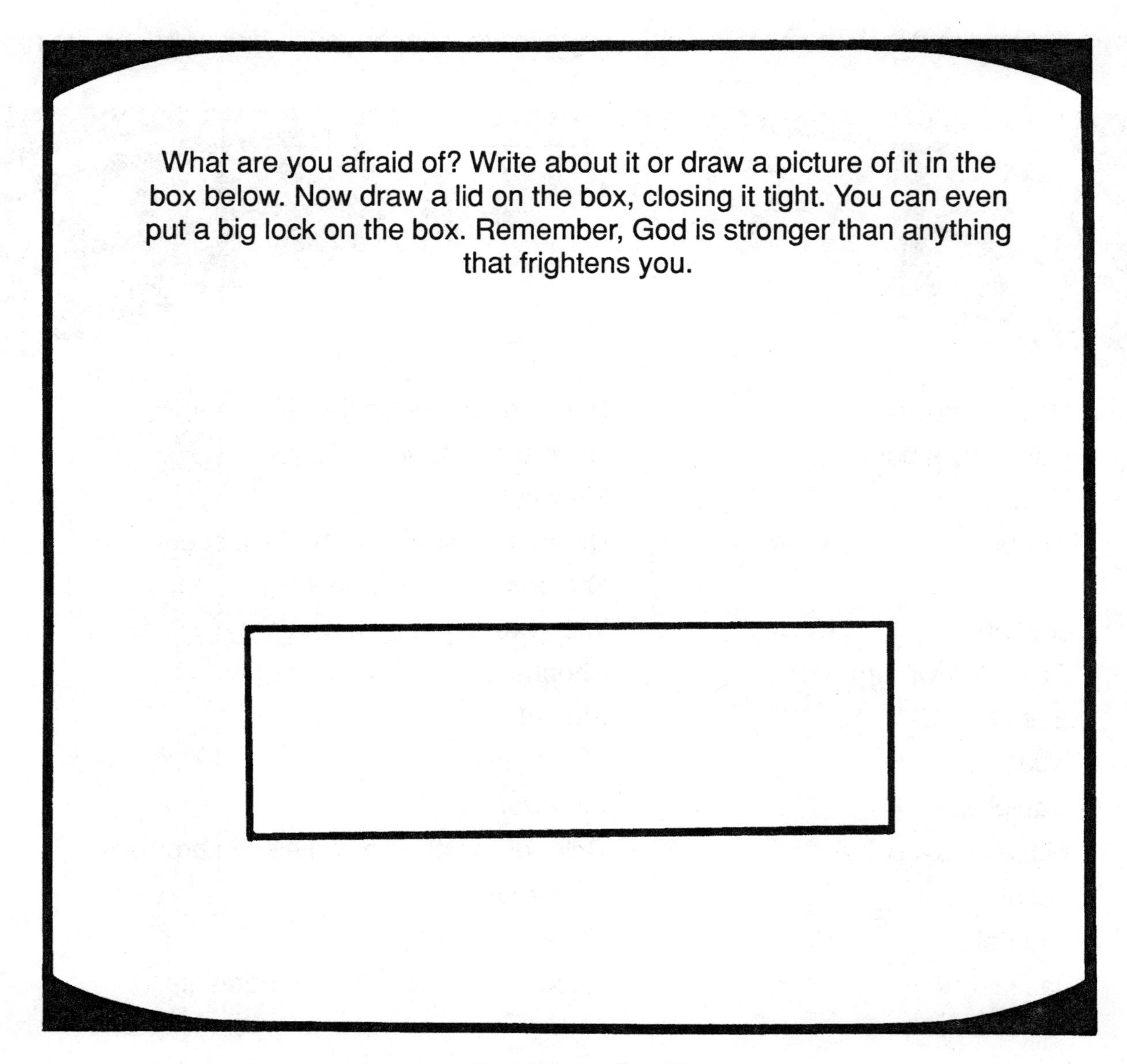

Don't be afraid!

Luke 2:10

Dear God,

Thank You for Your love for me. Please take away all my fears.

December 15

Good friends help make life special. They help take care of each other. But what does God have to say about the wrong kinds of friends? Look up the Bible verses below and write down the dangers of having the wrong kinds of friends.

Proverbs 16:28,29 ______________________

____

Proverbs 22:24,25 ______________________

____

Proverbs 24:1,2 ______________________

____

Proverbs 24:19,20 ______________________

____

Proverbs 25:19 ______________________

____

A friend loves at all times.

Proverbs 17:17 (NKJV)

Dear God,

Help me to find friends who love You and will help me love You more.

God makes sure winter arrives right on time every year. But did you know that winter is not the same in all places? It gets cold and snowy in the north, but closer to the equator, winter is hot and sunny! And places in between are cool and rainy.

In each space below, draw a picture of what winter looks like in each location.

Winter in Hawaii	Winter in Alaska
Winter in South Carolina	Winter Where You Live

The breath of God freezes the waters, and turns them to solid ice.

Job 37:10

Dear God,

Thank You for wonderful winter days.

The Bible tells us that children are a blessing from the Lord, and grandchildren are like a crown on your head. God blesses families who love Him. That means His blessings will continue in the lives of your children, your grandchildren, great-grandchildren, and so on.

Draw a picture of your great-grandparents when they were your age. Where did they live? What did they wear? What would they be doing?

Children's children are the crown of old men.

Proverbs 17:6 (NKJV)

Dear God,

Thank You for all my ancestors who have loved You and obeyed You.

December 18

Every day, year after year, God heaps His blessings on us—too many to count! Always remember that every good gift comes from God.

Inside each present below, write a blessing that God has given you. Then color the picture.

Blessed be the Lord, who daily loads us with benefits.

Psalm 68:19 (NKJV)

Dear God,

You are so good to me. I am glad that You will always love me.

Did you know that no two snowflakes are exactly alike? When you watch snow falling, the snowflakes may look the same, but if you look closer, you will see the differences. No two people are alike, either. So don't try to copy the ways of people who don't know or love God; be the special person God created you to be.

Design your own special snowflake.

Don't copy the behavior and customs of this world, but be a new and different person with a fresh newness in all you do and think.

Romans 12:2 (TLB)

Dear God,

Thank You for making every person special and different. Help me to be the kind of person You want me to be.

One day, an angel came to Mary and told her she would have a son named Jesus. He would be the Son of God.

Can you find the name Jesus in this picture?

The angel came to her and said, "Peace be with you! The Lord is with you and has greatly blessed you!"

Luke 1:28

Dear God,

Help me to trust You and always do what You want me to do, just like Mary did.

December 21

•

The angel, Gabriel, told Mary to name the baby Jesus. God was telling Mary what Jesus' name would be, even before He was born!

What is your first, middle, and last name? Write them in each section of the banner in the picture on this page. Then draw a picture of the person or persons you are named after in the space under the banner.

You will become pregnant and give birth to a son, and you will name him Jesus.

Luke 1:31

•

Dear God,

Thank You for the love You showed me by sending Jesus to earth.
Jesus is the Name above all names.

Everyone, then, went to register himself, each to his own hometown. Joseph went fron the town of Nazareth in Galilee to the town of ________________ in Judea, the birthplace of King David.—Luke 2:3,4

Discover the town that Joseph and Mary traveled to the night Jesus was born. Follow the path through this alphabet maze. Then fill in the missing town in the verse above. Hint: There is a beautif Christmas song about this town.

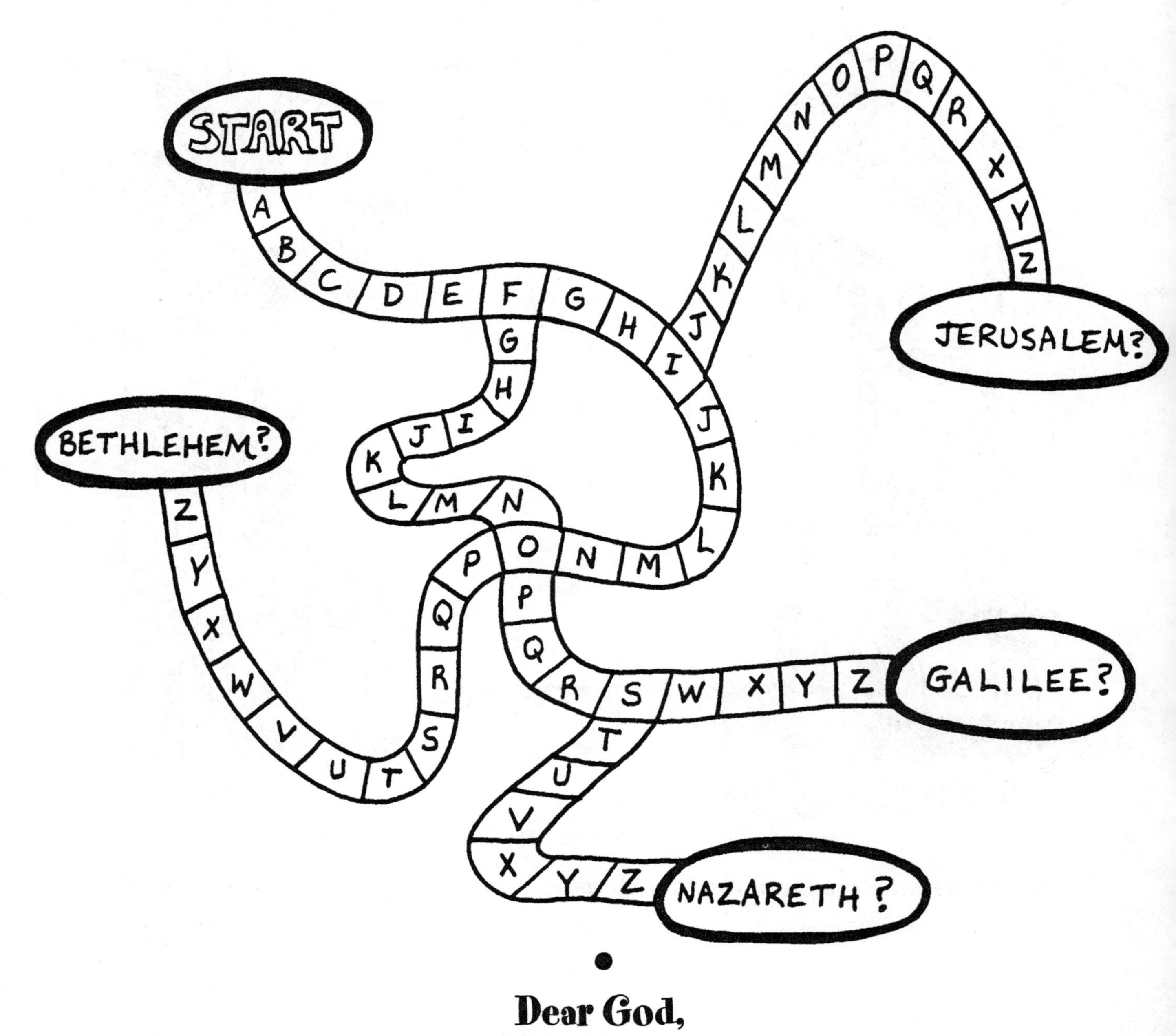

Dear God,

Your prophets said Jesus would be born in the same town that King David was born in — Bethlehem. Thank You for always keeping Your promises.

December 23

The angel's first words were, "Don't be afraid. The Messiah is born." What an exciting message for the shepherds! What an exciting message for the whole world! Finally, the promised Messiah had been born. God always keeps His promises.

Follow the lines from the top row and put each letter in the right place on the bottom. Now read part of the angel's message.

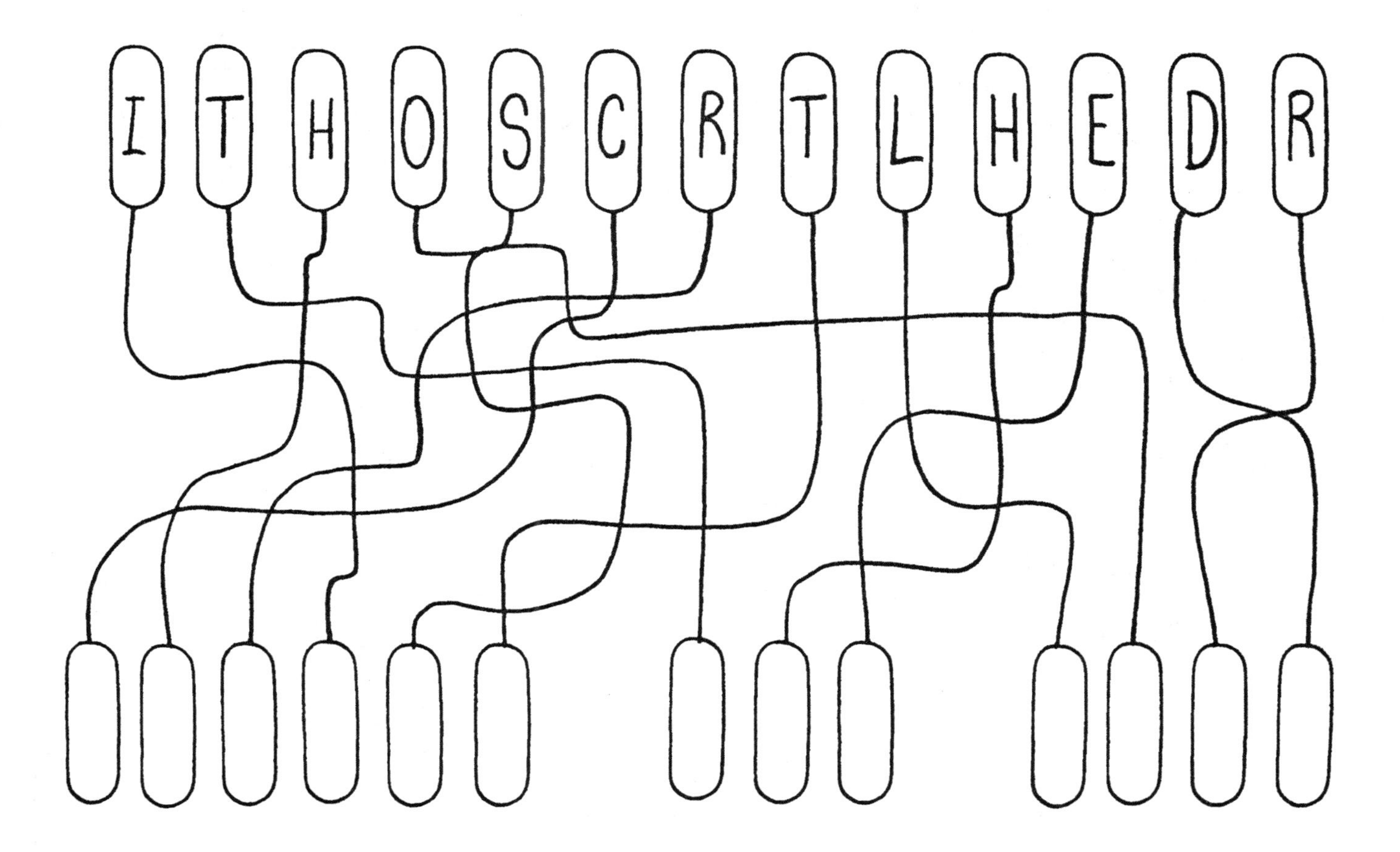

The angel said to them, "Don't be afraid! I am here with good news for you, which will bring great joy to all the people. This very day in David's town your Savior was born—Christ the Lord!"

Psalm 2:10,11

Dear God,

Thank You for always keeping Your promises ... especially the promise about Jesus.

December 24

Suddenly a great army of heaven's angels appeared with the angel, singing praises to God. How amazed those shepherds must have been the night Jesus was born in Bethlehem!

Make these angels look the way you think they looked that wonderful night.

Glory to God in the highest heaven, and peace on earth.

Luke 2:14

Dear God,

I am thankful Jesus came into the world. I know He came out of love for me.

When Jesus came to earth, He left the power and glory of His heavenly home and was born as a tiny baby. He was born in a stable full of animals in a tiny village called Bethlehem.

Color this picture.

And Christ became a human being and lived here on earth among us and was full of loving forgiveness and truth.

John 1:14 (TLB)

Dear God,

Today, as the whole world celebrates the birth of Jesus, may there be peace on earth.

•

God wanted you to be in heaven with Him forever, so He sent Jesus to earth to tell you all about God and how much you are loved. If you love Jesus, He will make sure you get to heaven one day.

Fill in the areas that have a dot • so you can read this special message for you from Jesus.

For God loved the world so much that he gave his only Son, so that everyone who believes in him may not die but have eternal life.

John 3:16

•

Dear God,

Thank You for making a way for me to be with You and Jesus forever in heaven.

December 27

Now after Jesus was born in Bethlehem of Judea in the days of Herod the king, behold, wise men from the East came to Jerusalem, saying, "Where is He who has been born King of the Jews? For we have seen His star in the East and have come to worship Him."
—Matthew 2:1, 2 (NKJV)

Draw yourself here with the present you would bring to Jesus.

Dear God,

Thank You for Your greatest gift of love...Jesus!

The wise men were excited when they saw the star in Bethlehem because they knew it would tell them where Jesus was.

Don't you love the day you were born—your birthday? Decorate your own birthday cake.

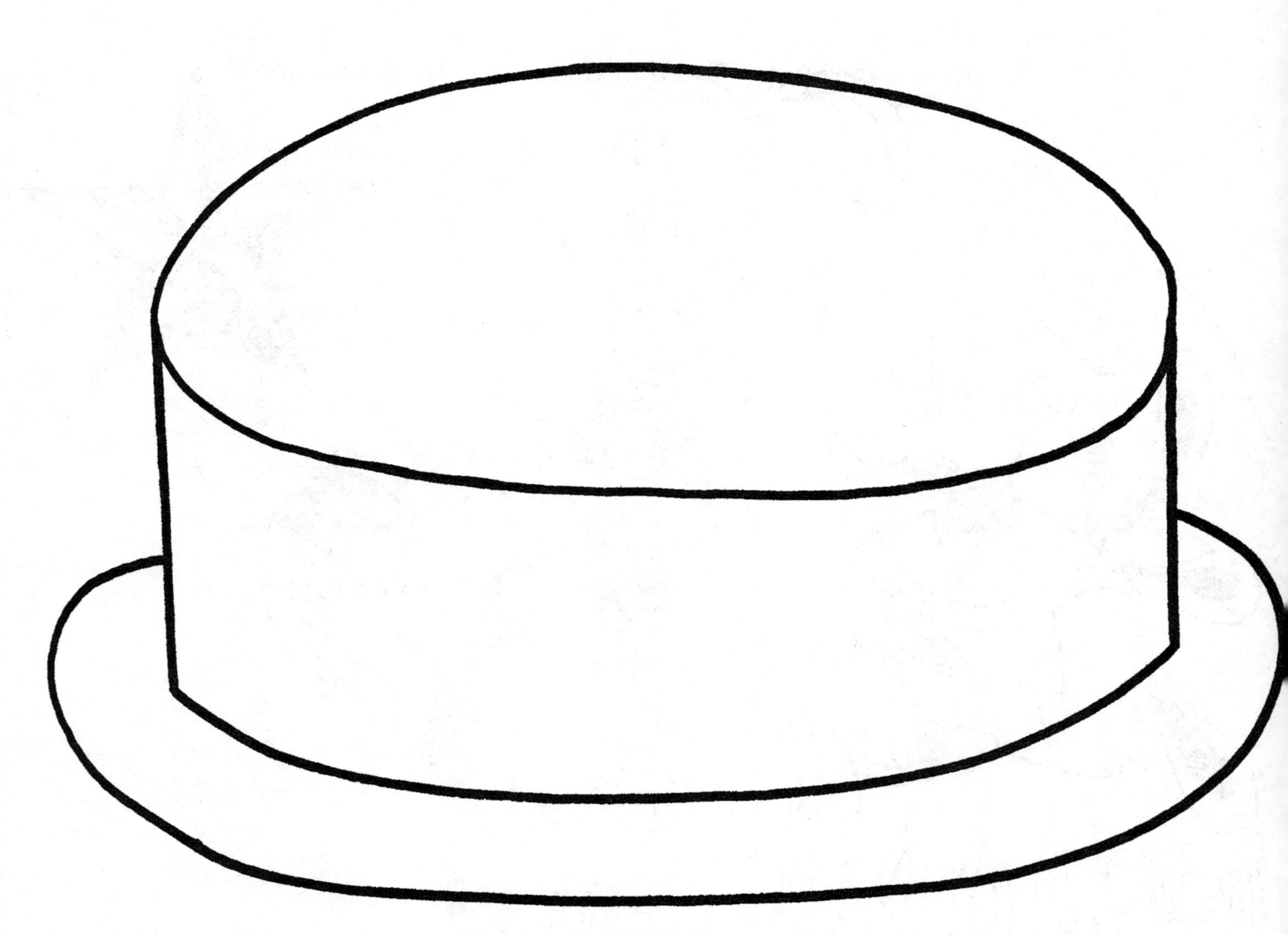

When they saw the star, they rejoiced with exceedingly great joy.

Matthew 2:10

Dear God,

Thank You for birthdays. I want to know You more and more each year.

   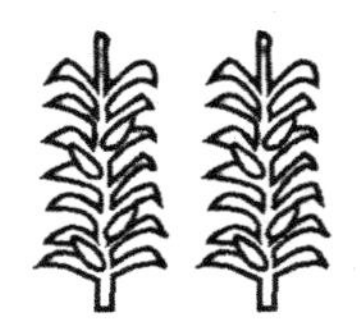

December 29

The year is nearly over, and what a year it has been! Every single day you have been in God's care. He holds your life and your times in His hand!

What are your favorite memories about this year?

____

____

____

____

____

____

____

My times are in Your hand.

Psalm 31:15 (NKJV)

Dear God,

This year and every year, help me to stay close to You.

 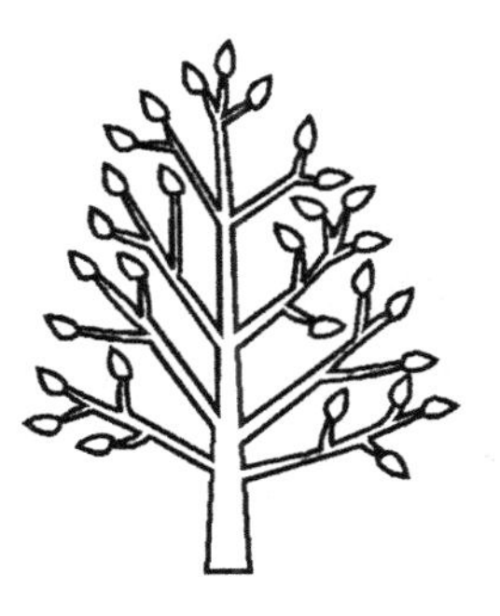  

DECEMBER ☆ DECEMBER ☆ DECEMBER ☆ DECEMBER ☆ DECEMBER ☆ DECEMBER ☆ DECEMBER ☆ DECEMBER ☆ DECEMBER ☆ DECEMBER ☆ DECEMBER ☆ DECEMBER

December 30

•

December is always such an exciting month! Parties, holiday celebrations, visits with loved ones, and, of course, celebrating the birth of Jesus! In all the excitement, what is one memorable moment you never ever want to forget?

Glue or tape a photograph or draw a picture of December's memorable moment in the space below. Write (or have someone help you write) all about that special time.

Honest people will lead a full, happy life.

Proverbs 28:20

•

Dear God,

Thank You for my happy life.

December 31

Think about all that has happened in 365 days. Now ask yourself these questions: Were you always as kind and loving as you could be? Did you always obey your parents quickly, without complaining? Did you always tell the truth? Now is a good time to ask God to help you grow stronger and wiser as a child of God this next year.

MY NEW YEAR'S RESOLUTION

In the frame above, write what you would like to try to do better next year.

But God will give glory, honor, and peace to all who do what is good.

Romans 2:10

Dear God,

Thank You for loving me each and every day. I love You.